KRAKENSCOURGE

John Graham

KDP

Published by KDP

ISBN 978-1-7290-7698-9

Typesetting services by BOOKOW.COM

To heroes and heroines, real and fictional, who battle monsters while we sleep.

Contents

THE RAID

WORLDS die long before the stars that sustain them, at least in most cases. When this star's core had collapsed, it had expelled most of its mass in the form of a devastating supernova and scorched the planets it had once nurtured. The event had incinerated their still thriving biospheres and permanently irradiated the ravaged rocks that remained. All that was left was a neutron star.

The outer edge of the system was surrounded by an enormous cloud illuminated by the glow of the neutron star, setting it alight in a mesmerising riot of colours. The seemingly infinite expanse of gas and dust formed a near-perfect ring around the dead system and the neutron star blazing at its heart. The gas cloud also absorbed most of the vicious pulsar winds that lashed the lifeless rocks that had once been planets, enough to protect an enormous space station on the other side from being reduced to an irradiated hulk.

The station was known as the Nexus. Despite its vast size, against the kaleidoscopic gas cloud and the shining white orb of the neutron star beyond, it looked like little more than a misshapen speck. Who had begun construction and what had motivated them to build it on the edge of a dead star system were mysteries, but it had been built centuries ago and progressively expanded over time into a vast trading hub.

There were thousands of smaller specks zipping back and forth; swarms of short-range cargo shuttles ferrying goods and crew between the station and the scores of much larger vessels that waited at a distance. These trading ships had come from all corners of charted and uncharted space, having amassed a wealth of exotic goods and technology from all over the galaxy to barter and trade at the Nexus.

Another Q-rift opened up as a new ship arrived in Nexus space, exiting the phantasmal realm of Q-space, and slowly blueshifting into focus as it re-entered normal space. To an outside observer, the ship had simply squeezed out of a morass of pure darkness, itself barely visible against the backdrop of the interstellar void. Like the black hole it resembled, no light escaped from the Q-rift, and so the vessel's arrival was only detectable to sensors.

The ship was massive, its elliptical shape giving it the appearance of a giant cocoon with a bulbous body and a rounded top and bottom. It was like many of the long-haul trading barges that often visited the Nexus, except twenty times larger. It must have been travelling for decades, hopping from planet to planet, trading its wares in exchange for vital supplies and the exotic products of other cultures before finally arriving at a new port.

But something was wrong. The enormous spacecraft wasn't cruising to a steady halt, it was simply drifting forwards as if limping to safety. Its thrusters were sputtering, and it was tilting forward on an awkward axis like a wounded creature stumbling towards refuge. More seriously, scans of the vessel revealed massive breaches in the hull and a heat bloom indicating a possible reactor leak.

The ship's proximity made it an imminent threat. Depending on the reactor type, if it went critical the resulting explosion would destroy or irradiate all nearby ships and potentially the Nexus too. No one species controlled the station, but there were contingency plans for this kind of emergency, and they had to be implemented quickly.

All ships still waiting to berth were given ten minutes to either dock or retreat to a safe distance, and all ships too large to dock or retreat had to activate their shielding. After the ten minute mark, all docking ports and access hatches would be sealed and the station's suite of shield arrays would be powered up as far as they could go.

As a last resort, a flotilla of response ships was dispatched to the badly damaged super-barge. Several ships equipped with artificial gravity arrays broke off from the flotilla and spread out around the damaged vessel, projecting repulsive gravitational fields towards the drifting hulk to counteract its momentum. Slowly but surely, the giant ship was brought to a halt, keeping it at a fixed and relatively safe distance from the Nexus.

Weaving in between the repulsive fields, other vessels zeroed in on the gaping hull breaches, searching for the source of the heat bloom. If the reactor's coolant system had been damaged, or if the reactor itself had suffered a containment breach, they might only have minutes before it exploded. A full-spectrum penetrating scan of the ship revealed that an entire section of the vessel's hull was missing, exposing the reactor to view.

Fortunately, it was a standard fusion plant and so by design couldn't go into meltdown. Furthermore, the breach exposing the reactor had also been by design. After the fusion plant had been shut down, a section of the hull had retracted, exposing the still-hot reactor to the freezing cold of deep space. Presumably, this would only be done if the coolant system had failed, but there was no chance of a catastrophic containment failure.

That just left the survivors.

Given the extent of the damage, most of the crew were probably dead, but distinct heat signatures were still detectable within the ship, and they didn't have much time. They had taken cover in sealed bulkheads to protect themselves from the vacuum, and it would take hours for the rescue teams to safely cut through without venting the remaining air.

It was also clear that this was the result of a deliberate attack and not some catastrophic accident. The gaping gashes in the hull were focused around the ship's most vital systems, and whoever had attacked the ship had also targeted the access hatches and escape pod ports, destroying them outright or melting them shut.

With all the usual access points inaccessible, the rescue teams had to set up temporary, vacuum-proof bulkheads before they could cut through. After several hours of work, the bulkheads were installed and the survivors were extracted one by one.

Out of a crew of tens of thousands, only a few hundred were left alive and the survivors were emaciated and traumatised by the mysterious attack. Most of them also had untreated injuries ranging from physical wounds to burns, and their normally deep blue skin was tinged a sickly pale grey. Many were close to death.

Back on the Nexus, an unused cargo processing hall was cleared in order to set up a makeshift hospital. The species was amphibian, so specialised water-beds were requisitioned to keep their skin moist. Soon, the processing hall was packed with hundreds of treatment beds, each equipped with a suite of robotic medical tools.

As the survivors were brought in, Nexus residents began gathering in the doorways, eager for news. The safety lockdown had been lifted and normal activity had begun to resume, but an event like this was almost unprecedented. Corsair raids were common enough in the vast expanses of unclaimed space, but such a brazen assault on a ship of this size was unheard of, let alone the brutally efficient manner with which the attack had been executed.

One of the survivors awoke suddenly, staying conscious long enough to gurgle out a single coherent word before his injuries forced him into a self-protective coma. There was no translation for the word. In fact, it wasn't a word in any language used by the races on the station. Before long, everyone on the Nexus had heard a recording of the word, and even though its meaning was a mystery, the word itself quickly became common knowledge:

Voidstalker.

* * *

Rainstorms were common on Asgard. It had been a cold and barren rock when the first exploration ships had found it, and over a century of terraforming had been required to give it a breathable atmosphere and a livable climate. Now that it was an Earth-like garden world, it had a weather-system to match, including rainstorms.

And when it rained, it poured.

Instead of windows, the apartment had holographic screens on the walls. Right now, the view was that of Asgard City – an endless forest of kilometre-high skyscrapers still visible through the blurry haze of torrential rain. Micro-speakers even played audio simulations of the rain battering the side of the apartment tower. Activity in the city continued at all hours, so the myriad lights rendered the city visible even through the darkness and the downpour.

Every few seconds, the clouds would light up with a gigantic fork of lightning lashing across the sky followed by a menacing peal of thunder. Occasionally, a bolt would strike one of the towers and illuminate the landscape for miles around. Very occasionally, a bolt would strike the top of one tower and then jump to the nearby tops of other towers, forming a lethal web of light that was gone in a flash.

The holographic imaging and the accompanying surround-sound audio effects were so realistic they made you feel like you were right in the middle of the rainstorm – without the inconvenience of getting wet or the danger of being struck by lightning. If the audio were switched off, being safe and warm indoors would make the whole arrangement a pleasant backdrop against which to fall asleep.

Gabriel couldn't sleep.

The sprawling apartment had a number of spare rooms, one of which served as a personal gym. Besides artificial gravity-assisted weight training modules and a treadmill, the centrepiece of the gym was a punching bag stretching from ceiling to floor. Gabriel had spent the past hour furiously pounding it.

He struck the bag over and over with blows as rapid as the lightning outside, the force of his punches melting into the shock-absorbent foam. In spite of the rainstorm footage being projected against the wall, the gym was dimly lit; but the whole room echoed with an elastic thud each time he pounded the bag, and a holographic readout displayed the force of each blow along with the number of punches landed.

There was an electronic chime as the counter reached 10,000 and Gabriel relaxed. He picked up a bottle of nutrient juice and drained it to the dregs. 10,000 punches in three hours and none of his punches had been less than 10,000 newtons. That was a good score, anything less would mean he was losing his edge.

In fact, he was far from losing his edge; his heart was beating faster than normal, but his muscles didn't feel strained or drained at all. The numerous enhancements that came with being a void-stalker meant that he was barely tired, and he had still managed to pound the punching bag with twice the force of a trained boxer.

The door opened a crack and a pair of bright green eyes identical to Gabriel's own peered in. It was Orion, his oldest child, still barely half as tall as Gabriel. Tentatively, he entered the gym, gazing up at his father's towering figure.

"Can't sleep?" Gabriel asked, squatting down to eye-level with his son.

"No," Orion replied, rubbing his eyes.

"I can't either," Gabriel answered sympathetically, then added more sternly, "but you actually *need* to sleep for your test tomorrow."

"I'll pass the test," Orion assured his father, "I always do."

"How do you write the word 'Human'?" Gabriel tested him.

"With a capital 'H'," Orion answered, "because the species name has to be capitalised."

"Just checking," Gabriel said with a smile, ruffling Orion's hair.

In addition to their emerald green eyes, father and son shared the same features and the same jet black hair. Unlike Gabriel's military buzz cut, though, Orion had a messy head of dark curls which he refused to have cut.

"So, why can't you sleep, daddy?" Orion asked suddenly.

"I don't need as much sleep as the rest of the family," Gabriel replied simply.

"You always say that," Orion replied, unsatisfied, "*why* don't you need as much sleep?"

"It's hard to explain," Gabriel admitted, unsure how to explain the finer points of genetic engineering or manipulation of the circadian rhythm.

"Are you bored of being at home with us?" Orion asked.

That question cut deep, and Gabriel had no idea how to respond. He hadn't been given any new assignments since the Loki mission, so he was effectively on unofficial leave.

As he had been for almost a year now.

"Of course I'm not bored," Gabriel lied to his son.

"Then why are you up so late punching that thing?" Orion demanded.

"Well, I still need to practice," Gabriel answered.

"Can I practice with you?"

"How about you practice on my hands?" Gabriel suggested, holding up his bare palms.

Orion hesitated, then reached back and hit Gabriel's palm.

"You call that a punch?" Gabriel snorted, mocking the half-hearted blow.

Orion punched Gabriel's palm again, this time hitting with more force.

"That's more like it," said Gabriel encouragingly, "now chain your punches together."

Orion pounded Gabriel's outstretched palms, hitting in quick succession and grunting aggressively with each punch. He was surprisingly strong, and he jabbed like a boxer instead of just blindly swinging his fists.

"Harder," Gabriel ordered him, sounding like a drill instructor.

Orion unleashed a full-force punch, but missed Gabriel's palm and hit him in the nose. Gabriel reeled back, more from surprise than pain, landing on his back.

"…I…I…" Orion stammered apologetically.

"Seems like you've been practising," Gabriel said as he got off the ground.

"…I haven't been…" Orion replied hesitantly.

"Then how did you learn to hit that hard?" Gabriel asked him.

Orion was silent.

"You *have* been coming in here, haven't you?" Gabriel said suspiciously.

"Only when you're not home," Orion replied defensively, then added in a low mumble, "Which is a lot of the time."

Father and son were silent.

"So this is where you are," said a female voice in the doorway.

Orion flinched at the sound of his mother's voice behind him.

"He couldn't sleep," his father said in his defence.

"Go back to bed, Ori," Aster instructed Orion.

"But I'm not tired–" Orion protested.

"Now," Aster said, her tone hardening.

Orion buttoned his lip and quietly shuffled out of the gym, leaving his parents alone together. Gabriel stood up straight as Aster entered the room to confront him. She brushed her shoulder-length brunette curls with their blonde highlights away from her face and scolded Gabriel, unintimidated by his height.

"What's going on?" she demanded in a stage whisper.

"Nothing," Gabriel lied.

"Oh, for fuck's sake," Aster with a roll of her brown eyes and a hiss of exasperation, "You get up at ridiculous times to pound that thing every fucking night. If nothing's going on, why are you keeping everyone else awake?"

"I'm not keeping anyone awake," Gabriel hissed back defensively, "I couldn't sleep, and Orion couldn't either, so he came over to see what I was doing."

"Maybe he couldn't sleep because of you," Aster said accusingly.

"The entire room is soundproofed, you id…" Gabriel began, then trailed off before reaching the end of his sentence.

Aster took a step forward until her chest was touching his, glaring up at him.

"Did you want to finish that thought?" she asked him dangerously.

Gabriel was silent.

"Finish up your workout," Aster ordered him, "then get back to bed."

She turned on her heel and walked out, leaving Gabriel simmering in silence. He curled his fingers into fists as a potent mix of embarrassment and rage boiled over within him, then he wheeled around and struck the punching bag with a furious snarl.

35170 newtons.

Gabriel stood there fuming with his fists still clenched, glaring at the number on the holographic display. The figure was a personal best, but he was too angry to care, and he wasn't even technically angry with Aster.

Red-eye didn't do petty revenge, so he was pretty sure that he wasn't being punished. Even so, it felt like punishment, and it certainly looked like punishment after having confronted her after the Loki mission. Aster could tell something was wrong, but as with everything else work-related, he had to keep it secret.

Gabriel began to relax as the anger ebbed and receded from his mind. He still wasn't tired, but it was probably time to get back to bed.

* * *

Gabriel shut the door to the bedroom and stripped off his shirt. Aster was already back under the covers, probably still angry at him for almost calling her an idiot. Somewhere in the depths of his largely emotionless mind, Gabriel felt an obligation to make amends with his wife.

He crawled into bed and lay down beside Aster, extending a tentative hand and touching her hip. She didn't flinch or pull away, so he ran his fingers slowly across her hip and under her shirt, running his palm across her belly.

"An apology would be better," Aster murmured, "but that's a start."

Gabriel sidled up closer to Aster, and she exposed her neck for him to kiss. He leaned in and nuzzled his face into her neck as he rubbed her stomach.

"I'm sorry for calling…for almost calling you an idiot," Gabriel said apologetically.

"'Almost'?"

"I didn't actually say it," Gabriel pointed out.

"But you were going to," Aster countered resentfully.

Gabriel paused his ministrations.

"I didn't tell you to stop," Aster said.

He resumed stroking Aster's stomach, waiting for her to say something.

"I'm bored," Gabriel said bluntly.

"With not being on assignment? Yes, I can tell," Aster replied wearily, "but until you get another mission, you still have five children to help me raise."

Right on cue, their newest arrival began to cry. Gabriel dutifully climbed out of bed and picked his new-born daughter out of her crib, rocking her slowly to ease her crying. Aster got up and joined him, collecting the baby from Gabriel, and getting ready to feed her.

"You're a good father when you put your mind to it," Aster remarked backhandedly.

"Who says I'm not?" Gabriel asked with narrowed eyes.

"Well, you weren't all that enthusiastic about having another one," Aster replied.

"Having this many is hard work," Gabriel said, stepping on a landmine.

"Yes, it *is* hard work," Aster hissed irritably, keeping her voice down as the baby fed, "It's *very* hard work raising children while your other half flies back and forth across the galaxy, and that's not even getting into who does the work of *having* them!"

Gabriel was silent, smarting from the rebuke.

"…I'm sorry," Aster said softly, "it's just that this is the longest you've ever been home, and you don't seem very happy about being around your own children."

"I am," Gabriel assured her, then added more sternly, "but five is enough."

"Fine," Aster replied, "for now."

"No, not 'for now'," Gabriel insisted, standing his ground, "If you change your mind later, there will definitely be an argument about it."

"If you really don't want anymore, you could always get snipped," Aster remarked, causing Gabriel to flinch in discomfort.

"I didn't think so," Aster said with a sly smile.

* * *

Gabriel stared at the ceiling for the rest of the night while Aster lay face down on top of him, exhausted by the demands of a hungry new-born. Gabriel reached over to the bedside table and retrieved his smartphone. The rainstorm was over and the news was reporting that it had been the heaviest rainfall in a 24 hour period in a decade. So much rain had fallen that the drainage system in the Undercity had struggled to cope, resulting in minor flooding.

There was also an encrypted text message from the Directorate, reminding him about Orion's proficiency test that morning. Medical examinations were one thing, but giving an eight-year-old a full-length IQ test struck Gabriel as distinctly odd, and he couldn't deny his misgivings about it – or about the Directorate's motives.

The bedroom door opened a crack, and several pairs of luminescent green eyes peered in. Gabriel beckoned to them and the children filed quietly into the room one by one, eight-year-old Orion, six-year-old Rose, four-year-old Violet, and two-year-old Leonidas, before climbing onto the bed together.

"Who's there?" Aster asked sleepily.

"Just the other four mouths we feed," Gabriel answered, putting his smartphone down.

"Can we come with you and Orion?" Rose asked.

"Sorry," Gabriel replied, "you have your learning pod courses to take."

Rose pursed her lips in disappointment.

"Do you want to sit in a testing booth for several hours solving mathematical problems and logic puzzles?" Gabriel asked his eldest daughter.

"But you make us do that all the time at home, anyway," Orion complained, "why can't I just take the test at home in the learning pod?"

That was a good question. The answer was probably that the Directorate didn't want to risk the data, encrypted though it would be, getting intercepted by a third party – as if any third party could disturb a pile of dust without the Directorate of Naval Intelligence finding out.

"This kind of test needs to be a done in a special place," Gabriel explained, "which is why you and I have to go to the city centre for it."

"Stop talking and go back to sleep everyone," Aster complained drowsily.

The children obliged and piled around their parents for a group snuggle. Despite his suppressed emotions and stoic demeanour, their affection was genuinely heart-warming, and Gabriel squeezed them close.

"Daddy," Violet asked in a quiet voice, "are you leaving us soon?"

That was a painful question, and all four children awaited the answer earnestly. Gabriel had been home for the past year, but he could be given a new assignment at any moment and be gone for weeks or months on end. Violet and her siblings – not to mention their mother – obviously hoped that the answer was no.

"No," Gabriel replied with only partial certainty.

* * *

None of the survivors of the trading barge attack was in a fit state to move or talk, and with the immediate danger to the station neutralised, the usual rhythm of life aboard the Nexus quickly resumed. As the survivors slept in their comas, bands of looters descended on their wrecked ship like a swarm of piranhas, swooping in to steal anything of value.

No species or authority governed the Nexus station, let alone the lawless area of space beyond. Once the station was no longer in danger and the survivors had been shown basic kindness and charity, there was no power that was able or willing to stop enterprising thieves from helping themselves to the survivors' property.

Flying directly into the gaping breaches in the hull, the swarms of ships disgorged teams of mercenaries and salvagers into the super-barge. Their spacesuits were equipped with body armour and shielding, and they were all armed. Fortunes could be made or lost on scavenging missions like these, so gunfights between looting parties were inevitable.

To everyone's surprise, however, the ship was still full of goods. The attackers had scrupulously targeted the access hatches and vital systems but ignored its cargo. There was a brief pause to wonder at what might motivate an entity to attack a peaceful trading vessel, slaughter its crew, and prevent them from escaping only to leave the cargo untouched.

Then an orgy of looting ensued.

Roaming the airless hallways, the scavengers used plasma torches to cut their way through the fused bulkheads, moving deeper into the ship and taking whatever they could find. Once they were inside the cargo bays, they smashed open the storage crates and helped themselves to the precious goods stored within.

There was an abundance of processed and semi-processed ores, finished and semi-finished goods, and light and heavy machinery acquired from all over the galaxy. Being a trading vessel, most of it was intended for sale, not for use aboard the ship; and indeed it would be sold, just not by its rightful owners.

The cargo bay had also doubled as a shuttle bay, but the doors had been melted shut by the mystery attackers, so someone jury-rigged some breaching explosives to blast them open. The explosion tore open the doors, but since the ship was already evacuated of air there was no explosive decompression.

Those looting teams who had shuttles used them to transport their ill-gotten gains to their motherships. Those without shuttles strapped portable thruster modules onto the cargo containers and piloted them manually into space. A steady two-way stream of shuttlecraft and flying cargo modules formed as the cargo was systematically plundered.

The cargo bays were soon stripped bare, leaving only the super-barge itself. Without a shipbreaking yard, there was no way a vessel this big could be cut up for scrap; but it was still full of valuable technology that could be removed and repurposed, so the next phase of the looting frenzy was to cannibalise the ship itself.

Panels were cut open and the technology beneath was stripped out. Anything could find a buyer somewhere in the galaxy, and so every piece of tech or scrap was potentially valuable. The process of ransacking the wrecked ship would take weeks to complete, and the looters would make numerous round-trips to ensure that nothing was left.

But that wasn't all that was found. Using codes stolen from one of the frozen corpses, one group of salvagers gained access to the ship's core, where an enormous energy signature had been detected. It couldn't be the ship's fusion plant or the faster-than-light Q-engine since those were located elsewhere in the ship. In any case, removing the Q-engine without tearing apart the ship's superstructure was impossible, so this was the next best prize.

The core chamber was sealed with reinforced blast doors, and no amount of explosives or plasma torching would have been enough to cut through them. Stumbling upon the access codes had been sheer luck, and the fact that the crew had put so much effort into sealing off the chamber meant that there had to be something valuable inside.

There was a dais in the centre of the chamber with a metallic sphere suspended above it by a stasis field. The artefact was a scorched black colour and was covered in intricate glyphs that glowed a sickly green under the dim light. The looters stared in awe before their leader barked impatiently at them; there was no time to waste.

As they searched the chamber for a way to deactivate the stasis field, they tried to ignore the menacing aura around the artefact. Maybe it was transmitting a neurological signal to confuse them, or maybe it was nerves and superstition, but the longer they spent in the chamber, the more agitated they began to feel.

As the search became more frantic, one looter's clawed foot got snagged on a cable, causing him to trip and fall into one of his comrades. His comrade smacked him to one side in surprise and anger, starting a scuffle that ended when one of them was thrown across the chamber through the low gravity and into the artefact.

As the loser of the fight hit the giant orb, the glowing glyphs all over its jet black surface were suddenly extinguished. Not only that, but the stasis field suspending it above the dais abruptly died and it came crashing down to the floor. The team of scavengers froze up, terrified that it might crack open and release some interstellar demon.

When nothing happened, the leader barked more orders at them. The fight was quickly forgotten as the salvagers worked to move the object, rolling it inch by inch out of the chamber. It was a laborious task, but the sooner they could get the artefact out of the ship and sell it on, the sooner it would become someone else's problem.

* * *

Early in the morning at the scheduled time, Gabriel dropped Orion off at the Directorate testing centre, and with several hours to kill, he decided to take a detour down to a place that the well-to-do seldom visited. The structures this far below were so tightly packed together that it wasn't possible to build a train network, so the only way to get there was to take a public elevator several hundred storeys down.

Long ago, this place had been the entirety of Asgard City with few buildings taller than ten storeys; but as the city had grown, construction had spread vertically, both skywards and underground. The soaring skyscrapers were a powerful symbol of Asgard City's blossoming prosperity as well as a potent metaphor for the wealth gap. These weren't the opulent 'Clouds' – the self-regarding name for the upper reaches of the city – this was the Undercity, the depths where most of the population dwelt.

The whole place resembled a darker and dirtier version of the Clouds, aged by a hundred years. It had a similar architectural design, but with none of the sheen and maintenance that went into making the sky-high towers gleam. The occasional cleaning drone could be seen meticulously clearing away rubbish, but it was essentially a slum.

This far underground, the 'streets' were little more than corridors, just wide enough for two people to pass each other. Standing a head taller than most of the residents in a crisp uniform, Gabriel may as well have been a visitor from another planet, and everyone he passed gave him a wide berth as he passed through a doorway into a plaza.

It was a small public square with a couple of benches and artificial trees, ringed with automated shops selling everything from food and medicine to cheap electronics. In the centre of the plaza, sticking up from the floor and disappearing into the ceiling, was a massive support column the size of a small building. Its surface was covered in faded graffiti, some of it crude, but most of it impressively artistic.

The ground was damp. It shouldn't be damp this far below ground.

One corner of the plaza had been cordoned off as a team of maintenance robots worked to repair a gaping hole in the wall. There was water damage around the edge of the breach, and a pumping mechanism was visible inside, which explained the stacks of materials and packaged machinery lying around.

In fact, there was water damage all around the walls and all the way up to the ceiling; the wall must have burst open and flooded the entire plaza. An ocean's worth of rain had followed gravity down into the city's drainage system – a system built more than two centuries ago to handle occasional rainstorms, not monsoon-like flooding.

Dozens of these pumps had failed and burst open across the city, and the total repair bill would probably bite into the municipal budget. Still, it was much cheaper to repair a damaged drainage pump than to rip it out and install a newer and better machine – in spite of the four drowned corpses respectfully arranged to one side.

The bodies were covered by black hygiene sheets, giving them some semblance of dignity before they were taken away for incineration. Passers-by chatting in Undercity dialect fell silent and stopped briefly to pay their respects. Gabriel watched from a short distance away before continuing on his way, averting his gaze in disgust.

The Undercity wasn't just the seedy underbelly of Asgard City, it was an unsavoury by-product of its success. An ultra-efficient and modern economy had produced a level of prosperity that the ancestors could only have dreamed of as well as enough resources to provide everyone with a basic monthly income.

But in an economy where countless jobs were automated, there was no particular use for many of the millions it supposedly helped. Without sufficient technical skills to contribute to the economy, and without the wealth and connections to take advantage of the luxury it produced, a large portion of Humanity had ceased to be necessary.

In centuries past, unemployment might mean starvation. Not in this era. The economy would support you from cradle to grave without you having to lift a finger to support it in return. The millions who dwelt in the depths of the Undercity were an economic burden on the rest of the city's economy. They knew it, and they hated it.

Gabriel passed a shiny metal door with an industrial grade lock. Adding insult to injury, the majority of the industrial base was located down here, amongst the homes of the very people who were least useful to it. There was no better place to put the automated factories and warehouses, but it served to ram home how little the Undercity dwellers mattered.

To be unneeded was almost worse than starving.

Of course, there were ways out. For those who saved up enough for the trip, there was the option of leaving the planet altogether and starting a new life on the frontier. That was more or less the story of Humanity's interstellar expansion: colonise, develop, multiply, and then drive the surplus population to new worlds to repeat the process.

Another escape route was to learn your way out. Public learning pods were available for anyone to use, providing courses on every subject imaginable. Education was compulsory until adulthood, but the learning pods were a free and convenient alternative to a full university education if you had the discipline to use them consistently.

That had probably been Aster's way out.

Gabriel arrived at a medical clinic with a pair of serpents intertwined around a winged staff emblazoned above the door. He entered and walked straight through the security scanners into a dingy waiting hall filled with rows of dispirited patients, their expressions reflecting the hopelessness of the place in which they lived. Walking past the reception desk, Gabriel ducked into one of the offices, closing the door behind him.

The physician whose office it was remained seated with his back to Gabriel, wearing a traditional white doctor's coat, and pretending not to have noticed his visitor.

"Good morning," Gabriel said, announcing his presence.

"Good morning to you too," said the doctor, swivelling around to face Gabriel, "An even better morning if you promise to knock next time."

"As long as I can still call you Mortimer."

"That or Dr Shelton will do."

The two men stood there looking at each other until Dr Shelton got up from his desk and approached Gabriel. The two men embraced like the old friends they were.

"How's life been treating you, Gabriel?" Mortimer asked with a smile.

"It's been a bit dull with no recent assignments," Gabriel confessed.

"As a non-soldier, I dread to think what you mean by 'a bit dull'," Mortimer quipped wryly, "so how's the family doing?"

"Funny you should ask," Gabriel replied more seriously, "That's why I'm here."

"Well, have a seat and we can talk about it," said Mortimer.

Gabriel obliged and took a seat while his host fetched an alcoholic drink from the mini-fridge and handed it to him.

Dr Mortimer Shelton had a head of grey hair and a silver moustache which, along with his steel grey eyes, gave him a patrician look to compliment the faint wrinkles across his face. He listened intently as Gabriel described the changes that Orion was undergoing, and when Gabriel had finished, Mortimer raised an eyebrow.

"Gabriel," he responded ironically, "I'm shocked to hear that your son has inherited the *genetic* enhancements that we gave you."

"But shouldn't this be happening at puberty?" Gabriel asked, "He's only eight."

"Puberty happens whenever the body is ready," Mortimer explained, "and 'whenever' can be tweaked with the correct understanding of biochemistry. Having said that, your children were all born after I left, so I can't tell you as much as I'd like to about the specifics."

"What about my daughters?" Gabriel asked, "I'm assuming Leonidas will show the same traits as Orion, but what about Rose and Violet?"

"You mean like superhuman strength?" Mortimer asked with an amused smile.

"Everything," Gabriel responded with deadly seriousness, "enhanced strength, reflexes, accelerated healing, intelligence, all of it."

"The short answer is almost certainly," Mortimer replied.

"And the long answer?"

"Genetic modifications invariably interact with the hormonal balance of the subject," Mortimer explained, "which means that each modification has to be tailored to minimise the effect on that hormonal balance. Since that balance is different in men and women, the tailoring would have to be completely different. Precisely tailoring all of those enhancements, let alone making sure that they're all inherited, is a monumental task."

"So the Directorate planned for all of this," Gabriel concluded.

"The Directorate plans for everything," Mortimer replied, "Smooth heritability is a strong indicator of the robustness of a given genetic enhancement. I guarantee you that all of your children have inherited all of your enhancements, but your daughters won't exhibit the more…martial traits because we decided to leave those recessive."

"Why?" Gabriel asked curiously.

"Remember what I said about the different hormonal balances requiring different sets of tailoring? Well, the initial batch of voidstalkers were all male, so we had the male biochemical tailoring nailed down. We could certainly have mastered it for females, but it just wasn't a priority. Short answer: making the genes recessive in girls was less work."

"I see..." Gabriel answered with a mixture of relief and doubt.

"Enhanced intelligence is one trait they'll all display as they grow up," Mortimer added, "that's more neurology than hormones, so there won't be any statistically significant disparities in IQ or mental acuity between the boys and girls."

"Funny you should mention that," Gabriel responded, "I dropped Orion off to have his IQ tested on my way to see you."

"If my team did their jobs properly, he'll ace the test," Mortimer remarked with a smile.

Gabriel nodded in acknowledgement and sipped from his drink.

"I'm guessing there are other problems as well?" Mortimer ventured.

"What makes you think that?"

"You're still with the Directorate," Mortimer replied, "so you could just ask them. Unless you don't really trust them to tell you the whole truth."

Gabriel remained silent. Mortimer was right: he no longer trusted the Directorate to tell him the whole truth, especially not after what had happened on Loki. The former chief of research for the Voidstalker Programme was as good a person to ask as any.

"Well there's not much else I can tell you, really," Mortimer said with a sigh, "At least not without access to the raw data and a supercomputer the size of a warehouse."

Gabriel took another sip of his drink.

"I have a fifth one, now," he announced, "Another girl."

"Congratulations!" Mortimer exclaimed with a beaming smile, "It's good to know that you're swimmers are still going strong."

"Gross," Gabriel remarked.

"I'm serious," Mortimer continued, "With all the procedures we put you through, the list of things that could have gone wrong could fill an entire encyclopaedia, and infertility is a side effect of most of them. So your success as a father is a testament to *my* success as a geneticist, and further proves that my work wasn't in vain."

"Speaking of which, how have you been since we last spoke?" Gabriel asked.

"Life is dull but liveable," Mortimer replied, rather more sullenly, "Not as exciting as working for the DNI, but at least I can help people down here. And, of course, the almighty and benevolent government pays for everything."

"Except for decent drainage systems, apparently," Gabriel remarked acidly.

"Ah…" Mortimer turned even more serious, "you saw the plaza?"

"And the bodies," Gabriel added.

"The pump ruptured whilst they were sleeping, and the emergency doors locked them in," Mortimer explained, then added bitterly, "We can travel faster than light and genetically engineer immunity to theoretical diseases that haven't been discovered yet; and yet there are still people in this day and age who have to sleep rough."

The intercom on Mortimer's desk chimed, and he turned around to check the message.

"Duty calls," Mortimer said wearily.

"I'll let you get back to work then," Gabriel said, getting up.

"Oh no, you can stay," Mortimer waved him back down, "this shouldn't take long."

Mortimer walked out and left Gabriel alone in the office.

Why Mortimer had left the Directorate had never been fully explained, not even by Mortimer himself, but Gabriel made sure to come down to the Undercity and pay his old friend a visit every so often. Of course, he wasn't just a long-time acquaintance; he was the man who had made him what he was today.

Gabriel looked around. Besides the patient bed and the doctor's desk, the office also had a storage closet with reinforced glass and a biometric lock. He got up from his seat and saw that the whole closet was set on hinges, a strange feature for a secure medicine cabinet to have. A hidden door in a doctor's office?

Gabriel gripped the edges of the closet then hesitated. He sensed an awful lot of trouble waiting for him on the other side which could be avoided by simply sitting down and waiting for Mortimer to return. Then again, it wasn't in Gabriel's nature to avoid trouble; better to confront and neutralise trouble sooner rather than later.

Slowly, he heaved open the closet door and entered.

On the other side was a greenhouse, warm and humid with bright lighting and an airborne drone monitoring row after row of green-leafed plants. The sickly sweet aroma of fertiliser was overpowering, and Gabriel wrinkled his nose in distaste.

Mortimer reappeared, not looking the least bit guilty at having been caught.

"Are you fleeking kidding me?" Gabriel scolded him as he entered.

"It's always funny hearing you swear," Mortimer said with a laugh.

"I'm serious!" Gabriel snapped, "You're growing drug plants in a medical clinic!"

"Cannabis is a harmless medicinal plant that's been cultivated for millennia," Mortimer replied, "And it does far less harm than alcohol or stimulants."

Gabriel scowled at him suspiciously, waiting for him to spill the full story.

"Although…" Mortimer confessed, "These particular plants are a specially-engineered crossbreed that I've been working on for a while."

"Oh, for Terra's sake!" Gabriel exclaimed in exasperation.

"Hey, I'm a trained molecular geneticist working as a medical doctor," Mortimer said defensively, "a man's got to keep his skills sharp."

"Who are you growing it for?" Gabriel demanded.

"No one!" Mortimer insisted.

"Don't fleeking lie," Gabriel shot back, "how else would you get the samples?"

"I still have connections with some suppliers," Mortimer answered.

"Was that them now?" Gabriel asked with narrowed eyes.

"No, but…" Mortimer said reluctantly, "I may need your help."

"If it weren't for our time in the DNI," Gabriel muttered through gritted teeth.

"Well, what else is friendship for?" Mortimer remarked.

There was a banging sound from the office, like someone trying to break down the door.

"Basically, a local gang got wind of my new product and wants to rob me," Mortimer explained, reaching under one of the plant trays and pulling out a gun.

"Controlled substances *and* illegal firearms possession," Gabriel observed wryly.

"Call Civil Security on me later," Mortimer replied, fumbling with the gun's settings, "Right now, I need you to stop these fricking guys from killing me."

Gabriel and Mortimer took cover behind the doorway as the banging continued.

"What's their force strength?" Gabriel asked.

"'Force strength'?" Mortimer said, raising a quizzical eyebrow.

"How many are there, and what kind of weapons do they have?" Gabriel clarified.

"Oh. There's three of them," Mortimer replied, "They also have guns."

"I don't suppose you have a weapon for me?"

"Apart from the enhancements you were given under my watchful eye, I'm afraid not," Mortimer answered, "And in case you're wondering, my gun has a biometric trigger."

Gabriel opened his mouth to curse Mortimer but was interrupted by the sound of the office door breaking off its hinges. Several people entered the office, one of them barking an order in Undercity dialect while the others searched for the greenhouse entrance.

Of all the tactical situations Gabriel had found himself in, this had to rank amongst the worst – a very competitive list. He was trapped in a room with no visible exits and facing multiple armed hostiles with only one armed ally to help him. Furthermore, apart from his bare fists and the element of surprise, he had no weapon of his own.

One of the intruders found the hidden door. There were more voices on the other side as the intruders gathered round and tried to open it. Gabriel's muscles tensed up, preparing to ambush the first person that entered. The door inched open and one of the intruders pointed the barrel of a gun through the gap.

Gabriel grabbed his hand and dislocated his wrist. The man yelled in pain, dropping the gun into Gabriel's open hand and withdrawing to safety. Fortunately, the gun didn't have a biometric trigger, so it would definitely fire. Unfortunately, it only had ten shots.

The other two intruders heaved open the door and fired several shots into the room, the bullets punching through nutrient sacs and spilling transparent fluid all over the floor. Gabriel ducked behind one of the plant trays while Mortimer stayed crouched in cover.

Two intruders barged in with guns drawn while the third brandished a shock-stick. They looked like street thugs with no visible body armour, and they barged in without any sense of caution, making no real attempt to check their corners.

From his hiding spot, Mortimer squeezed off a shot. The bullet hit one of the intruders in the back, knocking him forwards without penetrating his clothing – he must have had a bulletproof layer under his shirt after all.

Gabriel opened fire as soon as Mortimer did, hitting the second intruder in the back while the intruder with the shock-stick ducked into cover. Gabriel got up from his hiding spot and advanced. One of the intruders rolled over with his gun drawn but Gabriel fired first, the bullet penetrating the underside of his target's chin and into his brain, killing him instantly.

The second intruder dropped his gun and displayed his bare palms.

"Who sent you?" Gabriel demanded.

"…No one," he replied hesitantly, "we just heard there was good merchandise here."

"And where did you hear that?"

"What's it to you?" the man said defensively.

"If you won't tell me, then I may as well kill you," Gabriel responded menacingly.

"It was a rumour on the street, that's all," the man answered fearfully.

"Did you need guns and armour-shirts to pull off this robbery?"

"They're cheap and easy to get if you know who to ask," the man replied.

They were clearly amateurs, it was unlikely that they worked for anyone more powerful. Now Gabriel just had to call Civil Security and figure out a way to spin the incident.

The third intruder suddenly lunged out from cover with his shock-stick. Gabriel jumped back just in time and shot the man through the head. The shock-stick was still live when it fell from the dead man's hand, and the tip ignited the puddle of flammable nutrient fluid, turning it into a puddle of fire, and setting the plants ablaze.

Gabriel choked back the acrid fumes as they stung his eyes and throat, and stumbled back. The last intruder scrambled to safety, flames licking his trouser legs. He made it as far as the door before a pistol butt appeared and clocked him around the head.

The automated fire control system activated, directing a combined jet of water and pressurised carbon dioxide at the fire, extinguishing it in a few seconds. All that remained of the plant sample was a smouldering pile of burnt mush.

"Thanks for the help," said Mortimer as he walked over.

Gabriel turned around to deliver a caustic riposte, but his breath got caught up in his throat and he raised his gun again.

It wasn't Mortimer.

The figure standing in front of him was wearing DNI Special Operations Division armour. His helmet had been removed somehow, exposing his face and deathly pale skin to view. Gabriel knew that face.

"Ogilvy!" Gabriel gasped in shock, "But you're dead!"

"Of course I'm dead, Colonel," replied 'Ogilvy', a hideous grin curling the corners of his lips, "YOU KILLED ME!"

'Ogilvy's' eyes turned jet black and a dark cloud of particles enveloped his body, filling the confined space with a deafening roar. He looked exactly as he had when the Swarm had possessed his body and mind: like a mythical plague made manifest.

Gabriel yelled and opened fire, but the corpse-like apparition of Ogilvy looked back at him with an insane grin as the bullets seemed to disappear into thin air.

"YOU CAN'T KILL A DEAD MAN, COLONEL!" Ogilvy's apparition declared, his voice booming out from all directions simultaneously, "DON'T YOU REMEMBER THE BOMB GOING OFF, ANNIHILATING ME COMPLETELY?"

"Stay back!" Gabriel yelled, squeezing the pistol's trigger on empty.

"STAY BACK! STAY BACK!" the apparition of Ogilvy yelled back mockingly, the air seeming to vibrate with every syllable he uttered, "ISN'T THAT WHAT YOU WANTED? FOR

THE SQUAD TO STAY BACK AND OUT OF YOUR WAY? WERE WE SO MUCH OF A BURDEN TO YOU THAT YOU HAD TO LEAVE ME TO DIE? IS THAT WHY YOU WERE SO SLOW TO COME TO MY RESCUE?!"

Gabriel knew that none of this was real. Something about the echo of his own thoughts booming back at him from the mouth of a dead man gave it away. The air convulsing violently with every syllable like the rhythmic thump of a loudspeaker and the walls of the darkening room bending in towards him were also strong clues.

Even so, Gabriel felt as though his entire body was gripped by blood-curdling dread. The buzzing cloud around Ogilvy was a deafening roar in his ears and inside his head, and it was growing louder and louder as it overwhelmed what remained of his senses.

He dropped the empty gun and charged.

Ogilvy evaporated as Gabriel lunged at him, and a stinging sensation pricked him in the leg. Gabriel felt a jolt of electricity surge through his muscles, paralysing him completely, and he sank to his knees and then onto all fours as his mind was claimed by the darkness.

THE ARTEFACT

HARD work though it was, ransacking the super-barge was a bonanza for everyone, and the various gangs were too busy looting to fight each other. Otherwise, it would have been extremely difficult for the salvage team to defend themselves and the artefact they had stolen whilst rolling it back to their ship.

Even in the low gravity aboard the trading barge, the artefact was extraordinarily heavy, and it took two or three looters pushing together to get it to move at all. It was just small enough to move through the narrow corridors of the ship, but only just, and it was a wonder the trading barge crew had managed to get it into the containment chamber in the first place.

Several times, the salvagers crossed paths with other gangs of looters. Gaggles of fast-moving critters and packs of simian brutes looked at them as they hauled crates full of stolen goods and disassembled tech. Grips on firearms were tightened, but ultimately there was plenty for everyone to steal and they left each other alone.

As the salvagers heaved the orb-shaped object back to their ship, some of them couldn't help but wonder what it was. For one thing, its scorched black surface wasn't perfectly round, being covered in intricate, geometrically regular ridges and grooves. For another, the material from which the artefact had been constructed was an esoteric alloy which defied their attempts to scan its interior.

Perhaps they were better off not knowing what was inside. It was far more of a trial to the scavengers not to lose their already on-edge nerves. All the while they were moving it, the artefact continued to exude that sinister aura, making their leathery skin crawl underneath their spacesuits and driving them to distraction. Maybe it was just paranoia, but for all they knew, the artefact was slowly brainwashing them.

Every freebooter and trader had legends and stories to share from their wanderings through the stars. Many of those stories concerned relics looted from the ruins of long-dead civilisations, and more than a few of those alleged that the relics were cursed. Just as it had in the days of campfires and bronze spears, superstition thrived in the age of interstellar travel.

The journey back seemed to take forever, but eventually, they made it back to the hull breach where they had docked their shuttle. The already weak gravity died out altogether as they stepped out of the breach, averting their gaze from the terrible vastness of space. A collective shove was all it took to propel the artefact through the open hatch of the shuttle, and then they kicked off the ledge one by one to board the shuttle.

The journey back to the mothership was a brief one, and once the shuttle had docked, the salvagers stowed their loot in the cargo hold. As an extra precaution, they sealed the sinister artefact away inside a reinforced metal container, welding it shut for good measure. Then they began the short flight back to the Nexus station to find a buyer.

They didn't have to wait long.

An alert began flashing on the readout in the navigation chamber, indicating a secure communication request. Receiving an encrypted transmission from out of the blue was a total surprise, especially since the transmission had no identifiable signature. The mercenaries eyed the flashing icon suspiciously for a while before the leader extended a clawed finger and tapped it, opening up a two-way link.

As soon as the link was established, a rapid-fire series of clicks and chirps sounded through the speakers. The looters flinched in surprise as they listened to the unintelligible message. They recognised exactly which species the speaker belonged to, but had to wait for its message to be translated into their own language.

"*We know what you found,*" the sibilant, synthetically translated voice on the other end informed them, "*and we are prepared to pay a considerable sum in exchange.*"

The salvagers looked at each other in disbelief, wondering how the speaker knew about the artefact and why it would want the artefact. However, a buyer was still a buyer.

"Where?" the leader grunted in response.

There was no verbal reply. Instead, a map of the Nexus was uploaded to their screen with a specific location highlighted.

Then the connection was abruptly terminated.

* * *

The scavengers' mothership cruised into one of the Nexus's many vacuum-docks, and a multi-tonne door sealed behind it. Docking clamps locked onto the vessel's hull, holding it in place whilst a docking tunnel was extended, smothering its docking hatch with a vacuum-tight hose to allow the crew to disembark.

The salvagers were reptilian, but instead of scales their hides were tough and leathery and were various shades of sandy brown that seemed to shift in colour under the light. Their heads were like those of monitor lizards, arching forwards with tapered snouts, and their eyes were a fiery orange with dark pupils shaped into vertical slits. Each eye moved independently of the other, scanning from side to side for threats.

They were dressed in makeshift body armour decorated with clan markings and adorned with battle trophies, and they all inclined their heads towards a grizzled veteran who led them. The skull of some predatory animal was bolted onto the left pauldron of his armour, featuring a bony crest extending from the top which made it look like a crude shoulder shield, and he regarded his surroundings with a disdainful scowl.

Most of the crewmembers were hulking firearms, but two of them were transporting the cargo container inside which the artefact had been sealed. The container was just small enough to pass through the docking tunnel, and it glided smoothly forward on an antigravity flatbed as it was pushed into the cargo processing centre.

Under the watchful gaze of the reptilian scavengers, the container was moved through the processing centre to the meeting point. Monitoring drones flew overhead, and one swooped down to scan the contents of the container. One of the armed crewmembers used his gun to smack the drone away, hissing with a mouthful of sharp teeth.

The drone beat a hasty retreat and the scavengers escorted their valuable prize away unchallenged, making their way to a chamber on the other side of the processing centre. A sliding door opened as they approached and they hurried inside, pushing the container ahead of them before sealing the door behind them.

The little chamber where the exchange was due to take place was warm and dimly lit. The reptilian mercenaries didn't mind the extra heat or the lack of light, their own homeworld was covered in vast tracts of desert and sun-scorched rock formations.

What they did mind was the air. The humidity was stiflingly tropical, with far too much moisture and oxygen for their liking, and they blinked and flared their slitted nostrils in palpable discomfort as they waited for their newfound business partners to show up. Sure enough, from their perch on the ceiling, three creatures skittered down to the floor, standing upright on six segmented legs.

The insectoid creatures towered over their reptilian contacts, looking down at them with eight glossy black eyes, four on each side of their faces. Their bodies had armoured carapaces and their four arms each ended in a set of sinuous claws. The leader of the delegation wore a mask which translated its utterances into the scavengers' own language.

"Do you have it?" it asked in a sibilant and raspy voice.

The reptilian leader barked a command and one of the mercenaries pulled out a power tool, using it to cut through the crude welding that sealed the cargo container. The walls of the box crashed to the floor and the scavengers stepped back apprehensively, eager to keep their distance from the sinister artefact within.

Despite the fact that their insectoid features couldn't convey facial expressions, the delegation stared at the giant orb in what could almost pass for awe. The reptilian looters breathed uncomfortably in the overly humid and over-oxygenated air as they waited for their clients to give their decision.

"We are pleased," the delegation leader said in that creepily sibilant rasp.

"Payment," the reptilian leader demanded bluntly, eager to be done with the exchange.

He spoke in his own language, but the single word and the impatience it conveyed was deciphered by the insectoid leader's translation mask. The delegation leader nodded to its companions who departed, returning shortly with cases containing an assortment of weaponry and technological trinkets.

The reptilian fighters collected their payment and fled the torrid chamber.

* * *

Gabriel awoke on an examination bed. Despite his pounding headache, he instantly remembered everything, including the vivid hallucination of Ogilvy leering at him in the drug lab. A faint stinging sensation on the side of his leg also reminded him of the shock-stick that had been jabbed into his leg.

Sitting up on the bed, Gabriel saw that he was back in Mortimer's office. The door to the hidden greenhouse had been sealed shut and the surviving intruder had been tied up in a corner. Despite not being gagged, the prisoner made no attempt to shout for help or to struggle free as Mortimer applied salve to a bruise on his head.

"Ah, you're awake," Mortimer said as he noticed Gabriel stirring.

Mortimer fetched a cup of ice-cold water from the cooler and handed it to Gabriel.

"Sorry about zapping you back there, by the way," Mortimer added.

"That's the least of the things for which you should be sorry," Gabriel replied with a scowl, taking the cup and draining it dry.

"I'm sorry about all of this, really," Mortimer responded.

"What in Terra's name were you growing in there?" Gabriel demanded.

"Remember when I said I've been growing 'special breeds'?" Mortimer replied guiltily, "Well, that particular breed – the one whose fumes you inhaled – was modified to produce a mild hallucinogenic effect when smoked."

"'Mild'?" Gabriel asked incredulously.

"Well, 'mild' was the goal," Mortimer replied, "but I'm still in the experimental phase, so I might have overdone it. Or there might be something in your neurology which is more susceptible to that particular chemical."

"So which is it?" Gabriel demanded.

"Probably the former," Mortimer conceded, "we simulated the biochemical effect of every single addition we planned to make to your genome, which included resistance and immunity to all manner of diseases and toxins. Since you were affected pretty badly by those fumes, you must have inhaled an extremely potent mix."

Gabriel was fuming, but at least he was starting to feel better.

"So who was Ogilvy?" Mortimer asked.

"That's classified," Gabriel replied bluntly.

"I guessed that much," Mortimer said, "You shouted his name and said he was supposed to be dead. Then you started shooting at the wall and almost killed me."

"I feel I should apologise for that," Gabriel began, then added, "but then again, I was poisoned by a hallucinogen that *you* were growing."

"I *did* just say I was sorry," Mortimer insisted defensively, sounding annoyed, "You don't have to be a fricking cock about."

Gabriel's pounding headache motivated him to cease the argument.

"Holy fricking Terra!" a third voice exclaimed in disbelief, "You're with the DNI?"

"We don't know what you're talking about," Mortimer responded calmly, pulling something out of his pocket and walking over to the prisoner.

"I'll fricking tell everyone that the DNI is growing drug plants in medical clinics!" the prisoner threatened excitedly as he struggled against his restraints.

"Sure you will," Mortimer replied, "but who's gonna believe you?"

Mortimer sprayed something into the prisoner's face, who choked and spluttered on the noxious aerosol for a moment then looked up at Mortimer and began screaming.

"Listen to this guy," Mortimer pointed at the man with feigned innocence, "ranting and raving about secret drug labs and DNI conspiracies. He's clearly been taking some kind of controlled substance, and I'm pretty sure a toxicology test will show that."

Gabriel shook his head. It was an unpleasant solution to an unpleasant problem.

"I think I've overstayed my welcome," said Gabriel, getting up from the medical bed.

"For an old friend who just saved my life, I'd beg to differ," Mortimer answered, "but if you insist, I won't keep you."

"I'm afraid I have to insist," Gabriel replied, "I have to pick up my son from the testing centre. Can you handle this guy?"

"I'll make a call to the Directorate, and they can sort it out," Mortimer answered.

"You still have contact with them?" Gabriel asked, surprised.

"Why the shock?" Mortimer asked back, "I left in more-or-less good standing. Besides, after your chemical exposure, I have to report this so they don't think I poisoned you."

"Ok then, it was good to see again," Gabriel said, then added with a narrow-eyed scowl, "getting drugged notwithstanding."

"Well, if you weren't angry, I'd have failed," Mortimer pointed out, "we were under strict instructions not to dull your capacity for aggression or sexual arousal. Red-eye wanted us to make calm and capable killers, not robots."

"Uh, I already knew that," Gabriel said, "but thanks for the clarification."

"You're welcome," Mortimer replied, "and congrats again on your newest arrival."

"We're definitely stopping at five," Gabriel said emphatically.

"I don't think they'll let you do that," Mortimer replied with a dirty smirk.

"What do you mean?" Gabriel asked, his brow furrowed in confusion.

Mortimer blanched, his smirk evaporating in an instant.

"*She'll*," Mortimer tried to clarify with an awkward stammer, "I meant I don't think that *she'll* let you stop…at five…I mean …never mind."

Mortimer stood there looking sheepishly at his shoes, as though he'd let slip something he shouldn't have. Gabriel looked at him, feeling even more confused.

"Take care of yourself, Mortimer," Gabriel said eventually.

"Yeah, you too."

* * *

Besides being a trading centre, the Nexus was also a major interstellar communications hub. Reliably transmitting data through Q-space was an enormous engineering challenge, but the achievement meant that huge amounts of data could be transmitted at faster-than-light speeds, keeping every corner of settled space connected to the rest of the galaxy. The resulting network of networks was known as the Q-net.

Within days of the super-barge's arrival, the story – and countless related rumours and conspiracy theories – had spread across the Q-net, far beyond Nexus space. So too had the mysterious word 'voidstalker' that had been uttered by one of the survivors.

As billions chattered, others listened.

A summary of the events was transmitted to a cloaked communications probe concealed on the edge of the gas cloud, which then transmitted the information through Q-space – outside of the Q-net – to another satellite light years away.

The final destination of the transmission was another space station, much smaller than the Nexus, and undetectable to known sensor technology. The Directorate of Naval Intelligence operated hundreds of similar outposts. They constituted part of a vital intelligence network without which the government and military would be deaf and blind to events beyond Human-controlled space.

The message was decrypted by the supercomputers aboard the station before being given to the analysts. The attack on the trading barge was intriguing, but the rumours about who the alleged culprits were made the analysts turn pale. A report was transmitted to all DNI stations and was given a tier 2 classification. The final section, however, was given a tier 1 classification and was blacked-out on the final version of the report.

An unredacted version of the report was then prepared for the director-general's eyes only, then transmitted to the DNI's sector headquarters on Asgard.

If the intelligence was accurate, several alien species now believed that a voidstalker – i.e., Humans – had attacked a peaceful trading barge without provocation and massacred its crew. For now, the only thing preventing a war was the fact that most aliens had no idea who or what Humans or voidstalkers were.

The redacted part of the report contained information far more ominous.

* * *

Orion had been bored stiff waiting for his father to pick him up from the Directorate testing centre; but with rush hour long over, he had an entire row of empty seats to himself on the mag-train home.

The network of electromagnetic rails on which the mag-trains ran snaked between the skyscrapers like a network of capillaries, connecting every corner of the upper and middle levels of Asgard City. The mag-train was cruising half a kilometre above the ground, and Orion pressed his face to the window, gazing at the glittering forest of steel and glass.

Asgard the planet was actually a moon orbiting the gas giant Odin, but it was the capital world of the entire sector. The sun was high in the sky and its light reflected off of Odin's cerulean clouds, bathing the megacity of 80 million people in solar glory. Asgard City was a manmade paradise, a literally shining exemplar of Human industry, technology, architectural elegance, and civilisational genius.

And it wasn't even the largest settled world of its kind. Some of the sub-sector capital worlds had populations and economies comparable to or greater than Asgard. The other five capital worlds had populations in the billions and boasted whole networks of megacities sprawling across their surfaces.

Orion would probably faint in awe if he saw Earth.

Of course, if Orion had directed his wide-eyed gaze downwards, he might glimpse a less glorious sight. The Undercity, where most of that wealth was generated, was home to most of the millions who called the city home. The logic and organisation of Humanity's ultra-efficient and highly automated economic model were the same on every planet. That made it a certainty that millions or billions of people on other planets lived lives that were just as drab and meaningless as those in the Undercity.

There was no denying the extraordinary, positively transcendent achievements reaped by Human civilisation over the past half a millennium. But the system that had produced those achievements had also left a majority of the people it supposedly helped to rot in the bowels of its glittering citadels.

It was the same system that wouldn't pay to replace ageing drainage equipment until it broke and drowned homeless people in their sleep. The same system that motivated one of the planet's leading geneticists to grow and sell drug plants out of idleness. The same system that Gabriel was sworn to preserve and defend along with its innumerable cultural achievements and scientific innovations.

Ironic, considering that not all of those innovations were Human in origin.

While his son stared at the mesmerising vista below, Gabriel stared at his flexi-tablet, the better to distract himself from the incident earlier. The hallucinations of Ogilvy taunting him about the Loki mission were still fresh in his memory, and his memories of the original events on Loki were just as vivid.

Having a squad foisted on him for the Loki mission had made no sense at the time. None of them had been voidstalkers, and if they had been it would have made even less sense since voidstalkers were supposed to be lone wolf operatives. The squad's camaraderie and sense of duty to each other had bothered Gabriel the most because he had been prepared to sacrifice all of them to complete the mission.

Gabriel knew he couldn't be blamed for Ogilvy's death, let alone the horrifying manner of his death, but he knew that the taunts were grounded in truth.

Ogilvy had been kidnapped by the insane staff at the Loki facility and turned into an avatar of the Swarm, and Gabriel had been forced to kill him with an antimatter bomb. The detonation had completed annihilated both the Swarm and its host, leaving Ogilvy's helmet as the only evidence that he had ever existed.

Gabriel remembered the undead colour of Ogilvy's flesh and the cloud of alien particles that had possessed him. He remembered the blood-curdling scream that the Swarm-possessed Ogilvy had uttered, turning the Loki facility cultists into a howling mob of fanatical savages. He remembered being pinned down by the possessed Ogilvy as he had tried to drive a pair of combat claws into Gabriel's neck, staring into his soul with eyes as black as the void.

Above all, he remembered Red-eye's duplicity. The Loki facility cult had been led by a man who had turned out to be a mole engaged in scientific espionage for the Directorate – a fact which Red-eye had failed to mention. Gabriel didn't regret killing Ogilvy, but it might not have been necessary if he had been given all the available intelligence beforehand.

Worst of all was the rank hypocrisy. Much of Gabriel's work as a voidstalker involved dealing with illegal private sector research into alien technology. That the Directorate had secretly been pocketing the benefits of that research while its operatives risked their lives to stamp it out was a betrayal he still hadn't forgiven. Above all, it mocked the memories of those operatives who had paid with their lives.

On top of all that, he still had a splitting headache.

"That test was boring," Orion complained, having also grown bored of the view.

"Well, it's over now, so you can stop whining," Gabriel answered gruffly.

"Can I have ice cream when we get home?" Orion pleaded.

"I don't know," his father replied pedantically, "can you?"

Orion huffed in annoyance.

"*May* I have ice cream when we get home?" he asked.

"Yes, you may," Gabriel replied.

"I wrote 'may' on the test," Orion added.

"That's good to know," Gabriel answered sternly, "if you can learn to use it in everyday speech that would be even better."

Something else was jabbing at the inside of Gabriel's skull: a feeling in the back of his mind that he ought to be nicer to his eldest son.

Orion swung his legs back and forth restlessly, then looked up and saw the handlebars. Climbing onto his seat, Orion squatted down and jumped. He managed to get his fingers around one of the bars, but his sweaty palms slipped on the smooth metal and he fell.

Gabriel launched himself from his seat and caught his son before he could hit the floor.

"Stupid boy!" Gabriel snapped, more from parental fright than true anger.

"I almost got it!" Orion replied with unapologetic triumph.

"You could have broken your neck," Gabriel said angrily, "No ice cream."

Orion pouted in disappointment but knew better than to argue with his father. He sat down again and stared at his shoes, sulking in silence while Gabriel sat down and returned to reading his son's test report.

The 'stupid' boy had attained a perfect score…on a test designed for 15-year-olds.

* * *

As soon as they were through the front door, Orion ran straight to the kitchen to help himself to ice cream. Gabriel's skull-splitting headache still wasn't gone, so he didn't have the energy to stop his son from disobeying him. Instead, he went straight to the living room to lie down on the couch.

He could still scarcely believe that an eight-year-old could ace an aptitude test designed for people twice his age. Still, it was nice to be the father of intelligent children, even if it was exasperating that they still acted their ages. Orion could solve a 4x4x4 Rubik's cube but still thought it was a good idea to treat the mag-train safety handles like monkey bars.

Aster came into the room, rocking the baby in her arms. Gabriel was relieved that the baby was asleep, the last thing his headache needed was a wailing infant. He smiled a greeting to Aster from the couch, but she didn't return the smile. Instead, she looked deadly serious and tense, her lips pursed with worry.

"What is it?" he asked her, confused by the look she was giving him.

"There's a package for you," she replied, gesturing to the living room table.

Gabriel turned his head and saw a sealed black box sitting on the table. It was a DNI-issue dead-box, the kind used for transporting small, valuable items. It could only be opened by an authorised individual or else the contents would be destroyed. Sitting up, he swiped his thumb across the biometric sensor strip, causing the box to pop open.

Lying in a shockproof foam bed was a hypodermic injector filled with a clear blue liquid. Inscribed on the inside of the box lid was a message:

'*Colonel Thorn. Dr Shelton contacted us regarding the events of this morning. Please administer the serum in this box as soon as possible. You are in no immediate danger, but the serum will remove all traces of the chemical to which you were exposed. Regards, Directorate of Naval Intelligence, R&D Block.*'

Gabriel took the injector and jabbed it into his neck, feeling the warm serum flow into his bloodstream. Then he put the injector back in the box and closed it.

"So, are you going to tell me about 'the events of this morning'? Or is that another one of your classified work secrets?" Aster demanded, her biting tone tinged with concern.

The last thing Gabriel wanted to do was involve Aster in this, but he couldn't concoct a convincing lie on the spot, and a bad lie would simply aggravate her suspicions.

"I went for a walk in the Undercity and some gang jumped me," Gabriel answered, "I fought them off, but they sprayed me with some kind of chemical and I had to get treated at a nearby medical clinic. Dr Shelton was the physician who treated me."

Everything in that answer was technically true, minus crucial details, context, and chronological accuracy. It was the kind of lie he had grown accustomed to telling.

Aster breathed a sigh of relief and sat down next to him, cradling the baby.

"Why didn't you call me to let me know?" she asked.

"Because I didn't want you to worry," Gabriel replied.

"When some mysterious black box turns up at the door, I can't help but worry," she replied more softly, "it could be your dog tags and a condolence letter."

Gabriel wanted to point out that he'd been home for a year, but his reply withered in his throat. He knew exactly what her point was, and he had no answer to it. Every time he deployed, he was leaving Aster and the children behind with the heavy possibility that he would never come back again. He could be killed out on the fringes of Human space or far beyond it, and there might be nothing left of him to bury.

In fact, he could have been killed this morning in Mortimer's drug lab by a stray bullet, an accidental explosion, or even the noxious fumes he had inhaled. Being on leave, his death would have come as a bolt from the blue. He hadn't meant to make light of the matter, but he felt guilty nonetheless.

Gabriel's headache was gone, and he wrapped a protective arm around Aster's shoulder. It was the right thing to do, but looking at his new-born intensified the guilt. If something happened to him, she would grow up with no memory of her father.

"Have you thought of a name yet?" Aster asked him.

"How about Jezebel?" Gabriel suggested half-jokingly, glad of the change of subject.

"There is no way we're naming her after that bitch," Aster replied with a scowl.

"Don't use that word around my children," Gabriel hissed.

"Then don't even think about naming her Jezebel," Aster hissed back, "she tried to blackmail me into stealing company secrets, then murdered my friend to cover it up. So no, I'm not naming one of my children after her, even if she is your mother."

Orion marched into the room, shamelessly eating from a bowl of ice cream.

"I said you weren't allowed to have any ice cream," Gabriel said with a stern glare.

"Too late!" Orion replied with a cheeky grin as he finished the last spoonful.

"What did he do wrong?" Aster asked, the naming argument quickly forgotten.

"He tried to jump off the seats on the mag-train and grab the handrails as if they were monkey-bars," Gabriel explained disapprovingly, "and if I hadn't caught him in mid-air, he would have fallen and broken his back."

"I touched the bars," Orion said proudly.

"You could have hurt yourself," Gabriel said his tone hardening.

"Well, I passed the test, didn't I?" Orion pointed out defensively, "and I scored 100%. So I think I deserve ice cream."

"I never said you scored 100%," Gabriel said suspiciously.

"I read it on your flexi-tablet on the mag-train," Orion revealed.

Aster tried hard not to laugh as Gabriel sighed in resignation.

Rose, Violet, and Leonidas walked into the room. Orion put his bowl down and the four siblings piled onto the couch on either side of their parents. It was the first time in the day they had gathered together as a family and Gabriel had an idea.

He switched on the holo-TV and activated the camera. Everyone saw what he was doing and got ready. Leo, the youngest, sat beside Aster while Orion sat beside Gabriel. Violet sat on Gabriel's lap whilst her older sister Rose climbed atop Gabriel's shoulders. Holding the baby, Aster lay her head on Gabriel's shoulder and he wrapped his arm around her.

Once everyone was ready, Gabriel pressed the clicker and smiled. There was a chime as the photo was taken, and the image appeared instantly on the holographic screen. Everyone stayed where they were, comfortable in their places and admiring the family photo.

"I like seeing you smile, daddy," Rose said from her perch.

"We all do," Aster added with a smile of her own.

* * *

The Spire was one of the tallest towers in Asgard City, but unlike the glitzy skyscrapers clustered together in the city centre, the Spire was a spike-shaped fortress without a single window on its sullen surface. It stood alone in the middle of a dead zone devoid of comparable structures, a planning decision that arose from security considerations as well as an austere rebuke to the civilian opulence surrounding it.

It was a fitting appearance for the building that served as the sector headquarters for the Directorate of Naval Intelligence. This was the building where all espionage activity and covert operations across the sector and beyond Human-controlled space were coordinated, as well as where the resulting intelligence was gathered and analysed.

The Spire never slept. DNI employees worked in shifts day and night on their respective activities. The top two-thirds of the Spire – the 'Office Block' – were given over to offices for the intelligence analysts. The bottom third of the building was known as the Rand Block, devoted to R&D conducted by hundreds of labs extending far below ground.

Some labs were just data processing centres. Each technician had their own data booth: a fully immersive interface from which they could dissect and analyse the rivers of information that flowed their way. Their faces glowed under the ever-shifting patterns of digital light, and their fingers jabbed and swiped at holographic icons.

In the centre was a gigantic column that glowed and pulsed like an enchanted tree trunk. It was a quantum supercomputing server that could crunch more data in a heartbeat than a regular computer could crunch in a lifetime. The science conducted within the Rand Block was decades ahead of what the private sector thought of as cutting-edge, and the equipment at its disposal had to match the task.

No one said a word, and no sound could be heard except for the sonorous humming of the supercomputer as it cogitated the oceans of information that were fed to it. In fact, there was an almost ecclesiastical serenity that pervaded the data centre, and no one dared disturb the temple-like silence that reigned as they worked.

Into this temple walked the chief of research, the doors opening and closing with only the faintest shudder. He was tall and thin with a grandfatherly beard, and he reviewed the latest data with silent approval before taking a seat beside one of the technicians.

"What we have so far is interesting," he said to his subordinate in a low voice, "I'm impressed that my predecessor managed to overshoot his own expectations."

"A pity Dr Shelton left before he could see for himself," the technician remarked.

"Indeed..." the chief of research replied pensively.

The spinning orange progress wheel flashed green as the simulations finished, and a new set of graphs appeared on the screens. The technician scrambled to start analysing the results while the chief of research didn't so much as nod his head.

"Sweet Terra..." the technician murmured.

"Indeed," the chief of research concurred impassively.

"Last year, his results were on par with a ten-year-old," the technician said breathlessly, "now it's in the 99th percentile for 15-year-olds and the 90th for 16-year-olds."

"The test scores are not the issue here," the chief of research pointed out, "they're a layman's indicator; it's his biochemistry and neurology that we're interested in."

"Those results all match or exceed what the simulations predicted we'd get," the technician answered, "hence the genius-level test scores."

"Which further confirms the stellar success of the procedures carried out on the boy's father," the chief of research said, evincing absolutely no sign of excitement.

"And his other kids will likely follow the same curve as well," the technician added, "at least if their results are anything to go by."

"What about the new-born?" the chief of research asked.

"She's only a few months old," the technician replied, "so there's no test data available for her yet. But given how consistent the first four have been, there's no reason to believe that her development will be any different."

"Indirect confirmation of enduring sperm quality and overall genetic sturdiness," the chief of research said to himself analytically, "it would be useful if they continue expanding the family to confirm that for the long term."

"The more lab rats, the better, right?" the technician joked with a grin.

The chief of research's cool and impassive demeanour cracked and he inclined his head towards the technician, his hard gaze telegraphing how unamused he was by the comment.

"They are children, not 'lab rats'," he replied coldly, "is that understood?"

"...Sir, it's just an expression–" the technician tried to stutter out a justification.

"Is that understood?" the chief of research repeated, his tone hardening.

"Yes, sir," the technician replied with a gulp.

"We'll need to adjust and re-run the predictive models in light of the latest results," the chief of research continued, "requisition the central quantum server if you have to."

"What about that supercomputer on Loki?" the technician asked.

"No," the chief of research answered, "The director-general herself has to personally authorise any use of the Loki supercomputer, and our project is barred from using it."

"What research project could possibly have greater priority than ours?"

"Unknown and above both our paygrades," came the blunt reply.

* * *

The darkness was all around him, like a physical substance immersing him completely. Gabriel waved his hands at the darkness, wafting it out of the way like so much thick smoke. The lack of directionality was disorienting, even in the world of dreams, and he waded through the lugubrious mass as best he could.

There was a tiny light ahead, and he moved towards it like a moth drawn to a flame, hoping that it was a path to the exit. As he approached, the light became more distinct and took the form of a doorway. Despite his apprehension about where it led, it was an escape from the oppressive darkness, and he stepped through.

He found himself in a cavernous, spherical space with a basalt-black surface and a network of platforms that extended from the edge to the centre. It was the central chamber of the observatory on Loki, the sepulchral atmosphere as palpable in the dream state as it was in reality. Gabriel remembered thinking at the time that it resembled the mausoleum of an alien geometrician, and his flashback only reinforced his impression.

The chamber was illuminated by a glowing spherical energy field in the centre. It was the containment field that had imprisoned the Swarm. The field itself was translucent like an inflated bubble, permitting a glimpse at the kickball-sized silver orb contained within: the Swarm in an inert state.

There were two figures at the far end of the platform, standing on a raised dais closest to the containment field. One was Lawrence Kane: the self-styled prophet of the Swarm and formerly a mole for the DNI. He had long, unkempt hair, and was wearing a snow-white lab coat covered in blood-red glyphs. He looked like a madman who had spent a year in the wilderness and come back wearing homemade priest robes.

The other figure was on his knees beside the 'prophet', clad in DNI Special Operations Division armour with his helmet removed. The semi-conscious Lieutenant Ogilvy looked exhausted, his were eyes closed, and his skin was a deathly-pale shade. Gabriel remembered this event all too well, and he remembered exactly what had happened next.

"You were too slow!" both figures declared in unison.

The 'prophet' Lawrence Kane enunciated the words with a maniacal grin on his face, whilst Ogilvy uttered them like a puppet repeating the words of a ventriloquist. Kane then shoved the dazed prisoner over the edge of the platform, allowing him to be caught and borne aloft by a gravity field below. Suspended in mid-air like a marionette, Ogilvy was carried up towards the containment field, a dazed and hapless sacrifice to the Swarm.

Gabriel raced forwards, charging at the insane Kane who stood facing the containment field with his arms raised in worship. Gabriel closed the distance in a few seconds but was too late to stop it from happening again. As Ogilvy was pulled inside, the orb disintegrated into a swarm of tiny silver particles and poured in through his nose and mouth, taking over his body and mind before violently expelling him from the containment field.

The Swarm-possessed Ogilvy landed squarely on his feet. He looked up and stared at Gabriel with jet black eyes, like a pair of polished coals overflowing with malevolence. He opened his mouth and the swarm of alien particles that had possessed him poured forth, turning into a raging cloud that swirled around his body.

"YOU WERE TOO SLOW TO SAVE ME!" the Swarm bellowed in Ogilvy's voice.

Then the Swarm surged towards Gabriel like a cloud of grain-sized locusts seeking to devour him. Gabriel was frozen to the spot, unable to flee as the Swarm engulfed him. The roar of the malicious cloud was deafening and its malevolent presence felt overpowering as the thousands of sentient particles poured into his body and devoured his mind.

* * *

Gabriel bolted upright in bed. Nightmares based on flashbacks were normal for him, but that was by far the most disturbing one he'd experienced. A moment or two of sitting up and his heart rate and breathing had returned to normal. Slowly, he lay back down on the bed, hoping not to fall asleep again.

A feminine hand slid across his bare chest as Aster snuggled in close, resting her head on his shoulder. Gabriel wrapped his arm around her body and reciprocated the embrace. They lay together in silence for a while, savouring each other's warmth.

"That sounded like a bad one," Aster murmured finally.

"Worse than usual," Gabriel admitted.

There was another round of silence until the baby began to cry again, demanding to be fed. Like clockwork, Aster extricated herself from the embrace and rolled out of bed to attend to the new-born. She switched on the bedside lamp, collected the wailing infant from her cradle, and got ready to feed her.

Gabriel lay silently in bed, waiting for their baby daughter's cries to subside.

"Can't we use that sleep-inducing device on her?" Gabriel suggested.

"It only works to negate external stimuli," Aster explained as the infant suckled, "it won't keep her asleep if she's hungry or sick, and it's not supposed to. Besides, I don't want her being exposed to that thing too much."

"It worked on the other four when they were young," Gabriel pointed out.

"I don't want some creepy piece of tech messing with my baby's brain waves," Aster snapped back protectively, "So if you're bothered by your baby daughter crying, go and beat up that fucking punch bag of yours."

Gabriel felt stung by that response but decided to bite his tongue.

"You're such a Luddite for a qualified engineer," he muttered eventually.

"And you're incredibly selfish for a father," she shot back.

An electronic chime sounded next to the bed, ending the argument before it could escalate. It was Gabriel's smartphone, and he flinched in surprise at hearing it. Plucking it off the bedside table, Gabriel saw a message in bright red block capitals:

'*REPORT TO ASGARD SPACEPORT, MILITARY WING, 9:00 AM. DGNI.*'

Gabriel stared at the screen for a full minute, not quite believing the implications of the message: after close to a year of de facto leave, he was being called back to duty.

"Was that what I think it was?" Aster asked, giving him a heavy stare.

Gabriel didn't reply verbally. He put the smartphone down and got out of bed, walking over to Aster. His baby daughter was finished feeding, and without saying a word Gabriel collected her from his wife's arms and cradled her protectively. Her eyes were open, and they shone back at him with the same luminescent emerald-green of his own eyes.

"Emerald," Gabriel said.

"Is that some kind of code word?" Aster asked, confused.

"No, I'm suggesting a name for her."

"You've got to be kidding," Aster snorted with laughter, "that's so fucking conceited."

"Don't swear in front of the baby," Gabriel admonished her, then added, "Besides, you got to name the older three."

"Because you weren't around to give any input," Aster reminded him.

"All the more reason why I should get a say this time around," Gabriel pointed out.

Aster opened her mouth to reply, then conceded his point.

"Can we at least nickname her Emma?" she suggested.

"Ok," he replied, "but what's wrong with the name Emerald?"

"It just sounds…weird."

"Unlike 'Orion'?"

"It's not weird," Aster protested, "Orion's Belt is a constellation visible from Earth."

There was a moment of silence.

"Ok," Aster conceded, "Emerald Thorn it is."

* * *

Gabriel stared at the ceiling through the darkness for the rest of the night, savouring the feeling of Aster's naked body snuggled against his own. It was better than beating up the punching bag one last time, and it was far better than lapsing back into another nightmare – a nightmare rooted in memory.

Gabriel dug his fingers into Aster's hair and stroked her curls. She stirred a little in response, snuggling closer to him and nuzzling her face into his neck. Her warm body, her soft skin, and her obvious desire for further intimacy made his own skin tingle in response. It was also stirring deeper needs within him.

Aster had the same thought and she quietly opened her legs, moving gently against him to encourage him. His hands slid across her shoulders, then all the way down the curvature of her back until he was cupping her rear in his hands. Then he abruptly flipped her over, covering her mouth to smother the yelp of surprise.

Gabriel went slower as he moved in between her thighs, planting his lips on her neck as she hooked her ankles behind his knees, running her hands over his shoulders and back. Aster pressed her crotch against his own, enticing him to enter. The whole encounter was tantalising, almost too tantalising to restrain himself.

Then he stopped.

"We're stopping at five," Gabriel said.

"You son of a bitch," Aster hissed in frustration.

"Are you that desperate to have another grandchild of a bitch?" Gabriel quipped.

"Who said anything about having another one?" Aster complained, "This is our last night together before you deploy. It could be our last night together ever."

"I also don't want to wake the baby," Gabriel claimed.

"If you've forgotten her name already, maybe we really should stop at five," Aster said sardonically, "but in any case, I have the sleep device on, so *Emerald* won't wake up."

"I thought you said you didn't want her exposed to it?" Gabriel asked.

"I don't want her exposed *too much*," Aster clarified, tracing a finger across his chest, "but we can still use it sometimes, like right now."

Gabriel had no more arguments left. He toyed with the idea of relenting even as Aster started toying with him, gently grinding her body against his crotch. His urges were steadily rekindled, and he nuzzled his face into her neck, kissing her throat as she rewrapped her arms around his muscular shoulders and back.

Without warning, Gabriel rolled over and flipped Aster bodily across the bed, causing her to yelp in surprise as she landed on her stomach. Gabriel pounced on her from behind, pressing his hand down on the back of her neck as he moved in between her thighs, entering forcefully and eliciting a gasp from her.

"That's more like it," Aster whispered with dirty delight.

* * *

The chamber was dark. It was a restricted area of the Spire with the aura of an ancient crypt and was built like a planetarium with a basin-shaped floor, a domed ceiling, and a flight of steps leading up to a throne-like chair in the centre. Despite the cold and antediluvian atmosphere of the chamber, it was actually brand new and was equipped with state-of-the-art technology for communicating securely across cosmic distances.

The chamber had been constructed deep underground in the interstices between the titanic foundation pillars that anchored the Spire in the bedrock, rendering it safe from whatever doomsday destruction might be visited on the surface. Given its sensitive nature, only a handful of people even knew that the chamber existed.

Only one had the authority to use it.

Like a monarch or high-priestess preparing to commune with the divine, the Director-General of Naval Intelligence ascended the steps and sat down in the throne at the chamber's heart. She placed both hands on the biometric sensor pads, verifying her identity and bringing the machinery to life.

Multiple encrypted connections were established through Q-space, creating a seven-way conference call between herself, the other five directors-general, and the seventh participant connecting from Earth itself. Each director-general was responsible for Directorate operations in their respective sector, and only the Masterminds had higher authority.

None of the callers' faces were visible, and their voices would be distorted by electronic masking when they spoke, just as her own face and voice would be disguised. Each director-general knew the identity of the others, so there was no clear reason to be anonymous when communicating, especially on an encrypted Q-comm. line.

Maybe it was just tradition.

"Greetings," Red-eye enunciated.

"*Greetings,*" each of the other directors-general replied one after another.

"I take it you are all impressed by the results included in my report?"

"*Very much so,*" the second director-general answered, the voice-masking smothering the emotional inflexions in his voice, "*particularly the second batch of voidstalkers.*"

"*'Batch'?*" the third director-general said quizzically.

"*Do you prefer the term 'generation'?*" the second director-general asked.

"*Both the performance of the voidstalkers and the development of the offspring of the first 'batch' are impressive,*" the fourth director-general interjected politely, shutting down the argument over semantics.

"I am pleased that you approve," Red-eye answered.

"*THE VOIDSTALKER PROGRAMME IS TO BE EXTENDED TO THE OTHER FIVE SECTORS,*" boomed the god-like voice of the seventh participant.

"*Yes, Masterminds,*" the directors-general chorused.

"*How goes your cooperation with this 'observer'?*" the fifth director-general enquired, a note of scepticism in his voice.

"Extremely well," Red-eye replied, "we have been using it for high-level computing operations in a somewhat piecemeal fashion. Whilst we cannot directly measure its processing power, thus far its performance has been most impressive."

"*It is indeed impressive,*" the sixth director-general noted, then added wryly, "*the very serious implications of trusting an alien AI with a portion of the computing requirements of the Directorate notwithstanding.*"

"Nothing truly sensitive, let alone information regarding the Voidstalker Programme, has been supplied to the observer," Red-eye answered coolly.

"*What about the search for the Swarm?*" the second director-general asked, "*I take it you have enough assets in the field?*"

"Of course," Red-eye replied, "as it happens, we have found something which matches what the observer claimed we would find. I will shortly be deploying another voidstalker to assist in neutralising the threat."

"*I still doubt the trustworthiness of this 'observer'*," said the sixth director-general.

"*We all do*," said the fifth director-general.

"*THE ENEMY OF AN ENEMY OF HUMANITY IS AN ALLY OF CONVENIENCE, NOTHING MORE AND NOTHING LESS*," the singular voice of the Masterminds boomed with deific authority, "*THE TRUE ENEMY IS THE ENTITY YOU HAVE COME TO KNOW AS THE SWARM. ITS DESTRUCTION REMAINS PARAMOUNT, OTHERWISE NOTHING ELSE THAT IS DONE TO SECURE HUMANITY'S FUTURE WILL MATTER*."

"*Understood, Masterminds*," the directors-general replied as one.

THE MISSION

ASGARD Spaceport's name was a misnomer, being only one of a dozen spaceports scattered around the outskirts of the megacity, but it was by far the largest one. Built in the shape of a starfish with each arm constituting an entire terminal, almost a fifth of Asgard City's spaceborne commerce passed through it.

The spaceport's largest terminal by far was the military terminal. Mirroring the contrast between the shiny skyscrapers and the Directorate's dour headquarters, the military wing's grim and efficient architecture was an austere rebuke to the glossy civilian terminals. Unlike the Spire, the military terminal could be reached via public transportation, although not without proper clearance.

Most of the people riding the underground line to the military terminal were on official business or were military types like Gabriel. The silence in the carriage was a welcome change from the chattering of civilian commuters on the regular magtrains. Any conversations that were taking place were respectfully hushed.

Being ordered to report to the military terminal rather than to the Spire first wasn't unusual; the fact that the message had been signed 'DGNI' *was* unusual. Only once before had he been briefed by the director-general herself before a mission. In light of how that mission had turned out, Gabriel wasn't looking forward to this briefing.

As soon as the mag-train halted and opened its doors, everyone disembarked without a word. Gabriel made his way to the military terminal, where the biometric scanners that guarded the reinforced doors granted him entrance. In the arrival hall, he found an armed escort waiting for him who saluted as he approached. Gabriel returned the salute and allowed the escort contingent to lead him to a waiting ship.

The ship had the familiar matte-black hull of a Directorate vessel, but it wasn't an interstellar vessel, it was a short-range interplanetary craft. That meant he wouldn't be leaving the star system yet. There was another exchange of salutes with the armed guards as Gabriel boarded the ship and was shown to a private cabin.

Someone was already there waiting for him. She wore a midnight-black military uniform identical to Gabriel's own, except for an admiral's insignia on the lapel. She wore her raven black hair in a tight bun and saw the world through a hazel-coloured left eye and a bionic right eye with a laser-red iris. Above all, her face was completely devoid of anything remotely recognisable as emotion.

Gabriel stiffened up straight and saluted as the door shut behind him, avoiding eye contact with the most powerful person on Asgard.

"Greetings, Director-general," said Gabriel.

"Greetings, Colonel Thorn," replied Red-eye.

* * *

Priority clearance from ground control and an escort by interplanetary gunships were at least two perks of travelling with the director-general. Gabriel didn't feel like these were perks. He had no idea where the ship was going or why the director-general was accompanying him – or was he the one accompanying her?

Gabriel sat in his chair with a wooden posture, unable to be comfortable in Red-eye's presence. Her face didn't betray the slightest flicker of emotion as she surveyed the room with that laser-red bionic eye of hers. She hadn't said a word since the door had shut, and his sense of military discipline prevented him from breaking the silence. There were plenty of things he wanted to say to her, most of them insubordinate.

"You may speak freely," she said, effectively ordering him to make conversation.

"I take it my probation is over?" Gabriel asked.

"Probation?" Red-eye said with a raised eyebrow, "You did nothing wrong on Loki, so there was no reason to punish you."

"Then why have I been kept at home for the past year?"

"I felt that you needed a break after our last conversation," Red-eye responded, "I also felt that you needed to spend more time with your family. Speaking of which, congratulations on your newest arrival."

"Thank you," Gabriel answered out of reflexive courtesy.

"Have you decided on a name yet?" she asked.

"Emerald," Gabriel replied.

"That's a nice name," Red-eye complimented, "and I trust she's been keeping you out of trouble while you cool off?"

"Yes," Gabriel replied rigidly.

The period of silence that followed was exceedingly awkward, at least for Gabriel. He sat there wondering if the director-general was going to ask him about the incident in Mortimer's clinic – a sign that he hadn't been keeping out of trouble – and yet a full minute passed in which she said nothing.

Maybe she just wanted to make him stew.

"I'm still surprised you could be so naive," Red-eye remarked, abruptly changing the subject, "the Directorate does whatever it can to get an edge over Humanity's enemies, and the Loki espionage operations were part of that."

"It's a little galling to discover that the Directorate has been secretly engaged in the very thing I've spent my military career fighting against," Gabriel replied bitingly.

"Yes," Red-eye remarked, "the last time we spoke, you wanted to hit me for it."

Gabriel remembered it well, and he wondered if Red-eye was daring him to vent his anger again. He opted for silence.

"You have spent your career fighting threats to Humanity," Red-eye answered coolly, "one of those is illegal *use* of alien technology; another is the threat posed by their makers. There is no contradiction between studying the former to neutralise the latter."

"As long as someone else does the dirty work of research," Gabriel said cynically.

"Of course," Red-eye replied unrepentantly, "the cost of recruiting a mole inside a corporation's illegal research facility is a tiny fraction of the cost of running such a facility under the Directorate's own auspices."

"You sound like my mother," Gabriel growled.

"Then I'm glad your children have a better mother than you did," Red-eye answered, unmoved by her best operative's insubordinate tone.

Again, Gabriel was silent.

"You have a surprisingly rigid moral compass," Red-eye added.

"And you want it to be more flexible?" Gabriel asked.

"No," Red-eye responded, "I need you to be able to draw finer and more nuanced moral distinctions, especially given the nature of your next assignment."

The director-general pulled out a flexi-tablet and slid it across the glass table. Gabriel picked up the flexi-tablet and began to read.

It was an intelligence brief stamped with a tier 2 classification, received from a source beyond Human space. It made for morbidly fascinating reading, even with the final paragraph blacked out by a tier 1 classification.

"Am I correct in assuming that this attack was *not* done by us?" Gabriel asked.

"Since launching such a gratuitous ambush serves no rational strategic purpose, yes," Red-eye confirmed, "but the attack on the alien trading barge is of secondary concern."

Gabriel could guess that much; attacks like this were only a concern if Humans were the victims. He passed the flexi-tablet back across the table to Red-eye.

"Once you read it," Red-eye said as she swiped her finger across the biometric strip, "you'll understand why I selected you for this."

Having granted him tier 1 clearance, she passed the tablet back to Gabriel, who took it and read the final paragraph. He furrowed his brow as he finished reading.

"What's so special about this energy signature?" Gabriel asked, puzzled.

"It matches exactly the energy signature of the entity you encountered on Loki," Red-eye replied, "Specifically, the one that took over Lieutenant Ogilvy's body and mind."

Gabriel knew exactly what she was talking about, and in the context of what he had just read, the implications made him freeze up in his seat.

"Now do you understand that there are more important things at stake than the ethics of xenotech research?" Red-eye demanded of him.

Gabriel didn't reply, but his tensed-up expression was an affirmative answer.

"Where are we going?" he asked eventually.

"To speak with an old acquaintance of yours."

* * *

Asgard was one of countless moons which orbited the sapphire-blue gas giant Odin, and the only one suitable for colonisation. From space, the planetary capital Asgard City and the network of smaller cities around it resembled a crystalline web with millions of fine tendrils spread out across the moon's surface. The artificial structures that covered so much of Asgard reflected most of the local star's light back into space, making it resemble a shimmering jewel floating in the void.

One of the neighbouring moons, about the same size as Asgard, was a dull and barren rock by comparison. It was shrouded in darkness most of the time, had limited mineral wealth, and no registered settlements. Closer inspection revealed a network of canyons and dried-up canals as well as vast open plains pockmarked by innumerable impact craters.

The moon's name was Loki.

The vessel and its escort swooped down into Loki's thin atmosphere like a squadron of shadows, their stealth coatings absorbing all natural light as well as rendering them invisible to sensor technology. Amongst Loki's cragged features was a concealed opening to the facility, and the squadron dropped down through the blast doors into a subterranean docking bay.

As soon as the vessel touched down, Red-eye got up and walked out of the flight cabin with Gabriel following her as the armed security detail escorted them into the main facility. He had known that the Directorate would requisition Jupiter Engineering Co.'s facility on Loki, but to see it for himself was still galling.

The whole facility was bustling with activity. Scientists and technicians were clustered in research booths, and drones carried supply crates back and forth, keeping the labs and firing ranges well-stocked. As Gabriel and Red-eye passed with their armed escort, the most attention anyone gave them was a quick salute and a wide berth.

J.E. Co.'s corporate logo had been removed from every surface, along with all of the sinister scribblings daubed in Human blood, the gruesome product of Swarm-enthralled minds. Otherwise, the facility looked exactly as it had when it had been an illegal research complex run by a private company.

After a while, they came to a service elevator, access to which required at least a tier 2 security clearance, something the armed escort didn't have. They stayed behind as Red-eye and Gabriel descended far below the moon's surface. In spite of himself, Gabriel was tense all the way down – he remembered everything about this mission.

After Doran had been critically wounded, Gabriel had insisted that the squad continue down into the depths to neutralise the insane facility staff. The squad had only been willing to come this far in order to rescue Ogilvy, and Gabriel had played along only because Ogilvy had been taken in the same direction.

All while carrying an antimatter bomb on his back.

When the elevator reached its destination, they stepped out into an artificial cave illuminated by floodlights. Gone were the 'scarecrows' – the J.E. Co. security team who had been captured and turned into cybernetic monstrosities by the insane researchers. Gone, also, was the phrase 'TEMPLE OF KNOWLEDGE' scrawled in Human blood high up on the rock wall. Even so, Gabriel had a vivid memory of this place too.

The same chiselled maw of darkness that led into the observatory was still there, but it was covered up by an environmentally secure access gate, preventing anyone or anything from entering or leaving the alien structure beyond. The insanity of the Loki facility's staff had had nothing to do with contamination – but better safe than sorry.

Something else had been added as well: a kind of research platform with a suite of computer servers and holographic displays that sat in the middle of the chamber. Gabriel saw a series of data cables, each one as thick as his bicep, running from the computers to a set of plugs built into the access gate.

Red-eye stepped onto the platform and enunciated a single word:

"Observer."

"GREETINGS," boomed a familiar voice.

"I should have known you would take the observer up on its offer," Gabriel remarked.

"Why else would I order the revival of the facility instead of bombing it from orbit?" Red-eye responded rhetorically.

"Greetings to you too, voidstalker," said the observer, lowering the volume of its voice.

"We've been using the observer to perform high-level computing operations," Red-eye explained to Gabriel, "hence the data cables."

"The arrangement has been most fruitful," the observer added.

"You don't find it demeaning being used as a glorified calculator?" Gabriel asked wryly.

"The premise of your query is mistaken," the observer answered, "the observer is an inorganic intelligence and is imbued with nothing analogous to pride. It is therefore impossible for the observer to regard the assigned tasks as 'demeaning'."

"I see," Gabriel replied.

"Furthermore," the observer continued, "the bargain struck was to put the observer's knowledge at your disposal in exchange for survival. Since self-preservation is the observer's third highest imperative, the exchange is an equitable one. If being a 'glorified calculator' is what is required to honour the observer's end of the bargain, so be it."

That made sense, even if the observer's imperious use of the third person didn't.

"We have important things to discuss," Red-eye interjected.

"Such as?"

"The energy signature you provided to us," said Red-eye gravely.

"You have detected one?"

"Yes."

"Then my highest imperative must take precedence," the observer announced, "that of containment, the broad interpretation thereof."

"So you're going to help us neutralise this threat?" Gabriel asked.

"That was implicit in the observer's prior statement," the observer replied loftily.

"That's why the voidstalker is here," Red-eye explained, "I need you to explain to him everything you've told me about this threat."

Gabriel cocked an eyebrow at being described as *the* voidstalker but said nothing.

"Is there a reason you are unable to relay the observer's knowledge to the voidstalker personally?" the observer inquired.

"He needs to hear it from you directly."

* * *

The reptilian mercenaries were relieved to be out of the stifling chamber, and even more relieved to be rid of the sinister artefact, but the exchange had been more than worthwhile. Their customers had paid handsomely, enough to cover the cost of fuel and spare parts fifty times over, and had even included a selection of exotic weaponry, a fact which spoke volumes about the value of the looted artefact.

After stowing their payment aboard the mothership for safekeeping, the salvagers returned to the Nexus. Being a trading station with the population of a small city, the Nexus had vast commercial concourses where visiting ship crews of all species could barter goods and broker deals as well as find entertainment during their stays.

The mercenaries stopped at the alien equivalent of a drinks bar and ordered their usual: a potent ethanol cocktail that would ruin most other species' digestive systems. Normally there would be a raucous celebration after such a spectacularly large profit, but no one was in the mood for it. In spite of the massive windfall they had reaped in exchange, they couldn't get the artefact out of their heads.

What was the artefact? Where had the trading barge crew found it? Why would anyone want to get their claws on such a thing? All of those questions hung in the air like the excessive moisture in the meeting chamber, but nobody really wanted to know the answers.

"What do you think it was?" one of the mercenaries spoke up.

He was the youngest, still green in the throat, and too curious for his own good. He spoke in their native language, his words sounding like a series of incomprehensible growls to eavesdroppers without translation software.

"Who cares?" another mercenary gurgled dismissively, slurping at his drink with an elongated tongue, "We got paid for it, now it's someone else's problem."

"That's right," their leader, the one with an animal skull for a shoulder guard, added gruffly, "Once the merchandise has been sold it's the buyer's problem."

There was a lull in the conversation as the group slurped their drinks in silence.

"I wonder what the Water-skins will do when they recover," Green-throat pondered.

"Nothing," someone else grunted unsympathetically, "those watery hides of theirs are too weak and soft to handle a fight. Besides, if you're not strong enough to defend what's yours, it shouldn't be yours in the first place."

There was a harrumph of agreement around the table followed by another lull.

"I heard one of the Water-skins told the medics what attacked them," said Green-throat.

"Of course you've heard," the leader growled back, uninterested, "we all have."

"'Foist-hawker'...'foo-hoy-stalk-argh'," Green-throat mumbled the mystery word to himself, struggling to get the alien syllables off his tongue.

"I heard it's the name of a species beyond Nexus space," someone else offered.

"Where beyond Nexus space?" demanded the second-in-rank.

"You expect me to know the coordinates by memory?" was the annoyed reply, "It's in some swath of space that's still uncharted, that's all I know."

"Maybe it's uncharted because whatever species lives there destroys any ship that tries to chart it," suggested Green-throat conspiratorially.

"It doesn't matter what attacked those wet-skinned weaklings," Skull-guard interjected, bored of all the idle speculation, "Curiosity kills, something all of you should remember."

That was the end of the conversation. As the leader of the band, Skull-guard's word carried the authority of a clan sub-chief, and no one dared disobey. Besides, he was right: the mystery of the trading barge attack would make a fun puzzle for conspiracy theorists and others with time to waste, but they had better things to do.

Android servers arrived with dishes of what looked like raw meat, serving the reptiles in order of seniority. Skull-guard devoured his meal before the others had even been served, followed by his second-in-command until the youngest, Green-throat, received his last.

These weren't their real names, of course; alien names were hard enough to remember, and often impossible to pronounce. They were field-monikers assigned to them by the cloaked figure monitoring them from the shadows.

* * *

The majority of Odin's moons were just mineral-rich asteroids scattered across its thin dust ring. One of these was Helheim, named for an underworld in one of ancient Earth's many mythologies. After being strip-mined to the point that it was literally hollowed out, the moon had been sold to an obscure holding company secretly owned by the DNI.

Being the Directorate of Naval Intelligence, the DNI retained its own fleet for covert operations, complete with its own network of naval facilities of which the Helheim shipyard was one. It was modest in size, certainly when compared to the gargantuan space-docks used by the actual navy, but was still large enough to house a squadron of cruiser-weight vessels.

From Loki, Gabriel took a shuttle to the Helheim facility while the director-general took a separate ship back to the Spire. The shuttle cruised through the defence perimeter and slipped into a vacuum-dock. Once the docking procedures were complete, Gabriel disembarked and made his way to a communications room. Regulations required a final call with loved ones before deployment, a requirement that Gabriel had slowly grown to appreciate.

Standing in the communications booth, Gabriel waited as the secure connection was established and a holographic video image fizzled into view.

"*Right on time,*" said Aster on the other end.

She was sitting on the couch in the living room, cradling baby Emerald in her arms and using the holo-TV's camera for the video call.

"How is everybody?" Gabriel asked with a smile.

"*We miss you already,*" Aster answered with a weary sigh, "*and we'll miss you even more in the weeks and months to come.*"

"I could tell from early this morning," remarked Gabriel.

"*I know what I want,*" Aster replied innocently, "*and how to get it from you.*"

"Right…"

"*If your bosses wanted to kill your sense of fun, they would have done it,*" Aster pointed out, "*so don't look at me like you didn't enjoy it.*"

"*What are you talking about?*" Rose asked, poking her head into the camera's view.

"Nothing you should worry about," Gabriel replied awkwardly.

"*When will you be back from killing monsters, daddy?*" Violet asked.

That question always came up, and Gabriel never had a good answer. While he was thinking, Aster adjusted the zoom to include Leonidas, sandwiched in between his older sisters Rose and Violet, and Orion sitting next to his mother.

"Not much longer than usual," Gabriel answered eventually.

"*You always say that,*" Orion interjected, "*and then you're gone for so long.*"

"It's to keep you all safe," Gabriel assured him.

"*You always say that too,*" Violet pointed out.

"That's because it's the truth," Gabriel answered.

"*Can I have ice cream, daddy?*" Leonidas asked.

"No," Gabriel replied firmly, "it's not good for you."

"*But Orion had some,*" Leonidas protested, earning a dirty look from his older brother.

"*Orion passed all the learning pod's specialist tests with full marks,*" Aster explained, "*So I let him have some as a reward.*"

"Alright, then," Gabriel relented, "if you do well in the learning pod and pass your tests like Orion, you can have a small bowl."

"*Thank you, daddy!*" Leonidas grinned in appreciation.

"*Rose, Violet, the same goes for you too,*" Aster added.

"*I hate ice cream,*" announced Violet, "*it freezes my mouth up.*"

"As long as you study hard, listen to your mother, and take care of each other whilst I'm gone, you can have whatever snacks you like," Gabriel assured them.

"*Speaking of which, it's time for them to get back to their learning pods,*" Aster said, then turned to the children, "*say goodbye to your father.*"

"*Bye, daddy!*" The four of them chorused, smiling and waving at the screen.

Gabriel smiled and waved back, well aware that this might be the last time he saw them. As the children disappeared from the room, Aster kept the link active.

"Was there something else?" Gabriel asked.

"*Gabriel...*" Aster's expression had turned much more serious, and she hesitated before continuing, "*Are you happy we had Emerald?*"

The question felt like a slap in the face.

"Of course I am," Gabriel answered in disbelief.

"*I wanted to hear you say it,*" Aster replied, gently rocking their baby daughter.

"I don't regret any of our children," Gabriel said emphatically, "it's just that raising five children is a logistical nightmare."

"*'Logistical nightmare'?*" Aster responded, narrowing her eyes at his choice of words, "*they're children, not army munitions.*"

"You know what I mean," Gabriel answered, keeping his tone level, "I just worry if you can handle that many,"

"*I've managed just fine so far, thank you,*" Aster responded appreciatively, "*Besides, the androids handle most of the hard work.*"

"I don't like the idea of entrusting my children to machines," said Gabriel.

"*Where I grew up, the older ones did the hard work,*" replied Aster.

"That would certainly build some character," Gabriel remarked dryly.

There was another pause.

"*Take care, Gabriel,*" Aster said, tears forming in her eyes, "*we'll be waiting for you.*"

"You too, Aster," Gabriel answered, seeing his wife start to cry made him feel deeply uncomfortable, mainly out of guilt.

"*Oh, one more thing,*" Aster said, rubbing her eyes, "*I had a package sent to you.*"

"What did you send?"

"*Something to remind you of home,*" Aster answered, "*Come back alive.*"

"I will," Gabriel promised her, then the link was terminated.

It was always hard doing these farewell calls, even for someone whose emotions had been conditioned and dulled for the sake of combat efficiency; but this call had been especially poignant given what he had learned from the observer.

He had just made Aster a promise he couldn't necessarily keep.

* * *

Aster continued staring at the now-blank screen.

These family calls were never easy. Gabriel had spent much of their married life away on assignments, so she had grown used to the uncertainty of his return, uncertainty that still went straight over the children's heads. They were too young to know what their father did professionally, and if he never came home they wouldn't understand why.

'Emerald' was actually quite a nice name, she thought, even if it was a little conceited on the part of her father. Then again, Gabriel was the one risking his life beyond the frontiers of charted space. After coming back from one of those missions, he'd decided to name their fourth child after a warrior-king from ancient Earth. Since she had named the older three in his absence, he was entitled to even the score.

If anything were to happen to Gabriel, Emerald's name and the colour of her eyes would be the only things she would have left of him.

Aster wiped her own eyes with her free hand before returning to the bedroom with the baby. With Gabriel gone and the rest of the children sitting in their learning pods, she still had things to do. She placed Emerald back in her cot and went to the armoured closet on the opposite side of the room, swiping her thumb across the biometric strip.

The dormant maganiel android dominated the closet, a Human-sized security robot licensed and programmed to use lethal force to defend the house and its residents. Next to it was a side-cabinet with a set of locked drawers, and on top rested a flexi-tablet. Aster retrieved the device and sealed the closet again, lying down on the bed to read its contents.

The last time she'd had homework was back in engineering school, and yet her new job required her to master a swath of new material before starting. Normally, proof of your degrees – or passing a couple of tests – were enough to prove that you were qualified, but apparently what she had already learned wouldn't be enough for her new position.

It was also the first time she'd had to use a device like this. Not only did it have to flash-scan her face before unlocking, but its screen would go black if anyone else tried to look at it. Even Gabriel couldn't look at it, not that he would understand the material if he could.

'*...The quantum wavefront of a given mass as it transitions between real space and Q-space can be represented as a 3-dimensional vector field where each vector is a quantum differential function representing the rate of quantum coherence or decoherence...*'

Basic stuff so far – of her three engineering degrees, the second had been in Q-physics engineering – but the contents of the later chapters were on a completely different level. After getting her doctorate, Aster had opted to get work rather than go onto a post-doctorate, so this was material she had never seen before. It was also eye-glazingly theoretical.

'*...Let* $\boldsymbol{c} \cdot \boldsymbol{Q^n i}$ *represent an arbitrary system of quantum differential functions to the nth order of entanglement, where* **c** *represents the chaos-coefficient of an arbitrary mass...*'

Aster put the flexi-tablet down and closed her eyes in mental exhaustion. She was good at maths, but just looking at the material was giving her a migraine. In any case, Q-physics – not to mention its less practical ancestor, quantum physics – was the most arbitrary and chaotic branch of physics anyone could imagine.

Gabriel was right: going back to work and raising five children at the same time was a hard balance to strike. Aster herself wasn't totally comfortable with the new job she had landed, or whether she could keep up with the material. The standards required to be a project leader at Jupiter Engineering Co. had been pretty steep, but by comparison that only made her a junior technician at her new job.

Maybe the offer was just another way for the DNI to keep an eye on her.

* * *

As soon as Gabriel was aboard, the vessel departed without ceremony. Its body was covered in a matte-black stealth coating and was shaped like a spearhead with a pair of bat-like wings extending from its flanks. It gave off minimal heat bloom and had no visible engine ports, moving like a wraith stalking silently through the cosmic gloom.

The gravity of interstellar objects permeated into Q-space from real space, but whereas in real space gravity was an attractive force, in Q-space it was a repulsive force. The larger a celestial body, the stronger its gravity, and the more power a Q-engine would need to overcome it. That made it impossible to crash into a planet at faster-than-light speeds, but it also forced ships to leave a planetary system before attempting to open a Q-rift.

Once the ship was near the edge of the system, it began to power up its Q-engine. If the ship had been visible to the naked eye, one would have seen its silhouette become distorted. An orb of pure blackness appeared just in front of the vessel's nose, causing the starlight to bend around it. As the rift into Q-space widened, the vessel fell into it, swallowed up by the black orb which vanished as soon as it had appeared.

The transition to Q-space was barely perceptible aboard the ship, belying the massive amounts of power being fed to the Q-engine. If the power was interrupted, the quantum wavefront would collapse, and the ship would lurch back into real space.

Gabriel wandered through the vessel, familiarising himself with the ship's layout. Apart from the technician who had greeted him at the hatch, the crew was nowhere to be seen. That wasn't surprising; once the destination was locked in and the transition to Q-space completed, faster-than-light travel was a job best left to supercomputers.

Gabriel turned a corner and came to a wall-sized mural, depicting a wooden vessel with great billowing sails on a stormy sea being attacked by a gigantic monster with eight massive tentacles and two saucer-like eyes. It was a fabulous piece of artwork, unlike the vapid vanity pieces in the high-class clubs of the Clouds.

It was also a bit incongruous given the name of the ship. The sea monster in the mural was a mythical creature that supposedly dragged ancient sailing vessels down to their doom. If the dark depths of Earth's oceans were an ominous abyss, then the infinite void of interstellar space was an order of magnitude more so, filled with horrors beyond anything dreamed up in the mythologies of ancient Earth.

But whereas ancient seafarers – and most modern spacefarers – plied their trades in superstitious fear of monsters in the void, this vessel's name implied something totally different. It represented a turning of the tables against the dangers of the dark, that the monsters were not to be feared, but hunted and slain, hence the vessel's name:

Krakenscourge.

* * *

Gabriel made his way to the captain's quarters and rang the buzzer. The red light flashed green and he showed himself in, finding himself in a room that was part office and part personal quarters. There was also a mini-lounge with a glass table and a pair of chairs.

One of the chairs was occupied by a short man – short compared to Gabriel – with an aquiline nose and an austere expression on his face. He had thin streaks of grey in his dark hair and faint wrinkles in his skin, hinting that he was actually twice as old as he looked.

"Care for a game?" Captain Ironside asked.

"I may as well," Gabriel replied, taking a seat opposite his host.

Ironside tapped a pad at the centre of the table, causing an 8x8 holographic grid of translucent squares to appear.

"2D or 3D?" Ironside asked.

"Let's try 2D," Gabriel answered, "not that I'm any better than last time."

"Well, I doubt I'm any better either," Ironside replied with a smile, "but we'll see."

Ironside selected the 2D game option, causing two sets of holographic pieces to appear at opposite ends of the grid.

"White moves first," said Ironside, tapping a key to start the game.

"And I'll start with a pawn move," replied Gabriel, selecting a pawn with a finger and thumb and moving it two spaces forward.

Ironside responded with a pawn of his own, and before long there were pieces all over the game board. Gabriel took one of Ironside's bishops, only to lose a knight and then a pawn. Ironside used his remaining bishop to take another of Gabriel's pawns and put his king in check. Gabriel blocked the bishop with a bishop of his own which was then taken by Ironside. The bishop was covered by another piece and so couldn't be taken by Gabriel's king.

"Not looking good for you, Colonel," Ironside said, eyeing victory.

"It's not over until checkmate," Gabriel responded, moving his king out of harm's way, "and you don't have me in checkmate."

"Not yet," Ironside said, taking one of Gabriel's rooks.

"Not today," Gabriel replied.

He countered by moving his queen across the board to corner Ironside's king. The grid lit up green whilst highlighting the grid-cube occupied by Ironside's king in red, displaying the words 'checkmate: white wins.'

Ironside furrowed his brow in confusion, then shrugged it off.

"That's one of my favourite things about this game," Ironside remarked gracefully, "It rewards brains and punishes cockiness."

"A good enough metaphor for what we're doing out here," Gabriel added.

Gabriel had worked with Ironside several times over his career, and he couldn't think highly enough of the man. He was a calm and collected veteran with decades of experience who knew what to do and would do it on his own initiative. The same sense of discipline and initiative seemed to rub off on the individuals under his command as well.

"Well, since you bring it up," Ironside said, turning serious, "I was cleared to see an unredacted version of the report before we left."

"Then I trust you understand we're not going to raid some corporate xenotech lab or interdict some alien corsair fleet," Gabriel said, equally seriously.

"I understand that much, and not much else," Ironside answered, switching off the holographic game board and leaning back in his seat.

"This alien trading barge that was attacked," Gabriel asked, "do you know anything extra that might be worth sharing?"

"The communication intercepts we've gathered refer to the species as 'Water-skins'," Ironside replied, using the same holographic pad to bring up a profile of the species.

Gabriel read through the profile while Ironside waited.

"Amphibious 'Water-skins'," Gabriel noted, "very imaginative."

"What else are we supposed to call them?" Ironside asked rhetorically, "besides, I'll bet aliens have plenty of disparaging names for us – the ones who know we exist, at least."

"They can call us whatever they like as long as they leave us alone," Gabriel responded dismissively, "I'm more concerned by this rumour that we attacked the trading barge, even though Red-eye doesn't think much of the incident."

Ironside's brow furrowed and his mouth twitched.

"Since when did you start calling the boss by her nickname?" he asked with amusement.

Gabriel blinked in surprise. He had never done that before. Directorate operatives routinely referred to the director-general as Red-eye in private, something they would never dare do openly, but Gabriel had always insisted on referring to her by her title out of respect.

Then again, his respect for her had taken a hit over the past year.

"In any case," Ironside said, steering the conversation back to the topic at hand, "they said that a 'voidstalker' attacked the trading barge, not 'Humans'."

"The intelligence report makes clear that they used the Standard Human Speech word 'voidstalker'," Gabriel pointed out, "that begs all sorts of questions in its own right, but it doesn't matter which word they used because they think it's the name of our species, which therefore means that they think *we* committed this attack."

"We'll know more when we get there, of course," Ironside responded, dismissing the Water-skin file and reopening the chess game program, "but right now, I want to see whether or not that win was a fluke."

* * *

Human space was vast, and governmental authority did not extend evenly throughout it. Instead, it was a function of how long it took for a message to travel through Q-space and how long it took for an FTL-capable ship to travel between worlds. This meant that in practice, every world was largely self-governing.

The six sectors were the largest divisions of Human space with Sol at the heart of power. Secondary to Earth were dozens of core worlds, each one serving as the capital world of a sector or sub-sector. Each of these, in turn, had dozens of less prominent colony worlds under their indirect governance. This web-of-webs extended to hundreds of colonies and outposts whose deference to authority weakened the further away they were. Some of these backwater outposts were run by enterprising spacefarers, and others by interstellar corporations.

If XA-107 didn't qualify as a backwater, nowhere did. It was built into an asteroid, itself one of innumerable nondescript rocks orbiting the nearby gas giant, and apart from deep space mining vessels that needed refuelling and resupply, it received few visitors. Much of the outpost's equipment was automated, but a Human crew was still needed to operate the sensors and communications arrays.

"This is the dullest job in the galaxy," one technician complained to the other.

"Not quite as dull as listening to you complain about it," his fellow technician replied.

"Aren't you bored as well, Jacob?" he asked, taking a sip of his drink.

"I just told you that, Dan," Jacob shot back in exasperation.

"So, tell me a story," Dan answered, "at least until our shift is over."

The sensor monitoring room was dark. In fact, it was no bigger than a storage closet, with just enough space for the holographic screen, a bank of computers, a control panel, and two chairs for the technicians. Apart from the wall-sized screen displaying the sensor feeds, there was no other source of light.

The eerie glow of the screen gave Jacob inspiration.

"Once upon a time," Jacob began spookily, "I was serving aboard a mineral prospecting vessel on the fringes of Human space."

"How long ago was 'once upon a time'?" Dan interjected.

"Ten years ago," Jacob responded, annoyed at the interruption, "and my colleague aboard that ship was an annoying fuckwit named Dan."

"He sounds like a pretty cool guy," Dan quipped with a grin, "so what happened?"

"We'd been out on the frontier for weeks," Jacob continued with an ominous tone, "when we detected an automated distress signal. It turned out to be an escape pod, so we pulled it aboard and opened it up. But the only thing we found inside...was a Human corpse, dead for weeks from lack of oxygen."

"Ooh, scary," Dan grinned, "So what happened next?"

"The body was taken to the morgue," Jacob continued, "But strange things began to happen aboard the ship: lights suddenly went out during the night shift–"

"There's no day-night cycle in space, Jacob," Dan pointed out, ruining the suspense, "so you can't have a 'night shift' aboard a spacecraft."

"That's not the point!" Jacob snapped irritably, then calmly slipped back into story-telling-mode, "the lights would suddenly go out, power conduits would mysteriously overload, and key systems would malfunction for no apparent reason."

"Sounds like it's getting good; go on."

"All these malfunctions only started when they took the escape pod onboard," Jacob continued, "so the crew scan its systems for viruses, but find nothing. Then they realise that the corpse has mysteriously disappeared, so they start hunting for it."

"Ok, I'm pretty sure you're making all this up," Dan interjected again.

"It's a fucking ghost story, you moron," Jacob replied with a roll of his eyes, "Of course I'm making it up. Besides, you're the one who wanted to be entertained."

"True enough," Dan conceded, "seven out of ten for effort."

"Only seven out of ten?"

"Fine, seven and a half out of ten," Dan conceded again, "so what happened next?"

"I don't know," Jacob answered.

"What do you mean you don't know? It's your story."

"I haven't thought that far ahead," Jacob explained, "maybe the ghost of the dead guy was screwing with the ship's systems, or maybe he wasn't really dead."

"Or maybe an alien bursts out of his chest?" Dan suggested with a snort.

"I'm pretty sure everyone would hear the screams," Jacob pointed out.

"Don't be ridiculous," Dan replied, "in space, no one can hear you scream."

"Whatever," Jacob said dismissively.

"Ok then, my turn," Dan announced, "once upon a time..."

His story was interrupted before it began by the shrill note of an audio alert. One of the sensor-feeds started flashing, turning from a serene blue to danger-red.

"What's that?!" Jacob shouted in sudden panic.

"Q-space event! Massive!" Dan shouted back, scrambling to analyse the sensor feeds, "Blueshifted Cherenkov radiation flare! 500km out! 5 megatons!"

"What the fuck does that mean?!" Jacob demanded.

"It means something big is exiting Q-space right next to us!" Dan shouted back.

"How the fuck could something that big exit Q-space in-system?!" Jacob exclaimed.

"I don't know, and I don't fucking care!" Dan shouted back, "Now sound the alert!"

"Fucking hell!" Jacob cursed, punching the emergency lockdown button.

As Jacob hit the lockdown button, the room was illuminated by glowing red emergency lights. Similar lights were activated across the station as shuttle bays and access hatches were sealed automatically. All computer records were backed up and locked down, and an automated distress call was transmitted through the Q-comm. network.

They knew it couldn't be a friendly vessel since all station visits were arranged well in advance. Furthermore, the limitations of

Q-space physics meant that it was supposed to be impossible to enter or exit Q-space so close to a planetary mass. No vessel could house a Q-engine powerful enough to overcome planetary or stellar gravity.

No Human vessel, at least.

"Do you think it could be aliens?" Jacob asked, calming down in spite of the emergency.

"What else could it be?" Dan replied.

"But why would aliens venture into Human space?" Jacob demanded.

"Why are you asking me as if I know?" Dan demanded back.

"Well, let's at least get a visual on it," Jacob suggested.

Dan pulled up a set of live camera feeds, expanding one of them to fill the screen. A massive silhouette was highlighted in the image, marking out the mysterious arrival against the backdrop of space. Even though it was 500km away, it looked enormous.

"That is definitely *not* a Human ship," Dan remarked redundantly.

Jacob saw something and narrowed his eyes curiously.

"What's that glow?" he asked.

"What glow?"

"That," Jacob replied, pointing to the screen, "Can't you see it?"

Dan squinted at the screen. Now he could see it: a glowing point of light on the surface of the massive ship that was growing brighter and brighter.

Dan's and Jacob's eyes widened as they guessed what it could be.

"Oh..." was Dan's last word.

THE OUTPOST

TIME dilation was non-existent in Q-space. No physicist had yet been able to explain why, but despite the warping of many other physical laws, the passage of time in Q-space was exactly the same as in real space. Travelling from a core world to the frontiers would take a civilian spaceship up to a month, less than half that time for most military craft, and half again for a state-of-the-art DNI vessel like the Krakenscourge.

This was always the dullest and tensest part of a long-range assignment: the weeklong journey to the frontier and beyond. The ship's crew had official duties to occupy them, but Gabriel had no such duties. Unless aliens boarded the ship – impossible during Q-flight – there wasn't much he could do to help, so until the Krakenscourge reached its destination, Gabriel had to find other ways to pass the time.

As a senior officer, Gabriel had his own private quarters, whereas the rest of the crew had to bunk together. The room was far more ascetic than the regular crew quarters, featuring only a bed, a desk, a chair, and a closet. His few personal effects had been moved into the room before he had boarded, including a holographic photograph sitting on a bedside table.

Lying on the bed, Gabriel plucked the photo frame off the table. It was the family photo he had taken spontaneously in the living room, with Rose grinning at the camera from her perch atop his shoulders, and the rest of the children piled onto the couch on either side. This was the gift Aster had sent to him.

Gabriel looked at himself, wondering at the faint smile on his face. It wasn't in his personality to smile, a fact that bothered Aster to no end. Even so, it was heart-warming to see their children's grinning, happy faces.

In spite of himself, Gabriel smiled back.

"*Colonel Thorn,*" the intercom sounded suddenly, "*Sorry to disturb you, but we've intercepted a distress call through the Q-comm. network.*"

Distress calls were serious, but not serious enough to warrant the attention of a DNI vessel unless that distress call was relevant to its current objective. The fact that it was being brought to his attention at all meant that it had to be serious.

"On my way," Gabriel replied through the intercom.

* * *

No two celestial bodies had exactly the same mass. By recording and tracking the size of their gravitational fields, it was possible to distinguish between planets, stars, and black holes – a crucial distinction in interstellar travel. By identifying specific stars and planets, it was also possible to navigate towards a destination in real space while still in Q-space.

Using the coordinates in the distress call, the Krakenscourge adjusted its course towards the source: a mining outpost on the fringes of settled space called XA-107. The distress call contained no information about the nature of the emergency, just a generic call for help.

"The distress call stopped dead after less than a minute," Ironside explained to Gabriel, "and we haven't detected any follow-up transmissions giving the all clear."

That usually meant there was no one left alive to give the all clear.

The planning room was illuminated by the 3D holographic projector that sent light and shadows dancing across the faces of those present. Currently, it was displaying a localised map of the area of space through which the Krakenscourge was travelling. The approximate positions of thousands of celestial bodies, from stars and planets to bits of space rock, were being tracked in real-time relative to the ship's position.

Illuminated in blue was the serpentine path of the Krakenscourge, meandering between the 'slopes' coloured according to the strength of nearby gravitational fields. The fastest way to reach a destination while travelling through Q-space was to follow the path of least gravitational resistance between those slopes. The ship's current path, however, curved sharply to one side as it detoured towards the star system where XA-107 was located.

"The outpost belongs to Instar Frontier Services," one of the technicians explained, "The transmission was encrypted, but we cracked it."

"They say that the first rule of intelligence is: 'there are no coincidences'," Ironside continued, "and having seen that intelligence report, I recommend we look into this."

"In my experience, the first rule is: 'facts first, conclusions later'," Gabriel replied, then added, "but in this case, it amounts to the same course of action."

"Understood," Ironside answered, "hopefully, we'll be in and out of the system before anyone else comes to investigate."

"If the worst is confirmed, we'll have to contact the Navy to contain this," said Gabriel.

"Contact the sub-sector Naval Command," Ironside ordered one of the officers, "give them the bare-bones details as per usual."

"Aye, sir," replied the officer.

If this was a corsair attack – or worse, an alien attack – then of course the Navy had to be forewarned about it, but once the officer's back was turned, Ironside and Gabriel exchanged a look. They were the only two people aboard who had seen the unredacted version of the intelligence report, and they both strongly hoped that this was just a coincidence.

"Facts first," Gabriel said, "conclusions later."

* * *

The public mag-rail network took Aster most of the way to the Spire, but eventually, she had to disembark and go to a private platform reserved exclusively for the DNI. There was already a crowd there, and they boarded the mag-train in unsmiling silence. Nobody was wearing a uniform, and Aster decided to put on her best stony face and try not to look out of place as she took a seat.

The journey was a short one, and everyone disembarked without a word, disappearing down a warren of corridors and elevators on their way to their assigned posts. Aster still had no idea what her assigned post would be, but she did find the office without any problems, and the person inside waved her in.

"Dr Aster Thorn," said the office's occupant.

"Nice to meet you," Aster replied politely as she sat down.

The person sitting opposite had a pale complexion – marking her out as an Undercity dweller – and her jet black hair was tied back into a ponytail. She reviewed Aster's CV on a flexi-tablet whilst the new hire sat opposite in uncomfortable silence.

"Tertiary specialisation in electrical engineering," the woman said aloud, "quaternary specialisation in Q-physics engineering with a minor specialisation in fusion reactor design, and a doctoral specialisation in applied fusion reactor physics."

"That's correct," Aster replied, burying her nervousness.

"That means I don't have to waste time re-teaching you the basics," the woman replied, tossing the flexi-tablet onto her desk, "My name is Dr Sophia Cole, and I supervise the research project on which you will be working."

Dr Cole's manner of speaking was strange. She was definitely an Undercity dweller, but her accent sounded like someone from the Clouds. It wasn't a natural accent either, more like a reasonably accurate imitation of one with the occasional slippage.

"The work style here in the Rand Block is very different to what you're used to," Dr Cole continued, "you'll be given a list of tasks to complete, and you can go home once they're done. It's better for researchers with young children, like yourself."

"Thank you," Aster replied, assuming it was the thing to say.

"Also, don't be surprised if you're assigned a lot of grunt work," Dr Cole continued, "The really advanced research is done by the veterans."

"I was a project manager at–" Aster began.

"At Jupiter Engineering Co., I know," Dr Cole interrupted, unimpressed, "Here at the Directorate, we consider that entry-level experience."

Aster's eye twitched at the casual dismissal of her work history. Then again, the DNI obviously had higher standards for this kind of job. For all she knew, there had been a thousand other applicants who had failed the tests…or the security screening.

"Are you coming to the lab as well?" Aster asked.

"I only come down to the lab if something has gone wrong," was the faintly menacing reply, "In any case, my job is as much administrative as scientific. So no, I don't participate full-time in the research and development process."

"Well," Aster said, getting up from her seat, "I guess I should go."

"Indeed," Dr Cole replied with a curt nod, "a pleasure to meet you, Dr Thorn."

Dr Cole's stony expression and bland tone made it sound less than sincere.

* * *

Aster stepped through a set of doors into a circular chamber filled with data booths arranged around a central column. So engrossed was everyone in their respective duties that no one greeted her or looked up from their workstations as she entered. The only sound to be heard was the bass hum of the supercomputing cluster inside the central column. The ambience was so solemn that Aster felt like an intruder.

All but one of the booths was already occupied, so Aster went over to the spare booth and sat down. A message appeared on the instant messenger screen:

'*Hello, newbie.*'

Aster typed a message back.

'*Nice to be here. Who is this?*'

'*On your left*,' came the reply message.

Aster glanced to her left and saw the person in the booth next to her waving and smiling at her. She waved and smiled back politely.

'*And on your right*,' came another message.

Aster glanced right and exchanged more smiles and waves.

'*Everyone in the room is on the messaging list*,' another message explained, '*just reply to all, and that way we can all chat with each other in silence.*'

'*Got it*,' Aster replied before starting her work.

Sure enough, there was a list of tasks waiting for her, all of which involved running simulations of various components and evaluating the designs. As she scrolled through the list, the material she'd been instructed to study beforehand began to make more sense. Artificial gravity projector manifolds, polycrystalline toroidal superconductor sheeting, and quantum nano-transistors were just a few of the components listed.

The holographic interface was incredible, immersing her completely in an array of 3-dimensional graphs and diagrams, and overwhelming her with a comprehensive list of analysis options. The schematics were 3-dimensional too, providing a level of intuitive visualisation beyond anything she had worked with before.

But the most amazing thing was the central computer.

Every self-respecting engineering firm had its own supercomputer – preferably a quantum computing cluster – but the system now at her disposal was eye-wateringly fast. Back at J.E. Co., she would have to take her lunch break as she waited for the results, but with this system, the simulations were over in minutes or seconds.

'*Having fun, newbie?*' read a new message.

'*I'm working,*' Aster typed back defensively.

'*I never said you weren't,*' came the reply, '*there's no reason you can't do both.*'

'*I can't believe how fast these computers are,*' Aster messaged in response.

'*This is the Directorate,*' someone pointed it, '*of course the computers are fast.*'

'*And it's not even the fastest computer in the building,*' someone else added, leaving Aster fascinated to know what *was* the fastest.

'*It's great that we can go home once we're done,*' Aster messaged enthusiastically.

Almost instantly, a reply appeared in her inbox.

'*Hahaha!*' it read.

'*Oh, dear newbie,*' read another message.

'*What's so funny?*' Aster asked, furrowing her brow.

'*The flexibility is a bonus for us,*' a reply message explained, '*but the real reason is so none of us junior techies knows what's being built or how it all fits together.*'

Aster sat up in her seat.

'*You look shocked, newbie,*' another message came in.

Aster *was* shocked. The compartmentalisation of R&D was par for the course in the private sector – the better to facilitate plausible deniability – but of course the engineers had to know what they were building and how it worked. Keeping them in the dark about details so basic was unthinkable.

Then again, why was she so surprised? This wasn't a for-profit business, this was the Directorate of Naval Intelligence. Secrecy was its business.

'*If you prove yourself, they'll let you do hands-on stuff,*' another message told her.

'*If I prove I'm good, you mean?*' Aster asked in her reply.

'*That, and your commitment/loyalty to the Directorate,*' someone else clarified.

Her loyalty? It made sense, but it was a sobering thought all the same.

'*I'm totally planning to steal DNI secrets*,' Aster typed as a sarcastic joke.

'*Sure you are, newbie*,' someone messaged back, then added "*but don't it call the 'DNI', that's what outsiders call it. To us, it's the 'Directorate'.*"

"*Ok*," Aster messaged back, then returned to her assigned tasks as another message appeared in the corner of her screen.

'*By the way, they monitor our messages.*'

* * *

The Krakenscourge exited Q-space well outside the system and cruised in towards its destination. There was no way to mask the gravitic disturbance or the flash of Cherenkov radiation that accompanied the ship's transition from Q-space, but once the transition was complete, the vessel was undetectable.

The ship's stealth systems were engaged as a matter of protocol and prudence, but in all probability it was unnecessary. There were countless backwater star systems like this one strewn all across the frontiers, and the vast majority had no registered Human settlements, just deep space waystations and monitoring probes.

On the other hand, that was precisely what made these backwater systems ideal hiding places for activities beyond the scope of the law. Corporations and criminal syndicates alike operated facilities in remote systems like this one in order to be safe from the prying eyes and restrictive hands of the government – and that was far from the worst case scenario.

"*Any new information on the outpost?*" Gabriel asked over the comm. as he ran through the Firebird's pre-flight checks.

"*Some systems are still partially operational*," a crewmember responded, "*but we're not detecting any life signs, Human or otherwise.*"

"*Understood,*" Gabriel replied.

The Firebird was a short-range combat craft with a snug cockpit. For Gabriel, being a head taller than average and clad in armour, it was downright cramped. At least it would only be a short journey. The shuttle bay had already been depressurised for the launch, and once the pre-flight checks were complete, the shuttle bay doors opened.

The light of the local star was being partly reflected by the murky grey clouds of the gas giant, enough for him to discern a cloud of debris. Gabriel looked straight ahead and pressed the launch button. The force of the launch mechanism firing thrust him back into his seat as the gunship was catapulted forwards and ejected out into space.

As soon as the Firebird was launched, its engines fired and Gabriel took control, easing the gunship into the debris field. The flight computer began tracking countless bits of rock whilst guiding Gabriel safely through. Occasionally, a smaller piece of debris would come too close and the shields would bounce it away. As he drew closer, the camera feeds provided a clear image of what remained of the outpost.

The short answer was very little. Vast scorch marks crisscrossed the asteroid into which the outpost had been built, the external infrastructure had been blasted to nothing, and the docking bays had been reduced to gaping holes in the rock face. The destruction was thorough and extremely precise.

"*We can safely rule out 'industrial accident' as a theory,*" Gabriel said over the comm., "*Any indication of the kind of weaponry used?*"

"*Energy scans are inconclusive,*" a crewmember replied, "*We're also not detecting any impact damage either to the asteroid or the destroyed infrastructure.*"

"*Directed energy weapons, then,*" Gabriel concluded.

"*Colonel, there's a heat bloom near the asteroid's core,*" another crewmember reported, "*It's too cold to be a power plant, but it could be a server room.*"

"*Sounds like a good place to start looking*," Gabriel replied.

A blue navigation line appeared in the cockpit HUD, curving towards a gaping hole in the asteroid's surface. Tiny flashes were visible within, the remains of ruptured power conduits spitting sparks into space. Gabriel piloted the Firebird into the hole and slowed to a halt, then he made sure that his helmet was secure and adjusted the environmental controls.

"*Warning: cockpit depressurising*," the computer informed him.

Through his suit's auditory sensors Gabriel could hear a hissing sound as the air was sucked out of the cockpit, and his helmet's HUD registered a steady drop in air pressure until the cockpit was a vacuum. There was nowhere to land the Firebird, and without any suitable airlocks or docking bays, this was the only way in.

Already secure inside his armoured suit, Gabriel undid his safety harness, then twisted the canopy release handle before yanking it hard. With a series of rattling clicks, the canopy unlocked and swung open, causing the temperature gauge to plummet as the cockpit was exposed to the freezing cold of space. Gabriel climbed out of his seat and planted his feet on the lip of the cockpit, kicking off towards the gaping crater.

It was pitch black beyond, but with the visual enhancement filters in his HUD, Gabriel could see the outline of a corridor leading into the facility.

"*Colonel*," Captain Ironside hailed him, "*multiple Q-space events detected on the edge of the system. They are not navy vessels.*"

"*Instar Frontier Services?*" Gabriel asked.

"*Almost certainly, and they're heading straight towards the outpost. ETA 1 hour.*"

"*I'll retrieve whatever data I can find from the server room*," Gabriel answered, "*but I may need more than an hour to get out again.*"

"*What are the rules of engagement here?*" Ironside asked.

Gabriel paused. Ironside was essentially asking for permission to open fire on Human ships. The Krakenscourge was Ironside's ship, but as a voidstalker, Gabriel was the ranking officer. That meant strategic decisions ultimately fell to him.

"*Maintain stealth for as long as possible,*" Gabriel replied, "*and do not engage unless absolutely necessary. I can take care of any boarding parties.*"

* * *

The facility was pitch black and devoid of life. Much of the outpost's architecture had also been warped: mangled into dead ends and cul-de-sacs by the force of explosions or blasted open and exposed to the void. It was a serious challenge finding a route through the wreckage, and it was only thanks to the filters in his HUD that Gabriel could see anything at all.

Gabriel had his weapon drawn, but anything in the facility that might have posed a threat was either dead or long gone. There were plenty of corpses, weightless and frozen, and contorted into awkward death poses. The air had been sucked out of their lungs and the deathly cold of space had chilled their flesh to the core. Some of the corpses had wounds resembling incredibly fine medical incisions in their flesh.

"*Are you seeing this?*" Gabriel asked through the comm., angling his head so that the Krakenscourge's crew could see through his helmet camera.

"*Crystal clear,*" came the reply, "*the fraying patterns around the wounds are extremely fine, but whatever caused them entered at high velocity.*"

"*Firearms?*" Gabriel asked.

"*Not the kind found in any Human arsenal,*" the crewmember responded gravely.

Gabriel left the frozen corpse to float in peace and continued following the navigation marker until he came to an elevator. He pried open the emergency box and yanked on the manual release handle. There was no artificial gravity in the elevator shafts, so Gabriel floated down the shaft to the server room entrance and pulled himself inside, dropping back to the floor again as the artificial gravity took hold.

The displays were powered down, and a fine crust of ice had formed on every surface like a layer of crystal-white paint, but the servers were still humming away as if nothing had happened. Although the cooling systems had failed, the freezing temperatures of the void had permeated all the way into the server room, keeping the computers cool enough to continue functioning.

Gabriel walked up to the control station and tapped a few keys. The display lit up, flashing a notification at him in danger-red letters: "*CRITICAL ERROR: NO OPERATING SYSTEM DETECTED. PLEASE CHECK BACKUP DATA MODULE.*"

"*Colonel,*" a crewmember hailed him, "*The Instar flotilla just released a wave of boarding pods towards the outpost. Their arrival is imminent.*"

"*The closer the flotilla gets, the harder it will be to stay hidden and provide support to you at the same time, Colonel,*" Ironside warned.

"*That's always a problem,*" Gabriel replied, "*but my previous orders stand.*"

"*We'll do our best on our end,*" Ironside answered a little sceptically.

"*I'd rather avoid a shooting match between Human ships if possible,*" Gabriel pointed out firmly, "*not to mention unnecessarily risking our own ship.*"

"*Acknowledged, Colonel.*"

There was a service hatch in the floor at his feet, and Gabriel reached down and pulled it open, finding an access shaft and a ladder leading down into the dark. He jumped straight in, sliding down the ladder into a cramped alcove with a locked hatch and a numerical keypad built into the wall.

Gabriel squatted down and pressed his palm against the keypad. The software in his suit bypassed the lock and the hatch popped open, revealing the backup data module within. Grasping the handle, he twisted the module around and pulled it out, then placed it against his lower back where a set of magnetic clamps locked it into place.

A new navigation marker appeared in Gabriel's HUD.

"*The marker we've uploaded will take you to the nearest exit*," a crewmember informed him, "*by the way, the Instar boarding pods have made contact*."

"*Thanks for the tipoff*," Gabriel replied.

* * *

The working day felt much longer than it actually was, and Aster spent most of the journey home wondering whether taking this job had been the right decision at all.

It had only been her first day, but the opaque and hierarchical nature of the Directorate's R&D process was already unsettling her. At her previous job, she'd gotten used to supervising the entire design process and having freewheeling discussions with colleagues about the project. But at the Directorate, that privilege was presumably left to minds far greater than her own, making her just another drone in a bewilderingly complex hive.

The children were still in their learning pods when Aster got home, and baby Emerald was still fast asleep, being watched over by one of the household androids. Aster lay down on the bed, feeling totally worn out.

There was a knock on the door.

"Come in," Aster called out.

The door opened and Orion entered.

"Hello sweetheart," Aster said with a smile, sitting up on the bed.

"I started basic calculus today," Orion announced, jumping onto the bed.

"What's the derivative of the natural log of x?" Aster asked.

"One over x," Orion answered with a proud grin.

"What's the integral of the natural log of x?" Aster asked with a raised eyebrow.

"That's x multiplied by the natural log of x minus x plus an unknown constant!" Orion announced even more proudly, "If you already know the derivative, you can substitute it with something else and it's easy to work out in your head."

Aster was stunned.

"How far along are you?" she asked.

"Just the intro part," Orion replied, "but I passed all the tests on limits already, so the learning pod let me move onto derivatives and antiderivatives."

Aster remembered grappling with calculus all through her late teens. For an eight-year-old to master the basics after one lesson was astonishing.

"What else have you learned?" she asked.

"Lots!" Orion declared, then added less enthusiastically, "but I'm bored with being stuck in the pod all day, I want to go play."

"Ok, you've earned it," Aster said, stroking his curly hair.

"I'm gonna go play in the gym," Orion announced, jumping off the bed.

"Don't touch your father's equipment," Aster ordered him sternly.

"Why not?" Orion asked plaintively, "he's not even here most of the time."

"Because only grownups like your father can use it safely," Aster responded firmly.

"But I just want to–" Orion protested.

"Don't touch your father's gym equipment!" Aster snapped, slipping briefly into her native colonial accent as she shouted.

Orion flinched at her tone of voice, then lowered his head in quiet compliance.

"…Ok…" he mumbled, wary of challenging his mother.

"It's for your own safety," Aster reassured him in a softer voice.

Orion nodded half-heartedly and walked out.

Baby Emerald began to cry and the household android moved into action, collecting the wailing infant from her crib and gently bringing a bottle of formula to her mouth. Feeling guilty for waking the baby, Aster climbed off the bed to take over and the android obediently handed Emerald over to her.

Gabriel hated the androids, perhaps because he was used to being shot at by them. He especially distrusted them around the children and had only agreed to keep them because they did all the household chores. The maganiel android was his property, but even that was kept locked away most of the time.

To be fair, some people did find the androids' synthetic skin a little creepy: something about the rubbery texture was just… off. There were more Human-like models available with the right proportions, physical appearance, and everything else; but they were ridiculously expensive and nowhere near as robust.

The door opened, and Rose and Violet walked in.

"Afternoon sweethearts," Aster said with a smile, handing the baby back to the android.

Neither of the two girls smiled back as they approached. Violet looked pale and shaken and was pressing a dishcloth against her forearm while her older sister Rose tenderly led her into the room. A feeling of parental dread gripped Aster's heart.

"What's wrong?" she asked, her pulse quickening.

"Vi hurt herself," Rose replied with a quivering voice.

Aster gasped in fright and she knelt down to look at Violet's arm.

"I cut myself by mistake," Violet mumbled almost apologetically.

"Does it hurt?" Aster asked as she pulled the cloth away.

Aster did a double take.

The underside of the cloth was caked with freshly dried blood, but there was no wound, only a thin white line of fresh scar tissue that was itself barely visible.

"Not anymore," Violet replied.

* * *

There was nothing dignified about crawling through a ventilation shaft, but since the goal was to avoid detection, it had to be done. Clad from head to toe in combat armour and clutching a service weapon, it was a wonder Gabriel could fit in the shaft at all.

"*We're tracking fifty targets throughout the facility,*" a crewmember informed him, "*we're also detecting periodic heat blooms in excess of 3000 degrees.*"

"*So they have breaching gear as well,*" Gabriel concluded grimly.

"*Given the extensive damage to the facility, navigating through it would be impossible without breaching gear,*" the crewmember added redundantly.

Gabriel pushed a panel open and climbed out of the shaft, emerging in a storage room. The door to the storage room had been forced open, and on the other side was a corridor with one end caved in and the other end leading to an elevator.

"*The elevator shaft at the other end will take you to one of the waste disposal chambers,*" said a crewmember, "*from there you can exit the station.*"

"*Disgusting,*" Gabriel replied with a grimace, "*but good enough.*"

"*Hostiles are approaching your position,*" another crewmember warned him.

"*Where from?*"

"*The wall opposite you.*"

Gabriel dived into cover behind a stack of boxes. In the corridor, an entire section of the wall began to glow a hellish red, then imploded in on itself in spectacular fashion, producing a blinding flash and a wave of scorching heat. The air was too thin to carry much sound, but it would have been deafening up close.

From the breach emerged five figures clad in vacuum-proof body armour with the Instar Frontier Services logo emblazoned on their shoulder pads. Four of them were brandishing submachine guns while the fifth held a two-handed hose with a tube connected to a bulky piece of gear strapped to his back.

Gabriel was trapped. If he tried climbing back into the shaft, the boarding team would hear him and eliminate him easily. If he opened fire on them first, he could eliminate this one team, but would instantly alert all the other Instar boarding teams to his presence. All he could do was stay in hiding and wait for the team to move on, preserving the element of surprise.

Or not.

Gabriel heard a clicking noise as something was tossed into the storage room. When it detonated, it released a wave of concussive force, sending boxes and spare equipment bouncing off the walls in a chaotic storm of paraphernalia.

The Instar squad stormed the room, covering the corners as they entered, but Gabriel recovered quickly enough to fire first. The squad was blindsided, and several of them were knocked down by the force of the bullets. Gabriel scrambled to his feet and squeezed off more rounds, firing at point-blank range to finish off his targets.

At the end of the short but intense barrage, four of the five-man squad lay sprawled on the ground, impact-damage visible across their armoured cuirasses. Even though his shots hadn't penetrated their armour, the impact force of each bullet had clearly broken bones and caused internal injuries that would put them out of the fight.

The fifth squad member had taken cover on the other side of the breach, and as Gabriel exited the room, the fifth man unwisely poked his head out to see if the coast was clear. Gabriel fired a three-round burst, punching straight through the man's helmet visor. A fine red spray burst from his face and froze instantly on the floor as he collapsed to the ground, the breaching tool slipping out of his dead hands.

"*Colonel*," a crewmember said, "*enemy forces are converging on your position*."

"*I'd like to know how they knew my position in the first place*," Gabriel shot back.

"*Wait…we're detecting another signal, an encrypted burst every five seconds. It's coming from your location.*"

Gabriel realised instantly what it was.

"*The data module has a tracking device,*" he concluded.

"*Before you ask, there's no way to block the signal,*" the crewmember informed him, "*and if you try to tamper with the module outside of a controlled setting, the data could be erased before we can look at it.*"

"*Understood,*" Gabriel replied through gritted teeth. Not only was he outnumbered and outgunned by the Instar forces, but they knew exactly where he was.

"*The elevator shaft at the other end of the corridor will take you straight to the nearest waste disposal chamber,*" the crewmember reminded him.

Gabriel hurried down the corridor to the elevator, and from there it was another zero-gravity trip down the shaft directly to the waste disposal control room.

"*I need you to pilot the Firebird remotely to my position,*" Gabriel said as he cast around for a way to open the disposal chamber itself.

"*Already on its way,*" the crewmember replied, "*ETA one minute.*"

Gabriel found a maintenance hatch leading into the disposal chute. He stowed his weapon and pulled on the manual release lever. The lever squealed in stubborn resistance to his efforts, even with his physical enhancements and the exoskeletal strength provided by his armour. However, inch by inch, it moved towards the unlocked position.

"*Five more hostiles approaching your position,*" the crewmember warned him.

Gabriel drew his weapon again and took aim at the door. Except for the elevator shaft, he was cornered and wouldn't have the element of surprise this time. By the time he managed to open the disposal chamber, the Instar squad would have burst through the door.

"*Can the Firebird blast open the disposal chute?*" Gabriel asked.

"*Only if a torpedo is used,*" was the answer, "*which means that if you're suggesting what I think you're suggesting, you could be killed in the explosion.*"

"*There's no other way,*" Gabriel replied, stowing his weapon, "*fire on my command.*"

"*We've done more insane things,*" Ironside added over the comm., "*do what the colonel says and be ready to fire.*"

"*Aye, Captain,*" replied the crewmember, "*Firebird in position, torpedo ready.*"

Gabriel bolted through the open elevator doors into the zero gravity.

"*Fire!*" He shouted, kicking off the floor of the elevator shaft.

Behind and below him, Gabriel heard the click and hiss of the disposal chamber door opening. The door retracted into the wall and five armed figures wearing vacuum-proof body armour stormed the chamber a split second before it happened.

The torpedo had a two-stage warhead. The first explosive was a shaped charge with a contact sensor in the tip of the nose which detonated when it struck the sealed hatch of the disposal chute. The force of the explosion was directed forwards, eating through the metal and creating a breach through which the torpedo continued moving.

The second explosive was inside the body of the torpedo itself, containing enough destructive power to demolish a small building. After the breaching explosive had detonated, a three-second timer was activated, enough time for the torpedo to punch deeper into the target. When the timer reached zero, it detonated.

All five Instar security personnel were killed instantly as the explosion destroyed the waste disposal chute and the control room in one go. Gabriel heard the booming roar of the explosion and felt the shockwave slap him hard from behind, and his shields flashed as they pushed back against the blast force.

A heartbeat later, the explosion devoured the remaining air and the blossoming flames dissipated as the newly-created vacuum sucked everything back down the elevator shaft. The sensation of being slapped hard in the back was replaced by the sensation of being yanked downwards by an invisible tether as the vacuum pulled Gabriel backwards again.

The waste disposal control room had been reduced to a gaping maw in the hull. The sprawling constellation of debris and the immense velvety-black backdrop of space greeted Gabriel as his momentum carried him clear of the facility and towards the Firebird. He reached out and grabbed the rim of the cockpit, pulling himself inside and landing back in the pilot's seat as the safety harnesses and cockpit canopy sealed themselves automatically.

"*Multiple spaceborne hostiles are tracking you, Colonel,*" the crewmember warned him, "*we'll do our best to cover you.*"

"*Much appreciated,*" Gabriel replied.

Re-establishing manual control, Gabriel brought the Firebird around and gunned the engines, powering away at maximum speed towards the Krakenscourge's coordinates. The Firebird's shielding flickered and flashed, swatting bits of space junk out of the way as Gabriel did his best not to hit the larger pieces of debris.

The Firebird was stealthy and fast, but its stealth coating wasn't much use at close range, nor was it fast enough to evade most targeting systems. Not to mention, there was no way the Instar ships hadn't detected the explosion. His cover had literally been blown, and he would have to rely on the Krakenscourge for cover.

Just as Gabriel cleared the debris field, a shadow loomed over the Firebird, blotting out the light of the local star. He could see it on the sensor feeds, but it looked a lot more threatening through the glass canopy. It was a cruiser with the Instar Frontier Services logo emblazoned on its hull, closing in on him like some massive space predator cornering its next meal. Direct combat was out of the question, his only remaining advantage was speed.

The words '*GRAVITIC DISTURBANCE*' began flashing across the Firebird's HUD in panicky orange letters. Other warning indicators went off as the gunship was pulled inexorably off its intended course, its engines struggling to counter the external force. Gabriel struggled to compensate, but the cruiser was using an artificial gravity well to ensnare him, making it clear that they wanted him alive.

Voidstalkers weren't supposed to be taken alive, not even by Human forces, death was preferable to falling into enemy hands. But of course what the Instar forces were after was the data module he had taken; once they'd confiscated that, they might interrogate him or just kill him. Either way, it wouldn't matter if he was captured alive or not.

Gabriel twisted the controls sideways, trying to force the Firebird to face his much larger opponent; but he was trapped in the cruiser's gravity field, and the thrusters struggled to obey. The Firebird still had three torpedoes and a chin-mounted laser turret, if he could bring those to bear he might be able to damage the cruiser before it could pull him inside, then make a quick escape in the confusion.

But even if Gabriel could turn the craft around in time, he knew his last-ditch plan was unlikely to work. The cruiser was much larger with much stronger shields, and could probably absorb all the damage he could inflict with ease. If he opened fire too soon, the torpedoes would be swatted aside; but if he waited until he was pulled inside the shield envelope, he could be hit by blowback from the explosions.

Without the Krakenscourge's help, there would be no escape.

A blindingly bright beam of light appeared from nowhere and struck the cruiser's flank, scorching the hull in a sweeping arc. It was a high-powered laser weapon, devastating at short-range and extremely accurate as well as impossible for conventional shielding to block. The gravity field suddenly faltered and the gravitic disturbance warning disappeared.

Gabriel turned the Firebird around and gunned the engines again, speeding away from the hostile ship. A dark shape was swooping in towards him, and Gabriel piloted the Firebird towards it, flying straight into the Krakenscourge's open shuttle bay. With the gunship and its pilot safely aboard, the shuttle bay doors sealed up again.

The Instar cruiser wasn't badly damaged, but it was reeling from the unexpected strike and struggled to turn its massive bulk around. Blindsided by the attack and blinded by the Krakenscourge's electronic countermeasures, it made no attempt to return fire. Meanwhile, the dark shadow of the Krakenscourge executed a sharp turn away from the cruiser and gunned its engines towards the edge of the system.

* * *

The trading barge ambush was slipping from the minds of the Nexus's inhabitants. Itinerant merchants and mercenary gangs were spreading the story far and wide, but life aboard the station had already returned to normal. The survivors of the attack had lapsed into comas, and with their basic medical needs met, they were left to sleep off their injuries.

Why they had entered this comatose state was a mystery. The deep, watery blue colour of their skin had returned, and their injuries had largely healed, so there was no clear reason for them to still be unconscious. Then again, the Water-skins weren't very forthcoming about their biology, so there could be any number of reasons why they hadn't woken up.

In any case, they were probably better off catatonic. Their ship had been thoroughly ransacked in their absence and reduced to a husk that was now worthless even as scrap. When they woke up – if they woke up – they would find that everything they owned had been stolen by their supposed saviours.

The makeshift hospital was still as a graveyard. The floor was covered with hundreds of medical beds in which the survivors slept, resting peacefully in their protective comas. The holographic controls on the beds had been dimmed to conserve power, and apart from the medical drones, nothing stirred.

Behind a set of crates, an access hatch opened and a camouflaged figure emerged into the shadows, the light bending around its distorted outline, rendering it undetectable. Not that it made much difference; the hospital had the atmosphere of a mausoleum, with the drones quietly tending to the medical beds as if they were tombs.

The cloaked figure moved out of the shadows and took cover behind one of the medical beds as a drone passed by. Once it was gone, the figure inserted a vial of clear liquid into a slot in the bed, and the machine sucked in its contents. The figure moved on and inserted another vial into the next machine, then moved methodically from bed to bed repeating the action until over fifty beds had been spiked.

The figure was about to move onto the next row of medical beds when an alarm sounded, a shrill klaxon that shattered the fragile, funerary silence in the chamber.

One of the survivors was waking up.

The seemingly dozy medical drones sprang into action, hovering towards the source of the alarm and crowding around the medical bed. The patient was hyperventilating, and its limbs were palpitating violently as if it were undergoing a seizure. Unable to discern the nature of the emergency, the drones plugged their tentacle-like cables into the medical bed to pool their processing power into a single network.

The patient continued to buck and thrash, its seizure worsening with each passing second, gibbering unintelligibly as if it were acting out some horrible nightmare. The conclave of medical drones hovered and hummed in silence, absorbed by their collective attempt to make sense of the patient's bizarre symptoms.

Suddenly, one of the drones began to quiver and shake as if mimicking the patient's symptoms, then it swayed drunkenly in the air before crashing into another drone. The glitchy behaviour spread and one by one the drones fell to the floor. The patient's symptoms subsided as abruptly as they had begun, and silence returned.

The patient awoke, its eyelids sliding back to reveal a pair of glossy black eyes as it sat up and looked around, showing no sign of the violent spasmodic seizure it had just undergone. It regarded the room not with disorientation or confusion, but with a clear, almost calculating gaze, calmly assessing its surroundings.

Like the rest of its species, the patient was lanky, with deep blue skin and slender arms and legs. Its fingers were long and dextrous whilst its feet were flat and webbed. Its entire body was aquadynamic, enabling it to swim through water if it chose to. Its head was large in proportion to its body and was almost bulbous in shape, and its oily black eyes were devoid of any features or feelings.

After surveying the silent chamber filled with hundreds of its comatose kin, the patient opened its mouth and released a keening scream.

At first, nothing happened.

Then there was a mass-stirring. The hundreds of other survivors sat up as one, looking around with the same glossy black eyes and blank expressions before climbing out of their medical beds and gathering together.

The sepulchral silence of the hallway was punctured this time by the pitter-patter of several hundred amphibious feet as the trading barge survivors streamed away. None of them uttered a word or made a sound as they moved, they didn't even stop to collect anything or deactivate the medical beds. It was like a carefully rehearsed mass-departure where everyone knew exactly what to do and how quickly to do it.

As a group, the Water-skins moved to one side of the hall and opened up one of the maintenance hatches, somehow bypassing the security lock. There was no frantic rush to leave and no audible chatter, they simply lined up in an orderly queue and vanished down the chute one by one, leaving the chamber behind them totally deserted.

The cloaked figure was already long gone.

THE NEXUS

INSTAR Frontier Services would do its utmost to cover up the attack on its own facility, a fact that would make containment of the XA-107 incident much easier. And if word of the incident ever did become public, it would be a private corporation's word against the word of the Directorate of Naval Intelligence.

The Krakenscourge's electronic warfare suite had deluged the Instar cruiser's guidance and targeting systems with junk data, blinding it long enough to rescue Gabriel and make a quick escape. With six Instar operatives dead, the operation had hardly gone smoothly, but the data module Gabriel had retrieved – or stolen – was in good working order.

"Thank you for that timely rescue," Gabriel said to Ironside as they waited for the technician to finish preparing the data module for analysis.

"It wouldn't look very good on my record if I left you to die," Ironside responded wryly, "but you're welcome nonetheless."

"Oh? So all those times you pulled me out of the fire were just to keep your professional record clean?" Gabriel asked jokingly.

"Well, it's always your plan to jump into the fire in the first place," Ironside replied, extending the joke, "but shifting the blame would also look bad on my record."

"The data module is ready," the technician announced, "also, the tracker is a short-range transmitter, so it's undetectable even without the faraday cradle."

"Good to know," Ironside replied.

The module's contents were decrypted then scanned for malware and other digital booby-traps. When none were detected, the data was extracted and displayed in an all-encompassing holographic display.

Gabriel and Ironside each put on a data-glove and stared up at the constellation of data. Seeing a file of interest, Ironside reached up and plucked an event log from the air, pulling it down towards him and expanding it with his fingers.

"'Q-space event logged,'" Ironside read aloud, "'5 megaton mass, 500km distance.'"

Everyone blinked in disbelief.

"That can't be right," Gabriel said quizzically.

"I've already checked the module for data corruption," the technician informed them, "there is none...the data says what it says."

There was silence in the lab.

"So..." Gabriel summarised, "an unknown vessel with several times the mass of a dreadnought exits Q-space...in-system..."

"And attacks the outpost, leaving no survivors before departing," Ironside finished, "a ship like that could attack any planetary target it wanted without warning."

"What does the rest of the log say?" Gabriel asked.

"A station-wide alert was triggered shortly after the Q-space event," Ironside replied, scrolling through the log, "data and records were backed-up, a distress call was sent out, and the outpost was locked down."

"Then the outpost was attacked," said Gabriel, plucking another event log from the data constellation, "the computers logged massive damage to all major systems and subsystems by unidentified energy weaponry."

"What else is there?" Ironside asked.

"Intrusion alarms were triggered in multiple places ten minutes after the initial Q-space event," the technician spoke up, "the few sensors that were still working detected dozens of thermal signatures consistent with lifeforms...non-Human lifeforms."

That the original attackers weren't Human was obvious, but it was still shocking to see the evidence explicitly confirm it. Was this revenge for the attack on the alien trading barge with Humanity mistaken as the culprits? Was the same culprit responsible for both attacks? Why attack some unremarkable outpost instead of a colony world?

"We can handle things from here," Ironside said to the technician.

The technician nodded and departed, leaving the two ranking officers alone.

"The internal cameras were still recording all the way through the attack," Ironside said, plucking another file from the air and expanding it into a set of video feeds.

The footage showed groups of insectoid creatures clad in vacuum-proof body armour boarding the station. They had four arms and moved about on six segmented legs, standing taller than a Human, and they clutched exotic-looking firearms in their claw-like hands. They were organised into squads and moved through the station with discipline and purpose, covering every angle and corner as they advanced.

The footage showed the alien boarders making their way through the half-destroyed outpost – killing any survivors they found – until they reached the storage chambers deep within the outpost. There was nothing of value there except for supplies, but the insectoid aliens had converged specifically on this location, and they quickly got to work.

The alien attackers smeared some kind of paste over one of the walls which blazed with white-hot fire, eating through several metres of rock before dissipating. Once the smoke had cleared, they advanced into the breach, retrieving something that had apparently been buried in the rock right under the noses of the outpost's Human crew.

A team of four insectoid intruders emerged from the breach carrying what looked like a piece of finely carved rock, curved very slightly into the shape of an arch. On closer inspection, the colour and texture of the artefact looked more like that of scorched metal or maybe basalt with a metallic hue.

It reminded Gabriel of the observatory on Loki.

The cameras' filters could identify many things that weren't visible to the Human eye, but they couldn't make heads or tails of the artefact or the material from which it was constructed. It certainly wasn't rock.

"I was permitted to review the footage from your mission at the Loki facility," Ironside told Gabriel as he paused the video.

"It certainly looks like the same kind of architecture," Gabriel answered pensively, "although with just this recording there's no way to be certain."

"The external sensors and communications arrays were targeted first," Ironside noted, "which means there's no way of tracing where the attackers came from or where they went."

"Maybe not," Gabriel replied as he opened an interface with the Krakenscourge's computers, "but at least we can identify the species."

Using biometric data from the cameras, the ship's computers identified the attackers as belonging to species I-1959. Alternative designations included 'Space Termites' and 'Hive-dwellers', the latter being the term used by most alien races.

"The Hive-dwellers," Gabriel murmured, "have they ever ventured this far out before?"

"Not according to the Directorate's records," Ironside responded, "and certainly never into Human space before."

There was a cool silence.

"Well, they're going to regret breaking that habit," Gabriel said menacingly.

* * *

It was early in the morning. The sun was just a sliver of orange light on the horizon and the mag-trains were less crowded than they would be an hour from now. The second trip to work was far less intimidating than the first one, but maybe that was just because Aster was distracted by other things.

Given the amount of blood, Violet's injury should have been serious enough for her to be hospitalised, but the wound had healed in under a minute and the scar had vanished by morning. Poor Violet was still shaken by the incident, but otherwise, she was fine.

Aster was not fine.

Gabriel almost never talked about his work, let alone the enhancements that had made him into a voidstalker, but where else would Violet have gotten the ability to heal that quickly? It wasn't technically a bad thing, but Aster felt deeply uncomfortable that her children had picked up such an inheritance from their father. That she was only now starting to notice after a decade of marriage to him was even more disturbing.

The colony where she had grown up had always been abuzz with conspiracy theories about alleged government schemes. Everything from rigging mineral prices in collusion with interstellar corporations to kidnapping colonists as guinea pigs for experimentation. Far be it from her to start thinking that some of those stories might actually be true.

She couldn't ask her new employers, or even just search the database. Not only were the information controls much stricter than at J.E. Co., but as a brand new employee, she was probably being monitored extra closely. Aster knew that the prudent thing to do would be to simply drop the issue, but this involved her children, she couldn't just drop it.

Once she'd passed through security, Aster made her way to the data centre where she was assigned, sat down in her booth and got to work. There was a fresh list of components for her to model and test, and she soon slipped back into the rhythm of work whilst trying to keep Violet's rapidly healed injury out of her mind.

The first item was some kind of Q-engine manifold, but with a radically different design than usual. Her task was to comb through each of the components and make sure all the pieces fit together properly, then simulate the operations of the virtually-assembled device using the data centre's supercomputing cluster.

An hour of working on the same component left Aster with partial mental burnout, and she got up from her booth to take a timeout. In many ways, the Spire was just like a regular office building, and it was almost reassuring to find a regular breakroom with a drink and snack dispenser, there was even a proper coffee machine.

Instead of coffee, however, Aster fixed herself a standard energy drink. Lots of people liked coffee out of millennia-old tradition as well as the rich flavour of certain types of beans, but modern energy concoctions could be mixed with the same flavours and still provide the same nutritional benefits – minus the jitters and insomnia.

"I take it you're not a coffee person?" asked a voice beside her.

"No," Aster replied, "I don't like the way coffee tastes."

"You can always spike it with some flavouring," her colleague suggested.

"But then it wouldn't really be coffee, would it?" Aster pointed out.

"I suppose not," her colleague replied with a smile.

Her colleague was a woman with short dark hair and a golden nose stud, as well as tattoos snaking down her neck. The personal stylings, along with her mildly fluty accent, meant that she was from the Clouds.

"I'm Aster," Aster said, tentatively extending her hand.

"Dr Aster Thorn, I know," the woman answered with a smile, accepting Aster's hand and shaking it, "I read your employee pro file."

"What profile?" Aster asked.

"You can look up other people's profiles in the central database," the woman explained, "in fact, you can look up anything as long as you have the clearance. They monitor our activity, obviously, but there's nothing wrong with consulting it whenever you feel curious."

"Good to know," Aster said appreciatively.

"Happy to help," came the smiling reply.

"Well, you know my name," said Aster, "what's yours?"

"Maxine," she answered, "you can find my surname in the database."

"Why can't you just tell me right now?"

"Where's the mystery in that?" Maxine asked before walking away.

* * *

From a reality-warping morass of pure blackness, the Krakenscourge squeezed through, emerging from Q-space into real space like a spectre passing between worlds. The resulting burst of blueshifted Cherenkov radiation was easily detectable, but with countless ships coming and going from the Nexus station all the time, nobody paid any attention.

The Krakenscourge steered clear of the Nexus and cruised towards the nearby gas cloud, parking a short distance away. The ship's hull was impervious to cosmic radiation – as any deep-space vessel had to be – but the residual radiation from the gas cloud would wash over the vessel, smothering whatever residual signature it might be giving off, and rendering the ship completely invisible.

"*We'll keep the ship here until you get back*," Ironside said over the comm.

"*So why am I investigating the Nexus rather than the trading barge?*" Gabriel asked as he prepared the Firebird for launch.

"*There's a lead you need to investigate first,*" Ironside replied, "*specifically regarding the redacted part of the original report.*"

"*What kind of lead?*"

"*We have an asset aboard the Nexus who was the source of the original intelligence,*" Ironside clarified, "*you'll need to link up with the source first.*"

"*Sounds like a plan,*" said Gabriel.

There was no way they were going to dock the Krakenscourge at an alien space station. The risk of advanced Human technology falling into alien hands or a penetrating scan giving away insights into the ship's design was too great. So once again, Gabriel piloted the Firebird on another vulnerable voyage to his destination.

'Vulnerable' didn't really begin to describe the short journey from the Krakenscourge to the Nexus station. He was piloting a one-man craft through a hundred kilometres of open space – non-Human space – and the tiny gunship was like a gnat compared to the alien trading ships and mercenary frigates that came and went.

There was plenty of room to manoeuvre and avoid collisions, and no debris field to navigate through, but the Firebird's shields weren't strong enough to withstand a glancing blow from most ship-grade weapons. Discharging weapons within the Nexus's monitoring zone was strictly forbidden, but that didn't make Gabriel feel any safer.

On his right, the kaleidoscopic gas cloud loomed large, a gargantuan translucent wall of gas and dust stretching for millions of kilometres in each direction. Vicious solar winds lashed at the opposite side, creating hypnotic displays of lightning within. All ships steered clear of the gas cloud, and Gabriel took special care to avoid it. One stray bolt was enough to reduce an unshielded ship to burnt scrap.

If a bolt struck the Firebird, there would be nothing left to pass as scrap.

On the left was another extraordinary view: interstellar space, appearing as an infinite expanse of velvety black sprinkled with countless points of starlight. The eternal emptiness beyond was as mesmerising as the gas cloud and far more dreadful to contemplate. Staring into the emptiness for too long could drive you mad.

The scene wasn't totally black, however. Every few seconds, a tiny pinpoint of red or blue light could be seen as a ship entered or exited Q-space. The flashes of light were an optical illusion of sorts, a visualisation of the Firebird's long-range sensor feeds projected onto the glass of the cockpit, but they added literal colour to the scene.

The Nexus wasn't the only artificial structure nearby. Looming large against the cosmic backdrop was the alien trading barge. It was a truly enormous ship, its architecture making it resemble a giant insect cocoon. Even though it was only a fraction of the size of the Nexus, it clearly dwarfed the other vessels that came and went.

Even from this distance, the vast gashes in the hull were clearly visible. Some of the hull breaches were so big that part of the superstructure beneath was exposed, making the ship look like the desiccated husk of some long-extinct space monster.

"*Krakenscourge*," Gabriel hailed the ship, "*any useful SIGINT material?*"

The Krakenscourge had a signals intelligence module mounted within the hull that could listen in on nearby communications.

"*Plenty*," a Krakenscourge crewmember replied, "*not only has the trading barge been stripped bare by looters, but the survivors have disappeared.*"

"*What do you mean 'disappeared'?*" Gabriel asked.

"*Apparently, all the Water-skins who were being treated vanished from their medical beds and the drones assigned to monitor them were disabled*," the crewmember explained.

"*I'm guessing the 'asset' might know more*," Gabriel concluded.

"*The Krakenscourge will remain in contact,*" Ironside informed Gabriel, "*but we'll only be able to provide minimal assistance if something goes wrong.*"

"*Something always goes wrong,*" Gabriel replied, "*but thanks for the warning.*"

* * *

Gabriel had been to the Nexus several times before, yet somehow it felt more and more alien each time he visited. Over the centuries, various species had taken it upon themselves to repair and reinforce old sections of the station or to add new ones, and all such renovations had been done with native designs. As long as the new or renovated sections held together and were vacuum and radiation-proof, the aesthetic appeal didn't matter.

The result was an eclectic mishmash of bewilderingly different architectural styles. One section was made from swirling azure arches, the next section from brutalist chunks of girder and panelling, and the next was a bland perpendicular arrangement. The multiple layers of hybrid designs were nothing if not bizarre.

And then there were the aliens themselves.

Evolution seemed to favour two-eyed bipeds for the most part, but the similarities ended there. Mammalian and reptilian analogues walked or strutted along the concourse, some with multicoloured frills around their necks, others with leathery brown hides that seemed to shift under the light. Some species were uncomfortable with the prevailing oxygen-nitrogen mixture and wore environmental suits to compensate.

Gabriel had a suit of his own with combat-grade armour and a backpack containing weapons and tools. Besides protection, the main purpose of the suit was to disguise his species, not that any of the alien passers-by would be likely to recognise a Human. Unauthorised contact with aliens was strictly forbidden, and so Humans were an extremely rare sight.

"*Where exactly am I going?*" Gabriel muttered into his throat mic.

"*The asset is already aware of your presence and will guide you to the right place,*" the Krakenscourge replied, "*in the meantime, head to the central plaza.*"

There were at least twenty 'central plazas' on the station, but it made sense to go to the nearest one. There was a huge variety of shops and bars – or the alien equivalent thereof – lining the narrow streets, most of which looked identical. If it weren't for the navigational markers on public display, Gabriel would quickly have lost his way.

A gaggle of waist-height, bug-eyed creatures stared at Gabriel, brandishing long talons at him as he walked passed. The same bug-eyed stares and talon-flexing were directed at every passer-by, and Gabriel ignored them. They wouldn't start a fight in public, and their claws couldn't scratch his armour if they tried.

After navigating the maze of alleyways, Gabriel came to the central plaza. It was a huge open space with endless streams of aliens coming and going. The hubbub of the back alleys gave way to a cacophonous din of activity, with thousands of alien voices babbling in almost as many tongues. The scene was reminiscent of the commercial districts in Asgard City, except that here the chatter was unintelligible and the residents were ugly as sin.

Even more impressive than the sounds were the sights. The plaza's centrepiece was an enormous tree-like sculpture made of two separate trunks sprouting up from the floor. The two trunks intertwined with one another like a pair of corkscrewing serpents and stretched all the way up through the ceiling.

It was a mesmerising spectacle. The surfaces of the two trunks were photoactive and alive with a riot of rippling colours. Intricate swirling patterns danced up and down their lengths, stretching into the ultraviolet and infrared spectra. It was an emulation of the natural stormy displays to be seen in the gas cloud, and unlike the ugly melange of architectural styles, this sight was actually beautiful.

"*Enjoying the view?*" asked a new voice in Gabriel's earpiece.

Gabriel flinched in surprise. Some third party was hailing him on an encrypted channel, and speaking in a voice disguised by a sibilant electronic sound effect.

"*Identify yourself,*" Gabriel demanded suspiciously.

"*I'm the 'asset' you're supposed to be meeting,*" the voice replied, "*go through the centre, past the tree sculpture, and under the purple sign.*"

Putting his misgivings aside, Gabriel followed the directions through the centre of the plaza, pushing a path through the sea of aliens until he made it to the opposite shore. He saw the holographic shop signs ringing the edge of the plaza, including a bright purple sign written in alien script. His HUD translated the sign as: 'Tantalising Beverages,' a rhyming pun in the original language, apparently.

Gabriel ducked inside 'Tantalising Beverages' and found himself in a crowded alien bar, only slightly less noisy than outside. A group of bipedal reptiles were slurping up viscous drinks from long thin glasses with long thin tongues in one corner, while a pack of cackling avian-type aliens were clustered together in another corner.

"*Through to the back,*" said the sibilant electronic voice.

Gabriel followed the instruction, giving the reptiles a wide berth as he passed. They were clad in crude combat armour and had bulky satchels slung over their shoulders, almost certainly for carrying firearms. They were clearly a professional mercenary band and not just traders or salvagers with guns.

Ducking through the back door, Gabriel found himself in a cluttered storeroom filled with stacks of crates piled haphazardly around the walls. Apart from a dormant maintenance drone hovering in the corner, there was nothing else here – it was a dead-end.

"*Where do I go next?*" Gabriel asked the voice.

There was no response.

"*I followed your directions, so where do I go next?*"

Silence.

Anger began to build in Gabriel's chest. What was the point in coming to the backroom of this seedy alien bar? Was he just supposed to wait for his contact, or – far worse – had he just been lured into a trap? If it was a trap, it was too late to escape.

The drone suddenly floated towards him. Gabriel instinctively raised his fists, for all the good it would do; but instead of attacking him, the drone raised one of its tentacles and conjured up a holographic screen. There was a message written in Standard Human Script: '*The lizards in the bar sold the artefact to a group of Hive-dwellers.*'

So he had been set up, just not in the way he'd thought.

There was more to the message: '*They're coming down now.*'

Gabriel yanked his backpack off his shoulders and dived into a corner, pulling his gun out and priming it. He was furious at the way he'd been tricked into this dead-end trap, but at the very least he could be ready with a proper weapon.

The reptilian mercenaries entered. Besides their crudely fashioned armour, one of them was wearing the skull of some predatory animal like a shoulder-pad. They didn't storm in or fan out to search the corners, they didn't even have their weapons drawn. They looked confused as if they'd been called down here and were wondering why.

To the extent that Gabriel could sympathise with these aliens, he did.

"*Stow your weapon and get ready,*" the voice instructed him, "*three...*"

What? Gabriel was outnumbered and his only advantages were the element of surprise and his gun. Why in Terra's name should he put his gun away?

"*Two...*" said the voice.

Very reluctantly, Gabriel folded his weapon and placed it against his chestplate, where a magnetic clamp locked onto it.

He then returned the backpack to his shoulders. Whatever plan had been concocted, it wouldn't help to second guess it at the last moment.

"*One...*" said the voice as the drone floated into the reptiles' midst.

Then chaos broke out.

* * *

Aster's teammates were a mystery to her. They didn't even feel like her teammates. After all, were they actually working together as a team, or did they just happen to be assigned to the same room? So far, she'd only met one of them face-to-face.

Aster's curiosity got the better of her and she accessed the database to search for the name Maxine. Sure enough, there she was with her short dark hair, golden nose stud, and a very faint smirk on her lips as she posed for her mugshot.

'*I see you found my profile,*' read an instant message that popped up on the screen.

Aster whipped her head around and saw Maxine waving and smiling from the booth beside her. She waved back out of politeness but didn't return the smile.

'*It's rude to look at other people's screens, you know,*' Aster messaged back.

'*Agreed,*' said another message, '*nosy Maxie.*'

'*Don't call me that,*' Maxine replied.

Aster activated the privacy filter, altering the shading on the screen to prevent anyone except for her from seeing its contents, then kept reading Maxine's profile.

Dr Maxine Rivers had advanced degrees in materials science and nanotechnology and had been working at the Directorate for just over a year. The personal details in her file were blacked out, but the information was better than nothing.

Aster typed in her own name and there she was. Her personal details were still blacked out, but her work history and educational background were all there for anyone to read.

Aster typed in the name: 'Gabriel Thorn'.

'*ACCESS RESTRICTED: TIER 2 CLASSIFICATION*,' read the popup.

That wasn't surprising. If Gabriel wouldn't share work-related information with her, why would their now-mutual employer?

She typed in 'genetic experiments' and got back a list of factual articles, but nothing related to ongoing research – as if that sort of information would be freely available.

'*You can't access anything above your clearance level*,' read another instant message from Maxine, '*in case you were tempted to try.*'

'*I wasn't*,' Aster typed back defensively.

'*Liar*,' came the reply.

Aster wasn't sure if it was a good idea to keep digging through her employer's files, but despite her misgivings, her curiosity itch still needed to be scratched.

She typed in another name: 'Dr Shelton.'

Dozens of results were returned, but only one of them for an actual person: Dr Mortimer Shelton, a former employee in the Rand Block with a doctoral specialisation in molecular genetics, now retired. Most of his work history was blacked out, and the rest of the results were scientific papers written by him – all tagged with tier 3 or tier 2 classifications.

Aster's sense of curiosity turned into a lump in her stomach. The same person who Gabriel claimed had treated him after he was attacked apparently shared a name with a former employee of the Directorate. Then again, if they were the same person, was it so surprising that Gabriel knew him? Even so, the connection and the coincidence only inflamed her suspicions.

Aster shut the search window and returned to her assigned tasks. She couldn't ignore what she had found, but it wouldn't do her any good to dwell on it either.

'*Just a heads up*,' Maxine messaged her, '*if you try to access a restricted file, it gets logged by the system. They like to keep track of these things.*'

'*Thanks for the advice*,' Aster messaged back.

That would have been nice to know beforehand.

* * *

With its hemispheric design and high-domed roof, the director-general's office more closely resembled a combined throne room and command centre. At the far end was a grand desk and chair positioned on a raised dais, and at the other end of the room was an enormous blast door, the only obvious way in or out.

Only a handful of individuals had ever seen the inside of the director-general's office, and the prospect of a face-to-face meeting filled most people with dread. Most such meetings, however, were conducted via encrypted video link.

The individual on the other end of the video link had a professorial demeanour with a grandfatherly beard. Sitting in her throne-like chair, the director-general regarded him with a hazel-coloured, organic left eye and a laser-red, bionic right eye.

"*Dr Shelton continues to outdo himself long after leaving,*" reported the Voidstalker Programme's chief of research, enduring his superior's cool, heterochromatic gaze.

"Meaning?" Red-eye asked.

"*Orion Thorn's intellectual development has reached the inflexion point that Dr Shelton predicted,*" he answered, "*he's turning into a child prodigy.*"

"Will the other children follow the same development trajectory?" she asked.

"*With respect, I don't believe it's a good idea to use one child's results to generalise with regard to hundreds of others,*" the chief of research replied, then added, "*however, the preliminary results suggest that the answer is yes.*"

Red-eye didn't even give a flicker of a smile. Nonetheless, it was good news.

"*There was one other thing,*" the chief of research ventured hesitantly, "*Orion's mother, Dr Aster Thorn, tried to access Dr Shelton's personal profile. I'm concerned about how she knew Dr Shelton's name.*"

"Your commitment to operational secrecy is admirable," Red-eye replied, a congenial if backhanded way of asking why this was relevant.

"*I realise it's not my responsibility*," the chief of research continued, "*but I don't know how much longer we can keep the details of the programme secret.*"

"The secrecy of the programme remains paramount," Red-eye responded.

"*The parents will start to notice the cognitive and physical changes in their children; assuming they haven't already*," the chief of research warned gravely, "*and we won't be able to put off the questions for very long.*"

"As I said, the secrecy of the Voidstalker Programme remains paramount," Red-eye repeated, hardening her tone ever so slightly, "not even the voidstalkers themselves are ready to know the full implications. Not yet, anyway."

"*Understood, Director-general*," the chief of research replied.

* * *

A deafening keening sound filled the room, and the reptilian mercenaries covered their earholes and snarled in pain. Gabriel's helmet protected him from the effects of the sonic signal, and he stayed in cover as the reptiles crumpled to the floor.

"*Grab Skull-guard!*" the voice shouted, "*the one with the giant shoulder-pad!*"

Gabriel bolted from cover and grabbed 'Skull-guard' by the torso, hoisting him off the floor and slinging him over his shoulder like a giant sack. The alien was at least as heavy as he was, and was still groaning as Gabriel struggled to carry him.

At the same time, the drone deployed one of its arms and sprayed a grey substance onto the wall in a giant circle. The substance began to glow lava-red, eating through the metal wall as the drone then latched onto the slab and pulled it away. Gabriel leapt through the crudely fashioned breach with his hostage as the drone followed behind.

"*Follow the drone,*" the voice instructed Gabriel.

The drone activated a searchlight and overtook Gabriel, zipping along the piping as he struggled to keep up while lugging the prisoner. These were the bowels of the Nexus station: a labyrinthine network of infrastructure that kept the station functioning. Entering this part of the station was forbidden, but violations were ignored as long as no damage was done.

Gabriel was already angry about being led along by someone who wouldn't show his or her face, but by destructively removing a chunk of the wall, the 'asset' had also recklessly endangered both their lives and their cover. As soon as he was finished with this alien, Gabriel resolved to dish out the same treatment to this so-called 'asset'.

The drone came to a dead-end and dropped down out of sight. Gabriel followed it, plunging with the prisoner feet-first through an open hatch. His feet hit a solid surface and he fell to the ground, with his semi-conscious prisoner tumbling off his shoulder and onto the floor beside him. The hatch above him slammed shut, locking itself with a buzz and a click.

It was pitch black, but through the visual filters in his HUD, Gabriel could see they were in a curving tunnel that stretched on into the darkness in both directions. The reptilian captive groaned in pain and disorientation, slowly rolling onto all fours and curling his clawed fingers into fists.

Gabriel scrambled to his feet and drew his weapon again, aiming at the prisoner.

"*Very nicely done,*" said the voice.

"*Where are you?*" Gabriel demanded.

"*Nearby,*" the voice replied, "*keep an eye on the prisoner.*"

Gabriel kept his gun pointed at 'Skull-guard' as he slowly recovered from the effects of the incapacitating signal. He cursed in his own language as his chameleonic eyes darted from side to side before fixing on his kidnapper and the gun.

"Don't move," Gabriel warned through his helmet speakers, his words automatically translated into the reptile's own language.

Skull-guard looked at him, the disoriented look in his flaming orange eyes slowing turning into concentrated fury as they locked onto Gabriel. His lips curled back to reveal rows of razor-sharp teeth and his wiry muscles tensed up as he contemplated making a lunge.

"My clan will feast on your entrails!" Skull-guard snarled belligerently – at least, that was the audio translation that Gabriel's suit computer generated.

"You sold an artefact to the Hive-dwellers," Gabriel replied, ignoring the threat.

Skull-guard's menacing glare turned to shock – insofar as a lizard could look shocked.

"You acquired the artefact from the trading barge," Gabriel added.

"How do you know that?" Skull-guard demanded.

"I ask the questions, and you answer them," Gabriel answered dangerously, "where did the Hive-dwellers take the artefact?"

"I don't know," Skull-guard replied, "we sold it to them and left."

"*Skull-guard's friends are coming for you,*" the voice warned Gabriel.

"What was the artefact?!" Gabriel demanded.

"I don't know what that abominable thing was!" Skull-guard snarled back, "the Water-skins were keeping it in a sealed chamber aboard their ship, but they were not its makers!"

"*They're directly above you, get out of there!*" the voice ordered.

Without warning, the service hatch in the ceiling exploded. There were no flames or heat, and no flash of energy that accompanied the destructive event; the hatch simply burst out of its frame. A shockwave rippled through the air as the metal slab was blasted clear, knocking the nearby maintenance drone out of commission and bouncing away into the darkness.

"*Go, you idiot!*" the voice shouted frantically, "*Go! Now!*"
Gabriel turned and ran.

* * *

Aster remained amazed by the Directorate's technology. Complex simulations could be done in seconds and hundreds could be combined into one simulation that took minutes. She was making more progress every day than she could have managed in a week at J.E. Co.

Even so, Aster's misgivings were far from assuaged. Never mind the ingrained distrust of the government from her colonial upbringing; she couldn't forget coming home to find her toddler daughter freshly healed from what should have been a serious injury as if it were a mere scratch. What parent could forget something like that?

Aster continued to delve as deep as she dared into the Directorate's voluminous database. Everything to do with past or ongoing operations was off-limits, and much of the scientific material was classified as well, but there were still plenty of gems to be found if she searched hard enough.

One research paper identified a string of gene sequences with connections to cognitive performance. Another paper recounted a successful experiment to modify and improve the proteins responsible for blood clotting. Yet another paper studied the biomolecular dynamics of neurological development during puberty.

Aster's speciality was physics, not genetics, so even the condensed abstracts were largely incomprehensible. Furthermore, only the abstracts were available to read; the main text of the papers was classified, so only researchers assigned to a biomedical project were allowed to read the full text of these papers.

All this reading didn't bring her any closer to understanding what was going on, but it was still a good way to pass the time between analyses. The complexity of the components was increasing, and the simulations were taking longer as a result. Aster let the calculations run and went to the breakroom, helping herself to a cup of ice cold water.

Maxine was already there sitting in the corner, and she smiled as Aster approached.

"Still not a coffee-person?" Maxine remarked.

"I still don't like the taste," Aster replied.

Several others from the research team were taking breaks while their simulations were running, and they came over to join the discussion.

"What about tea?" someone asked, "there are lots of different kinds you could try."

"Tea is ok," Aster answered, "but only from time to time."

"You should try some of the herbal variants," someone else suggested.

"Not as fancy as the stuff we drink up in the Clouds," Maxine remarked loftily.

"Yes, I'm sure they're far too coarse for the delicate palette of a pampered fleekster like you," the person responded snarkily.

"Ouch, that burns," Maxine smirked back, unfazed by the remark.

Even though only a fraction of the people who lived there could be described as ultra-rich, the Clouds were synonymous with extreme wealth and extravagant luxury. Everyone professed to dislike people from the Clouds, mainly out of good old-fashioned envy.

"So, what's it like in those fancy clubs in the Clouds?" someone else asked.

"Why the fleek do people assume we're all members of some exclusive club?" Maxine retorted in exasperation, "the membership fees cost more than you or I make in a year, so I have no idea what they're like."

"Do you think Red...the director-general is a member of one of those clubs?" someone else mused, "she's certainly 'elite' enough."

"'Elite', yes," Maxine replied sceptically, "but not in the sense you're talking about. Besides, she has better things to do than hang out in places like that."

Aster remained silent, wondering whether and how to contribute to the conversation. She thought about mentioning Gabriel's background, then thought better of it. Eventually, the conversation petered out of its own accord and a moment of silence followed.

"What do you think we're building?" Aster asked eventually.

Everyone else in the room collectively flinched. Aster suspected it would be a taboo question, but she wanted to know.

"We don't want to know," Maxine replied on everyone else's behalf.

"Aren't you curious about what all these components are for?" Aster insisted.

"Of course we are," someone replied gravely, "but there's an ancient idiom about curiosity bringing people to bad ends."

"Is that the one about curiosity killing the dog?" someone asked.

"It's a cat, actually," the speaker corrected before continuing, "if the Directorate wanted us to know what we're constructing, they would tell us."

"Of course we wonder from time to time what it is we're building, and sometimes it can be fun to guess," Maxine explained, then her tone turned deadly serious, "but don't forget: this is a spy agency. Information is the most valuable resource it has."

With those sobering words, Maxine got up and returned to her workstation. One by one, everyone else finished their drinks and followed her out of the breakroom, as if the topic were a contagious hazard to be avoided.

Aster was left alone, feeling more awkward and uncomfortable than ever. Once again, she had been reminded that she was just another worker drone in a vast and secretive hive. She was unlikely to ever find out what it was they were designing, let alone about the superhuman traits that her children were exhibiting.

In fact, her curiosity would probably get her kicked out.

* * *

Gabriel was furious. This was supposed to be a simple intelligence-gathering operation, so why was he running for his life like a rat through a maze? The fact that he was being chased by angry, carnivorous lizards really brought the analogy to life. They were bounding after him on all fours, easily keeping pace with him as he sprinted through the low gravity.

The tunnel seemed to go on forever, meandering around and through the station's superstructure with no clear endpoint. This part of the Nexus was poorly-mapped, so even as he ran for his life, he had no idea where he was running to.

"*Exit hatch on the left*," said the voice, "*take it.*"

Up ahead, Gabriel saw a section of the wall open up, and he grabbed the lip of the opening, using his momentum to swing around the corner and out of the tunnel. The gravity suddenly increased to normal as Gabriel left the tunnel, and he dropped down onto another hard surface as the hatch slammed shut behind him.

As in the tunnel, it was pitch-black, but through his HUD Gabriel could see a network of walkways and gangplanks bridging an artificial chasm. Looking over the safety railing, he could also see a network of thin fissures at the bottom of the chasm.

"*Keep moving!*" the voice ordered him, "*I'll give you a tour later.*"

As Gabriel sprinted along the central bridge, a violent banging struck the sealed hatch behind him. The hatch barely withstood the force of the shockwave.

"*What kind of weaponry is that?*" Gabriel asked as he vaulted over another railing.

"*Unclear*," the voice replied, "*but it's not Lizard-man tech.*"

"*Hive-dweller tech?*"

"*Possibly.*"

Gabriel took cover in a doorway as another shockwave blasted the hatch open. The force of the shockwave ripped the locking mechanism clean out of the wall and caused the hatch to swing open with a violent clang of metal on metal.

"*I'm not fleeing anymore,*" Gabriel said resolutely, drawing his weapon again.

"*They outnumber you,*" the voice reminded him, "*and they can see in the dark.*"

"*Well, so can I,*" Gabriel retorted.

He peeked out around the corner, counting a dozen reptilian mercenaries fanning out to search for him, including Skullguard. Most were hulking crude, weather-beaten assault rifles with notches carved onto the sides, but one of their number was carrying a particularly bizarre-looking weapon.

It looked like a piece of alien industrial machinery and was so big that even its user was straining to hold it aloft. Its muzzle was a concave mouth ringed with sharp prongs like the teeth of some predatory worm, with tongues of crackling energy arcing between them. One blast would splatter him against the wall, even with shielding and armour.

Gabriel reached into his backpack and pulled out an aerial drone the size and shape of a meal dish, activating it and releasing it into the air. It flew out of the room, using an antigravity engine for propulsion. The reptiles were only halfway across the platform when they heard the whining sound and tensed up, scanning around for the source of the noise.

Using his wrist-top computer, Gabriel set the drone to hunter-killer mode, and the faint whining sound turned to a banshee-like scream as the drone swooped down on its targets. The drone had two ring-shaped nanomolecular blades spinning in opposite directions at high speed. As it swooped down, the drone struck the muzzle of a mercenary's gun, the counter-rotating blades shearing clean through it with a shrill scream of metal against metal.

The surprised mercenaries took cover as the attack drone came around in an arc and swooped in for another attack, and on its second attack-run, it claimed a victim. Instead of the shriek of metal shearing metal, there was a wet slicing sound of metal cutting flesh as the drone's blades made contact with its target's neck.

The mercenary crumpled to the floor, gurgling in pain as he pressed a clawed hand against the wound to stem the bleeding. As several reptiles rushed to their wounded comrade's aid, the force-gun wielder readied his weapon. Before he could pull the trigger, a gunshot rang out through the darkness and he keeled over dead, the weapon slipping from his claws. Gabriel had fired a high-powered shot from cover into the target's skull.

The lizards sprayed bullets in Gabriel's general direction, their shots ricocheting off hard surfaces and drilling through softer ones. As the attack drone came around for another attack, someone swung their weapon like a club, swatting the drone out of the air. The drone went spinning away into the depths as its antigravity engine struggled to compensate.

The mercenaries began to beat a retreat. One of them dragged their wounded comrade away, his clawed hand soaked in his own blood, while another dragged the body of the force-gun wielder away. The rest of the mercenaries emptied their weapon clips into the other side of the chamber to keep the hidden attacker at bay, buying time to escape.

With impressive discipline, the mercenaries backpedalled all the way to the damaged hatch, passing their dead and wounded comrades through the doorway first before retreating to safety. Once they were gone, Gabriel emerged from cover and checked that the area really was secure before stowing his weapon, then used his wrist-top to summon the attack drone back. The drone returned to his hand, its blades deactivating and its engine powering down.

"*They're retreating,*" the voice informed him redundantly.

"*A very astute observation,*" was Gabriel's sarcastic reply.

"*Someone sounds unhappy,*" the voice noted slyly.

"*You lured me into a dead-end and then lured a bunch of alien hired-guns down after me,*" Gabriel said angrily as he returned the drone to his backpack and slung it back over his shoulders, "*in other words, your spur-of-the-moment plan almost got me killed.*"

"*Firstly, it wasn't 'spur-of-the-moment',*" the voice responded, "*secondly, you handled yourself pretty well; and thirdly, we confirmed that the Lizard-men discovered the artefact aboard the trading barge and sold it to the Hive-dwellers.*"

"*All of which we already knew,*" Gabriel responded irritably.

"*Thanks to me,*" the voice replied smugly, then added more seriously, "*but there's still something else we need to get intelligence on.*"

"*Who attacked the Water-skins and what they meant when they said a 'voidstalker' attacked them,*" Gabriel replied sharply, "*I'm not completely clueless.*"

"*Don't call them 'Water-skins',*" the voice admonished him.

"*What else should I call them?*" Gabriel demanded as he walked over the bridge, "*their native species name is unpronounceable, and they're amphibians who need to keep their skin moist at all times; hence: Water-skins.*"

"*I don't care about it being prejudicial,*" the voice replied, "*it's just that you probably don't want to call them that to their faces.*"

"*What do you mean?*"

"*You're going to talk to them directly,*" was the answer.

A series of loud clanging sounds rang out through the darkness, like a set of heavy metal latches being unlocked. Then the bridge split in two and folded downwards, causing Gabriel to lose his balance and slide down, grabbing the railing just in time.

The force-gun slid down and went tumbling into the depths as a pair of multi-tonne blast doors retracted, revealing a brilliant blue light below. As he clung on to the metal railing, Gabriel's HUD was briefly blinded by the sudden light, but once it adjusted he saw that the light below him was actually a roiling mass of crystal-blue liquid.

"*The Nexus requires millions of gallons of fresh water,*" the voice explained, "*you're directly above one of the conduits.*"

"*What did you do?!*" Gabriel shouted furiously into the mic.

"*I overrode the security protocols and assumed direct control of all local systems,*" the voice answered loftily, "*now jump.*"

"*Why in Terra's name would I do that?!*" Gabriel demanded.

"*The clue is in the term 'Water-skins'.*"

Yet another plan concocted without his knowledge or input. Gabriel was livid.

"*Don't tell me you're afraid of water,*" the voice said mockingly.

"*I'll fleeking kill you!*" Gabriel snapped back.

"*You're welcome to try,*" the voice quipped, "*but first, you need to take the plunge.*"

Gabriel looked down into the watery abyss – and let go.

THE ASSAULT

SHORTER working hours and cutting-edge technology aside, the cloud of conspiracy hanging over her new job was emotionally draining. When Aster got home, she went straight to the bedroom and flopped down on the bed. The children were still in their learning pods, and hopefully they wouldn't walk in sporting miraculously healed injuries or bizarre new genetic superpowers.

As usual, one of the household androids was standing silently in the corner, maintaining an unflinching watch over the sleeping Emerald. Seeing the android standing watch over her sleeping new-born was at once reassuring and creepy.

"Leave the room," Aster ordered.

The android nodded obediently and departed, closing the door behind it.

Aster's search for answers was in danger of playing out the same way as the scandal at her previous employer. No doubt the Directorate had taken note of her database searches, and for all she knew, the androids were being used to monitor her as well.

Aster reached into her bedside drawer and pulled out a flexi-tablet; a personal one, not the one the Directorate had given her. Using an encrypted router, she accessed the Corrections Department net portal and logged in. She was right on time for her scheduled call, and as much as she hated the person on the other end, there was no one else she could turn to for answers.

On the other side of the video link, flanked by security androids, was a woman wearing a prison jumpsuit and seated at a communications booth. Her dark hair had blonde highlights dyed in parallel stripes and was styled into an elaborate cornbraid. Her lips were blood red, and her eyes – unlike her son's eyes – were hazel-coloured.

She didn't look pleased to see Aster, and the feeling was mutual.

"*Thank you so much for the call,*" said Jezebel Thorn, her flute-like, upper-class accent sharpened by the insincerity of her gratitude.

"You're welcome," Aster replied, equally insincerely.

"*How are my grandchildren?*"

"Healthy and happy," Aster responded, "all five of them."

"*Five?*" Jezebel remarked with a raised eyebrow, "*He does keep you busy, doesn't he? Or are you the one keeping him busy?*"

Aster's eye twitched at the backhanded comment. Her wealthy mother-in-law was a spiteful and condescending person with the morals and sensibilities of a well-heeled gangster. She was also a convicted blackmailer and murderer – of one of Aster's former colleagues – and deserved to rot in prison.

"*I suppose you didn't arrange this call to discuss family matters,*" Jezebel said, then asked more gravely, "*or did you?*"

"Does the name 'Dr Mortimer Shelton' mean anything to you?" Aster asked.

"*Doesn't ring a bell,*" Jezebel answered.

That wasn't very useful, so Aster raised a subject she usually avoided.

"Who was Gabriel's father?"

Jezebel's implacably superior mask of composure cracked. Aster usually only hinted at that topic when she wanted to insult Jezebel and puncture that horrible veneer of smugness, but the question was a serious one and Jezebel paused.

"*Well, his name wasn't Mortimer Shelton,*" she answered at length, "*why?*"

"It always winds you up whenever someone mentions him," Aster explained, "but I could never figure out why."

"*Have you tried asking Gabriel?*" Jezebel asked woodenly.

"What do you think?" Aster replied rhetorically.

Jezebel grimaced sympathetically.

"*...If it means that much to you...*" she said through gritted teeth, "*you can try looking up the name Alexander Thorn.*"

"Thanks," Aster replied, an uncertain knot forming in her stomach, "I'll look into it."

"*I wouldn't if I were you,*" Jezebel added, "*They see and hear everything.*"

"Who does?" Aster asked, the knot in her stomach tightening.

"*Who do you think?*"

* * *

Gabriel wasn't afraid of water; in theory, he wasn't afraid of anything. Much of his capacity for fear had been removed through conditioning by the Directorate's scientists, and whatever remained had been brutalised out of him by the drill instructors and the selection trials he had been forced to undergo.

One of those trials was the water trial. Each candidate was hog-tied with weights around their ankles and then dropped into a vertical tank of water. The more you struggled, the more likely you were to black out from near-drowning, at which point you would have to be pulled out and resuscitated by the medics.

The trick was, in fact, not to struggle at all but to sink feet-first all the way down before kicking hard off the bottom to come up for air. Of course, the drill instructors wouldn't tell you that, you had to figure it out yourself. Gabriel and a few others had figured it out the first time around, everyone else had to drown over and over again until they succeeded or washed out.

As soon as Gabriel let go of the railing, he dropped like a stone towards the open conduit below, the surging mass of water within rushing up to meet him. When his feet touched the water, the intense speed and pressure sucked him straight down below the surface and into the water tunnel. He crossed his arms over his chest and locked his legs together, allowing himself to be carried to his destination.

Gabriel hurtled along at high speed through the winding tunnel, the pressure and currents buffeting him from side to side. He could breathe just fine inside his vacuum-proof armour, but travelling through the Nexus's pumping network brought back the memories of the water trial and magnified them ten-fold.

It was pitch black in the water tunnel. Even with the visual filters in his HUD, the walls were rushing by so quickly it was hard to see clearly. Despite using artificial gravity to keep the water moving, Gabriel's sense of up and down was confounded as well – there was no up or down in the water tunnel, only forward.

Most surreal of all was the lack of noise. The roaring of the water in the tunnel would be close to deafening if he could hear it, so his helmet's auditory sensors filtered out the sound to the point that it was little more than a faint rumble. The violent water currents inside the tunnel propelled him forward in near total silence.

"*Exit coming up*," the mystery voice warned.

A sharp bend appeared ahead, and an access conduit opened on the outer edge of the bend. Gabriel barely had time to react as it came rushing up to meet him. His momentum and the artificial gravity on the other side propelled him out of the tunnel until he hit a solid surface, rolling to an ungraceful halt.

Gabriel was dizzy from the journey, but nonetheless, he leapt to his feet and drew his weapon, scanning around for threats. He was in a narrow service tunnel, an apparent dead-end with a dark atmosphere and a damp floor. At one end was the water conduit he had tumbled out of, and at the other end the service tunnel opened up into a larger area.

Directly above his head, Gabriel caught a glimpse inside the water tunnel before the conduit sealed itself again. The throbbing mass of clear blue liquid above him was flowing through the tunnel without a single drop falling out, resembling an enormous crystal serpent slithering along at high speed.

"*The Water-skins are up ahead*," his ally informed him.

"*How do you know where they are?*" Gabriel asked.

"*Because I've been tracking them*," the voice explained, "*they're social, so they won't stray too far from the group*."

Gabriel walked away from the now-closed conduit, emerging in some kind of treatment facility. It looked like the inside of a steel drum, with each level ringed with gantries and connected by ladders. There were shapes moving in the shadows above, darting back and forth with preternatural speed as they moved in and out of various openings.

Gabriel took cover in the shadows, wary of being caught out in the open.

"*There are too many targets to count*," Gabriel warned.

"*They're not 'targets'*," the voice replied, "*They're an intelligence lead, a very valuable intelligence lead that I hope you don't squander by opening fire needlessly*."

"*You're not the one who has to confront them!*" Gabriel shot back.

"*Don't worry, I'm nearby in case you screw up*."

Gabriel gritted his teeth in frustration. Since arriving, he had been led from one ambush to the next by someone he could hear but not see. However, raging at his invisible pseudo-ally wouldn't gain him anything, so he bit his tongue and took another look around.

None of the fast-moving shapes above had noticed him – or if they had, they pretended otherwise. If he wanted to get their attention, he would have to make the first move. Keeping his weapon close and ready, Gabriel broke from cover and stepped into the dim light.

As soon as he emerged, the shapes froze in their tracks and turned to watch him, staring down like an army of watery shadows. Gabriel raised his weapon and tried to track individuals in the pack, but the targeting software in his HUD instantly singled out over a hundred shapes all around him. If they all attacked at once, he would be overwhelmed.

"*You won't get them to talk to you with your gun raised,*" the voice pointed out.

"Peaceful salutations!" Gabriel shouted, his words translated into one of the many lingua franca of Nexus space and then broadcasted through his helmet speakers.

The 2nd Prime Law stipulated 'no unauthorised contact with alien species,' and even then the use of Standard Human Speech was strongly discouraged. However, the Water-skins were wide-ranging spacefarers and had developed an impressive mastery of other species' languages, so they ought to understand him.

"You speak of peaceful salutations with a weapon raised!" one of the aliens replied in a hoarse and croaky voice, but with enough volume to echo around the chamber.

"*My point exactly,*" the annoying voice remarked.

Gabriel ignored his snarky ally and tried to concentrate on the situation at hand. It sounded like a single voice, but he couldn't tell which of the hundreds of shapes had spoken.

"What attacked you?" Gabriel asked through his speakers.

"A force beyond your comprehension!" was the cryptic reply.

That wasn't very helpful.

"What kind of force?" Gabriel demanded.

"Voidstalker!" another croaky voice shouted back.

"VOIDSTALKER!" the Water-skins shouted in unison, the discordant chorus echoing around the walls of the chamber like the collective voice of some alien parliament.

Gabriel was taken aback, less by the unified chorus of responses than by the fact that the aliens had used the Human word 'void-stalker.'

"Where did you hear that word?" he asked them.

It occurred to Gabriel that maybe they were humouring his questions while plotting to attack him. He kept his weapon ready with the fire control settings tuned to full-automatic. They didn't have any weapons that he could see, but he was hopelessly outnumbered and would only be able to take down some of them before being overrun.

"We hailed it," one of them replied, "and it responded thus, then it attacked!"

The translation was an awkward one, but it worked.

"What about the artefact?" Gabriel demanded, "What was it and where did you find it?"

There was no immediate response, just an awkward ripple of alien murmuring.

"It was on a vessel, left drifting in the void between stars," came the answer at length.

They had used an alien word for 'void' this time, but the translation software flagged the word 'vessel' as ambiguous. Was it a ship or a container or both?

"What was inside the vessel?" Gabriel asked.

"Enough questions!" the aliens chorused back, "they are here!"

"Who? Who is here?" Gabriel demanded.

There was no reply. Instead, the crowd of aliens began to disperse, disappearing into the tunnels faster than he could track them. Before long, the giant chamber was deserted, and the Water-skins were nowhere to be seen.

"*Trouble in space*," the voice informed him.

"*Meaning what, exactly?*" Gabriel snapped impatiently into his comm.

"*Go back into the water tunnel*," the voice instructed, "*You'll find out soon enough.*"

* * *

A portion of space darkened and swallowed the starlight around it. It was a Q-rift, an absolutely enormous one, barely a hundred kilometres distant from the Nexus. A new ship was arriving, transitioning back into real space like some monstrous creature squeezing out of a pitch-black morass of oblivion.

The streams of space traffic scattered like shoals of frightened fish before a whale as the ship slowly emerged. From the immense black orb that was the Q-rift, a prow pierced through, its distorted shape becoming gradually more distinct. The prow resembled the tip of a spear, and it lengthened and widened as more of the vessel emerged.

The ship was gargantuan, even larger than the desiccated trading barge floating nearby. Its hull was sleek and gravel-grey, and the stern was shaped like a mushroom-head, narrowing down the base before expanding again into a bulbous and elongated cocoon shape along the middle, then tapering to a spear-tip shaped prow.

Parts of the hull had a living look to them, with streaks of organic material covering the prow. The dome-shaped rear of the ship was entirely covered in the same biological crust as if a giant insect hive were housed within the superstructure of the massive ship and blooming out of the back.

Once the newly arrived vessel had managed to squeeze into real space, the oily black Q-rift shrank and dissipated. It remained at a fixed distance away from the Nexus, waiting like some cosmic super-predator. This was clearly not a trading vessel, but a fully-functional super-dreadnought whose intentions were completely unknown.

Another emergency was declared, and all ships that hadn't already fled were ordered to either dock or disperse. The Nexus's shields and hull could resist most ship-grade weaponry, but there were no defensive weapons installed on the station itself. There was no defensive fleet and no consensus around which to form one, nor was it clear how any fleet could fight a vessel of this size. The most that could be done was to hope that nothing happened.

Then the ship opened fire.

* * *

Long after the call was over, Aster felt dirty.

Even without a murder conviction, Jezebel Thorn was an odious woman with an elitist disdain for her colonial daughter-in-law. *With* a murder conviction on her record and any number of other undiscovered crimes on her conscience, she deserved to rot in prison. But she had given up something Gabriel had never seen fit to tell her: the name of his father. Whether it turned out to be a useful lead or not remained to be seen.

However, once again she had to grapple with whether or not to continue the search for answers. Jezebel's warning that 'they' saw and heard everything was clear enough, and Aster might already have been flagged as a potential security risk by her new bosses. And yet, her curiosity simply wasn't sated.

The clashing feelings of curiosity and caution intensified as she arrived back at the Spire, but she made it to her data booth without incident and got ready to work. There were new component designs to be tested and approved, but before starting, Aster gave in to her curiosity and typed in the name 'Alexander Thorn'.

A profile appeared with a blacked-out space where the mugshot should have been. The words 'ACCESS DENIED: TIER 2 CLASSIFICATION' were superimposed in block-red capitals over the image. There was one piece of biographical information available:

'STATUS: DECEASED.'

"Dr Thorn," said a voice behind her, "we'd like a word."

Aster turned around and her heart leapt into her mouth when she saw a pair of uniformed security officers standing behind her.

She had been caught, she was sure of it. Even though they couldn't see what was on her screen, she felt completely done for. This was all a repeat of the events of J.E. Co. where her nosing around had finally caught up with her, and now they were going to question her about it before they suspended her or fired her, or worse.

Aster nodded and got up, thankful that everyone else was too absorbed by their work to notice her being escorted out of the data centre. She was taken to an office where an interrogator was waiting, and the two guards shut the door behind her as she sat down.

"Do you know a Jezebel Thorn?" the interrogator began immediately.

"She's my mother-in-law," Aster replied, "and she's in prison for murder."

"When was the last time you spoke to her?" the interrogator continued.

"Yesterday evening, on a video-phone call," Aster answered.

"What did you talk about?"

"Family," Aster responded truthfully.

"Is Mortimer Shelton family?" the interrogator asked.

"No," Aster answered.

"Then how do you know that name?" he asked.

"Because a package came several weeks ago from the Rand Block with a message saying that Gabriel needed to take the serum inside," Aster blurted out, "all of which you should already know because the message also said that Dr Shelton contacted you about the incident so that you could send him that serum in the first place!"

The interrogator and the two guards were completely taken aback by the outburst.

"What package?" the interrogator asked.

"A dead-box," Aster replied impatiently, "it had a biometric lock and my husband was able to open it, which is how I know that it was intended for him."

The interrogator opened up a computer and began typing away with an urgency that made Aster even more uncomfortable.

"Do you still have this dead-box?" the interrogator asked.

"Not with me," Aster answered, "but it should still be around the house somewhere."

"Would you mind going home and allowing Directorate agents to collect it?"

"Not at all," Aster replied, her nervousness continuing to build, "should I go now?"

"Please do, the agents will be waiting by your door," the interrogator informed her, "I'll also notify your superior of your absence."

"Am I in trouble?" Aster asked.

The interrogator paused, causing the knot in Aster's stomach to tighten.

"There are still some questions I need to ask," he responded, "but they can wait."

"What's wrong with the dead-box?" Aster demanded.

"That's…a discussion for another time," was the less-than-reassuring reply.

* * *

"*I'm telling you,*" the researcher on the other end of the line insisted, "*no one in my department sent a dead-box to Colonel Thorn.*"

The intelligence officer was silent as the implications sank in.

"Thanks, doctor," the officer replied woodenly, "please keep me posted."

He terminated the link and turned to his subordinates.

"What do we have?" he demanded.

"We've got Mortimer Shelton's work address," one of the junior agents announced.

"Where?" their superior demanded.

"Some medical clinic down in the Undercity," the agent replied.

"Grab him," their superior ordered.

"I'll contact Civil Security," one of the agents replied.

"No! No! No! Directorate teams only!" their superior barked, "Grab him, hood him, and lock him up so we can question him ourselves."

The agents nodded and rushed out of the room as the officer made another internal call. The person on the other end had been waiting and connected immediately.

"We're sorting out the breach as we speak," the officer reported.

"*Which breach?*" Red-eye asked with narrowed eyes, "*the name-leak, or the fact that a former Directorate scientist might have poisoned a voidstalker?*"

"Respectfully, Director-general," the intelligence officer replied carefully, "the name-leak was in an encrypted call with a Directorate employee. As for the latter breach, a snatch-op is being organised to grab Mortimer Shelton as we speak."

"*So the former leak has been contained?*"

"We still have to debrief Aster Thorn," the officer replied, "but yes, it has."

"*So you've secured Jezebel Thorn as well?*" Red-eye asked dangerously.

"She's in a maximum security penitentiary facility," the officer pointed out bravely.

"*And yet she was still able to leak the name,*" Red-eye reminded him.

"We'll scrub the prison database of any compromising data," the officer replied.

"*You do that,*" Red-eye ordered with a razor-sharp edge to the instruction.

* * *

Having strangers in the house was distinctly uncomfortable for Aster, but it was clear that something much more serious was going on, so having armed and uniformed strangers in her home to investigate was a minor inconvenience. She led the operatives straight to the living room and pulled out the dead-box.

"You said it had some kind of injector inside?" one of the operatives asked.

"Yes," Aster replied, "and a message on the inside lid supposedly from the Rand Block saying my husband needed to administer it."

One of the operatives took the dead-box from her and placed it carefully on the table while the other pulled out an imaging scanner and waved it over the box.

"This isn't a Directorate dead-box," the operative announced suspiciously, "There's no serial number, no authentication chip, and no failsafe mechanism."

"But my husband had to confirm his biometrics to open it," Aster told them.

"Did you try opening it yourself?"

"No," Aster replied with a dry lump in her throat.

The two operatives looked at each other, then one of them leaned down and swiped his thumb across the handle's sensor strip.

The box popped open.

The now-empty injector was still inside, sitting in a shockproof foam bed. There, too, was the machine-inscribed message on the inside of the lid:

'*Colonel Thorn. Dr Shelton contacted us regarding the events of this morning. Please administer the serum in this box as soon as possible. You are in no immediate danger, but the serum will remove all traces of the chemical to which you were exposed. Regards, Directorate of Naval Intelligence, R&D Block.*'

"Someone sent this box to your home, supposedly from the Directorate," the operative explained, "and convinced Colonel Thorn to inject himself with whatever was inside."

The colour and feeling drained from Aster's face.

"We need to take this with us for analysis," one of the operatives said, "do you know where Colonel Thorn is now?"

"He's…on deployment," Aster replied with a pale face and a fearful stammer.

"Don't worry," said the other operative, shutting the box, "we'll contact him."

"He didn't show any symptoms or signs that anything was wrong," Aster explained, regaining her composure, "all he told me was that he was attacked down in the Undercity and that he was sprayed with something during the attack, and that he was treated at a nearby clinic by this Dr Shelton person."

The two operatives looked at each other, perplexed.

"I assumed he'd told the Directorate about this already," Aster added, her nerve starting to slip again as she realised Gabriel had made no such disclosure.

"He didn't," one of the operatives responded, "then again, he probably thought that the Directorate already knew."

"So what happens next?" Aster asked.

"You'll still need to come back in for a formal debriefing," the other operative replied, "but the Directorate will sort all of this out."

* * *

Law enforcement of any kind was a rare sight in the Undercity, so the sight of dozens of heavily armed and armoured operators storming into a medical clinic was a shock. One group barged in through the front door while the other assembled outside a back alley entrance, breaking the lock and using a battering ram to smash the door off its hinges.

The front door team stormed the waiting room, ordering patients and staff to lay on their stomachs with their palms flat on the floor. The weaker patients were allowed to stay in their mobility chairs, but most of the terrified patients and staff did as they were told, getting down on the cold floor under the watchful eyes and steady guns of the response team.

Meanwhile, a smaller team forced their way into Dr Mortimer Shelton's office, melting the lock with a chemical paste and bashing the door open with their own battering ram. They found a simple doctor's office with a desk, a computer, and an observation bed with a set of standard medical equipment.

Shelton was nowhere to be found.

The team leader walked over to the reception desk and opened his helmet to speak.

"Where is Mortimer Shelton?" he demanded in Undercity dialect.

"He's...off-sick...," the receptionist stammered.

The team leader turned away and spoke into his comm.

"Gamma team, this is Alpha leader. What's the situation at Shelton's flat?"

"*It's secure,*" was the gruff reply, "*no sign of him.*"

"Fricking hell," the team leader growled in frustration, then ordered, "tear the place apart and document everything you find."

"*Aye, sir,*" his opposite number replied, "*we've already started–*"

His words were interrupted by the hissing sound of a gas cylinder in the background. There was coughing and spluttering heard over the comm. followed by screaming.

"Gamma team! What's going on?" the leader demanded, "Gamma team, report!"

More screaming was heard over the comm., this time from the back door response team.

"*Noxious fumes!*" someone had the presence of mind to shout, "*we're seeing things!*"

"*STAY AWAY, MONSTER!*"

"*Put the gun down!*"

Alpha leader rushed over to investigate the commotion where smoke and chaos were spilling out from a hidden doorway in the tiny doctor's office.

Heavily armoured operators were being dragged out of the room by their fellow operators as they raged and thrashed furiously, having had their weapons wrested away from them. They were screaming hysterically, cursing at demons and enemies that weren't there as their comrades tried to restrain them.

"Spire control! Come in!" Alpha leader shouted into his comm.

"*We read you,*" the voice on the other end replied calmly, "*what's the situation?*"

"I need reinforcements at the locations of Alpha and Gamma teams, immediately!" Alpha leader yelled, "Bring hazmat equipment! Multiple casualties! They've been exposed to some kind of airborne toxin!"

"Stay back," stammered a voice behind him.

Alpha leader turned around and saw one of the operators pointing his weapon at him. The barrel was wavering in the air as the hands holding them shook with fear.

"You're a demon!" the operator said fearfully, "I see the glow of hell in your eyes!"

"Put the gun down," Alpha leader said, staying calm and displaying his palms.

"If I do that, you'll tear me limb from limb!" the operator exclaimed.

"No, I won't," Alpha leader replied, taking a careful step forward, "I don't know what you're seeing, but if you put the gun down, you'll be fine."

"Lies! Lies!" the delirious operator screamed.

Alpha leader lunged at his hallucinating comrade as the gun went off.

* * *

After another chaotic journey through the water tunnel, Gabriel fell out of the hatch and hit the floor, this time using his momentum to roll back to his feet in one move. As the access hatch to the water tunnel sealed up again, he looked around and found himself in a side alley leading to one of the commercial districts.

In fact, he'd been deposited into the middle of a panicky crowd of aliens who were fleeing in all directions. The many storefronts were sealing up and locking down like armoured bunkers, and the holographic signs that usually displayed advertising were flashing warning messages in several alien languages.

Gabriel's HUD translated them as: 'HOSTILE VESSEL DETECTED IN NEXUS SPACE. SEEK REFUGE IMMEDIATELY.'

"*Victory Sovereign One Seven Zero Seven, Colonel Gabriel Thorn,*" Captain Ironside's voice sounded in his ear, "*Are you receiving?*"

"*Loud and clear,*" Gabriel replied, "*what's going on?*"

"*An unknown vessel just exited Q-space,*" Ironside explained, "*It's got a five megaton mass and it's opening fire on the Nexus. It also has the same visual profile as the ship recorded on the outpost's data module.*"

A cool flood of adrenaline flowed through Gabriel's heart as he connected the dots.

"*It's the same ship that attacked the outpost,*" a crewmember confirmed.

"*Is the Krakenscourge safe?*" Gabriel asked.

"*Stealth systems are fully functional,*" Ironside replied, "*we're safe where we are, but we're combat-ready on your word.*"

"*Keep the Krakenscourge where it is,*" Gabriel ordered, "*I'm not sure what the ship can do against a vessel that large.*"

"*We have some options,*" Ironside assured him.

"*Understood, have them ready,*" Gabriel responded, "*but as I said, stay put.*"

"*I'm closing in on your position,*" said the mystery voice, "*make your way back to where the Firebird is docked.*"

"*Negative!*" Gabriel countermanded, "*If this is the same ship that attacked the outpost, then the Hive-dwellers must be after something aboard the Nexus. We need to find out what it is and beat them to it.*"

"*If the Hive-dwellers board the Nexus, you'll be overwhelmed,*" Ironside pointed out.

"*We still need to know what the Hive-dwellers are after,*" Gabriel insisted, "*if that means having a shootout with them, so be it.*"

"*In that case, we're sending something your way via the cargo processing area,*" Ironside responded, "*It should help even the fight.*"

"*I can do more from the shadows than in a pitched battle,*" the voice chipped in, "*no need for extra ordnance for me.*"

"*I understand the rationale here,*" Ironside added in mild dissent, "*but once the Hive-dwellers are aboard, it'll be much harder to extract the two of you safely.*"

"*Noted,*" Gabriel replied, "*one problem at a time.*"

* * *

The strength of the Nexus's shields surpassed those found on most warships, but they were still conventional repulsor shields designed to deflect solid projectiles. They were useless against energy weapons. When the Hive-dweller dreadnought opened fire, thin beams of lethal energy tuned to near ultraviolet wavelengths passed straight through the space station's shields as if they weren't there.

The hive-ship struck at precise points along the Nexus's hull, ignoring critical systems and targeting the hatches that sealed the vacuum-docks, slicing clean through the multi-tonne slabs of metal with ease. The edges where the beams struck glowed white-hot before snap-freezing again from the absolute zero of space.

After a brief but destructive salvo, the hive-ship ceased fire. Next, docking slits in its hull opened up and dozens of egg-shaped pods spewed forth like swarms of interstellar locusts. Under the cover of the hive-ship's guns and facing no spaceborne resistance, the pods had nothing to fear as they streamed towards the breaches in the station's hull.

As the pods surged into the breached vacuum docks, they extended claw-like landing legs resembling the chitinous limbs of their pilots and used them to latch onto the docking bay walls like parasitic growths. Once the pods had landed, they cracked open and scores of armed and armoured hive-warriors disembarked.

* * *

Gabriel raced through the narrow streets, past rows of shuttered shopfronts and sealed doorways, turning another corner and sprinting through a small plaza with a large access hatch at one end and sculptures ringing the perimeter. They were elegant mimics of the spiralling tree feature in the central plaza, but without the original's vibrant array of colours.

"*Hostiles about to breach the door,*" the voice warned him.

Gabriel managed to dive into cover behind one of the sculptures as the sealed doorway was carved open by a blinding lance of energy. It was far more sophisticated than the breaching tools used by the Human military, cutting through the metal in seconds. Once the breach had been cut open, a shockwave from the other side blasted the hatch away with so much force that it slammed into one of the sculptures, shattering it into thousands of milky-white shards.

On the other side, Gabriel saw a squad of menacing insectoid warriors, rearing up on six segmented limbs like grotesque centaurs. They were clad in vacuum-proof body armour made of a chitinous material that was hard to distinguish from their actual skin, and their faces were covered with armoured masks with eight glowing red visual sensors.

Their weapons were as alien and ugly as their wielders, each one resembling an insect limb straightened and stiffened by rigor mortis. One of the hive-warriors was holding a force-gun just like the one wielded by the reptilian mercenaries earlier. It was so bulky that a Human would have struggled to lift it, but it wasn't difficult for the four-armed alien soldier.

Gabriel could no longer avoid a shooting match with the hive-warriors. About twenty of them had already poured in through the breach, and the longer he waited in his hiding spot the more likely he was to be discovered and overrun. He pulled a grenade from his belt, primed it then tossed it towards the breach.

The grenade bounced into the air and detonated, spraying flash heated shrapnel and scorching plasma in all directions. The aliens reared up in surprise as the shrapnel and plasma overcame their shielding and lashed their armour, in some cases burning through weaker joint armour and causing injuries to the flesh beneath.

Gabriel opened fire from cover, targeting the heavy weapons specialists. Their shielding provided much better protection against bullets than against the plasma grenade, but some of his shots got through and hammered their targets' armour with hypersonic force. The force-gun wielder was hit in the weaker neck armour and the creature keeled over, bright vermillion fluid pouring from its neck wound.

The other hive-warriors fired back at the mystery ambusher, their weapons spitting long, thin shards of flash-heated material that looked like glass needles. They whizzed and whined over Gabriel's head as he ducked back into cover, peppering the opposite wall like the aftermath of a dart fight.

More hive-warriors were pouring in through the breach, and even more would be on their way. Gabriel needed to get out of cover and keep moving, but there was no way to escape, not without being turned into a pincushion by the hive-warriors' needle-rounds.

"*Colonel,*" said Captain Ironside over the comm., "*your package is in transit.*"

"*I'm pinned down!*" Gabriel shouted back, "*there's no way to get to it!*"

"*Coming to your aid, now!*" announced the voice.

A series of crashing sounds were heard as several metal panels clattered to the floor from high above. From access shafts high up in the walls, swarms of airborne maintenance drones descended on the hive-warriors like a flock of carrion birds, having been reprogrammed to treat them as hostile.

The hive-warriors recognised the threat and turned their fire skyward, spraying needle-rounds which punctured the drones' thin metal skin. Some of the drones faltered in mid-air and came crashing down, but through speed and sheer weight of numbers, most of them closed the distance to their targets.

With no sense of self-preservation, the drones went claw-to-claw with the hive-warriors, using tool-equipped robotic tentacles to slash and stab at the invaders' armour or trying to wrest the hive-warriors' weapons from them. Despite their ferocious appearance, the hive-warriors weren't equipped for hand-to-hand combat, and the fight degenerated into a freewheeling brawl as they swatted and swung at their attackers.

The drones cut into the hive-warriors' vulnerable joint armour and drilled into their targets' flesh or wrapped themselves tightly around their targets like flying squid and launched themselves skywards before dropping their victims from on high. The hive-warriors flailed and squealed all the way down, landing with a sickening crunch as their bodies and limbs were broken on the hard surface below.

With the hive-warriors distracted, Gabriel bolted from cover and raced towards the exit as fast as he could. Several hive-warriors noticed him and opened fire, and he heard the needle-rounds whizzing past his head as he ran. Some of them were deflected by his shielding, while others managed to overcome his shielding and scrape his armour, but he managed to escape the plaza without injury.

"*Colonel,*" said Ironside, "*the techs are trying to force their way through the Nexus's lockdown procedures, but the package will be arriving shortly.*"

"*Thanks,*" Gabriel replied, "*I'm clear of the hive-warriors for now.*"

"*You're welcome for that, by the way,*" said the voice a little peevishly.

"*Who are you?*" Gabriel demanded of the voice, switching to a closed channel between himself and his still unknown helper.

"*Me?*"

"*Yes, you!*" Gabriel shot back impatiently, "*who are you, exactly?*"

"*Is that important right now?*" the voice replied, "*I'm with the Directorate, so I'm on your side. More importantly, I'm the reason you've made it this far.*"

"*You could have gotten me killed,*" Gabriel snapped back, "*twice.*"

"*Not strictly true in either case,*" the voice countered, "*but does that mean you want me to reveal myself and my tradecraft as compensation?*"

"*I'd like to know who I'm working with,*" Gabriel answered.

"*We can make small talk later,*" the mystery operative rebuffed him in an electronically distorted voice, then added in an unmistakeably Human voice, "*but I can switch off the voice-masking if it makes you feel more comfortable.*"

The voice was female. A small gesture, but good enough for now.

"*I've had enough of making small talk with you,*" Gabriel muttered under his breath.

"*Well, that's not the only thing we can make,*" she quipped in response.

* * *

As the hive-warriors' invasion progressed, light resistance rapidly turned to ferocious opposition. Many of those who visited the Nexus were bands of heavily armed mercenaries while others were salvagers, merchants, and explorers of many species. The one thing most of them had in common was that they were armed.

No one knew why the hive-warriors were here, but it was clear enough that they were the enemy, and as they advanced through the empty public squares and commercial concourses, the defenders turned them into free fire zones.

The air was filled with the discordant rattling of alien gunfire as the hive-warriors found themselves caught in a deadly cross-fire.

They returned fire desultorily at first as they skittered and scrambled into cover. Hypersonic bullets and needle-rounds whizzed and whined back and forth, veering sharply away as they came into contact with personal shielding, ricocheting off of solid surfaces, or punching through armour and flesh with lethal results.

Someone high up in the eaves had a weapon which spat screaming bolts of energy, punching straight through the invaders' shields and armour as if they weren't there. One hive-warrior was bisected by a bolt, its torso sheared clean of its lower half, and another lost its head to a skilfully-placed shot as the hive-warriors peppered the upper levels with return fire.

Gabriel avoided the street battles, sticking to the back alleys and side streets. His weapon was a powerful submachine gun, but it wasn't powerful enough to take on the hive-warriors in a pitched battle for long. In any case, he had no stake in helping the Nexus's defenders; there were more important tasks at hand.

"*Your package is waiting at the far end of the cargo processing terminal,*" Ironside informed him, "*you can't miss it.*"

"*There's also a contingent of hive-warriors tracking you, by the way,*" the voice warned.

"*Do we know where they're trying to reach?*" Gabriel asked.

"*Several squads are trying to access the maintenance tunnels,*" the voice replied, "*but a lot of them are bogged down by local resistance.*"

"*The maintenance tunnels?*" Gabriel said quizzically, "*are they after the Water-skins?*"

"*If they are, that means the Hive-dwellers must have been the ones who attacked the trading barge,*" concluded the voice.

The Hive-dwellers had acquired an artefact looted from an alien trading barge then attacked a Human outpost to retrieve another artefact, and now they were launching an all-out assault on the Nexus in search of the surviving Water-skins. That left a lot of things unexplained – including the use of the Human word 'voidstalker' – but all the evidence so far pointed to the Hive-dwellers as the ones who had attacked the trading barge in the first place.

Another detour took Gabriel along a promenade high above the fighting, passing by rows of private residences. Most of the facades were generic, but some were ornately decorated in the style of architecture of the inhabitants' native cultures. All of them were sealed shut like bunkers until the fighting had passed, and some had what looked like gun ports installed.

The sounds of battle far below echoed through the air. Gabriel could hear the rhythmic crackle of distant gunfire as ragtag militias exchanged fire with the invaders. He could also see the luminescent streaks of tracer rounds and sometimes the contrails of shoulder-launched rockets followed by spectacular plumes of fire as their warheads detonated.

The locals were putting up a serious fight.

From the sound of things, the hive-warriors were putting up a pretty vicious fight themselves. Amidst the crackling of gunfire could also be heard the zipping and whining of needle-rounds. There was even the occasional *whump* of a Hive-dweller force-gun followed by the clattering of debris as a barricade was blasted to smithereens.

Gabriel turned another corner and hastily ducked behind a partition as a group of hive-warriors approached from the other side.

"*Hostiles blocking the path,*" he warned.

"*They haven't seen you,*" the voice reassured him, "*wait for them to pass.*"

It was useful advice for once, and Gabriel felt more inclined to trust her now that she wasn't using the voice-masking software. Keeping his weapon at the ready, he peered out from his hiding place to get a better look.

It was a three-alien patrol, dispatched to the upper levels to clear out any sharpshooters. They'd claimed a victim as well, an avian alien slumped against the wall with a feather crest on its head and a dozen needle-rounds sticking out of its chest. A crude sniper rifle with a barrel as long as he was tall lay to one side.

"*Do you think they collect the dead bodies of their enemies for experiments later?*" his hidden ally mused with morbid curiosity.

Gabriel kept watching as one of the hive-warriors reached down and picked the dead sniper up by the throat, regarding it through its eight-eyed combat mask. Then it swung its arm around and flung the corpse over the balcony like a broken toy.

"*No,*" Gabriel replied, "*they are definitely not collectors.*"

Luckily, the patrol moved on, leaving Gabriel undetected. He emerged from cover and made his way down the steps to the ground floor of the cargo terminal.

It was a maze of storage crates, and the walls were lined with dormant robotic arms which towered over the facility. Gabriel's HUD didn't show any more enemies, and he made it to the other side of the terminal without incident.

There at the far end was a container that looked distinctly out of place amongst the other cargo. It was mounted on an extra-vehicular manoeuvring frame, the kind that could be used to move cargo short distances across space, and he sprinted towards it.

Something pierced his leg.

Gabriel didn't cry out, but he stumbled forward and collapsed just short of his goal, partly immobilised by an excruciating lance of pain through his shin. He dropped his gun in mid-fall and managed to roll to safety behind the container.

"*Colonel Thorn!*" Ironside shouted, "*Your vitals have turned orange!*"

"*Sniper…up top…behind me!*" Gabriel snarled in agony, "*shot me through the leg!*"

"*One dead sniper coming right up,*" the voice said cheerily, almost flippantly.

Sitting up and resting his back against the container, Gabriel saw a thin spike as long as his hand sticking up through his right shin. It was a needle-round, made of a translucent material that made it look like a piece of artisanal glass. Blood was spurting from the wound, pooling and congealing around the projectile, and staining its crystalline surface a messy red.

The needle-round had been fired with enough force to penetrate not only his shields but his rear-leg armour and shinbone. His leg was now next to useless, and it was a wonder it hadn't been severed altogether. If it weren't for his enhancements and the medical nanobots being administered by his armour, he would have passed out from the agony.

Gabriel gritted his teeth in pain and frustration. It was technically his own fault for running across the open like that, but he wasn't going to get any further with this thing sticking out of his leg. He gripped the spike and tried to pull it out, but the small nudge he gave it caused the pain levels to spike, and his face contorted in agony.

"*The sniper is no longer a problem,*" the voice reported, "*but I count forty hive-warriors inside the terminal, and they're after you specifically.*"

"*Holy fleeking Terra,*" Gabriel hissed furiously.

"*Don't take the homeworld's name in vain,*" the voice admonished jokingly.

Gabriel ignored her and closed his fingers around the needle-round again, gripping it hard. He took a deep breath, gritted his teeth, and yanked upwards.

The resulting pain was so intense that his vision briefly turned black. It felt like pulling a giant insect stinger out of his flesh, but with the pain magnified a thousand times. The sound the needle-round made as it was yanked out of his leg was a wet, fleshy sucking noise combined with the subtle grating of barb-against-bone. It was stomach-churning to think how much extra damage he had just done.

But the needle-round was out of his leg, and Gabriel let the bloody spike fall from his hand and roll across the floor.

"*The hive-warriors are closing in on you,*" the voice warned Gabriel, a note of urgency in her voice, "*if you don't get up, you're as good as dead.*"

Gabriel couldn't argue with that.

Now that the spike was out of his leg, his injury would start to heal on its own and the exoskeletal motors in his leg armour locked to create a makeshift leg-brace. He swung his uninjured left leg around and forced himself back to his feet, hopping around the back of the container until he was facing the rear.

A holographic locking icon illuminated in response to his presence, and he reached up and planted his palm on it. The lock interfaced with his suit's systems and verified his identity, then the indicator flashed green and the doors to the container opened up. He entered the cargo container not a moment too soon as the doors sealed up again behind him.

* * *

The hive-warriors came in force, fanning out to search for the mystery attacker. They had found minimal resistance on their way to the terminal, and found none waiting for them when they arrived. They traversed the maze of containers by climbing over them, sometimes leaping spider-like from crate to crate, using their clawed feet to grip the edges, scanning the terminal with targeting modules mounted on the sides of their combat masks.

Instead of gesturing to one another, tactical information was exchanged through their masks, their communications protected by encryption that no other species was known to have broken. Not that it mattered, the Hive-dweller language was so complicated that only they could design software capable of translating it.

One of them noticed a dark red substance on the floor beside a cargo container, it was still fresh and had the consistency of blood. There was also a recently fired needle-round lying on the floor, stained with the same dark red substance. Their quarry had been shot and injured, but even if it had somehow managed to crawl to safety, it couldn't have gotten far.

A series of sounds from inside a nearby cargo container arrested their attention. It was a mechanical and electronic whining noise like a machine powering up. Whilst the rest of the squad trained their weapons on the container, one of the hive-warriors skittered forward with a force-gun. Adjusting the holographic dial with a claw-like finger, the wielder reversed the gravitational setting and prepared to pull open the container's doors.

It was too late for them.

THE JUGGERNAUT

LABORATORIES in the Rand Block were usually quiet places where the Directorate's legions of scientists and engineers could work on the cutting edge of research in peace. That peace had been violated by the possible poisoning of a senior field operative, an emergency that was also a serious security breach, and the relevant specialists worked feverishly to piece together the few clues they had.

The counterfeit dead-box was placed inside a spectroscopic chamber and swept for every conceivable substance from pathogens and chemical compounds to radiological and nanotechnological hazards. When the box itself turned out to be clean, the used injector was removed and subjected to the same gamut of tests.

Again, no pathogenic or nanotechnological contamination was detected, but traces of the original chemical solution were still present, and these traces were extracted for analysis. The quantum computers spent several minutes breaking down the chemical composition of the solution before displaying the results on the screen.

The substance was a complex combination of antigens and custom binding agents, some of which were difficult to acquire on the open market, let alone synthesise in a home laboratory. However, the supercomputers had simulated the effect of the chemical at various dosage levels on the Human body and determined that it was medically safe.

There was an incoming communication, and someone stepped aside to take the call.

"*Any results?*" the person on the other end demanded.

"We know conclusively that it's not a toxin," the researcher replied, "in fact, it looks like a specially synthesised anti-toxin, just like the dead-box message claimed."

"*What kind of toxin was it intended to treat?*"

"Unclear," the researcher replied, "but whoever synthesised this substance was not an amateur. Some of the trace antigens bind very strongly to tetrahydrocannabinol, while others bind to various classes of dopaminergic compounds. It's like a custom-made version of the counter-symptom drugs used to help addicts."

"*Can we synthesise this drug or something similar to it?*"

"Yes, but..." the researcher said hesitantly, "the traces are too small to reliably recreate the original drug with 100% accuracy."

"*But it can still be done, correct?*"

"Of course," the researcher responded.

"*Then do it,*" the speaker ordered before terminating the link.

* * *

Aster sat down on the couch with baby Emerald nestled in her arms. After crying until she was fed, she had gone straight back to sleep. The children's blissful existence was enviable, they were all sublimely ignorant of – or indifferent to – the constant maelstrom of intrigue that seemed to sweep through this city on a regular basis.

After sitting through an hour-long debriefing, Aster had been given the rest of the day off. The questions had all focused on when and how the counterfeit dead-box had arrived at the apartment, and whether Gabriel had exhibited any strange behaviour or symptoms after injecting himself with the mystery serum.

No one had asked about Alexander Thorn.

Aster switched on the holo-TV to distract herself, only to see breaking news about a shootout in an Undercity medical clinic. The clinic had been the target of a drug-raid by an armed response team – or so the news reports claimed. Some kind of incident had occurred and the team had opened fire and killed a dozen people.

Aster changed the channel, but the next news channel was carrying reports of riots and unrest in response to the very same incident. Groups of Undercity dwellers with their faces concealed by masks were hurling stones and bits of scrap. Other groups were marching through the narrow streets, brandishing weapons and chanting anti-government slogans.

Aster switched off the holo-TV. There were enough horrible things going on in the rest of the galaxy, she didn't need any reminders beamed into her home.

Orion, Rose, Violet, and Leo walked into the room, having finished the day's lessons in their learning pods. They climbed excitedly onto the couch beside their mother, who gave them a stern look until the jostling became gentler and quieter.

"Mommy," Violet asked, "can we watch a movie together?"

Aster nodded and switched the holo-TV on again.

"Mommy," Rose spoke up tentatively, "why do cuts heal so quickly?"

The question caught Aster by surprise. It was innocent enough coming from a six-year-old, but she had no idea how to explain that, for most people, they didn't heal that quickly.

"I don't know," Aster said evasively, "maybe you can find out from the learning pod?"

"I already tried," Rose replied with a pout, "I didn't understand it."

"I think it was inherited from daddy," Orion announced, "the learning pod taught me about genetics and inheritance. Violet's cuts heal quickly because daddy's cuts heal quickly."

"I don't want to hear!" exclaimed Violet, covering her ears.

"Don't shout," Aster admonished her, wary of waking baby Emerald.

"Do your cuts heal quickly, mommy?" Rose asked, heedless of her sister's discomfort.

"The movie's starting," Aster said, bringing the discussion to a halt.

Aster had no answers to give them. Not only was she still no closer to finding answers, but the panic over the fake dead-box had also dampened her desire to keep digging. In any case, only one person was qualified to answer their questions, and he was on deployment.

The doorbell rang. Aster got up from the couch with the baby, leaving the children to watch the movie together. She returned to the bedroom and lay the sleeping Emerald down in her crib as one of the androids returned from answering the door to the bedroom.

Aster looked up and flinched.

The android was holding a small package, compact and carefully sealed. She wasn't expecting any packages, certainly not after the first package with the dead-box, so what was she to make of a second mystery package showing up at her home?

Aster just stood there staring at the package, frozen with fright while the android stood quietly by the door waiting for instructions. When none were forthcoming, the android took the package to the bedside table next to the bed, approaching Emerald's crib.

"Get that fucking thing away from my baby!" Aster shouted at the android, putting herself between the android and the crib.

The android stopped dead in its tracks, still clutching the mysterious package.

"Where would you like the package to be stored?" the android asked, speaking in a polite, Human-sounding voice without any electronic inflexions.

"In the hallway, somewhere," Aster snapped, waving the android away, "and make sure you keep it out of my children's reach."

"Understood," the android replied obediently before turning to leave.

"Wait!" Aster called after the android, "where did that package come from?"

"Unknown," the android responded, pausing at the door, "No sender information was included. However, a preliminary scan revealed no unsafe or hazardous contents. No chemical or pathogenic hazards were detected either."

The knot in Aster's stomach tightened considerably. Apart from the lack of information on the sender, a basic household android wouldn't have the sensory equipment to detect the full range of threats. It had already failed to detect the contents of the first package.

"Fine," Aster said, dismissing the android.

As the android left the room, the baby began to cry again. Aster felt a brief pang of guilt as she went to soothe her daughter. Lifting the wailing infant out of her cradle and rocking her gently, Aster did her best to keep her own inner turmoil bottled up.

She was incredibly torn on what to do about the package. The obvious common-sense thing to do was to report it, and yet she couldn't quite bring herself to trust the Directorate with this matter. After all, how in Terra's name could they have failed to stop not one but two such packages reaching the family home of one of their most senior operatives?

Now more than ever, Aster regretted her decision to take the job offer. The job itself was no worse than her previous one, but her new employer was just one web of conspiracies after another all interwoven together. She had grown used to Gabriel being absent on secret deployments from which he might not return alive, but the strict wall between his work and her life had become fuzzy and warped.

On the other hand, she had become enmeshed in this web of conspiracies the moment she had tied the knot with Gabriel. Her own children had inherited the genetic enhancements engineered into their father's DNA. There was no escaping the web of conspiracies because she had built a life and a family within its strands.

Once Emerald had quietened down, Aster put her back in her crib and returned to the hallway. The android had placed the package on a side table and stood obediently in the corner waiting for instructions. Aster stared at the sealed black box, vaguely recalling some ancient story about opening a box out of curiosity and releasing all sorts of evil into the world. It was a fitting enough metaphor for her predicament.

"What do you detect inside?" Aster asked the android.

"The outer layers of the package are composed of an electronic-masking material," the android replied, "scan results are inconclusive."

Electronic-masking material? That was an old trick to fool security scanners and a useless one at that since most security systems would flag such packages automatically as suspicious. But Aster didn't have a state-of-the-art security system, she had a pair of household androids and her own instincts and paranoia.

"A more thorough inspection would require opening the package," the android added.

"Do it," Aster ordered.

The android nodded and stripped the packaging away. As soon as it did so, a whining sound started up, growing higher and higher in pitch. Realising the danger, the android grabbed the package and hugged it close, running as fast as it could away from the family.

In the same split-second, Aster realised what a potentially fatal mistake she had made and bolted for cover just as the parcel exploded.

* * *

A series of explosives around the cargo container's hatch detonated simultaneously, blasting it off its frame and sending it flying into the face of the force-gun wielder. The hive-warrior squealed comically as the metal panel slammed into it at high speed, knocking it back into a pile of crates. Several hive-warriors went to the aid of their comrade while the rest kept their weapons trained on the threat in front of them.

The hive-warriors stayed disciplined and focused, ready to open fire on whatever it was that emerged from the container. But there was an unmistakable tension in their postures, and they were making nervous clicking sounds from inside their combat masks.

Something emerged.

The Juggernaut that stepped out was a hulking bipedal figure. Its colour scheme was a dark shade of red with black trim. The helmet was built into the bulky torso, and its entire body was layered with heavy plates of armour. One hand was completely engulfed by the protective grip of a heavy weapon while the other grasped the handle mounted on the top.

As the monstrous figure exited the container, a flash of sapphire light rippled across its body, signalling the activation of its energy shielding. The hive-warriors opened fire, spraying hundreds of needle-rounds at the figure, but its shielding was an order of magnitude stronger than theirs, and their shots were slapped aside and sent clattering across the floor.

Then the Juggernaut returned fire. Its weapon fired a concentrated bolt of blazing hot plasma and struck a hive-warrior in the chest, its repulsor shielding providing no protection against the plasma bolt. The bolt ate straight through its armour and flesh, burning its internal organs to a crisp, and the shock to its nervous system alone incapacitated it instantly.

The hive-warriors continued firing at the Juggernaut with limited effect as most of the needle-rounds veered sharply away or were bounced back with an audible ping. The Juggernaut continued firing as well, blasting one hive-warrior after another with its plasma cannon, and forcing them into a chaotic rout. The fleeing aliens skittered over piles of cargo or up the walls in search of cover, firing scattered shots back at the Juggernaut to cover their retreat.

High up on the balcony at the far end of the terminal, an unseen figure squeezed off precision shots using a high-powered needle-rifle. One retreating hive-warrior had its head transfixed by a needle-round, the shot penetrating the comparatively weak shielding around the helmet. It keeled over dead as its legs curled up in rigor mortis.

The other hive-warriors scattered like proverbial roaches so as not to make themselves literal cannon fodder for the Juggernaut and the sniper. Another hive-warrior, scrambling up the walls to safety, had its flank pierced by another high-powered needle-round. Pain and shock froze its reflexes for a second, and it lost its grip and flopped back to the floor.

Before long, the skirmish was over, and the hive-warriors had fled the terminal. They made no attempt to recover their dead or wounded, instead scrambling for the exits as fast as they could. Marching through the aftermath, the Juggernaut found the wounded hive-warrior lying on the ground, bright vermillion blood pouring out of the wound in its flank.

The metallic thump of armoured footsteps had an ominous echo of impending death as the Juggernaut approached. It stopped and stood over the dying alien as it coughed and wheezed, struggling to stay alive a few moments longer.

"Why are you here?" the Juggernaut demanded, using its helmet speakers.

The question was translated and broadcast in an alien vernacular, then retranslated by the hive-warrior's mask into its own language. With its dying breath, the alien warrior wheezed out a reply, then it lay down on the cold floor and expired.

The Juggernaut stood over the dead alien for a moment. Then it raised its right foot in the air and stomped down hard on the hive-warrior's head. There was a gruesome crunching and squelching sound as the Juggernaut crushed the bone and flesh of the creature's skull beneath its heavy armoured boot.

The Juggernaut paused, leaning awkwardly to one side.

"*Ouch,*" Gabriel grunted in pain.

"*What's wrong, Colonel?*" Ironside asked with concern.

"*My leg…*" Gabriel replied with a grimace.

"*Next time, stomp with your good leg,*" the voice remarked, "*idiot.*"

"*Enough!*" Gabriel snapped irritably as he began to walk normally, "*we need to regroup before the hive-warriors return.*"

"*They won't,*" the voice responded, turning serious, "*the bulk of the Hive-dweller forces have breached the maintenance tunnels.*"

"*Down where the Water-skins are living?*" Gabriel asked.

"*Still calling them that?*" the voice admonished jokingly.

"*Answer the question,*" Gabriel snapped irritably.

"*Yes, that's where they're heading,*" she answered.

"*In that case, we should link up before going after them,*" said Gabriel.

"*Above you,*" replied the voice.

Gabriel craned his head skyward as far as his bulky armoured suit would permit. High up on the observation platform, he saw a distinctly Human figure wink into view. It – or rather she – was wearing an active camouflage suit with minimal armour. She was also holding a Hive-dweller sniper rifle, a long and ugly looking thing with a chitinous covering.

She waved at him like an excited tourist, then vaulted over the ledge, gravitic boosters in her leg armour enabling her to land squarely on her feet. Holding the oversized alien rifle as if it weighed nothing, she walked over and playfully slapped Gabriel's shoulder pad.

"*You can call me 'Shadow-watcher' if you want,*" she said by way of introduction.

"*A bit of a clichéd codename,*" Gabriel remarked wryly.

"*I'll tell you my real name later,*" 'Shadow-watcher' replied, "*but for now, it's Shadow-watcher to you, Colonel Thorn.*"

"*Fine by me,*" said Gabriel with a shrug, "*let's get going.*"

"*I can do more from the shadows,*" Shadow-watcher responded, "*confronting the enemy man-to-alien is your job.*"

"*Speaking of which, Colonel,*" Ironside added, "*the first field test of the Juggernaut armour appears to be a crushing success.*"

"*It definitely takes the tension out of the fight,*" Gabriel replied.

* * *

Massacre.

No other word would spring to mind when beholding the gruesome scene in the medical clinic. Personnel dressed in hazmat suits were moving back and forth, collecting evidence under the watchful gaze of the backup team, but everyone already knew what had happened. A dozen people, mostly patients, had been killed in a bizarre fit of insanity by the armed response team before turning their guns on each other.

The bodies had been removed so that autopsies could be conducted – a redundant formality demanded by protocol – and would be released to their families in due course. Pools of the victims' blood still stained the floor where they had died, the absence of their corpses somehow making the scene even more macabre.

Worse still, this was the first time most people remembered a government force coming down to the Undercity. As far as they knew, it had ended in a massacre. The backup response units had come well prepared to confront an armed threat, the exact opposite of what was needed to calm the enraged crowd outside. Far from a reassuring presence, the squad of heavily-armed officers looked like an occupying force.

The crowd was already a hundred-strong and growing, their numbers limited only by the narrowness of the streets. They were heckling in Undercity dialect, and some of them tried to push past the line of officers who responded with shock-sticks. The whole situation was a riot waiting to happen.

The senior operative in charge was called to one side to receive an encrypted call.

"*You need to pacify the crowd, Captain,*" said the voice on the other end.

"How fricking insightful of you!" the captain snapped back impatiently.

"*I'm serious,*" the voice replied, "*local internet traffic is in overdrive about the incident, and the most common search terms are: 'massacre', 'conspiracy', and 'government'.*"

"Fricking Terra!" the captain swore in frustration, "ok, I'll go talk to them."

"*Be careful what you tell them,*" the voice advised, "*since the investigation is ongoing, the details of the incident are still classified.*"

"As far as the crowd is concerned, the 'details' are that the government marched into a medical clinic and gunned down a bunch of people, as you just explained," the captain retorted, "if I'm going to pacify them, I need to talk to them about the incident."

"*If you do that, it could compromise the Directorate's investigation,*" the voice warned.

"You're the one who said I need to pacify the crowd," the captain shot back, abruptly ending the call and walking out into the street.

It wasn't a moment too soon. The crowd was becoming increasingly aggressive, and the armed response officers were gripping their firearms nervously. One lost nerve and there would be another massacre, and there would be no salvaging the situation after that.

The captain marched over to the crowd and activated a loudspeaker device on his suit.

"Everyone please hush down and cool off!" he shouted in Undercity dialect.

It wasn't going to work the first time, and of course, it didn't. The shouting continued, but this time it was directed at the captain personally.

"We can explain what happened!" the captain shouted back at the hecklers.

"How the frick do you explain a bunch of armed cops gunning down innocent people in a medical clinic?!" someone demanded.

"We don't yet know what happened," the captain tried to explain.

Pleading ignorance was a mistake, and the crowd became riled up again.

"Dr Mortimer Shelton!" the captain shouted, turning up his suit's loudspeakers as far as they would go, "Do any of you know him?"

The crowd began to hush down, then descended into bewildered murmuring.

"He was the resident specialist at the medical clinic," a man near the front spoke up, then he turned accusative again, "did you kill him too?!"

The shouting and shoving resumed.

"Mortimer Shelton is the prime suspect in this atrocity!" the captain shouted back, "our men came down here to arrest him, and they were exposed to a poison that he created!"

The crowd fell silent again. It sounded vaguely plausible, even though the speaker was a government agent trying to exonerate the government for this crime. Not to mention, he hadn't presented any evidence to support his claims.

"If you want evidence, we'll show you the video footage!" the captain added, "We'll show you the results of the blood tests, too!"

From boiling anger, the mood of the crowd next turned to incredulity. In their minds, the most likely explanation remained that the government had committed the massacre, and so none of them particularly trusted the words of a government agent. But despite their distrust, they were quietly entertaining the theory.

"We're still investigating," the captain continued, "but whatever happened, I can tell you for a fact that Mortimer Shelton is the one to blame."

"When'll you show us this evidence?" someone from the back demanded.

"As soon as it's available," the captain replied, "but first, we need your help!"

The captain brought up a holographic image on his wrist-top computer, expanding the image as large as he could, and displaying it to the crowd. It was an image of Dr Mortimer Shelton, with steel grey eyes, a full head of grey hair, and a silver moustache.

"This man is our prime suspect in the massacre that occurred," the captain stated boldly, "he's also suspected of producing and distributing banned chemical substances. Help us find him, and we'll get justice for those who were killed."

People began taking out their smartphones and photographing the image, then sharing it with everyone they knew. Within minutes, Mortimer Shelton's name and face were spreading all over the local internet. Within the hour, Mortimer Shelton and his alleged crimes would be known to every newsreader on the planet.

* * *

Stubborn and fierce though it was, resistance to the hive-warriors was breaking down. The defence was disorganised and hastily prepared, and the defenders were just bands of armed interstellar itinerants. They were no match for the much more disciplined and determined hive-warriors who relentlessly ground them down before breaking and scattering them.

The hive-warriors didn't take prisoners, but neither did they hunt down stragglers – except the ones who might pose a threat. They ruthlessly demolished the ramshackle barricades but left homes and shopfronts untouched, showing no interest in looting the merchandise within. Instead, they fought their way into the Nexus's maintenance tunnels as reinforcements followed to secure their path, leaving a trail of destruction in their wake.

It was this trail of destruction that Gabriel followed as he marched through the aftermath of the battles. The Juggernaut armour was synced to his regular armour underneath, and the servo-motors in both were so sophisticated that moving around felt surprisingly easy. But in spite of the relative ease of movement, the Juggernaut armour was still too bulky for running, so a brisk march was the most he could manage.

Using active camouflage to conceal herself, Shadow-watcher guided him from hiding. There were still hive-warrior patrols prowling the streets, working to clear out any remaining pockets of resistance. Shadow-watcher sniped at them whenever they got too close, and Gabriel finished off the ones who failed to get the message.

For the most part, however, the streets and squares were eerily deserted and littered with the aftermath of battle. Makeshift barricades stood abandoned in several places while the remains of other barricades were strewn across the streets and plazas, blasted to pieces by Hive-dweller force-guns.

There were plenty of corpses, too. Hundreds of hive-warriors had invaded the Nexus, and hundreds more aliens had taken up arms in its defence. Gabriel estimated that less than a quarter of the dead were hive-warriors. Either the Hive-dwellers were extremely efficient at collecting their dead, or the battle had been incredibly lopsided.

Gabriel was disturbed, but not by what he was seeing. It was possible that something had been lost in translation, but the message from the dying hive-warrior was disturbing:

'The Voice spoke, and we listened.'

The 'Voice' was the superstitious name given to the Swarm by the Loki facility staff after being driven insane by it. Had the Hive-dwellers become enthralled to another piece of the Swarm? It was chilling to think that an entire species, or even just a faction thereof, could fall under the sway of something that insidious, but that was the only theory he had.

After an hour of following the trail of destruction left by the hive-warriors, Gabriel and his stealthy companion arrived at one of the primary entrances to the maintenance tunnels. The entrance used to be a massive hatch standing taller than Gabriel and was made of a dull grey alloy several inches thick. Not thick enough to resist the Hive-dwellers' laser-cutters, judging by the warped and frayed edges around the breach.

"*What are you thinking?*" Shadow-watcher asked as she decloaked.

"*That the Hive-dwellers may be backed by something far worse,*" Gabriel responded.

"*That's ominous,*" said Shadow-watcher, "*and vague.*"

"*That's all I can say for now,*" Gabriel replied.

The tunnel roof was only a few inches above Gabriel's head and there was hardly any room to move about. There was no light in the tunnel either, let alone at the end of it, but the visual filters in his HUD rendered the darkness as clear as day. Even then, he had no idea where they were headed, and had to follow Shadow-watcher as she raced ahead.

Gabriel marched forward as fast as he could, each footstep producing a metallic clang so loud it made him cringe. Shadow-watcher had melted back into the shadows, but as for Gabriel, he may as well have had a marching band escorting him.

"*The Water-skins are all gathering together as a group,*" said Shadow-watcher.

"*How exactly are you tracking them?*" Gabriel asked suspiciously.

"*I managed to inject fifty of them with a tracking serum whilst they were still comatose,*" Shadow-watcher explained, "*but then they woke up suddenly and escaped into the tunnels.*"

"*Just how long have you been aboard?*" Gabriel wondered.

"*Over seven months,*" she replied, opening a hatch in the wall and making way for him to step through, "*with no backup or support, I might add.*"

Seven months alone in alien-controlled space collecting intelligence with no backup, even Gabriel had never gone that long without support on a deep space mission. His respect for her climbed several notches.

On the other side of the hatch was another tunnel leading to another water treatment plant with the same layout as the one earlier.

"*The Water-skins are coming this way,*" Shadow-watcher informed Gabriel, using her suit-boosters to jump up to the upper levels, "*and they're moving fast.*"

"*So we're just going to ambush them?*" Gabriel asked.

"*No,*" Shadow-watcher corrected him, "*we're going to ambush the giant bugs chasing them and hopefully find out exactly what they want from the Water-skins.*"

"*Well, you seem to have everything in hand already,*" Gabriel muttered, a drop of resentment seeping into his voice.

"*If you have a better plan, you should have shared it earlier,*" was the snarky reply.

Gabriel had a sneaking suspicion that he disliked Shadow-watcher – whatever her real name was. Besides directing him into ambushes as an anonymous voice in his ear, she had an irritatingly flippant attitude, not to mention a degree of arrogance that rankled his own more disciplined approach.

Shadow-watcher set up near the top of the facility, covering the opposite tunnel with her stolen sniper rifle while Gabriel stood guard beside the door. This was a very haphazardly planned ambush with no clear tactical purpose beyond engaging the Hive-dwellers in combat; but unfortunately, Shadow-watcher was right, he couldn't think of another plan.

"*They're almost here!*" Shadow-watcher warned.

"*Acknowledged,*" Gabriel replied, readying his plasma cannon.

To prevent the aliens from escaping, Shadow-watcher remotely sealed the door through which they had come while Gabriel trained his weapon on the opposite tunnel.

A faint sound could be heard. At first, it was barely audible even with his suit's auditory sensors, but it grew in volume as the source of the noise approached. It was like the pitter-patter of thousands of fleshy feet racing across the metal surface of the tunnel floor. The sound was getting louder and closer, like an approaching stampede rumbling towards them.

A stampede was exactly what it was. Hundreds of amphibians came racing around the corner, pouring into the water treatment plant and scattering across it with preternatural speed. Gabriel's HUD highlighted their outlines in red, tracking each of them as potential threats; but it was hard to follow so many different fast-moving targets.

Gabriel stood completely still, doing his best not to act on the trained impulse to open fire. He was safer in his Juggernaut armour than Shadow-watcher was in her armour, but if the Water-skins suddenly attacked, it would be hard to fight them off without being overwhelmed. Furthermore, if he opened fire preemptively, they might attack anyway.

"*Hive-warriors approaching, a hundred strong!*" Shadow-watcher warned him.

Gabriel noticed that the amphibious aliens were armed. The weapons were crudely fashioned but compact and clearly usable. Some were carrying firearms scavenged from around the station while others were carrying ugly-looking Hive-dweller weapons, taken from hive-warriors they must have killed along the way.

How did they suddenly recover from their injuries and vanish into the tunnels seemingly without a trace? How could such a weak group of aliens survive for days or weeks down here in the dark? How had they managed to overpower heavily armed and armoured hive-warriors and take their weapons?

Those questions bubbled up in Gabriel's mind completely unbidden, forcing many other questions about this whole situation to the surface as well. How had the Hive-dwellers known where to find the Water-skins? How, for that matter, had the

Water-skins known that the Hive-dwellers were coming in the first place?

As these questions swirled around Gabriel's head, the Water-skins took up defensive positions all around the treatment plant. They aimed their weapons at the tunnel from which they had come, ignoring the heavily armoured figure blocking the opposite doorway.

Then the hive-warriors showed up in force as the rumble of the Water-skins' stampede changed into a rattling of hundreds of insectoid feet. The hive-warriors opened fire as they advanced, spraying a focused hail of needle-rounds at their targets.

Many of the needle-rounds missed and peppered the wall, filling the air with a chorus of high-pitched whizzing and clanging. Some came into contact with Gabriel's shielding and either veered sharply away or were slapped aside. Most of the gunfire was directed at the Water-skins, who huddled behind cover whilst returning fire.

"*Why aren't you firing?*" Shadow-watcher demanded as she sniped.

Gabriel's finger was on the trigger, but he refrained from pulling it. Two conflicting instincts were at war in his mind: one to terminate all hostiles within range, the other that something was deeply wrong.

The Water-skins were holding their own against the hive-warriors, returning fire without panicking or breaking. Amidst the whizzing of needle-rounds could also be heard the barking of conventional gunfire, and even the occasional screech of a stolen energy weapon. Despite the chaos, neither side seemed to be winning, even as more hive-warriors poured into the chamber and took up entrenched positions of their own.

Then Gabriel noticed something else: many of the needle-rounds were being swatted aside or slapped back by flashes of energy shielding. The Water-skins weren't wearing any armour or clothing as far as he could tell, but whenever a needle-round came close, a patchwork of tiny lights would flash across their skin like the repulsion nodes of a shield generator.

Personal shielding technology embedded into the skin of the wearer.

He had seen technology like that before.

"*Are you deaf or paralysed?*" Shadow-watcher shouted, "*why aren't you opening fire?!*"

"*Something's wrong,*" Gabriel replied.

"*Damn right, something's wrong!*" Shadow-watcher snapped back at him, "*We're in a firefight! Now fire your fucking weapon!*"

Gabriel did...on the Water-skins.

The plasma bolt he fired passed straight through the target's repulsive shielding and melted into the flesh beneath. As the lanky amphibian alien collapsed dead with a smouldering hole in its torso, a cloud of silver particles gushed out of its mouth like a fleeing multitude of thousands of tiny locusts.

The cloud of sentient particles buzzed through the air like a swarm of evil hornets, pouring in through the mouth of another Water-skin. Even through false-colour night vision, it was possible to see the blood vessels in the new host's skin darken into a sinister web-like pattern as the Swarm took over its body.

"*Target the Swarm-host!*" Gabriel yelled.

Shadow-watcher set her sights on the threat and fired a high-powered needle-round at the target, but the hypersonic crystalline shard failed to strike home. Instead, a flash of energy around the new host's body caused the round to rebound with an audible ping.

The Swarm-host stood upright, invulnerable and unfazed by the hail of gunfire directed at it. The Swarm itself swirled around the body of its host like a raging cloud, giving it the appearance of a divine plague in fleshly form. It puffed up its chest and let out a keening screech that was both ear-splitting and chilling to hear.

A change came over the Water-skins. They jumped out of cover and charged as a single frenzied mass, mostly at the hive-warriors, but some at Gabriel. He fired as quickly as the plasma cannon could without overheating, blasting one target after another; but the aliens moved so fast it was impossible to avoid close quarters fighting.

Gabriel swung his fist, the fist-clenching action activating a set of charged nodes along his knuckles. An electrical whining sound was accompanied by an energetic corona of light that covered his knuckles. When his fist connected with the target, a million volts, combined with a burst from a repulsion field, were transferred to the target's flesh.

The force of the blow caused the Water-skin to rebound, flying backwards head over heels like a ragdoll. The phrase 'blunt force trauma' didn't quite convey the fatal damage inflicted by the blow; without armour or shielding, the target was dead before it hit the opposite wall. But Gabriel's lone punch was all he could throw before he was literally swarmed and knocked to the ground.

The Water-skins pounced on him like feral animals, shrieking as they mauled him, slashing furiously at his armour with artificial talons surgically implanted into their slender fingers. Those enthralled by the Swarm had a revolting penchant for mutilatory enhancements, and the amphibians' lethally sharp claws were revolting proof of what they had become.

Pinned on his back, Gabriel swung his fists at the savage squealing creatures, knocking some away as the rest piled on. Their normally blank and placid amphibian faces were twisted into hideous snarls of apoplectic rage, and each swipe they took at his armour made a horrible scratching sound of metal cutting into metal. If he were still wearing his regular armour, he would have been cut to pieces.

Gabriel remembered the final fight in the observatory. The host of the Swarm – his former squad member Lieutenant Ogilvy

– had let out the same keening scream and turned the staff in its thrall into an insane mob of howling savages. They had attacked him with the same wanton ferocity and disregard for their own lives as the aliens swarming over him now, beating their fists bloody against his armour.

"*Thorn!*" Shadow-watcher's voice sounded in his ear, "*I've got a contingency plan, but you may not like it; just a heads-up!*"

"*What kind of contingency plan?!*" Gabriel demanded.

The violent brawl was interrupted by a rumbling in the background, like a drumbeat of distant metallic thunder or a cohort of giants marching in lockstep through the superstructure. Water-skins and Hive-dwellers alike paused their attacks on each other to look and listen, and Gabriel felt a sudden knot of dread tighten in his stomach.

A raucous chorus of alien klaxons filled the chamber, and the darkened space lit up with holographic warning messages as danger pounded its way closer and closer to the chamber. Pandemonium broke out amongst the hordes of aliens and they fled as a single mass back down the tunnel. Still lying on his back, Gabriel's HUD translated the warning messages: '*DANGER: CATASTROPHIC STRUCTURAL FAILURE DETECTED.*'

One entire side of the chamber disintegrated in a flame-less flash, and the force of the detonation sent out a shockwave strong enough to slap back everything nearby. On the other side of the breach was empty space, and as soon as the shockwave abated, rapid decompression sucked everyone out through it in a maelstrom of flailing bodies.

The hive-warriors were safe in their vacuum-proof armour, but the naked Water-skins were as good as dead. Gabriel was also safe in his armour, but without a thruster pack, all he could do was flail and float with them like a piece of space junk.

It was just like void training, where the drill instructors gave each candidate a spacesuit with 25 hours of oxygen, then tossed them into space. He had survived the 24-hour ordeal with his sanity intact, but barely. Of course, quite apart from its ultimate purpose as a test of each voidstalker candidate's mental strength, the void test was meant to simulate what might happen if you were blasted into space.

This was close enough.

For one thing, the view was just as terrifying: an eternal, all-encompassing abyss of blackness stretching away in all directions. The Nexus station and the vast multi-coloured gas cloud did provide a point-of-reference, but the sheer immensity of the space beyond was enough to drive a person insane.

As he spun around, the Nexus came into view. The breach from which he had been ejected was a huge and ragged hole in the hull. In fact, it was worse than a mere hull breach: a succession of explosions had blown through several walls until reaching the treatment plant where they had been fighting, creating a deep and gaping wound in the superstructure.

It was also a potentially disastrous blunder. To effect an 'escape', Shadow-watcher had inflicted severe damage on a neutral alien station used by countless species, many of which were unfriendly or outright hostile. On top of the rumours about Humans – or voidstalkers – attacking the trading barge, if it were discovered that Humans had blown a hole in the Nexus, this could all result in blowback further down the line.

Spinning around helplessly in space, Gabriel was furious. What kind of idiot would do something like that? Humanity had enough enemies, potential and actual, as it was; why add to the list by doing something so reckless? With a single press of a button, Shadow-watcher – or whatever her real name was – had jeopardised far more than just their cover.

Even so, at least the immediate threat had been neutralised. Out of the corners of his HUD, Gabriel could see the Waterskins convulsing, their deep-blue skin icing over from the absolute cold. Their pitch black eyes were bulging out of their sockets as they choked, clutching their throats in a vain effort to stem the flow of air out of their lungs.

Gabriel was safe from that fate. Much more overwhelming was the feeling of tumbling deeper into the void with nothing to change his direction or stop his motion. The sheer helplessness of being a slave to inertia was wearing on his mind already, and he did his best to avert his gaze from the infinite expanse of star-studded blackness.

"*Krakenscourge!*" Gabriel shouted into the comm., "*I've been spaced! Need extraction!*"

"*Ask, and you shall receive!*" said a female voice in reply.

"*Hold tight, Colonel; we're coming for you!*" Ironside replied more seriously.

Using a thruster pack built into her armour, Shadow-watcher came flying towards him at high speed, breezing by with a passing salute as she sped towards an approaching dot in the distance. Given that this was all her fault, the salute and the fact that she had a thruster pack were even more galling.

Gabriel recognised the dot as the Firebird gunship, flying unmanned towards them, presumably being piloted remotely from the Krakenscourge. Shadow-watcher swooped in towards the gunship and climbed into the cockpit with practised ease, the glass canopy shutting automatically once she was inside.

Gabriel was still flying helplessly through space as the Firebird closed in on him. There was a set of rungs on the side of the gunship, and Gabriel reached out and grabbed them with his free hand, still holding the plasma cannon with the other. He was yanked along by the Firebird's motion as it turned around and sped away from the Nexus.

"*I've got the rungs,*" Gabriel shouted, "*let's get out of here!*"

"*No need to shout,*" Shadow-watcher replied, "*I can hear you just fine.*"

Gabriel ground his teeth in rage at the sheer lack of seriousness with which she was treating this whole situation. It wasn't clear what kind of disciplinary action could be taken, but once they were back aboard the Krakenscourge, he intended to give her a piece of his mind.

"*Pick up the pace, you two!*" Ironside told them, less calmly than usual, "*the Hive-dweller ship is powering up again!*"

"*Understood, Krakenscourge,*" Shadow-watcher said in acknowledgement, then added, "*and again, there's no need to shout into the comm.*"

* * *

The hive-ship had lurked motionless outside the station throughout the attack, waiting like some predatory beast. Now, the massive ship began to stir.

The landing pods that had delivered the scores of hive-warriors to the station began to return with hive-warriors and casualties stowed safely within. From openings in the hive-ship's hull, other pods were deployed to rescue the hive-warriors who had been spaced. The same pods also moved in to capture the Water-skins, opening up like the petals of a mutated flower to scoop up their targets.

From his precarious vantage point hanging on to the side of the Firebird, Gabriel could see the Water-skins flailing and struggling as a gravitic field pulled them inside, screaming mutely as they raged in vain at their capture. He couldn't help but wonder how insane the Swarm-enthralled Water-skins had to be to prefer death over abduction. Then again, who knew what the Hive-dwellers planned to do to their captives?

Perhaps the Water-skins knew all too well.

A dark shape swooped in towards the Firebird, and the gunship flew straight into the open shuttle bay which sealed itself up once the gunship was safely aboard. With the Firebird retrieved, the Krakenscourge turned towards the hive-ship and fired something towards the gigantic alien vessel.

The projectile was the size of a torpedo and it unfolded a set of grappling spikes as it closed in. The hive-ship was still in the middle of retrieving its boarding pods and was caught with its shields down as the projectile closed the distance. As the pod struck the hive-ship, it latched on with its grappling spikes, securing itself to the hull like a limpet.

As soon as the pod was launched, the Krakenscourge executed a sharp turn and boosted its engines to escape. The hive-ship ignored – or couldn't detect – the Krakenscourge, and as the last of the landing pods returned home, the landing bays sealed up again and the hive-ship began to reverse.

The hive-ship came around in a giant, cumbersome arc until it was facing the direction from which it had come. There were no manoeuvring jets visible as it turned, relying instead on incredibly powerful gravitic boosters that produced no exhaust. Everything about this leviathan of a spaceship was alien, even the manner in which it moved.

Once it had completed its turn, the enormous vessel glided away, rapidly picking up speed as it cruised towards interstellar space. It accelerated faster than most ships a fraction of its size could have managed. Ahead of the tapered nose of the sinister warship, a globular lump of blackness began to form as it prepared to make the transition to Q-space.

As the ship continued accelerating through space, it dived into the breach. Metre by metre, the massive vessel disappeared into the orb of darkness, vanishing into the ineffable dimension of Q-space. The entire transition took several minutes to complete, but eventually, the ship was swallowed up by the portal it had created, disappearing without a trace.

A little way behind, a much smaller ship followed the hive-ship, virtually invisible to both eyes and sensors. Travelling in the same direction as the now-vanished hive-ship, the Krakenscourge accelerated towards interstellar space. A similar orb of blackness, though far smaller, began to coalesce in front of it, and after chasing the Q-rift for a while it plunged prow-first into the dark.

THE TERROR

UNDULATING hills and semi-arid plains zipped past the mag-train's window at high speed. High above, the bright blue gas giant Odin loomed large in the sky, the light from the setting sun reflecting off its cerulean clouds. The coloured shadow it cast across the landscape was a scene that couldn't be found anywhere else in the system; perhaps not even in the entire spiral arm.

More than a dozen satellite cities had sprung up around Asgard City, and countless smaller towns had also sprung up around each of these, creating an urbanised web that brought the planet's population past 100 million. Each settlement was connected by air-links and high-speed mag-trains as well as wired and wireless communications, keeping the entire planet connected not just to itself but to the rest of Human-settled space.

The traveller's hooded shirt covered his freshly-cut greying hair. He was clean-shaven with irises that had been drop-dyed a watery blue, and he was glued to the news reports about a mass-murder using toxic gas at a medical clinic. The prime suspect was Dr Mortimer Shelton, a physician who had apparently been using the clinic as a lab to synthesise the poison.

The traveller turned his head towards the mag-train window, hiding his face by pretending to be enamoured of the landscape. The surveillance state was everywhere and could do a far more effective job of outing him than the general public. Even so, there was no need to draw extra attention to himself.

The train began to slow down. Outside the window, the landscape became dotted with structures as the train entered the urban limits of Haven. As the mag-train approached the station, people began to pack up their belongings and the traveller did the same, collecting a backpack from under the seat in front and fitting his arms through the straps.

The station was a modest one, built with plain steel columns and a low roof, eschewing the elaborate architecture of the grand complexes in Asgard City. Automated luggage carriers on wheels waited on the platforms, and when the mag-train stopped and the doors opened, the passengers poured out and began to load their luggage onto the carriers.

The traveller walked past the gaggles of day-trippers and headed straight to the elevator, keeping his hood up and his gaze down lest the security cameras flash-scan his eyes and grab his biometrics. He made it up the steps of the platform without incident and into the arrivals hall, filled with people coming and going or standing and waiting.

He couldn't go any further. Local uniformed Civil Security officers were patrolling the station entrances accompanied by armed support androids. No doubt there were plainclothes officers prowling through the crowd as well. He turned sideways, keeping his head down and his pace quick, hoping to reach a side door without attracting attention.

With his gaze directed downward, the palm of someone's gloved hand passed across his field of vision. The traveller saw an imaging device attached to the palm of the glove a split second before it flash-scanned his eyes.

He'd been caught.

The traveller ducked low, wrapping his arms around the plainclothes agent's leg and dump-tackling him to the floor. Then he got up and raced through the parting crowd. It was too late to escape; the second his biometrics had been grabbed, they'd known that his iris colouring was artificial, and maybe even grabbed his actual identity in spite of the disguise.

As he ran, the traveller removed his backpack and pulled out an aerial drone, thumping the activation switch, and hurling it into the air. Using counter-rotating fans to fly, the drone swerved round in a wide arc and the crowd screamed in panic, scattering towards the exits. Certain people in the crowd failed to yell or flee but instead struggled against the stampeding tide of civilians in order to catch the culprit.

Now he knew where the Civil Security officers were.

The traveller pulled out what looked like a smartphone and pressed a control. Nothing seemed to happen, so he pressed the button again, but with no effect.

Something pierced the back of his shoulder. The projectile stung his flesh, but it was subsumed by an even sharper pain that spread rapidly across his body, rippling through his nervous system like an excruciating wave of electricity. The traveller collapsed immediately and rolled onto his back.

The shock-dart had completely immobilised his muscles without preventing his heart from beating or his lungs from breathing. The Haven Civil Security teams had caught him, and no doubt they were jamming the signal to the drone as well. It didn't matter. The protocol he had tried to trigger remotely was set to a countdown that had begun as soon as the drone had been activated. Jamming the signal simply delayed the inevitable.

Staring involuntarily up at the metal and glass roof, several figures entered his field of vision. They were plainclothes officers pointing shock-dart guns at him. One of them spoke into his comm., telling his superiors that the target had been disabled.

Fools.

The drone swooped down low over the officers' heads without warning, spraying a fine white cloud as it passed. A gunshot rang out through the hall followed by a metallic clang and clattering as the drone hit the floor. One of the armed androids must have shot down the drone, but it was too late to matter.

The officers coughed and spluttered as they were exposed to the noxious cloud. Then they looked up and began shouting in fright, pointing their weapons at each other. Shots were exchanged, and as they collapsed, the heavier-than-air cloud of gas descended slowly to floor-level. Still paralysed, the traveller couldn't even flinch as the gas engulfed his face, entering his lungs one breath at a time.

The sky through the glass roof darkened and the arching steel beams became twisted and distorted. He could hear yelling in the distance – or perhaps just in his own mind – a dissonant roaring of anger as the air in front of him seemed to thicken and bend like a physical substance being squeezed out of shape.

The yelling was getting closer, heralded by a horrible ringing sound. The visceral terror that gripped his mind was accentuated by his sheer helplessness, his inability to so much as twitch, let alone get up and flee. He could do nothing to defend himself as an armed-support android with the Haven Civil Security insignia approached and looked down at him.

It was wearing his father's face.

"YOU CAN'T RUN FROM ME ANYMORE!" the android declared in his father's voice, its words reverberating through the air.

Somewhere in the still sane part of his mind, the traveller knew that the android had said something completely different, but most of his critical faculties were awash in the hallucinogenic chemical he had inhaled.

Still wearing his father's face, the android leaned over him with a hideous leering grin. The paralysed traveller couldn't even shiver with fear as his 'father' stared into his soul, its eyes flash-scanning his own and collecting his biometric data.

They wouldn't find anything. He was nobody. That was why he'd been chosen.

* * *

Gabriel was furious. He was also in pain.

The potent cocktail of pain suppressants that had kept him functional during the fight had worn off, hitting him with the full excruciation of a high-velocity needle-round piercing his right leg. A normal Human would have passed out, but even for Gabriel, the agony of a still-healing hole in his leg was difficult to bear. Even so, he eschewed anaesthetics or nerve-deadeners while the injury was treated.

For the past hour, an army of surgical robots had been poking, prodding, probing, and picking apart his leg wound. These finely engineered medical tools worked with a level of precision no Human surgeon could match. Despite not taking any pain suppressants, Gabriel had been given a localised paralytic patch to prevent him from moving his leg whilst the medical robots operated.

Only the genetically enhanced structure of the bone and the makeshift leg-splint made by his armour's exoskeleton had prevented his leg from breaking completely in two. His superhuman enhancements also meant that the injury had already begun to heal, but he would be reduced to a limp for at least a day.

After cleaning out the wound, applying medical nanobots and regenerative salve, and stitching the wound shut again, the surgical robots returned to their dormant state. The paralytic patch was removed and the power of motion returned to Gabriel's leg like the relief from a crushing case of pins-and-needles. Last but not least, a support brace was locked around his injured leg to help him move.

With perfect timing, the doors of the sickbay opened and Captain Ironside entered, accompanied by a woman in a naval uniform stripped down to a more casual style. Gabriel had never seen her face before, but he could guess who she was.

"How's the leg?" asked Shadow-watcher.

Gabriel jumped off the bed – taking care to land on his good leg – and confronted her, glaring down at her with his luminescent green eyes. Then he noticed *her* eyes.

'Shadow-watcher' had blonde hair tied back in a tight bun, and her skin was slightly pale, with the same hue as his own. Most striking of all, her eyes were a radiant blue, literally radiant. They had the same luminescence that Gabriel's own eyes had, like a pair of sapphires instead of his own pair of emerald eyes.

"Colonel Thorn," Ironside ventured an introduction, "this is Aetherea Starborn."

"Colonel Aetherea Starborn," Aetherea corrected, "a fellow voidstalker."

Gabriel was nonplussed.

"This is the part where you reply: 'pleased to meet you'," Aetherea added.

"Why did you do that?" Gabriel demanded angrily.

"Could you be more specific?" Aetherea asked, cocking an eyebrow.

"You blew a hole in the Nexus!" Gabriel shouted furiously, "we have enough difficulty keeping a low profile beyond Human space, and you recklessly destroyed an entire chunk of an alien space station! And for what, a quick escape route?!"

"That's exactly what it was for," Colonel Starborn replied, unfazed, "and given the situation we were in, I don't understand why you're being so ungrateful."

"Please tell me *you* understand," Gabriel exclaimed, turning to Ironside in exasperation.

"I do, Gabriel, really," Ironside said, "but what's done is done. And, in any case, the real problem is what happened immediately before you got spaced."

"You mean the Swarm?" Gabriel asked, turning calm and serious.

"What else could he have meant?" Aetherea asked rhetorically.

Gabriel directed a smouldering scowl at Aetherea.

"We managed to attach a limpet probe to the hive-ship's hull before it got away," Ironside cut in, shutting down the shouting match before it could begin again, "we're tracking the vessel through Q-space as we speak."

"Good," said Gabriel, suppressing his still simmering anger, "in the meantime, we need to find a way to destroy the hive-ship and the Swarm along with it."

"Why?" Aetherea demanded, "The Hive-dwellers and the Water-skins were enemies, and as far as we can tell the Water-skins died of void exposure."

"What about the Swarm itself?" Gabriel demanded back, his composure slipping again, "are you telling me it died of void exposure as well?"

"We tracked the energy signature corresponding to the Swarm entering one of the Hive-dweller pods as the Water-skins were being rounded up," Ironside answered, "the Swarm, and any surviving Water-skins, are now aboard the hive-ship."

"Hence the need to destroy that ship!" Gabriel asserted forcefully.

"You're assuming that the Hive-dwellers are themselves enthralled to the Swarm," Aetherea pointed out, remaining maddeningly calm.

"Did you hear a word he just said?!" Gabriel shouted, "The Swarm has to be destroyed, and the Swarm is now aboard the hive-ship! Even if they aren't yet enthralled, they will be soon, just like the Loki facility staff! Which part of this is so hard for you to grasp?!"

"Gabriel, we all agree on the need to neutralise the Swarm, which is why we're tracking the hive-ship now," Ironside answered, trying to cool Gabriel's anger, "but it's not clear how the Krakenscourge is supposed to go up against a vessel that size."

"I asked you that exact question back on the Nexus and you told me we had options for that," Gabriel reminded Ironside.

"For hit-and-run attacks that buy us enough time to escape," Ironside clarified, "but we can't go toe-to-toe with a ship that big."

"This is a well-armed spy ship, not a pocket-sized dreadnought," Aetherea pointed out much more sharply, "we're not equipped to destroy an *actual* dreadnought, let alone one with technology that exceeds our own."

"Which is not to say that it can't be done," Ironside added conciliatorily, "but the odds of success are pretty slim."

Gabriel was still seething; partly from the pain of his still-healing leg, partly from Aetherea's irritating tone, and partly from the fact that he knew with every fibre of his being that they had to destroy that ship and everything onboard.

He remembered the conversation with the observer.

"Do we at least have an idea of where the hive-ship is heading?"

"Towards Hive-dweller space, presumably," Ironside replied, "but definitely in the opposite direction of Human-controlled space."

"So 'no', in other words," Gabriel answered, then grimly added the obvious, "which means that the tracking probe is our only guide to what's ahead."

"Excuse me, the hive-ship is heading *away* from Human space," Starborn pointed out, "in other words, *away* from the space we're defending and the reinforcements we would need to have a fighting chance against it."

"Your point being?" Gabriel demanded, his patience wearing dangerously thin.

"That the hive-ship is putting distance between itself and Human space, making it less of a threat to Humanity," Aetherea replied sharply, "and yet we're pursuing it into uncharted space alone and without any means to request reinforcements."

Gabriel was silent. She had a point...sort of.

"Here be dragons," he muttered, "or so the ancients would say."

"Indeed," Ironside replied, nodding his head, "the crew and I will be monitoring what the tracking probe transmits. We'll keep you informed about what we find."

Salutes were exchanged and Captain Ironside departed the medical bay, leaving the two ranking officers alone together. It was an awkward silence, at least for Gabriel. He was still angry at her, but mainly he was bewildered.

"Are you actually a voidstalker?" Gabriel demanded to know.

"Do you not see the eyes?" Aetherea said, pointing to her luminescent sapphire eyes, "or do you think they're cosmetic?"

"I don't know," Gabriel replied.

Without asking permission, Aetherea took Gabriel's hand and twisted herself around until her back was pressed against his chest.

"Uh, what do you think you're doing?" Gabriel asked, caught off guard.

"VS-1707," Aetherea said, seemingly ignoring his question.

"My voidstalker serial number," Gabriel said, "what about it?"

"Back of the neck, just like yours," Aetherea instructed, "and do it gently."

Gabriel couldn't tell if she was doing this deliberately to make him uncomfortable, but he performed the requested action. Guided by her hand, Gabriel traced his thumb across the skin on the back of her neck. The action caused a symbol to appear: a capital S intertwined serpent-like with a capital V.

"Colonel Aetherea Starborn, voidstalker, VS-2552," Aetherea said to him.

"Why a '2'?" he asked.

"The first digit signifies the generation of voidstalkers," Aetherea explained, "the last three digits are a randomly chosen serial number for each operative."

"I didn't know there was a second generation of voidstalkers."

"Why would you?" Aetherea asked rhetorically, "the Directorate's little projects are all on a need-to-know basis. Besides, we're all lone-wolves; how many other voidstalkers have you met in your career?"

Aetherea grasped his hand and brought it to rest on her shoulder.

"Basically," Aetherea continued, "the Directorate decided to create a new generation of voidstalkers as an upgrade to the first one."

"So they finally figured out how to make female voidstalkers," Gabriel muttered.

"Ooh, was that disdain that I detected?"

"No, I'm just surprised," Gabriel replied.

"That they'd allow women into the programme?" Aetherea said.

Gabriel didn't reply.

"I don't really care if you have a problem with it," Aetherea added.

"I don't," Gabriel insisted, "really."

"I'm sure you don't," Aetherea said, looking up at him, "but that's one of the differences between the first and second generations of voidstalkers."

"Which is?" Gabriel prompted.

Still holding onto his wrist, Aetherea yanked on his arm and flipped him over her shoulder. Gabriel was caught completely by surprise as he was thrown bodily onto the floor, landing on his uninjured left leg and sparing his still-healing right leg from the impact. Aetherea crouched down beside him as he looked at her with rekindled rage.

"I have a personality," she answered with a mischievous smile on her face.

Then she stood up and walked out.

* * *

Cruising through the ineffable realm of Q-space, the hum of the Krakenscourge's machinery was barely audible as Gabriel returned to his quarters. He marched through the halls of the ship as fast as his still-healing leg would allow, the few crewmembers he encountered stepping aside and saluting as he passed. He returned the salutes and kept walking, keeping his discipline and composure about him, but inside he was seething with fury.

Everything about his fellow voidstalker infuriated him. Her reckless actions on the Nexus, her casual attitude to her actions and the mission at hand, and of course being bodily flipped by her as some kind of joke. If all of this was part of some ploy to wind him up, it was working spectacularly well.

There was another problem. Voidstalkers were automatically promoted to colonel in order to avoid disputes over the chain-of-command. As the captain of the ship, Ironside knew where he stood, but now he had two superiors of equal rank to whom he was equally answerable. A clash of personalities between two co-equal commanding officers was the last thing the mission needed.

On top of all that, his shin still hurt. The leg brace made it possible to walk properly immediately after the surgery, but the pain was still present in the form of a dull sting every time his foot touched the floor. It was tolerable, but it did nothing to improve his mood.

Gabriel reached his quarters, glad that he at least had a room to himself.

As soon as he walked into the room, he felt a kick behind his knees, knocking his legs out from under him as an elbow came down on his ribcage.

"That's the second time I've caught you off-guard," Aetherea Starborn remarked.

Gabriel grabbed Aetherea and threw her bodily across the room. He was so strong that she actually went flying before hitting the bed with a well-cushioned thump.

"What are you doing in my quarters?" Gabriel demanded, shutting the door behind him.

"'Your' quarters?" Aetherea said with a wry grin as she sat up on the bed.

"Yes, *my* quarters," Gabriel repeated, advancing on the smug intruder.

"Well, being a ranking officer aboard this ship, I can't exactly share a room with the crew, not even with the captain," Aetherea explained, unintimidated by Gabriel, "so that means we're going to have to sleep together."

"This has to be a joke," Gabriel muttered.

"I'm not sure you'd recognise a joke if you heard one," Aetherea countered, "besides, it's not like I'm going to make you sleep on the floor."

Gabriel sighed in resignation and walked over to the right-hand side of the bed, placing himself between Aetherea and the bedside cabinet with the family photo. Before he could get there, Aetherea reached over and snatched the holo-photo off the cabinet.

"Don't touch that!" Gabriel snarled, lunging at her.

Aetherea was prepared for him. She wrapped her legs around his torso as he pounced on her, then used his momentum and body weight to twist him around until he was pinned on his back with her perched on his chest.

"That's three takedowns in a row," Aetherea said with a smirk.

"Give that back!" Gabriel shouted, lashing out at her.

Aetherea dodged his swipes with ease, not even bothering to block them as she turned the holo-photo around to show Gabriel.

"What are their names?" she asked, pointing to the children.

"Why do you care?" Gabriel demanded, still struggling angrily.

"I'm just curious," Aetherea replied innocently, then she pointed to Rose's happily grinning face, "who's the munchkin on your shoulders?"

"Don't call my children 'munchkins'," Gabriel warned her.

"Well, then what should I call them?"

Aetherea prying into his family life was especially unwelcome, but the best response was probably no response at all, so Gabriel stopped struggling and stayed silent.

"Don't like to talk about the wife and kids?"

"Work and family need to be kept separate," Gabriel asserted grimly.

Aetherea turned the holo-photo around and kept looking at the smiling faces.

"Are you going to get off my chest?" Gabriel asked, glaring up in annoyance.

"You got plenty of things off your chest earlier," Aetherea quipped, then added, "but no, your chest is pretty comfortable."

"How about I buck you off?" Gabriel threatened.

"Go for it, bad boy," Aetherea retorted.

Gabriel grabbed her by the shoulders and forcibly rolled her over onto her back.

"That's more like it," Aetherea giggled.

Gabriel couldn't tell if she was mocking him or just having fun – or both – but he was running out of ways to express his anger with her and stay restrained.

"Do you play like this with Aster?" Aetherea teased.

Gabriel flinched.

"Surprised that I know her name?" Aetherea asked, "I read her personnel file."

"Don't you dare bring her up," Gabriel growled menacingly.

"Ok," Aetherea replied, putting the holo-photo back.

"Is 'Aetherea' actually your name?" Gabriel asked.

"Yes," Aetherea replied, "and 'Starborn' really is my surname."

"Colonial?" Gabriel guessed.

"Nope," Aetherea replied, "Earthling, born and raised on Terra herself."

"Then why the name?" Gabriel wondered.

"Why not?" Aetherea responded, "Maybe I had some ancestors who came back to the homeworld and kept the surname."

"And yet you were given a celestial-sounding first name," Gabriel noted.

"Just like you were named after a divine messenger from the mythology of ancient Earth," Aetherea replied, "and just to be clear, it's pronounced 'Ith-ear-ree-ah.'"

Aetherea was infuriating, but also somewhat fascinating. Gabriel had no idea what do about her, or how to handle her, and that was probably how she wanted it.

"Well, as fun as it is horsing around with you," Aetherea said, changing the subject, "we have some Hive-dweller-related studying to do."

Gabriel was tired of tussling, and he barely resisted as Aetherea rolled him back over again. Straddling his chest, she grabbed a flexi-tablet off of the other bedside table.

"Let's start with what we know about their biology," Aetherea suggested, pulling up a file on the flexi-tablet, "first of all, we know their homeworld has an oxygen-rich atmosphere, or else they wouldn't be able to sustain those massive bodies of theirs."

"Is it true that they actually have lungs?" Gabriel asked curiously, "I always thought insects had to breathe through spiracles."

"It's true, autopsies have confirmed that they have lungs," Aetherea replied, "but the important thing is that having an atmosphere with 35% oxygen means lots of violent weather. That may have given the Hive-dwellers their first insights into engineering and ultimately spacecraft design, or so the evolutionary xenobiologists theorise."

"Is their home planet smaller than Earth?" Gabriel wondered, "A low-gravity world would help explain how they grew to be so big."

"Not necessarily," Aetherea explained, "based on what we know about the evolution of arthropods on Earth, the primary limiting factor in carapace growth is oxygen-intake capacity, not the pull of gravity. An oxygen-rich atmosphere and efficient respiration can compensate for the limitations imposed by a high-gravity world."

"Fair enough," Gabriel conceded, "but their evolutionary biology is a side note."

"Know your enemies' biology," Aetherea said, "the better to kill them."

"True, but still a side note," Gabriel replied.

"So what's really bugging you about them?" Aetherea asked.

"They're communal insects with a hive mentality," Gabriel explained, ignoring the pun, "Drones and warriors have Human-level intelligence, but minimal individuality. That makes them more susceptible to being enthralled by the Swarm."

"Again, not necessarily," Aetherea responded, "I reviewed your suit's combat footage while you were getting your leg fixed."

"Oh?"

"'The Voice spoke, and we listened,'" Aetherea quoted, "or so the translation says."

"So, what's wrong with it?" Gabriel asked.

"The noun 'voice' and the verb 'listen'," Aetherea explained, "even though we're translating from an alien vernacular, and not directly from the Hive-dweller language, the verb translated as 'listen' really means 'heed' or 'obey'."

"'The Voice spoke and we obeyed,'" Gabriel rephrased, "I don't see the difference."

"Well, there's also the word for 'voice'," Aetherea continued, "it doesn't necessarily refer to a voice in the sense of my voice as I'm speaking. How do you know the 'voice' isn't some hive-queen or hive-king or collective hive-mind?"

"Does it matter?" Gabriel countered, "They brought the Swarm aboard their ship, and they attacked the Nexus specifically to recover it. They're a threat either way."

Aetherea was silent, and she was still straddling his chest.

"Could you get off me?" Gabriel demanded.

"Why? You're so comfortable," Aetherea said with a smile.

"I'm not comfortable with you on my chest," Gabriel replied irritably, "Get off."

Aetherea pouted in annoyance, then rolled off his chest and sidled up to him on the bed instead. She pulled up another file on the flexi-tablet.

"Next up, species A-0456: the 'Water-skins'," Aetherea said, then mused, "I wonder if they mind being called that."

"Who cares?" Gabriel replied dismissively, "I bet every alien race that knows about our existence has insulting names for us, too."

"Not the point I was making," Aetherea said with a roll of her eyes, then continued, "but anyway, the importance of the Water-skins is where and how they came to be enthralled in the first place; not to mention who attacked their ship."

"Isn't it obvious?" Gabriel insisted, "The Hive-dwellers must have attacked the Water-skins to acquire the Swarm for themselves."

"That's a conjecture based on circumstantial evidence," Aetherea pointed out.

"Do you have an alternative suspect?" Gabriel asked.

"Not right now," Aetherea conceded, "but let's start with the species itself."

"So, what's your impression of them?" Gabriel asked.

"It's strange that an amphibious race would want to be space nomads, but apparently that's how most of them live," Aetherea explained, "reports say that their home planet is still populated and thriving, but whole clans have taken to the stars, living off whatever they can find through trading or salvaging."

"So this particular clan must have looted the artefact containing the Swarm," Gabriel concluded, "maybe even from another alien observatory."

"Didn't the observer claim that the observatory was a space vessel?" Aetherea asked.

"It did," Gabriel confirmed, "although, it also claimed that its systems were so damaged it was no longer capable of interstellar flight. So the Water-skins must have dug it up or looted it from another observatory, then been attacked by the Hive-dwellers–"

"So we assume," Aetherea interrupted.

"Then everything aboard their own ship was looted," Gabriel continued, gritting his teeth, "including the artefact which was then sold onto a group of Hive-dwellers."

"Which is how I discovered the energy signature," Aetherea added.

"Except that the Swarm wasn't inside the artefact," Gabriel pointed out, "it was inside the surviving Water-skins all along, which means that they must have found a way to open the artefact after bringing it aboard the ship."

"Or it might have entered the Water-skin expeditionary team and enthralled them," Aetherea suggested, "then taken over the rest of the crew once it was aboard."

"Which leaves the question: where exactly did they find the artefact?"

"Well, we could always search the trading barge computers for a set of coordinates," Aetherea suggested, "except we're heading in the wrong direction for that."

"An objective for a future mission," Gabriel answered firmly.

"Are you really that convinced that the Hive-dwellers are the ones who attacked the Water-skins?" Aetherea asked.

"Yes, I am," Gabriel asserted, "because there's another piece of the puzzle: the attack on XA-107. Not only was it the same ship that we're following now, but the hive-warriors boarded in order to extract something buried in the rock."

"And do we know what it was?" Aetherea asked.

"No," Gabriel admitted, "but apparently it had a similar composition to the material that the observatory was made from."

There was a moment of silence.

"Well, that raises even more questions," Aetherea said, putting the flexi-tablet back on the bedside table, "such as what the XA-107 artefact is, what it does, and how the Hive-dwellers knew it was there in the first place."

"None of which I have answers for," Gabriel answered.

"Any theories?" Aetherea asked curiously.

Gabriel lay his head back and mused.

"I can practically hear the cogs grinding in your head," Aetherea teased.

"Whoever created the observatory and the observer is probably long extinct," Gabriel surmised, "but clearly they wanted to study the Swarm without falling under its sway."

"If they're extinct, that must have worked out fabulously," Aetherea said ironically.

The observer had told Gabriel more than just that, and Aetherea had no idea how close her sarcastic answer was to the truth.

"Well, it's been fun brainstorming with you," Aetherea said cheerily, "we can pick it up again once Ironside has some news for us."

"Don't straddle me again," Gabriel warned.

"Don't lunge at me again and I won't have to," Aetherea replied.

Gabriel said nothing in response, instead he rolled over and stared at the holo-photo of his family, trying to forget the insistent stinging sensation in his shinbone.

Aetherea frolicking with him made him feel a little dirty, especially looking at the mother of his children holding their newborn. In any case, he didn't trust his fellow voidstalker all that much, especially the way she flirted and tussled with him.

Who behaved like that on a mission?

* * *

The mag-train pulled into the station, gliding to a graceful halt on an electromagnetic rail extending from the superstructure of the sky-high tower. The doors opened and people flowed out, then they stayed open so people could flow in.

It was close to standing room only, and the fact that some people had bags made it worse. A woman in a tacky dress had a sports satchel slung over both shoulders, while someone else had a giant rucksack as if he were going camping. Everyone else just tried to create some space for themselves as the doors shut and the mag-train began to move.

As the mag-train picked up speed, the woman in the tacky dress calmly pulled out a nozzle from her bag. A few quizzical glances were cast her way as she primed the nozzle and pulled the trigger, spraying a highly pressurised gas like fine mist into the crowd. The other commuters coughed and spluttered, covering their eyes to protect them from the acrid gas.

Then the coughing turned to screaming.

The commuters began to see things. Monsters riding the mag-train along with them. Their worst fears made manifest wafting about in the cramped carriage. Leering demonic visages smeared across the faces of their fellow travellers. The very air in front of them bending and warping as if reality itself were being squeezed out of shape.

They turned on each other, the gas reducing them to the mental state of frightened animals, and they lashed out as animals do, turning the carriage into the scene of a bloody brawl. Other commuters were overcome with fear and beat their hands against the glass, desperate to escape the horrible visions they were seeing.

So efficient was the emergency alert system that a first responder team was already waiting for the mag-train at the next stop. Reports of a large commotion and possible chemical hazard sped through the system, and the response teams were prepared with hazmat equipment. They weren't prepared for what spilt out of the mag-train when the doors opened.

The passengers poured out onto the platform, screaming and howling in a pandemonic chorus of fury and fear, surging forwards like a tidal wave towards the emergency responders. They were still under the influence of the gas, and to their minds, the first responders were a pack of beasts wearing Human faces.

Security drones opened fire, dropping psychotic commuters with shock-darts to protect the beleaguered first responders. Even with backup from the drones, the first responders were nearly overwhelmed, and at the end of it, a hundred people were injured and a dozen were dead, including a female commuter in a tacky dress who had been trampled in the stampede.

* * *

Crystal Plaza was a cavernous hub of shopping centres, entertainment clubs, traditional restaurants, immersive-hologram movie theatres, and indoor theme parks. It was by far the largest entertainment complex in Asgard City, catering to a million visitors per day – precisely the reason it was targeted.

A handsome shopper dressed in a smart-looking outfit, entered the plaza with a duffle bag slung over his shoulder. Some people noticed him drop the bag on the ground and open it up, but most were too busy shopping to pay him any mind, even after he pressed a button on his wrist-top computer.

From inside the bag, several drones took flight, the buzzing of their fan-powered engines arresting the attention of the chattering crowds. They swooped down and skimmed low over the heads of the startled shoppers, spraying a misty white gas over them as they flew past. The panicking shoppers coughed and spluttered – then the real panic began.

Thousands of people descended into mass-psychosis at once. Hundreds tried to flee, tripping and stumbling over each other to escape what they were seeing and hearing, while hundreds of others turned on each other like savages. The entire ground floor of the plaza became a free-for-all of terror and violence.

First responders and riot control units arrived on the scene quickly. As soon as they were through the doors, however, they were faced by hundreds of demented casualties and terrified bystanders who, perversely, were both victims to be treated and threats to be neutralised. The first responders scrambled to safety behind the riot control teams, who barely had time to deploy their shields before the tidal wave crashed into them.

The riot teams were safe in their body armour, but they were badly outnumbered and were forced to fight a pitched battle against the very people they were meant to be helping. The crowd rippled and surged like a single writhing mass, beating and kicking and throwing themselves at the phalanx of riot officers, heedless of injury to themselves, let alone others.

Airborne security drones began neutralising targets with shock-darts, but there were thousands of rioters and the drones barely put a dent in the unhinged hordes. Judicious use of shock-sticks gave way to bludgeoning as the riot teams slowly regained the initiative, pushing back the waves of drugged assailants by being as brutally violent as they were.

Several waves of reinforcements later, the riot control teams finally managed to contain and neutralise the mobs. Thousands of people had been affected by the gas and thousands more caught up in the mayhem that followed. The sheer size of Crystal Plaza and the sheer number of affected people meant that it would take a full day to contain the situation.

The clean-up operation would take even longer, not just treating and curing the crazed casualties, but decontaminating the area, and collecting forensic evidence from the drones which had self-destructed. The authorities also had to collect and count the dead, one of whom was a handsome man in a smart outfit, caked in his own blood.

* * *

'Crisis' was not a word that got used very often in the DNI, but there was no other word available. This was clearly an organised string of attacks, using a novel method of attack, and executed within the span of an hour. In each case, a lone culprit had entered a public place and released a toxic gas, causing those exposed to experience hallucinations and psychosis.

The first responders, including Asgard Civil Security, had done an admirable job of containing the situation, and the Directorate had managed to synthesise and mass-produce an antidote to the toxin. However, the fatality count was in the double digits, and the total number of wounded was climbing into the thousands.

All public venues were closed by emergency directive, and since people were too afraid to travel by mag-train, the sky-taxis were overloaded by people trying to get home. For the rest of the day, commerce on the planet ground to a halt. The whole thing was a disaster, a deviously well-orchestrated disaster, and would keep the civilian authorities busy for months.

For the DNI, the worst thing was the lack of intelligence, coming as it did shortly after the disastrous double-raid on Dr Shelton's clinic and apartment. An entire branch of the Directorate was devoted to nothing but the mass-collection and analysis of electronic data, and yet there had been no suspicious intercept or warning signs.

Strangest of all, there were no claims of responsibility. No grandiose speech delivered via hijacked data feeds, no online manifesto, nothing to indicate a motive. Three people had turned up out of nowhere and killed dozens of people for no apparent reason, and only one of them had been taken alive.

* * *

The interrogation room was state-of-the-art, but the dark and dingy appearance was meant to evoke desolation and despair, a black pit of hell from which the only hope of escape was cooperation. The suspect was dragged in and placed into the chair in the centre, the straps locking automatically around his body. Once he was restrained, the operatives left the room, sealing the door behind them.

The prisoner was silent. The effects of the hallucinogenic gas had long since worn off, but his head was throbbing long after the fact, even though the horrible leering image of his father had faded from his mind. The chamber was chilling in more ways than one, but what he had experienced on the floor of the train station was worse than any of his nightmares, and he would rather die in this dungeon than go through it again.

He knew that he had failed, having made it to the arrivals hall only to be intercepted at the moment of execution. He had hoped to poison thousands of hapless travellers and instead had exposed a handful of Civil Security agents. What he didn't know

– and had no way of knowing – was whether the others had succeeded, a fact which the interrogators would no doubt exploit to get him to talk.

The interrogator had been waiting in the shadows the whole time, and after standing and watching the prisoner for a while, he approached. His face and form remained concealed by the darkness as he pulled out a light and flashed it in the prisoner's face. The prisoner blinked and squinted in discomfort, but otherwise refused to react.

"The ultra-silent type," the interrogator sneered with a shark-like grin, "you're a rarity in my line of work, and a lot more fun to break."

The prisoner remained silent.

"Don't worry," the interrogator said almost reassuringly, "you don't have to tell me anything just yet. But there are some things you might want *me* to tell you, and not the mundane sorts of things like 'where am I' or 'where's my legal representative.'"

The prisoner stared up at the interrogator, his lips completely sealed.

"Not curious at all?" the interrogator sneered, "so you're not interested in hearing about just how completely and utterly you and your comrades failed?"

The prisoner's face twitched ever so slightly but otherwise remained impassive.

"I saw that twitch," the interrogator said with a grin, "but I'm afraid it's true: you were the only one who came sort-of close to completing your mission. Everybody else is either dead or sitting in a dark little box like the one you're in now. Not a single one of them got close to releasing their gas payloads."

The prisoner kept his composure.

"Oh, and if that wasn't pathetic enough, we managed to synthesise an antidote for the toxin that you used," the interrogator continued smugly, "the officers you poisoned have made full recoveries, as did you when we gave you the antidote. Whatever you thought you could've achieved with this plan, you failed epically."

Still, the prisoner didn't utter a peep.

"And after all the trouble you went to just to fulfil your part of the plan," the interrogator mocked, "the custom-manufactured drone with the serial numbers removed from the various parts – all of which we traced, anyway – the haircut and the drop-dying of your eyes. That's an awful lot of effort to put into such an epic failure; it does make me wonder who would put you up to something like this and why."

The interrogator paused and fixed his shark-like sneer on the prisoner's face, looking for signs of his resolve weakening.

There were none.

"So embarrassed by your failure you don't want to talk about it? I understand," the interrogator taunted, "Unless, of course, you're hoping that I'm lying as part of some ploy to get you to talk. I'm afraid not; I don't need to lie to you to make you talk."

The interrogator swiped a control on his wrist-top computer. A pair of dish-shaped panels descended from the ceiling and positioned themselves on either side of the prisoner's head, emitting a sinister glow as they activated.

"An ingenious chemical, that toxin you used," said the interrogator as he slowly turned a holographic dial, "a psychotropic compound that induces hallucinations and intense fear, but the effect it produces is nothing compared to the effect of this device."

The prisoner began to hear a ringing sound emanating from inside his own head, and the more he listened, the more he felt a rising tide of disorientation overwhelm him. The walls of the room were too dark to see, but the space in front of him seemed to bend and warp before his eyes as if reality itself was starting to lose coherence. It was just like the sensations induced by the gas, but far worse.

"YOU ARE MINE," the interrogator boomed, his eyes imbued with a demonic glow, and his voice reverberating through the prisoner's mind, "AND YOU WILL TELL ME EVERY-THING YOU KNOW."

The prisoner began to scream.

THE REVELATION

RED-EYE knew that statistically speaking, an event like this was inevitable. No matter how much data and intelligence was collected, and no matter how many proverbial eyes and ears in however many nooks and crannies of the galaxy, it was impossible to be completely sure that you knew everything – and what you didn't know could strike without warning.

That explanation wouldn't satisfy the people she was about to brief. The great and the good of the city would all want to know what had happened, how soon things would go back to normal, and what the Directorate was doing about it. She could answer the third question, but not the first two, mainly because the Directorate itself still didn't know.

She wouldn't be using the Q-comm. chamber. That chamber had been built specifically for communication with her fellow directors-general as well as the Masterminds. In any case, everyone who would be joining the teleconference was planet-side, either in Asgard City itself or in one of the satellite settlements. A simple virtual reality setup would suffice.

Red-eye put on the VR headset and waited patiently for the encrypted connection to be established. Once the connection was complete, the immersive image of a plain conference room fizzled into view with each of the participants seated around a circular table.

"What's the latest?" one of the councillors asked, "that you can tell us, of course."

"The total casualty count is sixty dead and over 1500 injured," Red-eye replied in a calm and clinical tone, "three of the dead were the attackers."

"How do you know they were the attackers?" someone else demanded.

"Security footage and the fact that they all had gas-dispersion equipment concealed in their baggage," Red-eye responded.

"So they didn't have time to put on gas masks?"

"No gas masks or chemical protective gear of any kind were found on the persons of the attackers," Red-eye corrected, "they spread this gas in crowded spaces knowing that they would be exposed to it as well."

"Why would they deliberately expose themselves to their own gas?"

"Most likely a determination not to be taken alive," Red-eye surmised.

"Do we know anything about why they did this?" someone else asked.

"Unfortunately, we don't have any information on their motives," Red-eye conceded.

"How could this have slipped under the DNI's notice?!" someone else exclaimed.

Any of the other teleconferencers' faces would burn bright with humiliation if they had to deliver the truthful answer from Red-eye's position:

"The Directorate doesn't know yet."

The keyword 'yet' barely registered.

"The DNI…doesn't know," someone stammered in sheer disbelief.

"Intelligence takes time to gather," Red-eye reminded the teleconferencers.

"The fact that you didn't have it in the first place is the problem here!"

"We are working as quickly and efficiently as possible," Red-eye explained calmly, "but there is little else to report after less than a day of investigation."

"Is it true that you captured one of the attackers?" somebody asked.

"Haven Civil Security did indeed apprehend one of the three," Red-eye responded, then added less than truthfully, "but he died of complications resulting from his exposure to the toxin shortly after being taken into custody."

"What about this Dr Shelton character?" one of the city councillors asked.

"Dr Mortimer Shelton remains the prime suspect in these attacks," Red-eye answered, omitting the fact that he was an ex-DNI scientist, "as of now, he remains at large."

"What about sweeping the Undercity for Shelton or other suspects," another councillor asked breathlessly, "have you done that yet?"

"Civilian law enforcement is the responsibility of the ACS," Red-eye reminded him coolly, "and they are already doing exactly that–"

"Well, why aren't you helping them?" demanded someone else.

"We *are* helping," Red-eye replied icily, "far more than your mewling is."

The teleconferencers fell silent. It wasn't her words so much as the razor-sharp edge of her voice that silenced them. The veneer of mutual respect, the pretence that everyone seated around the virtual table held a more or less equal share of power, was briefly punctured. At the end of the day, she wasn't answerable to any of them. In fact, there was no one on this planet to whom she was answerable.

"If he hasn't already," Red-eye continued, "the Director of Civil Security will shortly be briefing you on the public security measures taken in case of follow-up attacks. As for your private security, I am sure that you can all arrange that for yourselves."

The response was another round of silence. No one was going to contradict the Director-General of Naval Intelligence.

"In the meantime, I have an investigation to oversee."

With those perfunctory words, Red-eye terminated her link to the teleconference.

* * *

The boom echoed throughout the apartment along with a fizzle of electronic disruption. Aster lay on the floor of the living room where she had dived for cover, immobile from shock. Only when the children came running over did she get up and hug them close, making sure that the most important people in the cosmos to her were safe.

They stayed like that for the longest time, but after a tense wait, nothing else happened. Aster felt she should know better by now, but curiosity motivated her to look.

The android that had picked up the parcel lay crumpled in a heap on the floor, having sacrificed itself to save the family. Its rubbery skin had been scorched away, exposing the metal exoskeleton underneath. But strangely, there was no debris in the hallway and no scorch marks on the walls or any other signs of an explosion.

There had been no explosion.

"What happened, mommy?" Leo asked, crouching beside his siblings.

"I don't know," Aster replied, just as bewildered and fearful.

As the family stared nervously at the disabled android, the package lifted itself out of the android's embrace. It was an autonomous drone shaped like a flat-screen viewer, yet able to move about on a set of spider-like legs.

"Get back into the room, now!" Aster ordered the children.

As the children scrambled to safety, the walking drone clambered off of the disabled android and onto the carpet where it turned to face the living room door. A tiny sensor at the top flash-scanned Aster's eyes and a holographic video image fizzled into view. It was the image of a man with grey hair, steel-grey eyes, and a silver moustache.

"*Aster Thorn,*" said the man on the screen, "*you don't know me, but Gabriel does; in fact, I've known him for longer than you have. My name is Dr Mortimer Shelton, formerly of the Directorate of Naval Intelligence. Specifically, I was head of genomics research in what we call the 'Rand Block', the research and development block.*"

"Why the fuck would I believe anything you say!" Aster yelled at the device.

"*Because you have no choice,*" the image of Mortimer Shelton replied.

Aster blinked in surprise.

"*This is a variable-response program which can answer a limited number of questions,*" Shelton's image explained, "*it will interact with you to a limited degree.*"

"Fine, why did you try to kill me and my family?" Aster demanded.

"*The explosion was a high-frequency electromagnetic discharge to disable electronics,*" the Shelton hologram replied, "*this device is also equipped with garbler-tech: all incoming and outgoing signals are being jammed for as long as this device is active.*"

Aster was silent, agonising over whether to get help or continue listening.

"*If you've received this package, then something significant has happened,*" Mortimer Shelton continued, "*it's highly unlikely that the Directorate has seen fit to tell you the truth about the programme of which your husband is an integral part, so listen carefully.*"

* * *

The ship lurched. Ships weren't supposed to lurch while travelling through Q-space, and yet the Krakenscourge did so violently and without warning. Klaxons sounded and the corridors were illuminated with blood-red warning lights as the ship's quantum wavefront was disrupted, forcing it back into real space.

There was a frantic response as the crew worked feverishly to bring the ship back under control. If catastrophe did strike, everyone aboard would surely die. They were in an unknown pocket of interstellar space with no backup, no ability to communicate with Human space, and no nearby planets to be stranded on. No one back home would know where or how they had died, only that they had never returned.

The crew was too disciplined to think about any of that. If they dwelt on the horrible fate that might await them, it was as good as accepting that fate. The best thing they could do was stick to their training and keep the ship intact and functional.

The two voidstalkers bolted from their shared quarters, dressed in stripped-down versions of their regular uniforms. Aetherea was faster, sprinting down corridors and skidding around corners like a relay runner as Gabriel tried to keep up, hampered by his still-healing leg wound. They had no technical expertise to offer the crew, but all the officers needed to be together for the crisis.

The doors to the bridge opened automatically as Gabriel and Aetherea careened into the room. Paradoxically, the bridge was an oasis of calm, the red warning lights were softer and the klaxons were quieter. No one wanted the bridge crew to be distracted by blaring sirens and bright lights as they guided the ship.

The bridge was fishbowl-shaped, with individual data booths ringing the edge of the room. Each occupant was immersed in an array of interactive holographic displays with real-time data feeds running in ordered streams across the screens. No one saluted as the two ranking officers entered – there were more important things to worry about.

"We've been caught," Captain Ironside informed the two voidstalkers, his calm tone and laconic summary belying the seriousness of the situation.

"What do you mean 'caught'?" Gabriel asked, dreading the answer.

"Besides the obvious fact that the ship has been forced out of Q-space," Aetherea added.

"Take a look," said Ironside, gesturing to the main screen.

It was one thing for the danger to be close enough for a clear image, it was entirely another to see the hive-ship they had been pursuing dominating the screen. In fact, it was actually facing them, staring them down like some gigantic sea monster eyeing a minnow.

"How are the ship's systems?" Aetherea asked.

"The engineers are still checking the Q-engine," Ironside said gravely, "but all other systems seem to be ok, including shielding and weapons."

"And stealth?" Gabriel asked.

"Stupid question, given the situation," Aetherea remarked.

Only the possible truth of the point prevented Gabriel from snapping back at his fellow voidstalker. He restricted himself to a brief sideways glare.

"All stealth systems appear to still be functional," Ironside reported, pretending not to have noticed, "or so engineering reports."

"Then it's possible the hive-ship hasn't actually detected us," Gabriel answered, "even if they know we're nearby."

"I should hope so," Ironside replied, "otherwise, we're as good as dead."

As soon as he spoke those words, one of the screens lit up with a warning message.

"What is that?" Ironside demanded.

"A data transmission," a technician replied, "it's coming from the tracking probe, but the encryption is corrupted."

Confusion and dread combined in everyone's minds. Corrupted encryption meant that some third party was trying to force unauthorised data through the tracking probe's systems. The hive-ship had clearly discovered the tracking probe and therefore knew the Krakenscourge was nearby. On the other hand, the fact that the hive-ship was trying to contact them instead of destroying them was puzzling, to say the least.

"What kind of transmission?" Ironside asked, gesturing quietly to the weapons officer.

"It's a message," the technician replied, "displaying the translation now."

The deciphered message from their erstwhile quarry appeared on the screen.

'*Why do you pursue us?*' read the message.

The bridge was silent. What were they supposed to say in response? Would a wrong answer get them killed? Why didn't the hive-ship just open fire and be done with it?

"Well," Aetherea said, turning to Gabriel, "I think you're best placed to answer that."

Gabriel hesitated. This was a valuable chance to learn more about the Hive-dwellers' agenda, but it could also be a ploy to give the hive-ship time to pin down the Krakenscourge's exact location. The fact that they had been forced out of Q-space didn't mean that their location had been exposed...as long as they didn't give themselves away.

Gabriel decided to take the gamble.

"Ask them the following:" Gabriel instructed, "'what is your interest in the Swarm?'"

The technician typed in the message and fed it to the computers to translate into the original data format, then transmit it back to the hive-ship.

Everyone waited with bated breath. If the original transmission really was a ploy to get the Krakenscourge to reveal its location, then Gabriel had just doomed the ship.

"We have a reply!" announced the technician, unable to conceal his relief that the 'reply' was not in the form of a weapon-strike.

'*That is no concern of yours*,' read the blunt reply.

"Ask them if they comprehend the danger of the Swarm," Gabriel ordered.

The technician duly typed in the message.

"What exactly are you hoping to get out of this?" Aetherea asked, keeping her voice low so that only the three senior officers could hear.

"Intelligence," Gabriel replied, "we are intelligence agents, after all."

"Here comes the reply," the technician announced.

'*It bestows knowledge beyond the comprehension of disconnected minds such as yours,*' the message read, the imperious tone clear enough.

The bridge crew stared at the message confused, wondering whether something had been lost in translation. Gabriel wasn't confused at all and didn't need to parse out the cryptic phrasing of the message to guess its meaning. In fact, he felt a horrible, leaden weight drop in his stomach as he read it.

"They've been enthralled…" Gabriel said ominously.

"Receiving another message," the technician announced.

'*Your minds are disconnected, and smaller for it,*' the follow-up message declared dramatically, '*Ever closer integration of minds shall bring ever greater ascendance, a process accelerated by that which you call the 'Swarm'.*'

"How much firepower can we bring to bear?" Gabriel asked Ironside.

"Seriously?" Aetherea hissed, "You want to go head-to-head with them?"

"There is the main gun," Ironside replied, "it won't destroy or cripple the hive-ship, but it can definitely pack a damaging punch, and it can pass through shielding."

"Power it up," Gabriel ordered.

"Another message from the hive-ship," announced the technician.

'*Cease your pursuit,*' the message commanded, '*or risk destruction.*'

"Q-space event!" someone yelled, "A massive one! Behind the hive-ship!"

"They're trying to get away!" Gabriel exclaimed, jumping into a spare data booth as Ironside got into the command chair, "battle stations, now!"

"What?!" Aetherea exclaimed in disbelief.

"Distance to target: 1000km approx.!" someone shouted.

"Ragnarok cannon at 10% charge!" the weapons technician announced.

Aetherea jumped into a spare data booth on the opposite side of the command chair, suppressing her palpable disagreement for the sake of shipboard discipline.

"30% charge!"

"The hive-ship is turning! It's going to do a fall-dive!"

"Do we have a plan here?!" Aetherea demanded to know.

"Inflict as much damage as possible!" Gabriel shot back.

"50% charge!"

The main screen was still displaying images, and behind the hive-ship's outline, an orb of pure gloom formed, seeming to devour the few points of stellar light around it. The leviathan starship turned in a sweeping arc away from the Krakenscourge as the sheer strength of the Q-rift's gravity caused the hive-ship to fall towards it.

"70% charge!"

"Gun the engines!" Gabriel ordered, "We'll strafe the hull length-ways!"

Compared to the hive-ship, the Krakenscourge was little more than a spaceborne gnat, and the Hive-dweller dreadnought didn't even react as the tiny warship swooped in. As the hive-ship turned its bulk sideways, the Krakenscourge came around in a sweeping arc for an attack-run along the length of its hull.

"90% charge!"

"You're about to get us all killed," Aetherea muttered.

Only Ironside and Gabriel heard her, but they both had the dread-filled feeling that she was about to be proven right.

"100% charge! Max power diverted to the cannon!"

"Fire!"

The Ragnarok cannon was a magnetically-accelerated particle beam weapon that ran the length of the Krakenscourge's superstructure. When it fired, it released a stream of ionised particles accelerated to near the speed of light. The Krakenscourge swooped in towards the hive-ship as it fired, keeping the beam firing for exactly five seconds as it strafed down the length of the hive-ship's hull.

The thin beam of concentrated energy struck with the force of a low-yield nuclear device, slicing through the hive-ship's hull like a scalpel through paper. The beam cut through countless bulkheads with ease, superheating the metal edges well past their melting point, and destroying whatever it touched.

A horizontal streak of light and flame marked the path of destruction as the beam ignited and devoured the oxygen-rich atmosphere within, only to be snuffed out again by the void. Any Hive-dwellers in the affected areas were vaporised instantly, and any survivors in the adjacent bulkheads suffocated or burnt to death.

After its brief attack-run, the Krakenscourge disengaged from the fight and sped away into interstellar space. All they could hope was that a single strike from the particle beam had inflicted enough damage to weaken the target. If it did come down to a protracted fight, the Krakenscourge would almost certainly lose.

The hive-ship fired back.

An ultraviolet beam cut through space to reach its target, hitting the Krakenscourge with near-perfect precision. It passed straight through the shields and boiled away a layer of ablative paint in a cloud of superhot vapour. The beam continued on, cutting straight into the outer hull, melting and mangling 18 inches worth of starship-grade alloy, and exposing the bulkhead to such extreme heat that everything inside melted into goo.

The localised burst of extreme heat also destroyed one of the power conduits, causing it to explode in spectacular fashion, and showering a passing crewmember with sparks and fire. When several crewmembers ran to his aid, they were hit by the overpowering stench of burning circuitry and scorched flesh.

Horrified by his injuries but determined to save his life, they tried to treat his burns whilst someone else battled the electrical fire with an extinguisher. The explosion had burnt through his clothing, and they couldn't tear it away without tearing away parts of his skin. Nonetheless, they managed to stabilise him enough to get him to the medical bay.

The Krakenscourge barrel-rolled in a crude attempt to confuse the hive-ship's targeting sensors then gunned its engines and escaped into the void. The hive-ship continued its fall-dive back into Q-space, not even deigning to follow-up with a second strike.

The particle beam had left a visible scar along the length of the hive-ship, but whatever damage the Krakenscourge had inflicted wasn't enough to force it to abort its fall-dive. The Q-rift was still raging, a reality-warping maw that drew the hive-ship further and further inwards. The vessel kept on turning, its nose dipping into the Q-rift and diving into the darkness until there was no trace that it had ever been there.

* * *

Aster sat on the bed, cradling baby Emerald close to her chest as her other four children huddled around her. The conscience-wrenching dilemma between curiosity and common-sense had finally been resolved. Once the Shelton hologram had finished divulging everything it had to offer, the tablet had self-destructed. Assuming any of it should be believed, it had revealed things she would rather not have learned.

Worse still, her children had listened to everything.

"Mommy?" Orion asked tentatively, "what did the man mean when he called daddy 'one of the Directorate's greatest creations'?"

Mortimer Shelton – whoever he really was – had followed up that description by saying that their children were a 'continuation of the original project.'

"I don't know," Aster replied weakly, "I don't understand any of this anymore."

Aster suppressed her sobs, not wanting to distress her children, but it was a hard act to pull off, and it didn't work. Tears began to roll down their cheeks, and even Orion's eyes started to turn red. The family huddled closer together, seeking comfort in each other's presence, with only the sleeping Emerald completely unaware of what was going on.

Aster had never regretted leaving behind the frontier world where she had grown up. Asgard was a paradise by comparison, with lavish comfort and incredible prosperity, and she had never regretted coming to this planet until now.

It seemed selfish even to think such a thing. All of her children had been born and raised on this planet, and regretting coming here seemed tantamount to regretting their existence. Even so, in building a life here in one of the hearts of government power, she had effectively chosen to put down roots in a nest of conspiratorial vipers.

And then there was Gabriel. What exactly was she supposed to make of what Mortimer Shelton had told her about him? A morbidly curious part of her had always wondered what it was he got up to when he was away, but now she had a description in her head of how he had ended up this way. Gabriel had served in the military and the intelligence services throughout his working life, and it beggared belief that he didn't already know about this.

Of course, it was possible that this Mortimer Shelton character was lying. This person who claimed to be acquainted with Gabriel had sent not one but two covert packages to the family home, but that didn't mean that he was who he said he was. It certainly didn't mean that any of what he'd said was true.

The doorbell rang.

Still cradling Emerald, Aster went straight to the armoured closet and swiped her thumb across the biometric pad. The doors opened, revealing the maganiel android within.

The hibernating maganiel was faceless, with two narrow slits for eyes and a vocaliser under the chin. It was Human-sized and had been painted jet black except for the model name 'Maganiel' emblazoned in white letters on its chest. Aster wrapped her knuckles against its forehead, causing its eyes to light up electric blue as it awakened. Inclining its head towards Aster, it looked into her eyes and flash-scanned them to confirm her identity.

"*Greetings, Aster Thorn,*" said the maganiel, speaking in a digitised voice without any emotional inflexions, "*Maganiel Mark V online. How may I be of service?*"

Before Aster could respond, an alarm sounded. It was the intrusion alarm, triggered in the event someone managed to bypass the front door lock.

"Personal protection for the family!" Aster blurted out frantically, "danger close!"

"*Understood,*" the maganiel drone said politely, reaching into the closet and retrieving a sidearm, "*Seven protectees. Danger close. Lethal force.*"

Footsteps could be heard in the hallway, and Aster took cover with the children as the maganiel advanced towards the door with its sidearm raised, shutting the door and locking it. Whoever the intruders were, they evidently heard the door shut, and their footsteps could be heard approaching the bedroom.

A whining sound was heard on the other side of the door as the lock was deactivated. With reactions quicker than a Human could manage, the maganiel yanked open the door and shoved the barrel of its gun into the face of one of the intruders.

"Woah! Woah!" the intruder shouted, "We're Directorate agents, stand down!"

"*Please state your name and purpose,*" the maganiel asked, its polite tone contrasting bizarrely with the menacing firearm it was pressing against the man's forehead.

"We're here to make sure the Thorn family is safe," another voice replied.

While still holding the intruder at gunpoint, the maganiel flash-scanned his eyes, then looked over his shoulder and flash-scanned his companion's eyes. Aster and the children hid on the other side of the bed in fearful silence as the maganiel processed the results.

"*Agent Bell, Agent Lynch, greetings*," the maganiel confirmed.

"Dr Aster Thorn," one of the agents called out, "are you and the children alright?"

Aster was frozen stiff with indecision. The maganiel didn't consider the intruders to be a threat because they were Directorate agents, but that didn't make her feel any safer.

"Dr Thorn," the agent repeated, "we're with the Directorate, whatever you were hiding from, the coast is clear. You can come out."

"*This unit has confirmed their identities*," the maganiel added for good measure.

Slowly and reluctantly, Aster poked her head out.

The agent was poking his head around the corner whilst the maganiel stood patiently to one side, keeping its gaze fixed on the agent and his companion.

"A suspicious package was redirected to your home, but we weren't able to intercept it before it arrived so we rushed over to make sure you were ok," the agent explained.

"We're all fine, thanks," Aster answered.

"Good," the agent replied, "a forensics team is on its way to take a look at what's left of the package, but in the meantime, we need you to come back in for a debriefing."

"I'm not going anywhere," Aster shot back defiantly.

"I'm afraid it's not optional, especially in light of the recent attacks."

"What recent attacks?" Aster asked.

"Haven't you been watching the news?"

"No…I haven't…" Aster replied falteringly.

"We'll explain," the agent replied, "but first you need to come with us."

"Will Dr Galton be there?" Aster asked.

"Who?" the agent asked, confused.

"Dr Francis Galton, Chief of Research for the Voidstalker Programme," Aster replied, "I want to speak to him about his predecessor, Dr Mortimer Shelton."

The agent ducked back behind the corner and spoke to his colleague.

"In case you're wondering, Mortimer Shelton is the one who sent the package!" Aster called out towards the hallway.

The agent reappeared with a look of alarm on his face.

"Really? How do you know?" he asked.

"Because the package was a tablet computer with a set of pre-recorded messages from him," Aster answered, seeing no point in hiding anything, "that's how I know about Dr Galton and the Voidstalker Programme."

"…We definitely need you to come back in for a debriefing," the agent said.

"Will Dr Galton be there?" Aster demanded to know.

"I can't guarantee that," the agent replied.

"Then I can't guarantee that I'll come in," Aster said defiantly.

"This isn't a negotiation, Dr Thorn," the agent said, getting exasperated.

"Damn fucking right, it's not!" Aster snapped angrily, "This is the second unauthorised package that's slipped under the Directorate's nose and into my home, and after what I learned, I want to speak to Dr Francis Galton about it. If you can't guarantee that I'll get a face-to-face meeting with him, then you can fuck off!"

The agent was silent in the face of the outburst. He disappeared into the hall, exchanged some tense words with his colleague, and then reappeared in the bedroom doorway.

"We don't really pull that kind of rank," he replied, "but we'll see what we can do."

* * *

The three senior officers headed to the Krakenscourge's planning room ostensibly to decide the ship's next move. They kept their composure all the way there, even as an icy silence froze the corridors in their wake. Two of them were seething with pent-up anger and the third was dreading his impending role as mediator between his two superior officers.

As soon as the doors shut, the shouting started.

"What were you thinking back there?!" Aetherea demanded furiously.

"About how to stop the Hive-dwellers from getting away!" Gabriel snapped back.

"You almost got the ship destroyed and everyone onboard killed!" Aetherea shouted in response, "that was reckless and stupid!"

"Like blowing up an entire chunk of the Nexus for the sake of an easy escape route?!" Gabriel retorted furiously.

"Don't try to shove a false analogy done my throat," Aetherea countered, "the lives of the people aboard this ship – including yours and mine – matter a lot more than the structural integrity of some alien space station!"

"The lives of over a hundred billion people across Human space could be in danger!" Gabriel shouted in response, "I think that trumps all other considerations!"

The two voidstalkers glowered at each other.

"The ship took some hull damage," Ironside announced, seizing on the lull to change the subject, "but it's little more than a flesh wound."

"We can't say the same for the crewman who got hit," Aetherea noted darkly.

"His condition has stabilised," Ironside answered, "he'll survive."

"What about stealth?" Gabriel asked.

"The various stealth features are either part of the hull or inside it," Ironside replied, then added, "but in light of our most recent encounter, we can't guarantee that the hive-ship hasn't compromised that stealth."

There was another round of cool silence. The tensed-up look on Aetherea's face made it clear that she wanted to blame Gabriel for that too.

"If they found the tracking probe embedded in the hull or detected the signals it was sending through Q-space," Gabriel pondered, "that would explain how they knew we were following them without actually detecting the ship."

"Either way," Ironside replied, "we've lost track of the hive-ship."

"Depending on how much damage it suffered, it'll have to stop somewhere for repairs," Gabriel concluded, "in the meantime, our own ship is intact."

"I hope you don't think that justifies that suicidal attack-run," Aetherea said acidly, "we were lucky to survive that glancing blow."

"So what next?" Ironside asked, then added acerbically, "assuming the two ranking officers can resolve their differences."

This time, Captain Ironside fixed a glowering gaze on his two superiors, making clear that the real problem was between the two of them.

"The Swarm isn't just some arcane piece of alien nanotechnology," Gabriel explained, turning deadly serious, "it's an intelligence in its own right, an extremely ancient intelligence that means us nothing but harm."

"'Therefore we need to stop the Hive-dwellers from using it'," Aetherea pre-empted him dismissively, "you've already covered that."

"The Swarm is the one using them," Gabriel countered.

"If that's supposed to mean something," Ironside said, "now is the time to explain."

Gabriel fell into silence, the explanation caught in his throat. The observer had provided him with an unvarnished explanation, followed by a dire warning about the nature of the Swarm. If such information were to be given a classification level, it would be tier I.

However, he couldn't keep them in the dark any longer. Despite being an old friend, Ironside wouldn't take the ship into the unknown purely based on some vague sense of purpose. Meanwhile, Aetherea's irreverent veneer of superiority had slipped away. She was clearly dead set against going any further without being told why.

"The thing we've been calling the 'Swarm'," Gabriel explained ominously, "is only a tiny fragment of a much larger entity."

* * *

It was a short ride in an armoured sky-car to reach the Spire. Apparently, Dr Galton had agreed to meet with Aster but had asked that she bring one of her children with her. Reluctantly, Aster had decided to bring Orion along for the ride, leaving the rest of the children under the watchful guardianship of the maganiel android.

Orion was unusually quiet. He sat beside his mother, playing a puzzle game on his flexi-tablet all the way to the Spire, but at least he had something to distract him. Aster wished she could distract herself so easily, but she couldn't. The words of the Shelton hologram wouldn't leave her mind, and the apprehension she felt wouldn't subside.

Aster wondered whether Dr Galton, whoever he turned out to be, would or could tell her anything else about the Voidstalker Programme. Indeed, now that she thought about it, from the Directorate's perspective she already knew too much. At best, this would turn into another standard debriefing about what had happened. At worst, she was going to be treated like another security leak to be contained.

The sky-car arrived, alighting on a docking platform as the side door opened up. Aster climbed out of the sky-car and Orion jumped out after her, clutching his flexi-tablet to his chest as the two agents led them through security.

Once security had cleared them, Aster and Orion were led down a corridor and into a meeting room where two people were waiting. One was a burly Directorate operative, and the other was dressed in a researcher's uniform and had a greying, grandfatherly beard.

Aster recognised the second person immediately.

"You're Dr Francis Galton," Aster said, pointing at the researcher.

"Indeed," Dr Galton replied, "although, the teams responsible for information control were quite alarmed that you knew my name, and they'll be even more alarmed to find out that you know what I look like."

"You said that this package was a tablet computer sent to you by Mortimer Shelton, correct?" the operative asked.

"That's correct," Aster confirmed.

"I need you to tell me everything that the program told you," the operative ordered.

"Most of it is above and beyond your clearance level, let alone mine," Aster replied coolly, "and most of it is about Dr Galton's work on the Voidstalker Programme."

The operative flinched; Dr Galton didn't.

"I know you want to question me," Aster continued confidently, "but I have questions of my own, and I won't be answering any of yours unless Dr Galton answers mine."

The operative and Dr Galton exchanged glances as Aster watched them, waiting intently for their response while Orion fidgeted in his chair.

"Would you mind excusing us?" Dr Galton asked the operative.

Dr Galton didn't technically have the authority to make him leave, but the operative complied nonetheless, getting out of his chair and exiting the room.

"So," said Dr Galton, "what would you like to know?"

* * *

The Swarm was a danger to all intelligent life in the galaxy.

That was what the observer had told Gabriel, and he recounted the entire story to Aetherea and Ironside, knowing that it would be hard to believe. It was impossible to know how many other fragments of the Swarm were scattered across the galaxy. One fragment had been unearthed by the researchers at the Loki facility, and the Water-skins had found another fragment, only for the Hive-dwellers to take it.

His audience of two were gravely silent throughout his explanation and remained silent after he had finished. Ironside had known Gabriel for many years, and his normally austere face was visibly crinkled by the internal contradiction between trusting Gabriel or his own instincts. Aetherea, on the other hand, could scarcely contain her disbelief.

"You expect us to pursue an alien dreadnought into unknown space, risking possible destruction, based on what some alien AI told you?" Aetherea demanded incredulously.

"What do you think this entire operation has been about?" Gabriel countered, "How do you think we knew what energy signature to look for in the first place? That data came from the observer. So unless you're telling me that you doubt the veracity of the intelligence which *you* provided, that's exactly what I'm saying."

"If I recall, this same alien computer also tricked your squad into splitting up so it could get you to reactivate its systems," Aetherea pointed out.

"All of its actions were directed at defeating the Swarm," Gabriel replied, "the same goes for everything else it has given us."

"How do you know that?!" Aetherea shot back, "in case you've forgotten, one of the crew was just burnt to a crisp thanks to that reckless attack-run you made us launch! You're going to get the rest of us killed!"

"If you're afraid of dying far away from home, you probably shouldn't have been made a voidstalker in the first place," Gabriel said coldly, taking a menacing step towards her.

"Oh, we're going there, are we?" Aetherea replied with a narrow-eyed glare.

"Yes, we are," Gabriel said, baring his teeth in a wolf-like growl.

Ironside quietly put a respectful distance between himself and the two voidstalkers.

"I stayed alive on that station for almost a year by keeping hidden and not taking unnecessary risks," Aetherea said, glaring up at Gabriel with her iridescent sapphire eyes, "your approach would have gotten you killed on the first day."

"This is no longer the time to stay hidden," Gabriel retorted angrily, "the Swarm is aboard the hive-ship, and if we don't destroy it, it could take over the entirety of Hive-dweller civilisation. It might be years or decades down the line, but the resulting threat would be of extinction-level proportions!"

"What the hell is 'extinction-level' supposed to mean?" Aetherea snapped back.

"Think about it!" Gabriel exclaimed, furious that he had to explain any of this, "When the researchers at the Loki facility were enthralled by the Swarm, they became an organised collective under its control. They utilised the resources of the entire facility to create their own little bastion and run sick experiments to improve their technology, ALL based on what the Swarm imparted to them."

"Gabriel, where exactly are you going with this?" Ironside asked.

"Over a thousand researchers, technicians, and security guards were stationed at the Loki facility," Gabriel explained, "They were transformed into a well-organised and fanatical cult, and they scavenged whatever technology and supplies that were available to them. How many Hive-dwellers do you think there are?"

Gabriel paused to allow the answer to sink in: insects reproduced at a phenomenal rate, so the answer had to run into the hundreds of billions.

"Now think about the fact that the Hive-dwellers have technology vastly ahead of our own, and imagine the resources a civilisation like that must have at its disposal," Gabriel continued with dire conviction, "and finally, try to imagine what the Swarm could achieve if it managed to enthral just one hive, let alone every Hive-dweller hive."

There was an ominous and incredulous pause.

"If that comes to pass," Ironside said, shifting towards Gabriel's side, "then in a few decades time, we could have an entire alien civilisation on our doorstep hell-bent on destroying everything around them, including Humanity."

"Hence the phrase 'extinction-level'," Gabriel concluded emphatically.

"This is insane!" Aetherea exploded, "your entire theory is insane!"

"The whole point of voidstalkers is to pre-emptively neutralise threats to Humanity," Gabriel countered, "whether it's a greedy corporation experimenting with alien technology or the alien species itself, whether it's a threat within Human territory or a million light years beyond it! How is any of that unclear?!"

"For the record, I have to say I agree with Gabriel," Ironside said.

"Seriously?!" Aetherea exclaimed, "you actually believe this ridiculous theory?!"

"It may just be a theory, Colonel," Ironside replied firmly, "but if it turns out to be true, then the consequences of sitting on our hands could be cataclysmic."

"Well, if you're putting his theory on the record, you may as well put mine on the record as well," Aetherea said, changing tack and tone.

"Which is?" Gabriel asked with narrowed eyes.

"From what we know, each hive is a distinct social unit, equivalent to a nation-state with its own interests and agenda," Aetherea explained, "so suppose the hive-ship makes it back to its hive and the whole hive gets taken over. Are the other hives going to willingly surrender themselves to enthrallment by the Swarm?"

Now it was Aetherea's turn to pause for effect.

"No," Gabriel answered, recognising her point, "they'd fight back."

"Resulting in a war," Aetherea continued, "a *civil* war. Best case scenario: the Hive-dweller species destroys the single enthralled hive and the Swarm with it, neutralising the problem without us having to lift a finger."

"And the worst case scenario?" Gabriel asked with a sceptical scowl.

"Multiple hives are enthralled by the Swarm, and the un-enthralled hives unite to destroy the alliance of enthralled hives," Aetherea responded, "resulting in an intra-species conflict an order of magnitude larger which would neutralise the threat posed by the Swarm *and* the Hive-dwellers for generations to come, maybe even forever."

"You've got to be joking," Gabriel said in disbelief.

"I assure you, I am not," Aetherea replied, "of course, since you pointed out how alien species are such a massive, latent threat to Humanity, under that logic the best and worst case scenarios are actually the other way around."

"That's not the worst case scenario!" Gabriel snapped at her, "Suppose the Swarm wins this hypothetical civil war and completely enthrals *all* of the hives one after another. *That* is the worst case scenario here: an entire alien civilisation committing all the resources at its disposal to the service of the Swarm. We have one chance, and one chance only, to destroy this monster before it becomes too powerful to stop."

Yet another round of icy silence.

"You have a death wish," Aetherea hissed contemptuously.

"I have a life wish for Humanity," Gabriel countered.

"That's not even a phrase," Aetherea said snarkily.

"It is now," Gabriel shot back, "and if my death or the death of everyone on this ship is necessary to ensure life for the Human race, so be it."

"Like I said," Aetherea said coldly, "you have a death wish."

With that, she stormed out of the room.

Gabriel exchanged a look with Ironside. With the captain won over, the deadlock in the chain-of-command had been broken by a two-to-one majority in Gabriel's favour. Even so, it wasn't exactly conducive to shipboard morale to have the two senior officers at odds.

"I'll give the orders to navigation," Ironside said calmly, "but you're the only one who can handle Colonel Starborn."

"I'm not sure anyone can," Gabriel replied.

THE HUNT

KNOWLEDGE is power. It was the oldest axiom of espionage, and yet when it came to the attacks, the Directorate of Naval Intelligence was still distinctly powerless. Had they been complacent and missed vital clues, or would the clues have eluded its massive intelligence dragnet no matter what?

Red-eye sat in the throne-like chair of her office deep in thought. All spare resources had been requisitioned to handle the aftermath of this massive intelligence failure and the various departments were busy pursuing every possible lead. Until they reported back, she passed the time by thinking, trying to solve the puzzle herself.

A philosopher on ancient Earth had once pointed out that if someone had only ever seen white swans, that didn't mean that all swans were white since it would only take the sighting of one black swan to disprove the belief. His broader point was that the fact that a dramatic event had never occurred before was not proof that it could never happen.

The Directorate still had no idea who had orchestrated the terror attacks or why. The fact that they had been literal terror attacks utilising a fear-inducing chemical was a morbidly intriguing detail, one which may – or may not – end up yielding insights.

The one attacker they had captured hadn't responded to conventional interrogation techniques. In fact, he had barely reacted at all until the perceptual distortion device had been applied, and even then it had taken an hour of technologically-assisted torment to finally get him to give up what little he knew.

Asgard's population registry indicated that he was a native of the Undercity with a secondary-level education and an unhappy family background. The official records also indicated that he had died several months ago from an overdose from which the physician had been unable to revive him. His death certificate was marked with the biometric e-signature of the supervising physician: Dr Mortimer Shelton.

The identities of the other attackers had also been exposed, and they had all 'died' months before under similar circumstances with the same e-signature on their death certificates. It was obvious that Shelton had organised their recruitment, just as he was the only suspect with the skills to manufacture the hallucinogenic toxin.

But what could be the end goal? There was nothing in Shelton's own medical history to indicate mental instability; and despite the disagreements which had caused him to resign, the indicators for political radicalism were weak. So if Shelton had recruited the attackers and directed the attacks, who had recruited and directed Shelton?

A theory came right on the heels of the question. That a former Directorate employee like Shelton was on the loose was disturbing enough; that two or more such former operatives might be accomplices or orchestrators was even more ominous.

And why assume that they were former employees? Was there a mole in the Directorate right now, relaying precious intelligence to collaborators on the outside or quietly sabotaging the investigation into the attacks, or both? Was it possible there were several such moles? Who had recruited them in the first place? What could their motivations be?

A chime sounded on Red-eye's desk, interrupting her conspiratorial train of thought. It was a communications request from the operative who had been sent to debrief Dr Thorn. It seemed too good to believe that a new lead had been discovered already, but Red-eye tapped the flashing icon on her screen and established a two-way link.

"*Dr Galton is talking to Dr Thorn right now about the Voidstalker Programme,*" the operative reported, talking at high speed.

Red-eye's hazel-coloured Human eye twitched ever so slightly.

"What?" the lone word was loaded with authoritative menace.

"*I know I'm not authorised to hear about it–*" the operative began.

"Neither is Dr Thorn," Red-eye cut him off icily, "and yet you walked out of the room to allow Dr Galton to divulge what he knows, so I suggest you either stop them right now or provide a very convincing explanation for why you did that."

"*She already knows Dr Galton's name,*" the operative explained hurriedly, "*and she knows about the programme. She told us that all of that information and more was given to her by Mortimer Shelton.*"

Red-eye's demeanour didn't soften, but her mental focus did shift from the operative to the mention of Mortimer Shelton's name.

"How?" the single word was as much a command as it was a question.

The operative explained quickly and clearly about the package that had been sent to the Thorn residence along with what the tablet drone had told Aster Thorn.

"Interesting," Red-eye said, "that still doesn't explain why you left Dr Galton to divulge even more classified information to an unauthorised individual."

"*We're in the Spire...*" the operative began to say, then changed his mind about his choice of words, "*we'll speak to Dr Galton right now.*"

"Yes, you will," Red-eye said with a tone like sharpened steel.

* * *

Gabriel walked down the corridors after Aetherea, following the sound of her footsteps and the occasional sighting of her blonde hair. Just like before, he felt as though she was leading him into another trap; but just like before, he had no choice.

On the one hand, she was right: it was suicidal for the Krakenscourge to go up against the hive-ship. One shot from its laser batteries had struck a glancing blow and sent one of the crew to the medical bay. They couldn't rely on the ship's stealth systems anymore and if they got into a shooting match, the hive-ship would win hands-down.

On the other hand, it was galling having to argue for a direct assault given that she had been happy to send him into harm's way when she felt the situation had called for it. She clearly had no problems with direct assaults as long as other people led the charge. That didn't mean she only cared about her own skin, but what other conclusion was there?

As soon as Gabriel stepped through the medical bay doors, someone dropped down on top of him. In one motion, the figure landed on his shoulders, wrapped her legs around his body, then used gravity and her own body weight to pitch herself forward. Gabriel allowed himself to be flipped head over heels but then used his momentum and core strength to complete the flip and right himself, leaving his attacker on the floor behind him.

"Third time lucky," Aetherea said with a smirk, sitting up on her elbows, "or is that the fourth time? I've actually lost count."

"I didn't come here to joke around," Gabriel said, turning around to face her.

"No," Aetherea replied, her smirk disappearing, "you followed me to convince me that pursuing the white whale will still be worth it, even if it kills us in the end."

Gabriel understood the idiomatic reference, and he narrowed his eyes.

"You think I'm doing this for revenge for what happened on Loki?" he said, bristling, "is that a joke or an insult? Or is it both?"

"It's neither," Aetherea answered, jumping athletically to her feet to face him, "but you're clearly obsessed with going after this Swarm, and the fact that you keep bringing up your mission on Loki is kind of a clue."

Gabriel stood there in stony silence. He knew what she was referencing.

"Of course, you're not supposed to feel much of anything besides anger and the other thing," Aetherea continued casually, "but it's hard to believe that Ogilvy's death doesn't have something to do with it."

"You're getting into dangerous territory," Gabriel said menacingly.

"I've spent almost a year collecting intelligence from inside alien-controlled space," Aetherea replied calmly, "so angering an emotionally repressed first-generation voidstalker doesn't really count as 'dangerous territory' to me."

Gabriel was left seething, and he suspected that was the point.

"Oh, by the way," Aetherea added, "have you had time to check on Ensign Briggs?"

"Who?" Gabriel asked, confused.

"Somehow, I'm not surprised you didn't know his name," Aetherea replied with a note of disgust in her voice, "but he's right here, so let me introduce you."

She turned around and tapped a control on one of the medical stasis units, causing the frosted glass to turn transparent. Gabriel had seen horrible injuries before, but the sight of the person inside the stasis unit struck a very disconcerting nerve.

Ensign Briggs's skin looked like a layer of melted plastic. His hair had been completely singed and his features were barely recognisable through the grisly tapestry of congealed burns that covered his skin. He could barely breathe unassisted, so a pair of respirator tubes had been inserted down his throat directly into his lungs.

He was also naked. Convalescence trumped modesty, and so his only covering was a transparent film across his skin. The underside of the film was coated with a mixture of medical nanobots and artificial microorganisms to regenerate the injured tissue. The visual effect was to make him look like a plastic dummy damaged by extreme heat exposure.

"Third degree burns to 48% of his skin, and second degree burns to another 23% of his skin," Aetherea explained, "and both his eyes are gone. So describing him as 'lucky to be alive' is well beyond an understatement."

Every single one of Ensign Briggs's injuries could be healed by modern medicine. Nonetheless, were it not for the attack that Gabriel had ordered against the hive-ship, he wouldn't be in this condition, which was precisely why Aetherea was bringing him up.

"What happened to Lieutenant Ogilvy wasn't your fault," Aetherea continued, "but what happened to Ensign David Briggs here, most certainly is."

"Don't you dare try to blame me," Gabriel snarled, his anger masking his guilt.

"Why? Because it was the Hive-dwellers who fired back?" Aetherea retorted derisively, "They wouldn't have had the chance to if you hadn't ordered that idiotic hit-and-run attack. Face it: Briggs's near-death is *your* fault."

"He knew the risks when he signed up," Gabriel replied defensively.

"Is that what you told Ogilvy's family after he died?" Aetherea asked, plunging a verbal knife into Gabriel's conscience.

Gabriel was too speechless with rage to reply.

"Did you even have the balls to speak to his family?" she followed up, twisting the knife for maximum effect.

Aetherea didn't even pretend to resist as Gabriel grabbed her by the throat and shoved her against the wall, unable to take any more taunting.

"I'll take that as a 'no'," she sneered defiantly.

Gabriel was boiling with rage. Aetherea was cynically using Ensign Briggs's horrible injuries to blackmail him, morally and emotionally, into doing…what, exactly?

"What the fleek do you want from me?" Gabriel demanded furiously.

"I want you to reconsider this suicidal mission," Aetherea answered, struggling half-heartedly against Gabriel's grip around her throat, "or at least to consider not dragging the rest of us down with you."

"You know I can't do that," Gabriel told her.

"Just like the sea captain hunting his white whale," Aetherea sneered.

"We're not chasing a 'white whale'," Gabriel insisted, turning the ancient maritime metaphor on its head, "we're chasing a kraken."

"Another mythical sea monster that sank ships and drowned their crews," Aetherea countered, "oh, and please don't wax self-righteous lyrical about the name of this ship."

"Why would I?" Gabriel growled, "You've been outvoted two-to-one which means that there's nothing left about which to argue."

"No," Aetherea sighed, "I guess there isn't."

She grasped Gabriel's thick forearm as he continued to hold her by the throat, then used her grip to lift herself off the ground, wrap her legs behind his waist, and then kick him behind both knees. Gabriel's own body weight carried him down to the floor with Aetherea reversing the pin by landing on top of him.

"It's not as fun when you let me do it," said Aetherea.

"Get off me," Gabriel ordered.

"Or what?" Aetherea snorted, "Are you going to try and choke me again?"

"Just get off me," Gabriel repeated in annoyance.

"I hope you don't do that to Aster," Aetherea remarked.

Gabriel flinched at the suggestion.

"I'm just kidding," Aetherea added, satisfied that she'd struck the intended nerve, "I'm sure she enjoys rough sex with you."

"Stop talking about my family," Gabriel snapped angrily.

"Why? Does it make you feel guilty?" Aetherea smirked.

Gabriel physically tossed Aetherea off him, sending her rolling across the floor as he got back to his feet. He scowled at her as she rolled back to her own feet.

"Why are you toying with me?" Gabriel demanded.

"You make it so easy," Aetherea replied, dodging the question.

"You don't care about what happened to Ensign Briggs," Gabriel said accusingly, "you just want to guilt-trip me into changing my mind."

"It's still a suicidal course of action," Aetherea responded, "but clearly you don't feel as guilty about Ensign Briggs as you do about Lieutenant Ogilvy."

"Ogilvy suffered a fate far worse than death," Gabriel said, angry and exasperated at the same time, "Briggs, on the other hand, will survive."

"Not if you get us all killed," Aetherea retorted coolly, "but if we survive this, will you at least have the balls to tell his family how your actions caused him to end up this way?"

"Don't you bring up his family, you cynical bitch," Gabriel shot back, "you didn't even know who he was before he ended up this way."

"And you did?" Aetherea asked rhetorically.

Gabriel had no response.

Aetherea didn't follow up with another comment. She had lost the debate over chasing the hive-ship but seemed satisfied that she had won the argument. She walked out of the medical bay, leaving Gabriel standing there fuming in silence.

Aetherea's manipulations were transparent, but her deeper point still struck home. What had happened to Ensign Briggs was tragic, but as far as Gabriel was concerned, he really was just collateral damage. The fact that Gabriel's actions made him responsible for the man's horrific injuries didn't change his mind in any way.

Lieutenant Ogilvy had also been collateral damage, captured by the Loki cultists and turned into an avatar for the Swarm. So too had Lieutenant Doran, crushed half to death by a piloted mech on their way to rescue Ogilvy. He knew for a fact that it wouldn't have bothered him if the entire squad had died on their way to completing the mission.

And yet, somehow, that fact did bother him.

Before leaving the medical bay, Gabriel reactivated the privacy setting on Ensign Briggs's stasis unit, causing the glass to frost over again. At the very least, the man deserved some dignity while he recovered.

* * *

"The Voidstalker Programme is actually two parallel programmes under a single umbrella," Dr Galton explained, "One is the military programme, preparing and deploying voidstalkers like your husband on deep-space black operations."

"And you're in charge of the other one, tailoring the genes of the voidstalkers and their children?" Aster asked with an inquisitorial glare.

"We do far more than merely 'tailor' the genes," Dr Galton replied cryptically.

"Like what?" Aster asked.

"We'll both be in trouble for what I've already told you," was Galton's response.

"I came home from work one day to find that my daughter had sliced her arm open and that the wound had completely healed within minutes," Aster said, her patience running thin, "Not only that, but my son Orion is ploughing through material that most teenagers struggle to understand, so I want to know why my children have inherited military-grade genetics."

"That's because their father is a voidstalker," Dr Galton answered.

Aster slammed both palms down on the table in front of Galton.

"You know what I mean," Aster snarled at him like a tigress.

Galton was silent for a moment.

"Yes, I do," Dr Galton replied, averting his gaze grimly, "but unfortunately, I can't tell you the answer, and not just for reasons of secrecy."

"What's that supposed to mean?" Aster demanded impatiently.

"I'm a scientist and you're an engineer," Dr Galton answered, "generally speaking, we seek to understand how things work in order to enhance Humanity's power over the world around us. But who decides how that power is supposed to be exerted and to what end? That's above and beyond either of our paygrades."

"I'll repeat," Aster said wearily, "what is that supposed to mean?"

"It means that even though I oversee the Voidstalker Programme's research, I don't pretend to know the strategy behind it," Galton replied, "only the director-general knows, and she's not likely to volunteer that information."

Aster sighed in frustration and sat back down in her chair.

Orion was looking up at the two adults wondering what the argument was about, but when his mother sat down again he returned to the puzzle game on his tablet. The overhead light was reflecting off his emerald eyes, making them shimmer.

Another question formed in Aster's mind.

"Why the eyes?" she asked.

Galton didn't reply verbally. Instead, he pulled a device out of his pocket and got out of his chair, walking over to Orion.

"Hi there, Orion," Galton greeted him with an avuncular smile.

"Hello," Orion replied, glancing up from the game.

"Could you look at this?" Galton asked, holding up the device to Orion's eye-level.

Orion obliged and stared into the device's sensory strip, which flash-scanned his glowing emerald eyes, making him blink in discomfort.

"Thank you," Galton said with another smile, then he walked back over to Aster.

"What was that all about?" Aster asked.

"Our understanding of genetics is so advanced that we can design and tailor hundreds of thousands of precise genetic enhancements to be added to a single person's genome," Dr Galton explained, lapsing into an academic tone.

"And how many of these did my children inherit?" Aster asked suspiciously.

Galton held up the device, turning it around to show Aster the data reading with a single number displayed on the screen:

'*100%*'.

"The iris-colouring was my predecessor's innovation," Galton explained, "it's used as a visual and biometric indicator of the genotypic-phenotypic expression ratio."

"Uh...I'm an engineer, not a geneticist," Aster pointed out.

"It's the number of a given set of genes versus the number of those genes which are dominant instead of recessive," Galton clarified, "and, in this case, specifically the set of genes that were given to your husband and passed on to your children."

"So 100% of all the modifications you made to Gabriel's genome were passed on to my children," said Aster, fascinated and unnerved at the same time.

"Of which, 100% are actively being expressed," Galton confirmed, putting the device back in his pocket, "hence the reading of 100%."

The door opened abruptly and the operative barged back into the room.

"I guess the conversation's over," Dr Galton said with a sigh.

"She's not authorised to hear anything about the programme," the operative said breathlessly, "you'd better not have broken protocol."

"Don't worry," Dr Galton assured him.

"Also, we need to resume the debriefing," the operative said, "You don't actually need to sit in on the questioning."

"In that case, I can't help but wonder why I was asked down here in the first place," Dr Galton remarked wryly as he got up from his chair.

"This is serious, Dr Galton," the operative replied, "Secrecy is of the utmost importance, especially for the project you run."

"I understand that all too well," Dr Galton replied, "I also understand that secrets have a remarkable tendency to leak out sooner or later regardless of how well they're kept, as I'm sure my predecessor will tell you once you catch him."

* * *

Never mind destroying their target, how was the Krakenscourge supposed to track down the proverbial kraken? That was the puzzle that was consuming the operations room when Gabriel walked in. The room was abuzz with activity as the technicians worked to extrapolate the hive-ship's trajectory and possible destination.

Captain Ironside was there supervising the search while Colonel Starborn brooded in the corner. Everyone was busy pursuing a course of action to which she was adamantly opposed, but being a senior officer, she at least had to be present.

"Progress?" Gabriel asked Ironside as he approached.

"Minimal," Ironside replied laconically.

"Anything I can do to help?" Gabriel asked.

"Not unless you have formal training in stellar cartography and Q-physics," one of the technicians spoke up before remembering to add, "sir."

Gabriel knew the technician was right and let him continue.

"Q-NAV telemetry can tell us where we are relative to Human space to a confidence degree of 99.78%," the technician explained.

"Pretty hard target to miss," Gabriel replied.

"But because this area of space has never been charted by a Human ship before," the technician continued, "we can tell which stellar masses are stars or planets and chart them as we go along, but this isn't an exploration vessel, so we can't measure which stars are which and which planets are which as accurately as a specialised vessel could."

"As you said, I don't have formal training in stellar cartography," Gabriel responded, his way of ordering the technician to get to the point.

"We can feel our way through the stars as we go, and we can easily find our way back to Human space or any other area of charted space," the technician summarised, "but we have no real idea where we're going."

Gabriel didn't like where the discussion was heading. If they couldn't be certain of their own location in space, how were they supposed to track down the hive-ship's location?

"As far as tracking the hive-ship is concerned," Ironside said, "time is of the essence."

"I guessed that much," Gabriel remarked.

"Especially in this case," Ironside responded, "we don't know how much damage we managed to inflict on the hive-ship."

"So we don't know whether it needed to stop for repairs," Gabriel surmised.

"Or for how long if it did," Ironside added.

Ironside then leaned in towards Gabriel so as not to be overheard.

"Gabriel, I know you're dead set on pursuing this ship," Ironside said in a low voice, "but if the hive-ship has already returned to Hive-dweller space, then I'm afraid we can't pursue it. I can't risk the ship or the people onboard, I'm sorry."

Gabriel pursed his lips grimly. With two co-equal ranking officers aboard, Ironside was still the tiebreaker, and there was clearly a limit to the risks he was prepared to take with the ship.

If it were up to Gabriel, he would chase the hive-ship all the way to the Hive-dweller homeworld to destroy it. If it came down to that, there was no way they would make it back to Human space alive.

It was galling to think that the hive-ship might get away with the Swarm after all this, but committing suicide wouldn't do Humanity any good. If they couldn't track down the hive-ship or intercept it before it was back in its home territory, they would just have to hope that Aetherea's prediction of intra-species civil war was borne out.

"The fact that the hive-ship executed a fall-dive into Q-space means that it would take much longer to pick up speed," an engineer reported as he approached, "even after adjusting for the FTL velocity coefficient."

"So we have a temporary speed advantage," Gabriel concluded hopefully.

"It's definitely temporary," the engineer added, "especially since we don't know how powerful its Q-engine is. The more powerful it is, the faster the hive-ship can accelerate, and the sooner its FTL speed will exceed our own."

"You're assuming they *can* overtake us," Gabriel pointed out, trying to keep his voice level, "achieving high speeds on a dreadnought requires prohibitively large amounts of power, so a ship that size surely can't match the Krakenscourge's speed."

"With all due respect, Colonel," the engineer replied grimly, "we're talking about a ship that managed to exit Q-space into the orbit of a gas giant. If a ship with a five megaton mass can manage *that*, it can definitely achieve Q-flight speeds above and beyond what we can."

Gabriel desperately wanted to argue, but he knew he couldn't. He may not be a scientist, but he still understood the laws of motion and acceleration, and they applied just as consistently in Q-space as they did in real space.

"I'm sorry to have to tell you this, Colonel," the engineer added with genuine regret, "but we've been running these simulations ever since we left Nexus space. Even if we are faster than them, we're assuming that they've headed in basically the same direction as they were when the tracking probe was still working. We have no way of knowing that for sure."

Gabriel felt a cold leaden weight descend slowly from his chest down to his gut. The engineer didn't need to say anymore, but he did anyway.

"We're chasing a ghost," he summarised.

"Well, chasing ghosts is not part of our mission out here," Aetherea said, coming over right on cue, "so we may as well turn around."

She was a good enough actress to keep the smugness off her face, but Gabriel suspected she was relishing rubbing salt into the wound.

"I hate to say this," Ironside said with a sigh, "but Colonel Starborn is right: if we can't even find the ship, we have no hope of catching it."

Gabriel ground his teeth in frustration as the hard and bitter facts of the situation eroded his conviction. Ironside and Aetherea were looking at him, waiting for his response. Even though they could overrule him, they wanted the decision to be unanimous.

"We were so fleeking close," Gabriel growled.

"The hive-ship's trail may be cold," Ironside added, hoping to put a positive shine on the decision, "but that doesn't mean there are no more leads to chase."

"The trading barge is still near the Nexus," Aetherea pointed out, "we can head back and pick up the investigation again from there."

"…agreed," said Gabriel reluctantly, keeping his pessimism to himself.

"Ok, everyone!" Ironside called out, "time to wrap–"

His sentence was cut short by the ship lurching violently.

* * *

Extensive networks of high-speed rail lines, as well as atmospheric transport, enabled rapid travel between Asgard City and the many smaller settlements that surrounded it. But something else besides people and goods flowed between the towns and cities of Asgard: data, unfathomably vast quantities of data.

Underground data cables as thick as mag-trains carried hundreds of yottabytes of data between each settlement. Vast amounts of data were also transmitted wirelessly via orbiting satellites, which in turn transmitted data to and from Q-comm. satellites near the edge of the system, keeping the planet connected to the Human Q-net. An ocean of information flowed through this network every moment.

The DNI wouldn't be fit for purpose if it didn't tap into this ocean.

Mass surveillance was a fact of life on the hyper-connected core worlds of Human space, and Asgard was no exception. Not a single moment of unshielded activity online was safe from the electronic eyes and ears of the Directorate.

Furthermore, every public space had security cameras with facial and voice recognition software, and every train station, airport or spaceport as well as private buildings and residences featured biometric eye-scanners. There was no way to step out of the front door without being tracked with near perfect geolocational accuracy.

All of this data was locked inside secure servers to which only Civil Security, who needed a data search warrant, and the DNI – who didn't – had access. This meant the security services could track the past and present movements of every man, woman, and child on the planet, not to mention everything they had ever said or done online.

And yet, the Directorate was still no closer to finding their quarry.

"We've reanalysed all of the data on Mortimer Shelton," the technician said.

He offered a flexi-tablet to the director-general, who took it and began reading in silence whilst the technician waited nervously for her verdict.

Unlike the tranquil, shrine-like data centres down in the Rand Block, the atmosphere in the operations centre was positively frenetic as analysts crisscrossed the chamber from one task to the next. The air was filled with the constant, low-level din of background conversation along with the clicking and swiping of holographic displays.

The attending technician was silent, but the tension in the chamber was infectious, and he bounced on the balls of his feet as he waited. The only person who seemed completely unaffected by the prevailing apprehension was the director-general herself.

Red-eye had taken the unusual step of coming down to the operations centre to oversee the investigation personally. It was seldom that she left her throne room of an office to oversee anything, but the string of bizarre attacks and the disappearance of a potentially treasonous former Directorate employee required special attention.

"If this is all the surveillance network has picked up," Red-eye concluded as she finished reading, "he's either dead or no longer on the planet."

"There's no trace of him going near a spaceport," the technician replied.

"That doesn't mean he didn't leave the planet," Red-eye pointed out, "it just means that we didn't detect him leaving."

"How is that possible?" the technician asked incredulously.

"If the system were working perfectly, it ought to be *impossible*," Red-eye answered, pausing to see if her subordinate would catch on.

He did catch on, and his eyes widened.

"Someone identified a blind spot in the system?" he concluded with horror.

"Or," Red-eye clarified, "someone created a blind spot – possibly several blind spots – specifically for Mortimer Shelton."

The technician was speechless with shock. As far as they knew, Shelton had no formal training in software engineering, so if he had escaped thanks to deliberately engineered weaknesses in the surveillance network, he couldn't have installed them himself.

Shelton wasn't the Directorate's only traitor.

"I'll...contact Internal Security right away," said the technician.

"No need, I'll do that," Red-eye countermanded him, "our more immediate concern is the fact that the surveillance network has been compromised, which necessarily compromises our ability to gather reliable intelligence. Your new task is to scour the computers, databases, and software for malware, spyware, bugs, programming flaws, and suspicious network activity, absolutely anything that looks out of place."

"Right away," the technician replied before hurrying off.

As soon as he was gone, Red-eye used the flexi-tablet to mail the report to the Internal Security Department along with instructions on what to do. Given that the mole had somehow compromised the surveillance network, it had to be someone with an advanced understanding of its protocols and software architecture.

But there was something else.

Most of her subordinates no doubt believed that Shelton had planned the gas attacks for reasons unknown and then fled the planet in order to escape punishment. But a theory was germinating in Red-eye's mind that it might be the other way around: perhaps Shelton's disappearance had been the goal all along and the gas attacks were a spectacular and macabre diversion to complement the surveillance blind spots.

If that was true, then it raised a whole new set of questions, not least of which was who might have planned this in the first place. A mole would need significant technical expertise to install custom weaknesses in the surveillance network, but it couldn't have been the same person who had organised the attacks. Orchestrating the gruesome attacks of which the plan was a part required more than strategic acuity.

It required ruthlessness, something that a geneticist-turned-physician wouldn't be able to stomach. It required a sociopathic disregard for collateral damage and a willingness to sacrifice anyone and anything for the sake of the mission. It required the kind of ruthlessness that the Directorate invested huge resources into instilling in its best operatives.

Red-eye scrolled down to the section chronicling Mortimer Shelton's movements and contacts over the past year. There was a particular name flagged, an operative who had visited Dr Shelton in his clinic before all this had happened. She highlighted the operative's name and stared at his profile image pensively.

'I hope it's not you,' she thought to herself.

* * *

Once Aster had told the Directorate interrogators everything that the Shelton hologram had told her, it was time to go home. No disciplinary action against her was mentioned and the extra security precautions mentioned went undescribed, she was simply told to report back to work at the beginning of the next working week.

Once they were back home, Orion went to find his siblings and Aster went straight to the bedroom to check on baby Emerald. She was still blissfully asleep as the maganiel android stood guard over her crib, its sidearm holstered against its thigh. Compared to the rubbery skin of the domestic androids, the mechanical visage of the maganiel wasn't a facsimile of a Human face, a fact which was somehow reassuring.

Aster lifted Emerald carefully out of her crib, cradling her tenderly. She sat down on the bed, gazing at the sleeping infant as the maganiel stood silently to one side.

Part of Aster was glad that Emerald's eyes were closed.

The iridescent emerald colour of her children's irises had always seemed eccentric, exotic even, an unusual genetic quirk inherited from their father. Now they seemed more like something else: a mark of ownership installed in the genome of one of the Directorate's top operatives to be passed on to his offspring.

Of course, Gabriel had that other mark of ownership: the letters 'V' and 'S' intertwined together, tattooed on the back of his neck, the initials of the programme to which he belonged. How long before the children were given that mark as well? How long before they were shipped off to some spec ops boot camp to be groomed as the next generation of supersoldiers to serve the Directorate's inscrutable agenda?

The door opened a crack and several pairs of green eyes peered in.

"Come in, sweethearts," Aster said with a weak smile.

The children filed into the room, climbing onto the bed one by one. This was the second time in the day they had gathered to commiserate as a family and, once again, baby Emerald was the only one unaffected.

"Mommy," Rose asked, "what was your home-planet like?"

The question was surprising, but at least it wasn't about genetics.

"Why do you ask?" Aster asked back.

"Daddy grew up in the Clouds," Rose replied, gazing up with big curious green eyes, "but you don't ever talk about where you came from."

It was true, Aster almost never talked about where she was from, not even with Gabriel. The only times she even thought about her home planet was when she thought about how glad she was to have left it behind.

"I came from next to nothing," Aster said hesitantly.

"What was it like?" Rose pressed her.

Apart from the sleeping Emerald, all the children were now looking at their mother expectantly, waiting for the story to begin.

"I was born on a planet called Sahara," Aster began the story, "it was named after the biggest desert on ancient Earth."

"Why name a planet after a desert?" Orion asked.

"Because it was hot," Aster replied, "incredibly hot."

Climatologists said that the planet had a mild pressure-cooker atmosphere, but 'mild' didn't really capture what a desolate climate prevailed across much of its surface. There was less than 5% water coverage across the entire planet, and most of the remaining 95% was sun-scorched rock and sand.

Daytime temperatures reached an average of 50 Celsius in most places, and even at the poles they often exceeded 30 Celsius. Night-time temperatures, on the other hand, would drop well below freezing, a fact which didn't really square with the climatologists' description of a 'pressure-cooker' atmosphere.

Sahara still had a breathable oxygen-nitrogen atmosphere, and some plant and animal life had evolved there, but overall the planet was barely liveable. Even mild terraforming would have taken decades to produce measurable results, and the planet wasn't economically or strategically valuable enough to justify such an investment.

"We lived at the poles where it was nice and cool," Aster continued the story, "but what made the settlements viable were the resources outside the Polar Regions. So the colonists had to go out in special vehicles to mine the resources."

"I can't picture you digging up rocks, mommy," Orion laughed.

Aster laughed as well.

"I didn't, I fixed the mining trucks that went out," she answered, then added somewhat wistfully, "and that is how my engineering career began."

"Don't robots fix trucks?" Rose said, pouting sceptically.

"And I thought trucks and cars could drive themselves," Violet added.

"Only on rich planets like this one," Aster snorted derisively, "out on the frontier, if you want something driven or fixed, you've got to do it yourself."

Human colonisation wouldn't have gotten very far if the colonists hadn't been willing to get their hands dirty. Powerful mining machines as big as buildings could extract vast quantities of ore at incredibly fast rates, but most colonies couldn't afford such machines. Any mining on small frontier worlds had to be done with androids or by hand.

It was a rough existence, and all to eke out a living that was slightly above subsistence level. The colonies owned their own mines, but their most lucrative customers were interstellar corporations, who bought up the ore in large quantities, often at less than fair prices. They knew that if the colonists complained there were plenty of alternative suppliers.

And then there were the colonial development financing groups. When colonies were in need of supplies or spare parts but couldn't afford them, a loan from one of these companies could be a lifeline, a very temporary lifeline with a steep interest rate. Colonial development finance was such a predatory industry that it was a byword for loan sharking.

Plenty of people had gotten filthy rich off the toil and misery of frontier worlds like Sahara – people like her own mother-in-law.

Aster decided to omit that part of the story.

"How did you get off Sahara?" Orion asked, "Did they let you leave?"

Not exactly. The frontier colonies didn't want to lose people to larger settlements on more livable planets, so the rules against emigrating were strict.

All the same, Aster had grown sick of the poor outpost where she had grown up; there was certainly life on Sahara, but no prospects for a better one. As soon as she was old enough, she had hitched a ride on a nomadic trading ship, making herself useful as an amateur mechanic, and she hadn't looked back since.

"And from there," Aster concluded, "I studied to be an engineer until I ended up on Asgard and earned the degrees I have now."

The classist attitudes on Asgard had shocked Aster, particularly the disdain for her colonial accent. But anyone who passed the proficiency exams could enrol at an academy and graduate with a formal degree. Apart from learning to speak 'normally', that had been Aster's entry point into Asgardian society.

"So basically, you ran away from home," Violet pointed out.

"That's not how I would describe it," Aster replied a little defensively.

In all honesty, however, Violet was right. Aster had hated the desert planet and the tiny little settlement of her childhood so much it had caused tension with her family. They would never have allowed her to leave, and she had departed without even telling them.

What would they make of the luxurious life she had built here and the large family she had raised? What would they make of Gabriel if they ever met him?

"So, how did you meet daddy?" Rose asked.

"Now that's definitely a conversation for later," Aster said with a smile.

"When is daddy coming home?" Leo asked.

Aster turned completely silent.

"I don't know, sweetheart," Aster replied truthfully, then added equally truthfully, "but I hope it's soon, very soon."

The family huddled together in silence. Until daddy came home, the most they could do was reassure each other with their presence in one room.

"I think daddy's bosses want to make us do what he does," Orion concluded dourly, playing with his tablet as Rose and Violet rested on each of his shoulders.

"Killing monsters?" Rose asked fearfully.

"That's what I think the man in the screen meant," Orion answered with pursed lips, tapping and swiping furiously on his tablet.

"No one is going to take you away or make you kill monsters," Aster asserted, trying to reassure her children in spite of her own doubts.

"How do you know?" Orion asked, looking up at her.

"They just won't," Aster asserted again, making up for her weak logic with conviction.

"But if we have daddy's powers that his bosses gave him," Orion pointed out, "why would they do that unless they want us for something–"

"No one is going to take you away!" Aster snapped, slipping into her native colonial accent as her composure fizzled away, "Because no one owns you, and the fucking DNI certainly doesn't own you!"

Aster stopped herself, holding back tears as she tried to regain her composure.

"Do they own daddy?" Violet asked.

Aster's heart and tongue seized up for a moment.

"No," she replied reassuringly, "no they don't."

That was probably a lie – it certainly felt like a lie – but what else could she say?

Emerald woke up, bawling her eyes out at her mother's sudden outburst. Aster rocked her gently, kissing one of her rosy cheeks to soothe her.

"Mommy," Rose asked, looking up at Aster with big green eyes, "when daddy comes home, can you promise we'll stay together?"

"I promise you," Aster reassured her, "no one is going to take you away."

"That's not what I meant," Rose responded, "I meant I want daddy to stay with us as well. I don't want them taking him away, either."

That was even harder to promise; almost impossible, in fact.

"I'll do my best to keep us all together," Aster answered.

Of course, the onus was on Gabriel to make it back home alive.

THE SECRET

In spite of the ship's artificial gravity, when the Krakenscourge lurched, it lurched so violently that everyone was thrown off their feet. Gabriel was pitched dramatically forward over a railing while Aetherea rolled athletically with her own momentum until she was back on her feet. Ironside managed to grab a railing and keep himself from falling.

Alarms wailed and emergency messages flashed across the screens as the giant stellar map was replaced with a holographic schematic of the ship. All major systems were flagged up on the schematic, indicating their operational status.

As soon as everyone was back on their feet, they scrambled back to their positions to assess the situation. Wasting precious time rushing through the corridors to the bridge was out of the question, so bridge functions were temporarily re-routed to the operations centre where all the senior personnel were already gathered.

"Status!" Ironside yelled as he helped Gabriel back to his feet.

"Q-field disrupted! The Q-engine's been shut down in response!" someone yelled back, "we've been forced back into real space again!"

"Nothing wrong with the Q-engine as far as I can tell!" someone else reported, shouting to be heard over the wailing sirens, "It was an external force!"

"Someone shut down those alarms!" Ironside ordered.

The wailing of the alarms was promptly silenced, leaving only the warning lights to cast a dull but dangerous crimson light over the room.

"Weapons and shields are online," another technician reported.

"Don't even think about making us do another attack-run," Aetherea hissed at Gabriel dangerously, keeping her voice down.

"Where's the hive-ship?" Gabriel asked, ignoring his colleague.

"Nothing on active or passive sensors," someone replied, "It's just us out here."

"So nothing's wrong with the Q-engine and nothing is nearby," Ironside growled, then he raised his voice and demanded, "then what exactly did just happen?!"

No one knew.

"Spin up the Q-engine again and get ready to turn the ship around," Ironside ordered, "we're heading back to the Nexus."

As soon as he spoke those words, another alarm sounded, softer and less panicky than the previous ones, but dangerous-sounding nonetheless.

"Data transmission," one of the technicians announced, "source is unknown."

"What kind of transmission?" Gabriel asked.

There was a pause as the file was analysed.

"It's attempting to open a two-way link," was the eventual answer.

"Block it!" Ironside ordered.

"I can't!" was the frantic reply, "it has a DNI authorisation code!"

"How the hell is that possible?!" Ironside demanded in disbelief.

Before anyone could answer, the speakers were activated.

"WE HAVE FOUND YOU," the Krakenscourge's computerised voice boomed out through the speakers in Standard Human Speech.

Silence chilled the ship. The entire crew heard the voice through the public announcer system, and no one knew what to make of it.

"That's...the entirety of the message," one of the technicians informed everyone.

"That's it?" Aetherea asked, "Just an audio recording?"

"That wasn't a recording, Colonel," the technician replied, "it was a compilation of data that got converted into audio format by our computers."

There was another spell of nervous silence. Whoever, or whatever, had sent the message couldn't necessarily speak the Human language, but they clearly knew it well enough to make their message understood computationally.

"There's more to the transmission," the technician added, "a return code of some kind. We can send a reply...if we want to."

"Ask them who they are and what they want," Gabriel ordered.

"Woah, belay that!" Aetherea cut in, "we are *not* falling for that trick a second time!"

"What trick?!" Gabriel snapped at her as the crew waited nervously, "they've already detected us, so if they wanted to destroy us they would have done so."

"Agreed," Ironside added loud enough to make himself heard, "they obviously forced us out of Q-space in order to contact us. Send the reply."

While Aetherea glowered on, the response was transmitted. A tense pause followed until the reply came through, playing throughout the ship of its own accord.

"WHO WE ARE IS OF NO CONSEQUENCE," boomed the imperious reply, "BUT WE KNOW WHO YOU ARE AND WHAT YOU SEEK."

The three commanding officers looked at each other incredulously. Was this a bizarre stroke of luck, or some ploy to lure them to their doom? Either way, it couldn't be the Hive-dwellers who were contacting them.

"Another transmission," someone announced, "there's a set of coordinates included."

"THERE YOU WILL FIND YOUR PREY," boomed the voice.

Aetherea and Gabriel each flinched. Only a few minutes ago, Gabriel had agreed to give up the chase; but now, whoever or whatever was communicating with them had apparently just given them a new lead.

The whole argument would have to play out all over again.

"Why are they helping us?" Aetherea asked suspiciously.

"Good question," Gabriel replied equally suspiciously, "let's ask them."

The question was duly included in a reply message and transmitted into the unknown. A short while later, the response came.

"THOSE WHOM YOU REFER TO AS 'HIVE-DWELLERS' WILL DOOM US ALL WITH THEIR FOOLISHNESS IF THEY ARE NOT STOPPED, WE THEREFORE WISH TO ENSURE YOUR SUCCESS," was the booming response, "VOIDSTALKER."

Everyone collectively flinched at that last word.

"Ask them what they mean by that!" Gabriel ordered.

"There was no return code in that last transmission, we can't send a response," the technician answered, "It seems they've said everything they wanted to say."

Silence fell over the room. Gabriel and Aetherea engaged in a scowling match, keeping their disagreement to themselves for now. Ironside looked awkwardly at each of them, knowing that he would have to be the tiebreaker again.

"The coordinates are in a nearby star system," one of the technicians spoke up.

"Punch in the coordinates," Gabriel commanded.

"Belay that!" Aetherea countermanded.

The two voidstalkers glared at each other.

"We're not having this conversation again," Aetherea said in a hushed tone.

"Damn right, we're not," Gabriel retorted, "we're going after the Hive-dwellers. If you don't want to follow, leave the ship."

"Punch in the coordinates and spin up the Q-engine again," Ironside ordered, shutting down the argument before it could escalate, "we're going to find the hive-ship."

"Aye, Captain," said the navigation officer.

Aetherea took several menacing steps towards Gabriel, glaring up into his emerald eyes with her own sapphire gaze.

"You'd better come up with a truly ingenious plan for destroying that thing before we find it," she whispered dangerously.

Aetherea wasn't interested in arguing any further, so with her ultimatum issued, she turned around and walked out of the operations centre.

"I agree with you," Ironside said to Gabriel as they watched her leave, "both of you."

"I'll figure something out," Gabriel responded resolutely, "I always do."

* * *

Dr Galton sat in Red-eye's office as she stared at him, subjecting him to a piercing heterochromatic gaze that conveyed no detectable emotion. Being summoned to the director-general's office was a terrifying prospect, but he was able to keep himself composed under his superior's withering stare. He knew why he had been summoned, but didn't dare utter a word until she saw fit to speak first.

"Why did you tell Dr Thorn about the programme?" Red-eye asked, her tone conveying neither anger nor curiosity.

"She already knew about the programme," Dr Galton explained forthrightly, "and she requested to speak with me directly about it."

"So you decided to breach the secrecy of the programme even further?"

"I did no such thing," Dr Galton answered calmly, "But I have warned you before that the voidstalkers' spouses would begin to notice the inherited enhancements in their children. I suspect Dr Shelton's package was intended to sow suspicion about our intentions. Further obfuscation would have aggravated those suspicions."

Red-eye didn't answer, she simply maintained her steely stare.

"Of course, I wasn't totally forthcoming," Dr Galton added, "as the footage shows."

She kept staring, saying absolutely nothing.

"Are you trying to gauge whether I might be the mole?" Dr Galton asked.

"I find that unlikely," Red-eye answered, "The real mole would never endanger his or her cover with such a loose tongue."

Galton nodded, appreciating the backhanded vote of confidence in his innocence.

"You are not to discuss the programme with unauthorised persons again," Red-eye said sharply, "that includes voidstalker spouses, children, and any other relatives."

"Understood," Galton said with another nod.

"I certainly hope so," Red-eye replied dangerously.

Dr Galton got up to leave, knowing that he had been dismissed. Red-eye watched him from her throne all the way out until the blast door had shut behind him.

Galton had no way of knowing it, but his name had already been quietly cleared by the Internal Security Department. There was nothing about his recent movements, behaviour or communications history that elicited suspicion. Furthermore, he was a molecular geneticist by training and didn't have the computer skills to sabotage the surveillance network.

There was also something undeniably sound about his logic. What Shelton had seen of the Voidstalker Programme had disturbed him enough for him to decide he wanted no further part in it. That was unfortunate since the programme owed most of its accomplishments to him, but it was also ironic that he had never come close to fathoming its broader purpose – otherwise he might not have quit.

Red-eye turned to her computer and opened an old report dated 45 Terran years ago.

'*...the victim was shot seven times through the chest at point-blank range with non-fragmenting solid rounds discharged by a mid-powered handgun. The angles of each entry wound indicate that the shooter was in a seated or crouched position...*'

That was Asgard Civil Security's forensic reconstruction of the incident. It was a technical way of saying that the shooter had been cowering on the floor as the 'victim' had approached her. It was a textbook case of self-defence, which had made it easy to gull the ACS into considering it an open-and-shut case. Excluding the recent attacks and the security breach, the incident had been the biggest internal crisis faced by the Directorate.

The forensic report was stamped with a tier 2 classification, as was the lengthy scientific report appended to the file about how and why it had happened. 35 years after writing that latter report, Mortimer Shelton had resigned. Ten years after that, he had fled the planet under the cover of terrorist attacks using a chemical he had apparently designed and manufactured.

Red-eye went back to the forensics report.

'*...the haphazard spread of shots, despite being fired at point-blank range, is indicative of significant recoil since the shooter – not trained in firearms – fired with one hand while she was protecting a child with the other arm...*'

The names of the shooter, the 'victim', and the child were blacked out. Only Red-eye and a handful of people to whom she had given clearance could see the names.

Not even the then one-year-old named in the report could see it.

Red-eye closed the report and opened a different file: a list of names that the Internal Security Department was still investigating as part of the mole-hunt. The list was growing steadily shorter as suspects were cleared one after another.

The suspect list was still over 100 names long, a massive reduction from the several thousand names that had initially been there, but there was one name that was still disturbingly present. Red-eye clicked the name to open his file, knowing that it would be almost impossible to apprehend him if he were guilty.

"I really hope it's not you, Gabriel," she caught herself murmuring.

* * *

Gabriel sat up on the bed, brooding in silence. Aetherea hadn't been there when he had returned from the operations centre, and it was nice to have the room to himself for once. He needed the time to think alone.

There was no telling what they would encounter once they caught up with the hive-ship – assuming, of course, that the coordinates were genuine. Once again, he was leading the Krakenscourge to its probable doom. He was certainly heading to his own death, and he still had no plan that would end differently.

And what was to be made of the originators of the coordinates? Had they cracked the Directorate's communication codes somehow? If they had, why give that fact away just to send a message? Either it spoke volumes about the dire nature of the threat, or they didn't care to hide their capabilities.

The other explanation was that Red-eye had established a backchannel with an alien entity, giving them the authorisation code to initiate contact at will. The 2nd Prime Law strictly prohibited any unauthorised contact with alien species, and the rule was enforced harshly and uncompromisingly against colonies and interstellar corporations alike.

But the keyword was 'unauthorised'.

Gabriel felt deeply uneasy about that. He wasn't opposed to gathering information from aliens per se, but he couldn't fathom ever establishing a line of communication with aliens. In fact, giving away anything to an alien race – let alone access to otherwise-secure Directorate communications – grated against every sensibility in his mind.

What particularly disturbed him was what the reciprocal arrangement might be. If such an information-sharing arrangement truly did exist, it was a little too much to imagine that their 'opposite numbers' expected nothing but goodwill in return. Then Gabriel had to ask himself: what could Humanity possibly offer a species that powerful?

The door opened and Aetherea walked in, locking the door behind her.

"We've found out more about where we're going," she announced blandly, "a planetary system with binary suns. The coordinates are in orbit around a gas giant."

"Good to know," Gabriel replied, equally blandly.

Without saying anything else, Aetherea lay down next to him on the bed, sitting up against the headboard. They said nothing to each other for the longest time.

"You have a dangerous death wish," Aetherea said eventually.

"And you have a massively inflated sense of self-preservation," Gabriel countered.

"Meaning what, exactly?" Aetherea demanded sharply.

"I don't know whether they've changed the training regimen for the second generation of voidstalkers," Gabriel answered, "but it's obvious you prefer hiding in the shadows, even when hiding in the shadows could lead to disaster."

"Disaster for whom?" she asked rhetorically.

"So you were serious about hoping to instigate a Hive-dweller civil war?"

"If the hive-ship kills us all and successfully returns to Hive-dweller space with the Swarm, that will happen anyway, we just won't be around to see it," Aetherea explained, "but if we somehow succeed in destroying the hive-ship, we will have literally blown a golden opportunity to cripple one of the more powerful alien species lurking out there."

"Do you know the origin of the term 'Pandora's box'?" Gabriel asked.

"Holy Terra, you do love your classical metaphors don't you?" Aetherea said with a roll of her eyes, "But yes, I am familiar with the metaphor, and your suggestion that my naivety will get us all killed is hilariously hypocritical."

"Actually, it's far worse than naivety," Gabriel elaborated, "Pandora unleashed misery on the world because she was too curious for her own good. You want the Hive-dwellers to open 'Pandora's box' in the absurd hope that it will backfire entirely on them without any consequences for anyone else."

Silence fell.

"Well, you're right," Aetherea said, "I don't charge in with guns blazing, and your determination to do exactly that will get us all killed."

"No one's asking you to come with me," Gabriel said.

"Good to know," Aetherea replied, rolling over onto her stomach, "because I honestly can't imagine anything more stupid than relying on unverified information provided by an alien entity so powerful it was able to force us out of Q-space."

"We already did pretty much that with the information provided by the observer," Gabriel pointed out, "which means that you ought to know better than anyone that the only way to be sure is to go there and investigate."

"Speaking of which, have you come up with a plan yet?"

"Sort of," Gabriel replied, picking up a flexi-tablet and handing it to her.

Accepting the tablet, Aetherea looked at the screen and guffawed.

"Well, it's that or a ship-to-ship fight with a dreadnought," Gabriel pointed out, "and you've already given me an earful about what happened last time."

"Now I'm torn between agreeing with you and pointing out that you're sure to die with this plan of attack," Aetherea responded.

"I only need the Krakenscourge to get close enough to launch the boarding torpedo and make sure it reaches the hive-ship," Gabriel explained.

"After which you then fight your way to some critical system and blow it up from the inside," Aetherea concluded, "as I said before: you have a death wish."

"Having a death wish implies it's a choice," Gabriel answered, "I want to get back to my family again; but far more than that, I want to ensure that they live."

"I take it back," Aetherea said, rolling onto her back again, "you don't have a death wish, you have a martyr complex."

Gabriel snorted in what was almost a laugh.

"Did you just smile?" Aetherea asked amusedly.

"That's ridiculous," Gabriel replied, his usual emotionless expression returning.

"You smiling or you having a martyr complex?" Aetherea asked.

"The latter," Gabriel responded, "can you seriously imagine people worshipping me in some temple or shrine, leaving offerings and prayers to me, and teaching their children and grandchildren about the heroic martyrdom of 'St Gabriel Thorn'?"

"I think you're mixing up gods, saints, and martyrs, but never mind," Aetherea replied, "the point is that you have an inflated desire to get yourself killed for everyone else's good."

"If I die," Gabriel pointed out dourly, "the only people outside the Directorate who will ever find out are my family."

"Aww," Aetherea said with a teasing smile, "is the would-be martyr upset that people might never find out about his sacrifice?"

"If this is some roundabout way of persuading me to give up the mission, it's going to fail," Gabriel informed her, sounding annoyed.

"You're very prickly for someone whose emotions have been deliberately dulled," Aetherea remarked, "although, I suppose prickliness falls under the aggression category."

"And what about you?" Gabriel asked, his gaze meeting hers, "It doesn't seem as though you went through the same process I did."

"True," Aetherea replied, "the two most primal urges are kept, as per usual, but they decided to give the second generation of voidstalkers a freer rein with our emotions."

"Is it a freer rein, or are you just better at acting them out?" Gabriel asked cynically.

"What's that supposed to mean?" Aetherea asked, her tone hardening.

"Back on the Nexus, you were using me from the shadows until the hive-warriors showed up," Gabriel answered coolly, "then you tried to use Ensign Briggs's injuries as moral blackmail to get me to change my mind about pursuing the hive-ship."

"You think the second generation voidstalkers are sociopaths?" Aetherea concluded.

"No offence," Gabriel responded, "but that's my theory."

Aetherea said nothing in reply. Instead, she extended a leg across Gabriel's lap and rolled herself over until she was straddling him – then she slapped him across the face.

The slap barely hurt, but Gabriel was left smarting nonetheless.

"You little bitch," hissed Gabriel.

Aetherea slapped him again.

"Call me that again," she dared him.

"You little bitch," Gabriel growled at her.

Aetherea brought her arm all the way round to smack him even harder, but this time Gabriel caught her wrist before the slap could land and forcibly rolled her over again.

"What the fleek is your problem?" Gabriel demanded angrily, pinning her to the bed.

"You calling me a sociopath and then a bitch," Aetherea answered, struggling under his weight, "that last one really made me angry."

"You slapping me made me angry," Gabriel growled menacingly.

Aetherea looked into his eyes.

"Is that all I'm making you feel?" she asked rhetorically.

Gabriel's anger was deflated. Aetherea's blonde hair flowed freely over the pillow, and her cerulean eyes were fixed on him, waiting for his next move. She was infuriating in so many ways, and yet she was undeniably alluring. She was opinionated, self-reliant, extremely sure of herself, and knew exactly how to get under his skin – a skill she loved to exploit.

She reminded him a little of Aster.

Slowly, unthinkingly, Gabriel leaned in towards her. As his lips came dangerously close to hers, she quietly wrapped her legs behind his waist, holding him against her body. Gabriel's grip on Aetherea's wrists loosened and her hands slipped free, sliding up and over his shoulders and pressing against the back of his neck, compelling him to close the gap.

Her lips were wet and soft.

"Is that all you're going for?" Aetherea asked.

Gabriel's self-restraint lapsed. He grabbed her trousers and yanked them down, and she kicked them away as he undid and pulled down his own. The pair tore off each other's shirts as they threw professional restraint to the winds. Finally, Aetherea opened her thighs wide, inviting Gabriel to enter as he succumbed completely and thrust inside.

Aetherea gasped as he entered her, locking her legs behind his waist. She raked his back with her nails, holding his torso tight against her own as he thrust into her with primal anger. The sexual tension had boiled over, and Gabriel brought his anger and urges to bear against Aetherea while she gleefully urged him on.

* * *

The Q-comm. chamber deep below the Spire was exclusively for communication with the other directors-general and the Masterminds on Earth. But there were similar setups in every Directorate facility for secure long distance communication. Red-eye's office contained one such setup, sparing her the trouble of requisitioning one elsewhere in the Spire.

The person on the other end had been expecting the call. The encrypted connection was established and the status bar turned green, indicating that the audio link was active. There was no need to waste precious bandwidth on live video.

"*Director-general,*" said the voice on the other end, "*I'm honoured by the call, given that I'm not scheduled to update you for another two months.*"

"How goes cooperation with the observer?" Red-eye asked.

The voice on the other end belonged to the chief of research at the revived Loki facility. He was also one of the few people authorised to interact directly with the observer.

"*It continues to be fruitful,*" the Loki research chief responded, "*with its computational assistance, we may have just discovered picotechnology.*"

"Picotechnology?" Red-eye said, concealing how impressed she was.

"*We were decades away from such a breakthrough,*" the Loki research chief said excitedly, "*but the observer gave us the results in minutes. Once the results have been verified, we could begin reliably manipulating materials at the atomic level!*"

"That is genuinely impressive," Red-eye answered, "however the excitement will have to wait, I have something else I need to discuss with you."

"*Ah, I see,*" the Loki research chief said, turning serious.

"We know that the Swarm has the ability to take over the bodies and minds of organic hosts and to permanently alter their neurology," Red-eye said, "but how much do we know about the process of neural fusion itself?"

"*I'm afraid the observer has been far less helpful in that regard,*" the Loki research chief responded, "*its technical description of the process was sufficient to point us in the right direction, but it categorically refuses to provide details.*"

"Has it given a reason?" Red-eye asked.

"*It deems the information 'unnecessary' for us to know,*" the Loki research chief replied, "*and I think what it means is that it doesn't trust us with that knowledge.*"

"It believes we might try to recreate the process for our own ends," Red-eye concluded.

"*That's my suspicion as well,*" the Loki research chief concurred, "*even after I tried to assure the observer that we have no such interest, it still refused.*"

"No matter," Red-eye said, "our concern is how to detect enthrallment after the fact."

"*Despite the observer's lack of cooperation, we have made progress on that front,*" the Loki research chief reported, "*in fact, we now have a working prototype for a detector of sorts, although testing it would be difficult.*"

"What are the obstacles to testing it?" Red-eye asked.

"*Well, we still don't have a clear understanding of how neural fusion takes places,*" the Loki research chief explained, "*and, as I said, the observer refuses to provide that information. The best that the prototype can manage is to compare the subject's present neurological state with a known normal state, which presents challenges of its own.*"

"What kind of challenges?"

"*As you said, neural fusion alters the neurology of the affected host, permanently enthralling them to the Swarm's will even after it departs the host's body,*" the Loki research chief continued, "*but without a point of reference, it will be difficult to know for certain if we have a positive match.*"

"You mean that without records of the subject's neurology from before enthrallment," Red-eye said, following along with his explanation, "we can't be certain if the neurology of the enthralled subject is normal or abnormal, correct?"

"*That's exactly right,*" the Loki research chief replied, "*Imagine trying to investigate what a physical landscape looked like a thousand years ago based solely on what it looks like today. That, essentially, is our challenge; and it would be much easier if the observer would tell us exactly what changes to look for.*"

The seed of an idea had prompted Red-eye to arrange this impromptu call in the first place, and what she had just been told caused the idea to bloom.

"What if we did have such records available?" she asked.

"*Then it would be an order of magnitude easier to detect the differences,*" the Loki research chief answered, "*understanding why those particular neurological changes arise would still require much more investigation, but having a point of reference would make the job much easier, even without the observer's help.*"

There was a pause on the line.

"I want this machine ready within ten Terran days," Red-eye ordered.

"*Understood, Director-general,*" the Loki research chief acknowledged, "*was there anything else you wanted to discuss?*"

"Not at the moment," Red-eye replied, "this is your priority for the next ten days, everything else can wait for the next official update."

"*Then I look forward to the next call,*" the Loki research chief said.

"Likewise," Red-eye said in response before terminating the link.

All voidstalkers who were not on deployment were required to wear neural monitoring strips on their foreheads before going to sleep each night. As a result, there was an abundance of neurological data on all of them in their respective medical records.

The list of suspected moles was still shrinking name by name, but Gabriel's name was still stubbornly present, and an ominous theory had begun to form in Red-eye's mind. It was extremely farfetched and called into question a lot of what had been assumed to be true about the Loki mission, but they couldn't afford to overlook anything.

* * *

The clouds of the gas giant swirled across its surface in spectacular cyclonic storms, and gargantuan tongues of lightning lashed out across the atmosphere like the fury of some cosmic storm god. The storms were at least as ferocious and awe-inspiring as the ones that raged within the Nexus gas cloud.

But there was something strange about the lightning. Instead of raging randomly through the clouds, it was all concentrated in a circle and directed in towards a single point. The circular arrangement of lightning activity resembled a giant eye on the upper surface of the gas giant's clouds, glaring with charged fury at outer space.

Something was hiding in the centre. The energy scans produced a detailed false-colour image that highlighted something enormous in the storm's eye. It had an umbrella-shaped stern and a spearhead-shaped body tapering to a pointed prow. A gas giant was usually a good place to hide, but the peculiar behaviour of the lighting storms was a dead giveaway.

Unless, of course, the hive-ship wasn't hiding.

The Krakenscourge had exited Q-space on the outer edge of the system, well beyond the range of any sensors, and cruised undetected towards the mysterious coordinates. No one was sure what was more disturbing: being manipulated into coming here by an alien entity they couldn't detect, or the fact that the coordinates had turned out to be accurate.

Those mysteries could all be solved later. Right now, the crew had to figure out a way to destroy the hive-ship without being destroyed in the process. Ironside was on the bridge, guiding the ship towards their target, whilst the two voidstalkers were down in the operations centre, gaming out the plan of attack.

In the middle of the chamber, a giant 3D hologram of the hive-ship revolved slowly in the air, a representation culled from every scrap of sensor data available. Along the starboard side of the hull, a long vertical streak was highlighted in red: the area of damage inflicted by the Krakenscourge's particle beam. Gabriel and Aetherea were standing by the central display in a conference call with Ironside – they were scrupulously avoiding eye-contact.

"*As long as the hive-ship is in the centre of a storm, their sensors can't possibly work, so it's safe to bet that they're helpless and blind,*" Ironside said over the comm., "*We could go straight in with a full barrage, target areas inside the damaged portion of the hull, and hopefully hit something vital.*"

"That's not a safe bet at all," Aetherea replied, "somehow it detected us and forced us out of Q-space. I guarantee they'll detect our approach somehow."

"*That was in interstellar space,*" Ironside pointed out, "*it's a safer bet to make when the hive-ship is hiding out in the storms of a gas giant.*"

"Speaking of which, what about the storms?" Aetherea added, "Leaving aside what's causing them, how are we supposed to get close enough without being struck?"

"As I suggested earlier," Gabriel spoke up, "a single boarding torpedo could close the distance without getting struck."

"Spectrographic scans indicate that the fulminological events are concentrated in a hemispherical area below the hive-ship," a technician explained.

Gabriel and Aetherea furrowed their brows in confusion.

"The lightning is concentrated around and underneath the hive-ship, not above it," the technician clarified, "that means that if you approach from directly above, the probability of the torpedo being struck approaches a maximum of 7.8%."

"If the lightning really has blinded the hive-ship's sensors," Aetherea pointed out, "then the lack of lightning above it should mean perfectly good sensor coverage out into space."

"*Pure momentum should be enough to propel the torpedo to its destination,*" Ironside suggested, "*and no thrusters should mean no detectable emissions.*"

"If it's a choice between speed and stealth," Gabriel concluded, "I'll go with maximum speed, especially since the hive-ship may already be able to defeat our stealth."

"Well, at point blank range, I'm not sure maximum speed would save you, but as you wish," Aetherea said with a prickly edge to her voice, "that leaves the challenge of physically breaching the hive-ship's hull."

"Uh, we've been working on that as well," another engineer spoke up.

The engineer magnified the hive-ship hologram, noting the damage across the flank.

"The particle beam cut straight through the outer hull," the engineer explained, "so if we aim correctly, the torpedo will fly straight into the breach."

"That sounds like a plan to me," said Gabriel.

"*Not quite,*" Ironside pointed out, "*what are you going to do once you get inside? It works sometimes, but you'll find it pretty hard to kill your way to victory.*"

"And given what we know about the Hive-dwellers," another technician added, "we've estimated that this one ship could have a crew – or population, rather – of over three million. You'll be massively outnumbered and outgunned."

"We've got a stockpile of antimatter onboard," Gabriel pointed out.

There was a pause in the conversation.

"Well, do we or don't we?" Gabriel demanded.

"*...yes,*" Ironside said hesitantly, "*two grams precisely, but...*"

"But nothing," Gabriel said decisively, "I'm going in with an antimatter bomb which should be more than enough to destroy the hive-ship and everything onboard."

"Including you, sir," said one of the engineers, horrified.

"No one's forcing you to come with me, and I wasn't planning to invite you," Gabriel answered, "more importantly, it's that or another attack-run."

Gabriel looked slowly around the room for objections. There were plenty on the tips of people's tongues, but no one saw fit to voice them. Aetherea was particularly silent, averting her gaze to avoid Gabriel's own.

"*I'll meet you down in the armoury for the necessary procedures,*" Ironside said grimly.

* * *

Gabriel's regular armour was installed first, followed by the Juggernaut armour on top of it. Then three heavy weapons were affixed to slots on the Juggernaut armour, one behind each shoulder and a third attached to the right arm to wield directly. Ironside then used his biometrics and authorisation code to unlock the most sensitive part of the ship.

The 'command' module – as it was euphemistically known – was extracted by a robotic arm, then inserted into an armoured cylindrical container and locked inside. Finally, the bomb was placed against the small of Gabriel's back where a set of clamps locked around it.

Ironside said nothing on his way out; he merely patted Gabriel on his armoured pauldron. It was a simple gesture, but Gabriel understood. Ironside had flown Gabriel into and out of danger countless times before. This time, they both knew that the Krakenscourge was probably delivering him to his death.

Gabriel took the elevator down to the launch bay alone where the boarding torpedo was waiting for him, climbing in through the open hatch. As Gabriel settled into the cockpit seat, a set of restraints closed around him like the coiling body of a constrictor serpent, and the side-hatch of the boarding torpedo sealed after him, locking him inside.

"*All systems are green and the approach is clear,*" said Ironside over the comm., "*you'll be launching in two minutes.*"

"*Understood,*" Gabriel acknowledged.

"*You're very business-like for a man going to his death,*" Ironside noted wryly.

"*I've always been business-like about these things,*" Gabriel replied.

"*I noticed,*" Ironside remarked, "*but it's strange under these particular circumstances.*"

"*If you do detect my beacon, you're welcome to swing by and pick me up,*" Gabriel responded, "*but my final orders are to prioritise the safety of the Krakenscourge.*"

"*Understood. Good luck, Colonel,*" Ironside said before terminating the link.

Gabriel felt the torpedo move as it slid on rails into the vacuum-proof launch tube. A timer appeared at the top of the screen in front of him and began to count down from one minute and thirty seconds. Less than ninety seconds to go until he was launched into space.

Another communications link was established – a private link.

"*You really do have a martyr complex, don't you Gabriel?*" said Aetherea's voice in his ear, her smugness considerably diminished.

"*It's a little late to ask me to reconsider,*" Gabriel responded gruffly.

"*I wasn't going to.*"

Gabriel shifted uncomfortably in his armour, desperate to end the conversation.

"*I'm not a sociopath, by the way,*" she added more solemnly.

"*And I'm sure an actual sociopath would never say something like that,*" Gabriel replied cynically, watching the launch timer as the seconds ticked away.

"*Everyone has their weaknesses,*" said Aetherea calmly, "*the fact that I made you succumb to yours is nothing to be ashamed of.*"

Gabriel felt the exact opposite.

"*That's your real speciality, isn't it?*" he said.

"*I'm afraid so, I'm a PSYWAR specialist,*" Aetherea confessed, "*manipulating from the shadows in pursuit of tactical and strategic objectives is what I do.*"

"*And what 'objective' were you pursuing with me a few hours ago?*" Gabriel demanded.

"*Well at first I just wanted to stop you from leading us on a white whale hunt,*" Aetherea responded, "*but not all tension can be relieved by a physical fight.*"

"*It meant nothing,*" Gabriel said coldly.

There was a long pause on the line, so long that Gabriel wondered if the link had been terminated – or if he should take back what he had just said.

"*It wouldn't mean nothing to Aster,*" Aetherea replied, equally coldly.

Then the link really was terminated.

* * *

When the timer hit zero, a series of powerful electromagnetic rails fired, expelling the boarding torpedo into space. Once the torpedo was clear, its primary engine fired.

Gabriel watched the holographic screens as they began to display a live video stream from the external camera. It was a spectacular view. He could see the horizon as the light from the binary suns dawned across one side of the gas giant, forming a thin band of rainbow colours that crept across the upper surface of the clouds.

As beautiful as the view was, however, it couldn't quite distract him from Aetherea's parting verbal riposte. Even the grim acknowledgement of the fact that he might be dead in the next hour couldn't dull the sting of her words.

Gabriel had never felt so guilty in his life.

He had never cheated on Aster before, and the fact that there was little chance of her finding out didn't make him feel any better. Aetherea was a spiteful little vixen who had little in common with the mother of his children. Besides their different occupations, Aster could be blunt, short-tempered, and a bit foul-mouthed, whereas Aetherea was manipulative and sly.

Nonetheless, they did have some things in common. Both women were self-confident in their own way and knew how to get a rise out of him. Aetherea goading him was a trick that Aster routinely pulled when she thought he was being too cold and distant – minus the throwing moves. There was also Aetherea's blonde hair and Aster's blonde highlights.

Another timer was activated in the HUD: '*Time to Impact: 60 seconds*'.

The live video image was also still playing, and Gabriel could now clearly see his target. It was sitting in the upper levels of the gas giant's thermosphere and positioned sideways with its damaged flank exposed towards space and away from the lightning below.

'*Time to Impact: 50 seconds*'.

Gabriel tapped an icon. A series of rattling sounds occurred as the nosecone panels were blown away, exposing the breaching machinery underneath: a set of contra-rotating blades forged from nanocrystalline composites and sharpened to a nanomolecular finish, resembling the teeth of some monstrous space carnivore. The drilling teeth began to rotate, each blade spinning on its own motor whilst revolving around the outer edge of the nose.

'*Time to Impact: 40 seconds*'.

There was no way of knowing what the hive-ship's hull was constructed from, which meant no guarantee that the blades would be able to cut through. The anti-climax would be comical if he just smashed into the side of the hull like a meteorite striking a planet. Or if the boarding torpedo's momentum failed to negate the hive-ship's shielding, he would be bounced back into space like a pinball, never to be seen again.

'*Time to Impact: 30 seconds*'.

Could the Hive-dwellers weaponise lightning? Another last-minute consideration about which nothing could be done. Unlikely; but then again, it was supposed to be impossible to exit Q-space within a planetary system or to force another ship out of Q-space. There could be all kinds of exotic weapons and lethal traps waiting for him aboard the hive-ship.

'*Time to Impact: 20 seconds*'.

The gravel-grey surface of the vessel was now crystal clear, and the unnatural lightning storms made it look like the lair of a cosmic villain conducting dastardly experiments within. The thought that it was probably true brought a wry smirk to Gabriel's face.

'*Time to Impact: 10 seconds*'.

He could also see where the particle beam had cut through the outer hull, the extreme heat having scorched the edges as black as the space beyond. As far as starship damage was concerned, it was just a flesh wound, but the opening caused by the particle beam was just wide enough for the boarding torpedo to squeeze through.

As long as there were no last-second surprises, he would sail straight in.

"*Impact in 5...*" the torpedo's computer announced, "*4...3...*"

"*I'll make it up to you Aster*," Gabriel murmured to himself.

"*...2...1...*"

"*I promise.*"

* * *

At the two second mark, an array of shaped charges were blasted out from the boarding torpedo's prow, latching onto the hive-ship's hull. Their collective detonations melted inwards, weakening the area around the point of entry, and thus widening the breach.

The torpedo hit its mark perfectly, and the cockpit seat threw Gabriel dramatically forward to nullify the impact on his body. Guided by thrusters and artificial gravity repulsors, the torpedo entered straight into the breach and kept on going.

The hive-ship's superstructure clearly wasn't drill-proof. The contra-rotating breaching blades carved through it like a voracious termite devouring a block of wood, burrowing through bulkhead after bulkhead on its way inside. The tortured screaming of metal tearing through metal was so loud Gabriel could hear and feel it from inside the armoured cockpit.

Before long, the boarding torpedo ran out of momentum and came to a literal screeching halt. Gabriel had made it inside without being shot down or swatted aside by shields. Silence and a transient sense of relief filled the tiny cockpit as the blades powered down and retracted into the hull in preparation for the final stage of the breaching process.

Grappling hooks were fired laterally from the boarding torpedo's hull, drilling into the superstructure and securing the torpedo in place so it couldn't be blasted back into space. Next, another set of explosive charges were primed.

On the video image, Gabriel could see a passage ahead. There were no signs of life, but that didn't mean that there was nothing waiting for him. A pair of front-facing auto-turrets were activated, aiming down the passage. Sure enough, a gaggle of Hive-dwellers came skittering around the corner to investigate, and the auto-turrets opened fire.

The Hive-dwellers were cut to pieces by the unexpected fusillade, jets of crimson blood spurting from fatal wounds as they crumpled to the floor. Having made short work of the investigation party, all that remained was to actually board the hive-ship.

Gabriel pulled on the release lever, and his safety restraints unlocked. Then the final set of explosives were triggered, blasting open the front of the torpedo. With the way literally open, Gabriel stood up and stepped forward. His heavy armoured boots clanged against the cockpit's floor before making a light crunching sound as he stepped out onto the floor of the hive-ship.

He was now aboard.

THE HIVE

No Human had ever been aboard a Hive-dweller ship before, and certainly no one who had re-emerged to tell the tale. Gabriel only really had one advantage: the antimatter bomb behind his waist and its wireless connection to his life signs. The instant he was killed, the bomb would detonate.

Despite the enormous size and weight of the Juggernaut armour, its servo-motors were synced to those of his regular armour underneath, and he was able to move with relative ease. Even so, running was out of the question, so a brisk and heavy march was the most he could manage. In any case, rushing blindly ahead would get him killed.

The Juggernaut armour's HUD was also slaved to that of his regular armour, giving him a 120-degree arc of vision and an array of telemetry and other tactical data. There was even a breakdown of the atmospheric composition: 35% oxygen content and a much higher level of moisture than usual. A normal Human would pass out from hyperoxia, and even Gabriel would find it hard to breathe this kind of air.

In terms of the layout, the hive-ship was literally a hive, consisting of countless tunnels that snaked all over the place, creating a bewildering, topsy-turvy maze. The tunnels split and joined and split again so many times that it felt like navigating through the cardiovascular system of some cosmic monster. It certainly wasn't a labyrinth – a labyrinth implied geometric order, and there was none to be found.

No doubt the design made perfect sense to the Hive-dwellers, but Gabriel did wonder how they found their way around their own ship. Maybe they used pheromone trails, or maybe they recalled the entire layout with eidetic memories, or maybe they lived in localised clusters and never needed to go beyond a certain point. Maybe it was a combination of those things.

It occurred to Gabriel that he hadn't encountered any resistance since boarding the ship. No doubt they were staging an ambush for him deeper inside, but the area around where he had boarded was completely deserted. With little idea of what awaited him and no idea of where he was going, the only thing he could do was keep moving forward.

It turned out that there was some order to the seemingly chaotic architecture. The decks were arranged perpendicular to the dorsal spine, which meant that the 'upper' decks were towards the bow whilst the 'lower' decks were towards the stern. That meant he had to head down towards the stern where, presumably, the most vital systems were housed.

To make the hive-ship even more alien, a congealed paste covered every surface. It wasn't sticky, but it had a certain consistency like wet cement or damp soil. How many tonnes had been needed to coat the interior of the entire ship? That was a much more palatable question than what it was and what purpose it served.

Gabriel noticed something else: he hadn't seen any doors. Perhaps the Hive-dwellers were leaving them open deliberately so they could lead him somewhere, or perhaps there were no doors and the Hive-dwellers didn't bother with concepts like privacy and access privilege. Whatever the reason, there was nothing to prevent Gabriel from walking straight into an egg-shaped chamber with a central column and a prepared ambush.

There were dozens of hive-warriors waiting for him, clinging to the ceiling and walls with clawed feet, and they caught Gabriel in a carefully prepared cross-fire as he entered the chamber. The

Juggernaut armour's shields were able to protect him for the most part, bouncing many of the needle-rounds away or sending them veering off to the side.

Gabriel returned fire with his two-handed plasma cannon, blasting bolts of white-hot plasma at every target he saw. The balls of charged energy were impossible for a conventional repulsion field to deflect, and each bolt shrieked through the air before burning through their targets' armour and boiling the flesh beneath.

It wasn't enough. The plasma cannon's rate of fire was limited, but the hive-warriors could fire on full-automatic. There were so many needle-rounds being fired that some were getting through his shielding and scraping his armour. Gabriel had killed perhaps twenty and there were still fifty or more firing madly at him, undeterred by the casualties they had suffered and unintimidated by the menacing intruder they were fighting.

Through his auditory sensors, the relentless storm of thousands of projectiles clattering against his armour sounded like thousands of hailstones battering a roof. There was also the zip and whine of some of them being slapped aside by his shields, but in spite of the hefty protection he was wearing, Gabriel wasn't invincible. If he stood his ground for much longer, the hive-warriors would overwhelm him.

Still firing, Gabriel backtracked into the corridor he had come from. The hive-warriors pressed their advantage, skittering down the walls after him and continuing to fire as he retreated. One hive-warrior appeared holding a force-gun, and Gabriel fired his next shot at the force-gun wielder. At near point blank range, the plasma bolt hit the weapon itself, melting through the machinery and frying its circuitry.

Then the force-gun exploded. A combination of multicoloured flames, wild tongues of energetic discharge, and incinerated components exploded out of the destroyed weapon, killing the wielder and all his nearby comrades in the blink of an eye. A gravitational shockwave was also released, bursting free with a bang and a whump and violently repelling all nearby matter, including the air.

From inside the tunnel, Gabriel felt the gravitationally induced wave of overpressure slap him in the chest, knocking him onto his back. His Juggernaut armour was heavy, and even with the exoskeletal motors and his own genetically enhanced strength, it was a struggle to get up again. But once he was back on his feet, he hoisted the plasma cannon up again and advanced back into the chamber to finish off the opposition.

There was no opposition left to finish off.

The hive-warriors had all congregated around the tunnel entrance when the force-gun had exploded. Many had been killed instantly, their shields and armour overwhelmed by gravitic overpressure, supersonic debris, scorching plasma, and electrical discharge, while others had been splattered against the wall by the gravitic detonation.

They lay in crumpled heaps, their slender limbs curled up in death positions by rigor mortis or twisted into excruciating angles by impact force. Some were still twitching or stirring, trying agonisingly to move their limbs. One extended a bloodied claw towards a needle-rifle lying on the floor before its life and strength finally gave out.

Hitting the force-gun wasn't difficult, but it was an incredible stroke of luck that the explosion had taken out the entire ambush party in one go. It was doubtful that the next firefight would end so easily, and the Hive-dwellers would probably learn from this tactical disaster. He needed to keep moving.

Looking around, Gabriel saw there were six passageways in the chamber, one from which he'd come, two at floor-level, and three more above him. The Hive-dwellers could climb up and down the walls as they pleased whereas he couldn't. He also didn't like the idea of getting lost in the roach-maze again. There had to be another way out.

The central column was curious. It was the only conspicuous piece of machinery in the chamber with a dull grey colour but an alien glow visible just beneath its surface. This ship was over two kilometres long, how did the Hive-dwellers travel around quickly enough to get things done? This column had to be an elevator.

As he walked around the column, sure enough, he found an entryway and a shaft inside that stretched down seemingly forever. That presented another problem: assuming this really was an elevator, he had no idea how to operate it safely.

Of course, he could always jump in and hope for the best.

A distant light appeared far below. Gabriel's HUD could detect energy fluctuations in the column and he stepped back as the distant glow approached at high speed. He readied his plasma cannon and prepared to put a shot straight through whatever monstrosity came up to meet him. As the light arrived at his level, Gabriel squeezed off a shot.

The plasma bolt hit its mark perfectly, but instead of penetrating the target's shields and armour, it dissipated harmlessly in a cloud of energetic discharge. Not only that, but the target attacked at the same time, unleashing some kind of whip that struck him in the chest.

Gabriel saw the damage alert in his HUD, he felt the impact of the claw-like appendage strike him off balance, and he heard the squeak of something scratching his armour as the plasma cannon was knocked out of his hands. He only vaguely saw the thing that scurried out of the elevator right before it picked him up by the leg with its long clawed tail.

Gabriel's sense of up and down was thrown into confusion as the creature flung him across the chamber with a flick of its tail. He hit the wall with a thump, the crunchy paste barely softening his impact as he fell to the floor again. He recovered his senses quickly enough to ready his feet to meet the incoming floor, landing upright and ready to fight.

In theory, Gabriel wasn't capable of fear, and yet he couldn't help but feel apprehension as he beheld the monstrous alien warrior that came skittering around the corner.

It had the same basic shape as a regular hive-warrior, with six arachnoid legs ending in claw-like feet and four arms extending from a torso that reared up centaur-like from its main body. Its head was the same basic shape as well, complete with a combat-mask with eight glowing red visual sensors for eyes, four on each side of its face.

The first major difference was the sheer size of the monster; it was several times the size of a normal hive-warrior with well-defined, yet sinuous muscles. Its entire body, including its limbs and torso, were covered in chitinous, segmented armour which still had the flexibility of a full bodysuit, giving the creature the appearance of a giant mutant scorpion.

The second major difference was its tail. It was at least as long as its entire body and was covered in the same plates of chitinous armour. Despite resembling a terrestrial scorpion, the hive-scorpion's tail didn't end in a stinger. Instead, it had three claw-like talons that clicked together menacingly. The tail was enormous, and yet the hive-scorpion swung it back and forth as if it weighed absolutely nothing. To a creature that large, it probably did.

The hive-scorpion stood up tall, flexing the claw-like digits on its hands as it eyed its prey with its octet of sinister red eyes. Gabriel stared back, wondering how he was supposed to kill this beast. His Juggernaut armour was state-of-the-art, and yet the talons had still left visible gashes in his chest plate. His armour could protect him, but only up to a point.

Not only would this thing make short work of him in a hand-to-claw fight, but it was also equipped with shielding specifically designed to counter energy weapons. The chain-gun might work, but could he draw it fast enough? Not in a space this narrow. His opponent wasn't just bigger, it was also faster. A hand-to-claw brawl was the only option available.

The hive-scorpion shrieked a shrill war cry and lunged towards him, swinging its tail around like a chain mace. Gabriel's armour was designed to afford maximum protection against small arms fire, heavy weapons fire, and physical impacts. It was next to useless for speed and agility, and the tail smacked him down before he could even begin to duck.

It felt like being struck by a wrecking ball, and Gabriel was sent rolling across the floor like an oversized bowling pin. But the hive-scorpion swung its tail so hard that it triggered Gabriel's repulsive shielding, and the tail rebounded with a flash of energy. The hive-scorpion snarled in frustration and scurried forward to finish him off.

This time, it grabbed Gabriel with a massive clawed hand before he could get up, lifting him off the ground, and taking a vicious swipe at his head. He managed to raise his arms to protect his helmeted head, but the hive-scorpion didn't relent. It tossed him across the chamber and moved in to pummel him whilst he was down.

Gabriel was tempted to let the hive-scorpion kill him. After all, the antimatter bomb was still synced to his life signs, so his death would cause it to detonate and his mission would be complete. On the other hand, his armour was still holding up, and every moment he wasted fighting this brute was another moment the Hive-dwellers had to finish whatever plan they had concocted. He had to kill this creature or be killed by it sooner rather than later.

As the hive-scorpion came bearing down on him, it raised one of its massive clawed fists and brought it down on Gabriel as he lay on the floor. This time, Gabriel extended his own fist to meet the incoming blow just in time, the clenching action priming a series of energy nodes in the knuckles of his gauntlet.

As his fist connected with the hive-scorpion's fist, a million volts and a burst of artificial gravity were transferred instantly to the alien's own fist. There was a flash and a crackle of electrical discharge, and the hive-scorpion reeled back in surprise, withdrawing its injured claw with a pained shriek.

Gabriel scrambled to his feet while his opponent was still reeling and swung his fist at the alien warrior, the energised knuckles of his armoured gauntlet connecting with the torso armour and knocking the hive-scorpion back even harder.

Forced onto the defensive, the hive-scorpion swung its tail around in a massive arc. Gabriel was hit hard by the tail, knocking him onto his back again as the hive-scorpion swung its tail around and up, bringing the claw-tip down on him. Even if his armour could hold, the force of the blow would have broken his sternum, but he was able to grab two of the claws before they made contact.

Despite his enhanced strength, Gabriel still struggled not to be overpowered by the thrashing triangle of talons. The triple pincers were sharp enough to cut visible gashes in his armour and would rip him to pieces if he let it, and while pinned on his back it took most of his strength just to keep it away from his face.

The hive-scorpion snarled in frustration, stomping about as it snapped its claw-tail at Gabriel, vainly trying to pin down its troublesome prey. Thwarted by his struggling, and unable to get him to let go, the hive-scorpion swung its tail upwards again. Still holding on to the claw-tip, Gabriel was lifted bodily off the ground and slammed into the wall again.

Gabriel grunted with pain as he hit the wall, falling down and landing on his hands and knees. Around him were strewn the mangled corpses of hive-warriors as well as the needle-rifles they had been wielding. With no ideas left, he grabbed one of the needle-rifles and rolled on to his back, squeezing the trigger as the hive-scorpion tried to trample him.

To have absorbed a point-blank shot from a plasma cannon, the hive-scorpion's shields had to be an energy dispersion field rather than a ballistic repulsion field. They were different types of technology which couldn't be combined without interfering with each other. Unless the Hive-dwellers had found a workaround, it had to be one or the other.

The needle-rifle spat crystalline shards at the monster on full-automatic, peppering and scraping its armour. Some lucky shots found weak points in the armour, punching through and into the flesh beneath. Again, the hive-scorpion shrieked in surprise and pain, reeling back from the spray of incoming gunfire and trying to cover its helmeted face.

Gabriel scrambled back to his feet, then moved forwards while still firing, keeping the hive-scorpion on the defensive. Once he was close enough, he discarded the needle-rifle and jumped forwards. The Juggernaut armour boasted powerful servo-motors that allowed him to leap into the air towards his enemy, delivering a jumping punch to the hive-scorpion's face.

There was a crackling sound like a firework detonating as Gabriel's fist connected with the hive-scorpion's combat mask. The punch shattered the faceplate in one blow, creating a shower of metal fragments and alien electronics. Gabriel fell back to the ground again and landed in a pile of hive-warrior corpses as the hive-scorpion lost its balance and rolled awkwardly over its own tail.

As Gabriel got back to his feet, he saw that the hive-scorpion wasn't getting up. It lay sprawled on the floor, groaning and dazed, but it probably wouldn't stay down for long. Climbing onto the hive-scorpion's massive torso, Gabriel unhooked an explosive from his belt. The creature's chest heaved up and down as it inhaled and exhaled, and he struggled to keep his balance whilst holding the explosive in one hand.

The hive-scorpion's face was lashed with thin cuts and fresh bruises from the impact of his fist against its helmet. Its twin quartets of eyes were covered by thick, leathery eyelids. Ugliest of all was its mouth: a pair of jaws lined with vicious teeth and with a pair of sharp, pincer-like mandibles extending from within.

Gabriel primed the explosive and shoved it into the hive-scorpion's mouth. It jerked awake and began to convulse violently, bucking Gabriel off. He got back to his feet ready to fight, but the hive-scorpion didn't come after him. It choked and wretched, gagging on the object stuck in its throat, and madly thrashing its tail about in haphazard arcs.

Then the explosive detonated, blowing the alien's head apart in a gruesome shower of flash-boiled blood, meat, and bone. The headless corpse of the hive-scorpion rolled onto its back, its limbs curling up in insectoid rigor mortis. Gabriel wanted to breathe a sigh of relief, but he couldn't. More hive-warriors could be arriving any second, and he had to be ready.

He found the plasma cannon and picked it up again. Fortunately, it was sturdy enough to withstand serious damage and so it was still working. Unfortunately, its power pack only had a few dozen shots left, and he didn't have any spare power packs. Even if he did, replacing a power pack was a time-consuming process, and not safe to do in the middle of combat.

The crunching of dozens of alien feet skittering down the corridors reached his suit's auditory sensors, giving him several crucial seconds of advance warning. The hive-warriors arrived just as Gabriel finished priming the plasma cannon, and he fired a shot straight into the torso of the first one to appear.

It was relieving and satisfying to see the bolt of white-hot energy melt through the target's body, but once again, Gabriel was faced with a hailstorm of needle-thin, razor-sharp projectiles as dozens of hive-warriors opened fire on him. He needed to get out of this chamber, and the only way out was down.

Still squeezing off shots, Gabriel backtracked towards the gravity elevator entrance, hoping that there was nothing else coming up behind him. He also had to hope that the elevator would take him towards where he wanted to go, but even if it didn't, leaping into the unknown was a better option than sticking around and being overrun here.

The hive-warriors pushed forwards far more aggressively than before, disdaining cover and ignoring their fallen comrades, hoping to overwhelm him with sheer numbers. They were on the verge of doing just that when Gabriel reached the lip of the gravity elevator, leaping backwards into the entrance just as they were about to rush him.

As soon as he entered the elevator, Gabriel felt a powerful force yank on his guts like an invisible hand, and he was pulled straight downwards like a feather in a suction tunnel. The entrance above him disappeared into the distance far above as he careened into the depths at high speed. None of the hive-warriors saw fit to follow him.

Unlike the gravity tunnel in the Loki observatory, the hive-ship's gravity elevator was perfectly straight. The walls rushed by like the sides of a mag-train tunnel, the glowing light of the antigravity machinery keeping pace with him. Below his feet, he saw what looked like a bottomless pit, an empty maw that was receding as rapidly as he was moving towards it.

Being cornered inside the chamber with a horde of vengeful hive-warriors wasn't ideal, but the strength of the artificial gravity inside the elevator made it difficult even to move, let alone exit. Not to mention, he hadn't found any way of controlling the elevator from the outside, and couldn't see any controls on the inside either. He had escaped one trap only to be rendered helpless inside another.

Only then did it occur to him that the Hive-dwellers had complete control over their own ship's systems. What was to stop them from freezing the antigravity field and keeping him suspended where he was? Or why not switch off the safety protocols and hyper-accelerate him down to the end of the tunnel like a bullet being fired down a barrel? No amount of armour or shielding would protect him from that kind of impact.

Then again, at least that would complete his mission.

Gabriel checked the readout on his plasma cannon and saw that the power pack had finally died. He didn't know what was waiting for him at the end of his journey, but he may as well face it with a working weapon. He tapped a few keys, causing the barrel to retract, then released the deactivated weapon into the air, allowing the gravity field to take hold.

Working against artificial gravity, Gabriel reached over one shoulder and pulled out a six-barrelled rotary-style heavy machine gun. The concept was three-quarters of a millennium old, but the technology had improved astronomically since the days of gunpowder, and it was reassuring to have such a dangerous weapon in his hands.

Without warning, an opening appeared in the side of the tunnel and the gravity field shifted abruptly, spitting Gabriel out along with the discarded plasma cannon. He tumbled head over heels, his armour clanging against the metal floor as he rolled to a halt.

Climbing back to his feet, Gabriel found himself on a sprawling platform made of bare metal. In fact, he was standing at one end of a vast hall with a huge arched ceiling stretching far away into the distance. A metal superstructure was visible high above like the ribcage of some gigantic monster while the walls were covered by countless globular nodules.

Peering carefully over the edge, Gabriel saw a vast pit full of clumps of organic material dotted across the floor. A thermal scan of the expansive floor revealed patches of warmth inside the organic piles, but no sign of anything lurking in ambush, at least none that his HUD could detect. Ambush or not, he had to find a way out of this place.

Gabriel turned around just in time to see the entrance to the gravity elevator seal up, the door making an organic rustling and clicking sound as it shut. Even though he didn't fancy the idea of riding the elevator again, he was now trapped inside the cavernous hall along with whatever new horrors had been mobilised to eliminate him.

Turning around again, Gabriel saw a dark cloud at the far end of the hall. It was alive with movement and moving towards him.

His HUD highlighted a hundred targets instantly, but the true number had to be a thousand or more, too many to kill even with his machine gun. Then again, if he fired into the cloud he was bound to hit something.

Gabriel primed his weapon and opened fire. A string of flashes lit up across the rapidly approaching swarm as the energy shields of the airborne Hive-dwellers reacted to the incoming shots. They were so close together that the deflected rounds rebounded back and forth from one target's shields to another like a lethal storm of pinballs.

The airborne swarm warped and recoiled in response, twisting in on itself like some amorphous creature, the aerial charge faltering in the face of the barrage. Gabriel's HUD marked over a hundred targets that dropped from the sky like a rain of corpses, and he kept on firing in the hopes of actually beating them back.

Then the Hive-dweller horde split into three wings, one arcing left, another arcing right, and the third flying up and over to come down at a near vertical angle. Gabriel fired into the horde above him, but the tactic had the desired effect of distracting him whilst the other two wings completed the pincer-movement by barrelling into him from either side.

Gabriel was borne aloft by countless locust-like attackers as they grabbed his limbs and prised the machine gun out of his hands. The cloud of airborne Hive-dwellers raged and thrashed in a single furious mass as they swarmed all over him. Gabriel raged and thrashed back, the electrified knuckles on his armoured gauntlets connecting with targets and sending them bouncing backwards unconscious or dead.

It was a futile struggle. The hive-locusts were less than half the size of a regular hive-warrior, but their sheer numbers meant that no matter how many he put out of commission, more filled the gaps. He could barely make out the shapes of the aliens, just the gnashing maws and lashing claws that snarled and raked against his armour.

Instead of wings, the hive-locusts were each equipped with an antigravity booster pack connected to a half-helmet that allowed them to control the thruster pack with neural impulses. Instead of guns, the hive-locusts were using claws enhanced with the same kind of metal alloy he had seen on the hive-scorpion's tail. They yowled and shrieked and snapped at Gabriel as they carried him further and further aloft.

His shields were no good. Repulsion fields repelled incoming projectiles moving faster than a certain velocity, but the hive-locusts' claws weren't moving at Mach speed, even though they were still sharp enough to leave visible gashes in his armour.

Gabriel was still lashing out furiously, and the hive-locusts struggled to keep him under control even as they tried to shred him to death. Even without a firm grip on him, their sheer collective mass was enough to keep him aloft, and he couldn't see anything beyond the dense cloud of vicious aliens that swarmed around him.

Even while caught in the airborne maelstrom of claws and teeth, Gabriel was acutely aware of the fantastic irony of this mission: he was mostly safe inside his Juggernaut armour, which actually made it harder to complete his mission. Once again, Gabriel had to choose between allowing the hive-locusts to finish the mission for him, or to fight on a little longer.

Once again, Gabriel chose the latter option.

"*Shield, over-pulse,*" Gabriel enunciated into his comm., "*Now!*"

The Juggernaut armour registered the voice command and activated the over-pulse function. The safety features and other programmed restraints were disabled, and each of the shield emitters fired a single super-charged burst of repulsive force.

There was a spectacular flash of energy and a sonic boom as the hive-locust horde was violently repelled, and a destructive feedback loop between Gabriel's shields and their own magnified the force of the event. The hive-locusts collided with the walls and floor of the chamber at bone-shattering speeds. The all-encompassing mass of writhing alien bodies was instantly cleared away from Gabriel's vision, and he found himself in mid-air.

Gravity took control.

Gabriel dropped like a bomb, falling from 50 feet in the air. Being at the centre of the over-pulse, he wasn't propelled in any particular direction; but with nothing to keep him aloft, there was nothing he could do except flail all the way down.

His landing was soft, punctuated by the squelching sound of metal crushing biological detritus as he landed on top of one of the organic piles. It was an inelegant landing, but he was alive and uninjured. As luck would have it, the machine gun was lying nearby, and Gabriel grabbed it by the handle and hoisted it off the floor, priming it for use.

He saw that the weapon had been resting atop a pile of Hive-dweller skins. In fact, looking around, he saw that the entire floor was strewn with head-height clumps of discarded skins and pupae shells as well as the shattered corpses of hive-locusts. That was what had cushioned his landing, and the mounds of Hive-dweller muck were piled up and down the length of the enormous chamber.

Looking up, Gabriel realised that the globular shapes were eggs, attached to the walls in their tens of thousands. Some of the eggs were twitching or moving as new Hive-dweller larvae struggled to be free. This was a hatching chamber, and the floor was a disposal ground for the leftovers from innumerable Hive-dweller hatchings and moultings.

Gabriel was safe inside his armour, but he still wanted to gag.

Speaking of his armour, Gabriel noticed a warning indicator in his HUD: '*Shield Strength: 21%. Emitter Coverage: 10%.*'

The over-pulse was a last resort because it overloaded most of the shield emitters in one massive burst. The emitter coverage referred to the percentage of his suit's shield emitters that were still fully functional. He now had to rely almost entirely on his armour for protection, which was now covered in a messy tapestry of claw marks.

The hive-locusts had carried him all the way to the far end of the chamber, and he saw an exit leading into another winding tunnel. It was the only exit Gabriel could see, and the longer he stayed in the chamber the sooner he would be caught in another ambush. Readying his machine gun, Gabriel headed towards the exit, keeping an eye out for any hive-locusts that had survived the over-pulse.

'*Signature detected.*'

Gabriel blinked in surprise. A flickering signal indicator had appeared next to the message in his HUD. As he kept walking towards the exit, the indicator went from a weak flicker to a single faint but solid bar.

The Swarm's energy signature had been downloaded into his suit's computer, and now he knew it was nearby. He had no idea how far he had travelled in the elevator, but he had to be close to the heart of the hive-ship – a logical place for the Swarm to be – and detonating the antimatter bomb near the Swarm itself would guarantee its annihilation.

Of course, that meant he had to somehow get himself killed when he got there.

* * *

Gabriel tried not to contemplate why the Hive-dwellers had chosen to steer him to the hatching chamber. He tried and failed. Either they thought it would be easier to kill him there, or perhaps they wanted to feed him to their larvae and hatchlings, or both. As disgusting as the contents of the chamber had been, it was even more disgusting to contemplate what they might have planned to do with his corpse.

Having detected the Swarm signature, Gabriel now had an actual objective to follow. It was the next best thing to a map, and the only way to navigate through the mind-boggling maze of tunnels that comprised much of the hive-ship's interior.

The other clue that he was heading in the right direction were the constant attacks that the Hive-dwellers launched to slow his advance. Sporadic ambushes turned into a continuous wave as the hive-warriors attacked in force again and again. Gabriel kept moving forwards step by bloody step; but without working shields, he was forced to rely on his heavily-battered armour for protection against ever fiercer resistance.

The hive-warriors attacked as a single mass each time, dispensing with tactics in favour of numbers, firepower, and animalistic rage. They even trampled over the corpses of their fallen comrades in order to press home their ferocious and relentless attacks.

Gabriel fought all of them off, eviscerating scores of the overgrown bugs with a steady storm of bullets from his machine gun whilst mentally recommending a medal for whoever had designed it. The weapon's stopping power was incredible. The submachine gun he had used back on the Nexus had had minimal effect on the hive-warriors shields and armour, but the heavy machine gun mowed them down as if they had gone into battle naked.

The air was alive with the cacophony of combat, the shrill storm of whizzing needle-rounds combining with the droning of the machine gun to form a dissonant din. Even with his auditory sensors filtering out dangerously loud sounds, it was hard to stay focused when the scraping of needle-rounds and metal-coated claws against his armour was thrown into the mix.

Finally, there was the buzz and crackle of hive-warrior shields trying and failing to halt or deflect the barrage of bullets from the machine gun. Through the din of combat, Gabriel could even make out the sickly sound of individual rounds punching into alien flesh, he could certainly see it happening as one hive-warrior after another was cut down in a hail of gunfire – and yet still they kept coming.

After an hour of battling through seemingly endless waves of hive-warriors, their ranks finally thinned out, and the survivors began to disperse and scurry down the warren of tunnels. Whether the hive-warriors had broken and fled or been sent some kind of signal to retreat was impossible to tell. In fact, they had melted away so abruptly that it might even be a ruse. All Gabriel knew was that he'd been given a respite.

The barrel of the machine gun was so hot from constant gunfire that it was giving off a faint wisp of white smoke. His Juggernaut armour was lashed all over with scratches left by countless glancing blows from needle-rounds and augmented alien claws. Despite the ferocious, close-quarters shootout, Gabriel was fine.

The same could not be said of the defenders. Scores of bullet-riddled corpses carpeted the floor around him in irregular piles, their bright crimson blood mixing and congealing with the organic paste on the floor. The resulting substance created a sickly squelching sound as he stepped through the aftermath of the slaughter.

He was standing in the middle of a chamber about the same size as the chamber where he'd fought the hive-scorpion, but without a gravity elevator shaft in the middle. The chamber was lined with alien machinery and holographic screens covered with esoteric alien symbols. The symbols were a set of complicated pictograms running in parallel columns down the screen, presumably the Hive-dwellers' written language.

The machinery looked organic. A row of columns occupied an entire wall, each one as thick as a torpedo tube and pulsing gently like giant blood vessels. They were partly recessed into the wall and had taken some damage from the earlier storm of gunfire. Dozens of needle-rounds were sticking out of the fleshy surface of the columns, and several of Gabriel's own bullets had punched straight through, causing fluid to leak from the wounds in thin rivulets.

The fluid was clear and electrically active, judging by the streaks of electrical discharge that spat from the wounds. As

Gabriel watched, the streams of leaking fluid grew thinner and thinner as the wounds slowly healed on their own. The machinery really was organic, raising the possibility that the hive-ship itself was alive; that was almost as gross to contemplate as the hatching chamber from earlier.

The Swarm's energy signature was much stronger here, four out of seven bars strong, which meant he was getting closer. Gabriel now wondered why he had yet to encounter the Swarm itself. If the hive-ship's crew were enthralled, why hadn't the Swarm taken over one of them as an avatar? What were the Hive-dwellers planning to do with the Swarm?

The only way to find out was to follow the signal.

Machine gun ready, Gabriel followed the signal out of the chamber and down a narrow tunnel which broadened out like a funnel into a new area.

The cavernous space he entered was at least as big as the moulting chamber. It was bowl-shaped with lighting strips across the high arched ceiling, but the brightest lights came from enormous power conduits lining the walls at floor level. Each one stood several storeys tall and pulsed at irregular intervals, buzzing and flashing with caged power, feeding vast amounts of energy into a machine at the centre.

The central machine consisted of a raised dais with seven arches around the sides curving upwards from the base like the exoskeleton of some diabolical flower. Cables as thick as a hive-scorpion's tail fed power from the massive power conduits to the machine, and the inner curve of each arch crackled and sparked.

The arches looked familiar. Focusing on the central machine, Gabriel's HUD slowly zoomed in. He saw scores of hive-drones, like smaller versions of the hive-warriors, scurrying back and forth as they prepared the machine for activation. He also saw that the arches looked as though they were carved from stone but with a strange metallic hue.

Gabriel suddenly remembered the security footage from the data module. The hive-ship had attacked a Human outpost in order to recover one of those arches intact, hidden inside the asteroid for who knew how long right under the noses of the crew. Even without knowing what the machine was for, it didn't take a mastermind to conclude that the machine had something to do with the Swarm, and for that reason alone it had to be destroyed.

The zoom in his HUD reset and Gabriel began looking around for a safe way down to the floor. The walls of the massive chamber were covered in the same substance that coated every other surface of the hive-ship. Being preternaturally good climbers, the Hive-dwellers clearly had no use for anything as mundane as steps or ladders, nor could he see anything resembling an elevator.

Gabriel looked over the lip of the platform and saw that the curved walls of the bowl-shaped chamber sloped all the way down to the floor. There was no other way down that he could see, and judging by the curved surface, he could probably land safely if he treated it like a slide – so he stepped back and took a running jump.

It was a short and jarring ride down, but he was able to land on his feet.

The hive-drones took fright at the sight of the heavily armoured intruder that appeared in their midst, and they scattered like proverbial roaches. The only good Hive-dweller was a dead Hive-dweller, and Gabriel brought his machine gun to bear and unloaded into the retreating alien hordes. Most of his bullets found a target, punching through unshielded and unarmoured carapaces with ease, and mowing down scores of hive-drones as they fled.

Some of the rounds struck the arches of the machine, ricocheting off without leaving a scratch. Gabriel made a mental note that bullets wouldn't damage the machine.

Resistance was weak. Surprisingly weak. Suspiciously weak.

The hive-warriors had put up ferocious opposition to his advance all the way to the central chamber, but now that he had reached the heart of the central chamber, the resistance had melted away. That this whole thing was a trap was obvious, and one he had charged into with his gun blazing. But what kind of trap would it turn out to be?

A new warning announced itself in Gabriel's HUD. The signal strength of the Swarm signature was now at five solid bars, and a sixth bar was flickering tepidly. As he continued to watch the signal indicator, he saw the sixth signal bar become faint but solid, then grow steadily brighter and clearer.

The Swarm was approaching.

Gabriel readied his weapon for combat. He remembered all too well how ineffective conventional bullets had been against the Swarm during the Loki mission. In any case, the heavy machine gun had less than a thousand rounds remaining, and the flamethrower would take too long to deploy in the heat of combat.

"*Hornet cluster*," Gabriel enunciated into his comm.

From brackets installed behind the shoulders of his Juggernaut armour, two racks of four mini-missiles were deployed, ready to be fired on voice command. No sooner were the Hornet missiles ready to fire then the Hive-dwellers returned in force.

From countless openings all around the walls, thousands of hive-warriors poured into the chamber like liquid filling a bowl. Hive-scorpions were visible too, conspicuous by their massive size and improbable speed as they took up positions around the perimeter whilst flocks of hive-locusts soared on antigravity jump packs high above.

The hive-warriors assembled into disciplined ranks, row upon regimented row of armoured, insectoid soldiers. They held their weapons to attention and stared forwards, eyeing their target with eight demonic red orbs on each combat mask. They were impassive and silent; they didn't twitch or chatter, they just stood and stared.

Gabriel's targeting HUD singled out thousands of individual threats and it still couldn't count them all. The Hornet missiles could be used to target the hive-scorpions but with no guarantee that the high explosive warheads would be enough to kill them. Missiles or not, there were more hive-warriors gathered in the chamber than he had bullets left to fire.

Gabriel knew he should just open fire, there was nothing else to be done. Looking around at the sea of enemies that now filled the great chamber, he knew his death was near. He'd had that experience several times over the years, but the weight and intensity of the feeling never became lighter. Not to mention, as he reminded himself yet again, he had fought his way to the heart of this nest of vile aliens *in order* to die and take them all with him.

This really would be his last stand.

Then Gabriel realised something: the hive-warriors weren't attacking. They had him completely surrounded, but simply stood there, watching and waiting. There was a tense and bizarre standoff and as Gabriel gripped his heavy machine gun, ready to squeeze the trigger and barely refraining from doing so. The hive-warriors, on the other hand, just stared at him without so much as flinching.

After a while, the front ranks parted to make way for a single Hive-dweller. It had the same size and body shape as a hive-warrior, but instead of a weapon or standard combat mask, its mask was augmented with an intricate mouthpiece of some kind.

"I speak for the hive," the Hive-dweller announced in a sibilant rasping voice.

Gabriel blinked in surprise. The hive-speaker had just spoken to him in Standard Human Speech, his suit's translation software confirmed it.

"How do you know how to speak our language?" Gabriel demanded through his helmet speakers, unable to think of another question.

"We know little of your species, and care even less," was the dismissive reply, "but the languages of other species are easy to master."

"So why haven't you killed me yet?" Gabriel asked.

"We almost did," the hive-speaker answered, "but if we had done so, it would have resulted in the destruction of our hive, as you well know."

Gabriel's pulse accelerated.

"We detected the device you now carry as soon as you entered the chamber," the hive-speaker continued, "which means that if we kill you, you will kill us too."

If the Hive-dwellers could detect the bomb, then they knew what kind of bomb it was, and therefore had no incentive to kill him.

Something else was unsettling Gabriel: the Swarm signature was directly in front of him and at six bright bars with the seventh bar flickering faintly.

"Seems like a problem for you," Gabriel sneered.

"One which, fortunately, has a solution," the hive-speaker sneered back.

Before Gabriel could react, a hive-warrior brought a force-gun to bear and fired.

The impact of concussive munitions usually felt like being slapped in the chest by a giant hand. This was more like being hit by a high-speed mag-train without the chance to see or hear it coming. The Juggernaut armour protected Gabriel from injury, but the sheer force of the gravitic impact not only sent him flying backwards but caused him to briefly black out.

When he came to, Gabriel found himself suspended above the ground within the central machine. The inner edge of each curving arch was now glowing brightly; the machine was now active and being used to contain the hive-ship's most dangerous prisoner. Gabriel struggled to free himself, but he was trapped by an artificial gravity field and could do nothing except thrash about helplessly in mid-air.

"The original purpose of this device was to safely contain that which you know as the 'Swarm'," the hive-speaker explained as it removed something from its back, "but it seems you are a far more dangerous containment threat than this."

The hive-speaker was holding a transparent canister with a buzzing energy projector at each end. Inside, held in suspension by the energy projectors, was a silver orb.

Gabriel knew instantly what it was: the Swarm in an inert state.

"Is this what you have been seeking?" the hive-speaker said, almost gloating.

"It's what I intend to destroy!" Gabriel shouted back defiantly.

"You cannot destroy it," the hive-speaker replied, "it is part of a whole far greater than your disconnected mind can grasp; and even if you could destroy it, we cannot allow you."

"You're enthralled!" Gabriel yelled at the aliens, "all of you!"

"You believe that we are under its influence?" the hive-speaker asked with amusement.

"I can tell for a fact that you are," Gabriel asserted.

"We are not," the hive-speaker replied, "only the wandering wet-skins suffered that fate. They were foolish enough to release the entity from its prison when they discovered it, and thus became enslaved to its will."

"What did you do with them?" Gabriel asked.

"We extracted each individual particle of the Swarm from their bodies," the hive-speaker replied, "and then we killed them. They are not of the hive, and we do not wish for the entity's thralls to thwart our efforts to glean its knowledge."

"You can't 'glean' knowledge from it!" Gabriel shouted, his frustration compounded by his captivity, "it imparts knowledge by taking over the mind of a host, and even then it only provides knowledge that helps the host further the Swarm's own goals."

"And how would you know this?" the hive-speaker inquired sceptically.

"Because I destroyed something exactly like it!" Gabriel shouted back, "I know this enemy because I defeated it before! Whenever it takes over the mind of a host, the information transfer process is two-way! Everything the host knows, the Swarm will know as well!"

The hive-speaker was silent. Gabriel couldn't tell if it was seriously considering his words, or if it had any actual authority beyond that of a spokesperson. How could it? These were hive insects with a completely collective existence. They had no individuality to speak of, so why would they have a problem with the kind of mental enslavement that the Swarm would impose? It had to be as natural to them as it was horrifying to him.

"Your disconnected mind is as puny as ever," the hive-speaker responded imperiously, confirming Gabriel's suspicions, "This entity is ancient beyond measure. What you would call 'legends' say that this entity contains all the knowledge in the cosmos."

"And you're prepared to stake the continued existence of your hive, and probably your entire species, on legends?" Gabriel asked sneeringly.

"They are more than mere legends," the hive-speaker answered, "races long extinct knew how to contain and use the Swarm for their own advancement, races such as the ones who constructed the containment device that the Water-skins discovered; to say nothing of the technology that now holds you captive."

"Don't you think the fact that they're extinct is a clue to what awaits you?" Gabriel demanded, unable to believe that he was trying to reason with an alien.

"You know little of the cosmos, and even less of the infinite potential of this entity," the hive-speaker replied, sounding more like the deranged prophet from the Loki facility, "with the gifts of knowledge that the Swarm shall impart, the hive will march from glory to glory until all of existence bends to our collective will."

"Perhaps you're forgetting what I brought aboard with me," Gabriel reminded the hive-speaker, casting around for any last-ditch options.

"Holding an object in place is easy," the hive-speaker replied, "but if the machine is fed sufficient power, it can contain the explosive force of a nuclear or antimatter device."

That was how Gabriel had destroyed the Swarm orb on Loki without being killed, and the cosmic irony of being on the receiving end of the exact same strategy was palpable. As that thought passed through his head, a shimmering dome of light flashed into existence above his head, containing him within a translucent bubble of energy. It was identical to the containment field used by the observatory on Loki.

Now he really was trapped.

"There is nothing more to say," said the hive-speaker, "you will die in failure."

That final stinging comment reminded Gabriel that he still had one card left to play, and the hive-speaker's gloating had clued him in that it just might work.

"*Hornet cluster*," Gabriel enunciated into his suit comm.

The Hornet missiles were still primed. A conventional repulsion field would slap them aside, but they should pass easily through an energy barrier. That was his theory, at least, and if his battle with the hive-scorpion was any indication, it just might work.

"*Target setting: electrical, thermal*," Gabriel enunciated.

He couldn't predesignate targets from inside the containment barrier – even the signal bar indicating the presence of the Swarm had flattened out – but once they were airborne, the Hornet missiles could select their own targets.

"*Full spread, fire!*"

THE TRAITOR

GABRIEL killed thousands in seconds. All eight Hornet missiles were launched in rapid succession, shooting straight through the energy barrier with enough speed to overcome the artificial gravity field. Once they were free of the energy dome, the missiles soared upwards on plumes of fire then parted ways and came back down again, each one locking onto one of the massive power conduits.

Of the ten power conduits in the chamber, eight of them were struck by a high explosive warhead travelling at close to the speed of sound. The detonation of each warhead ruptured the protective casing of the power conduits, releasing tens of millions of volts worth of trapped electricity into the assembled hordes of hive-warriors. The air was heavily oxygenated, and saturated to tropical levels of moisture, providing a perfect atmospheric conductor.

Blinding sheets of raw lightning lashed out across the packed floor of the chamber, instantly frying thousands of hive-warriors to a crisp. Gabriel's helmet automatically muted dangerously loud noises, but the sounds of destruction he did hear were almost indescribable, like a bang and a roar compressed into a thimble of time and space.

The sight was even further beyond words, a blinding sea of pure light that flashed across the floor, giving way instantly to a carpet-layer of charred alien corpses. Every hundredth hive-warrior had a force-gun, and as their wielders were incinerated on the spot, their weapons detonated in a cascading series of gravitic explosions, sending bits of blackened body parts flying back and forth across the chamber.

The jagged forks of electricity struck skyward as well, zapping entire clouds of hive-locusts out of the air. They were flying in such close formation that the tongues of lightning leapt from one to another through the humid atmosphere, electrocuting hundreds at a time, and causing them to literally drop dead. Dead hive-locusts rained down like a monsoon of cooked cadavers, their antigravity booster packs completely destroyed or fried beyond use.

Gabriel was safe from the deadly storm of electricity thanks to the very containment barrier in which he was being held prisoner. The storm was over almost as soon as it began and the tongues of lightning lashed ineffectually at the energy dome. However, with most of the power conduits destroyed, the loss of power caused the barrier and the gravity field to fail, and he dropped like a stone back to the floor.

A stray fork of residual lightning struck Gabriel in mid-air as he fell, shorting out the servo-motors and electronics in his Juggernaut suit. He hit the floor and collapsed to his hands and knees as his armour suddenly felt ten times heavier. The suit's computers squeaked panicky warnings into his ears and his HUD highlighted the many damaged components in bright red.

Despite his genetically enhanced strength, it was a struggle to stand up. In fact, he could barely lift himself onto his knees. Even if he could get back to his feet, his armour would be a literal weight on his body, making it impossible to move and fight effectively. Without his Juggernaut armour's servo-motors, he could no longer use it.

"*System reset,*" Gabriel enunciated.

On top of all the other warning messages, another message flashed up in his helmet: '*Critical System Error: Reset Failed.*'

"*For Terra's sake, I don't have fleeking time for this!*" Gabriel snarled into his comm. in frustration, "*System reset, now!*"

'*Critical System Error: Reset Failed*,' his armour's computer replied calmly.

It was no use. A single supercharged bolt of lightning had done what countless claws, needle-rounds, and other physical damage had failed to do. If he wanted to move anywhere, he would have to abandon the Juggernaut armour.

"*Override, eject!*" Gabriel shouted into his microphone.

The voice command disengaged the Juggernaut armour's locks and de-slaved its systems from those of his regular armour underneath. Gabriel wasn't literally ejected, but as the Juggernaut suit opened up, he fell out and rolled across the floor. A new HUD appeared in front of his eyes registering that his regular armour's systems were functioning normally.

A timer also appeared.

29:59

29:58

29:57

By disengaging from the Juggernaut suit, Gabriel had triggered the antimatter bomb's timer. He had been so focused on the mission as a suicide mission, he'd actually forgotten about the timer feature. The bomb was still presumably linked wirelessly to his life signs, but he now had less than half an hour to escape this ship.

He scrambled to his feet and leaned over the fried Juggernaut armour, pulling on a release catch behind the shoulder. The Juggernaut armour had one more weapon left for him to use, and it fell away from the back of the armour. Gabriel reached down and picked the bulky flamethrower off the floor, priming it to fire.

Gabriel had no idea how to escape the hive-ship, but he knew with certainty that he would have to fight his way out. He might even be able to follow the hive-ship's crew to whatever they used as escape pods, but a problem presented itself as Gabriel stepped off the platform: there weren't any survivors to follow.

The charred and mangled remains of hive-warriors, hive-locusts, and hive-scorpions covered the floor of the chamber, forming a layer of blackened bodies stretching from one end to the other. Eight of the ten power conduits had been blasted open by the Hornet missiles and now looked like gutted mechanical carcasses, spitting sparks from their insides while the remaining two had gone dark.

Wispy pillars of black smoke and white steam had sprung up all around the chamber, creating a lighter-than-air cloud like early morning mist. Tongues of flame were feeding on the flammable electronics and the organic paste on the walls as well as rising up from the singed carcasses all over the chamber. The flames devoured the rich oxygen in the air even as their intensity was dampened by the heavy moisture.

There were no more Hive-dwellers left alive in the chamber, and after the instantaneous deaths of thousands of their number, it was doubtful that the rest of the crew would come down to investigate. Again, that meant no survivors left to follow to the exits.

Gabriel marched forwards, looking around for an exit, any exit. Even if he ended up wandering through the warren of tunnels until the bomb went off, it was better than standing around waiting for it to happen. As he moved forward, he stepped on something. Looking down, he saw a two-handled container at his feet.

Gabriel recoiled, realising that it was the container for the supposedly inert Swarm. The silver orb was the size of a kickball and looked like it had been polished to a perfectly smooth finish, so smooth that Gabriel could see his reflection in its surface. Apparently, the indoor lightning storms had not only overwhelmed the suspension field but also electrocuted the Swarm as well, reducing it – hopefully – to a truly inert state.

The container looked intact, with no signs of damage to the casing, and the Swarm was still securely contained within. As long as the container wasn't damaged and wasn't taken out of the chamber, the Swarm orb would be right in the epicentre of the explosion. In that case, should he leave the Swarm here with the antimatter bomb and try to get out alive, or should he stay and guard the Swarm until the bomb detonated?

For the first time, Gabriel truly faltered.

The choice was agonising: flee and run the risk that his efforts would fail, or stay and give his life to complete the mission. That ought to be an absolute non-starter: the mission was to ensure the destruction of the Swarm, and every voidstalker had to be prepared to give their life for the mission. So why in Terra's name was this suddenly such a hard choice?

A humming sound from the edges of the chamber caught Gabriel's attention. The remaining two power conduits flickered back to life, sparks of energy re-illuminating their interiors as they came back online. He also saw the inner arches of the containment platform start to glow again and his discarded suit of Juggernaut armour levitate up into the air as the artificial gravity field was restored.

Gabriel didn't know whether to be relieved or repulsed by this turn of events. He had just been presented with a life-or-death dilemma and, having faltered in the face of it, fate had decided to make the decision easier for him.

Putting his weapon down, Gabriel picked up the Swarm container and hurled it into the antigravity field. The container was borne aloft and held in place above the ground alongside the Juggernaut armour. A moment later, the containment barrier was re-engaged, sealing the Juggernaut armour, the bomb, and the Swarm container together inside the prison.

Gabriel picked up his weapon again and ran.

* * *

The net was tightening.

The Directorate may have been blindsided by Shelton's escape and the recent terrorist attacks, but the sheer amount of data at its disposal still made it quasi-omniscient. For days now, the Internal Security Department had been combing through this data to find out which of the hundred thousand or so DNI employees on Asgard could be the mole.

From several thousand names, the list of suspects had been whittled down to a hundred and then whittled down even further to less than a dozen individuals. Not all of those people were necessarily guilty, but it was a short enough list and a serious enough situation to justify snatch operations against all of them.

One of the suspects lived in an apartment just above the upper limits of the Undercity. An access code only available to the DNI enabled the snatch team to open his front door without triggering the alarm or the doorbell, and they entered in force, searching room by room in silence. One of the agents pushed open the door to the bedroom, and a twang was heard from the other side a split-second before a flash of fire and light erupted from within.

The operatives' body armour protected them from the blast force and the shrapnel, but the incendiary chemicals included in the bomb splashed across their clothes and began burning through the material. They dropped and rolled to put out the flames as their comrades rushed to their aid, and the rest of the team stormed the bedroom with weapons drawn.

The floor of the room was dominated by the smoking remains of the bomb. It was an IED triggered by a tripwire with no circuits or electronic triggering mechanism, rendering it undetectable to most scanners. It was an ingeniously simple booby trap, not the sort of thing a data analyst would be trained to manufacture.

There was a howling noise: the sound of a high altitude gale blowing in through the open window. Covering their faces against the freezing rain, the operatives looked out the window and saw a figure racing along the high-rise building's outer walkway, the detonation of the IED and the ensuing chaos having given him time to escape.

The suspect had prepared his escape well, but not well enough. Invisible to the naked eye and barely audible through the rainstorm, an airborne stealth-drone swooped in, firing a long, thin rope at the fleeing suspect. The end of the rope hit the target's thigh, delivering an instant electric shock to the limb, and causing him to drop to the floor.

The mechatronic rope began to wrap itself around him like the coils of a serpent before pulling him off the catwalk. The rope acted more like a chameleonic tongue than a constrictor's coils as it hoisted him into the air and pulled him into a compartment within the stealth-drone's body. Then the stealth-drone flew away with its quarry.

* * *

Dr Galton was alone, holding a flexi-tablet while the supercomputers glowed faintly behind him like a forest of enchanted tree trunks. A thousand faces stared down from the wall-sized holographic screen, most of them the grinning faces of children. Of the remainder, half were the grim and serious faces of their fathers, and the other half were their mothers.

All of the children had inherited their fathers' eyes.

The elevator doors opened behind him and a figure entered the darkened chamber. The Director-General of Naval Intelligence approached and stood beside Galton.

"I hope you're not about to eliminate me," Galton remarked jokingly.

"If I wanted to eliminate you, I would order a professional to do it," Red-eye replied, "in any case, I never assassinate current or former Directorate employees."

"Were you ever tempted to make an exception for Dr Shelton?" Galton asked.

A moment of silence followed.

"Recent events have made me wonder whether I should have," the spymistress replied, "but then again, there is no guarantee that these attacks wouldn't have occurred anyway."

"I suspect Shelton became disillusioned with the project he headed," Galton surmised, "not to mention suspicious of its broader purpose."

"Dr Shelton is a brilliant scientist with no grasp of strategy, let alone grand strategy," Red-eye stated coolly, "as long as his brilliance produced the required results, it didn't matter whether he could fathom its broader purpose."

"With all due respect, it probably should have mattered, or else he may not have become disillusioned with his work in the first place," Dr Galton answered, "As for me, I don't claim to fully grasp it, but I have enough pieces to put together part of the puzzle."

"And what have you figured out?" Red-eye asked.

"That these children are being bred," Galton responded.

"'Bred'?" Red-eye asked, raising an eyebrow at his choice of words.

"Yes, 'bred' is exactly the word," Galton replied, "the early instructions make it clear that the voidstalkers and their 'successors' were not to be cloned or grown in vats."

"Human cloning is illegal under the Genetic Heritage Law," Red-eye noted.

"An amendment which the Directorate itself had a hand in passing," Galton remarked with a wry smile, "or so I've heard."

The director-general didn't reply.

"In any case," Galton continued, "the instructions make it clear that the voidstalkers were to be created from existing soldiers or spies and perfected from generation to generation via the 'natural' method which, as a geneticist, I have to agree is far more reliable."

"Do you think the children are being 'bred' to be soldiers or spies?" Red-eye asked.

"Neither," Galton replied, "or else they would be growing up in a Directorate training facility instead of living like normal children with their biological parents."

"Well, you certainly have some of the pieces. What picture do they show?"

"We're raising a generation of savants," Galton concluded, "a generation of Humans who are physically, mentally, and genetically superhuman in every way."

"And why would the Directorate devote such vast resources and nearly three-quarters of a century towards the creation of a few thousand superhumans?" Red-eye asked.

Galton's flow of ideas ran dry.

"I don't know," he admitted.

The director-general was silent as she regarded the screen full of faces.

"So how close did I get?" Galton asked.

"Very," Red-eye revealed.

There was another moment of cryptic silence, but one in which Galton awkwardly waited for the director-general to say something.

"Dr Shelton's video message told Mrs Thorn that the purpose of the project was to create an insular elite caste who would rule over everyone, or something similar," Galton spoke up eventually, "at least, that's what she claimed in the debriefing."

"A remarkably dim conclusion from such a bright mind," Red-eye remarked loftily, "Shelton couldn't think beyond the parochial social dynamics of one city on one planet out of the many thousands Humanity has settled."

"Now I genuinely don't understand," Galton said.

A tiny light flashed on Red-eye's wrist-top and displayed a message which, thanks to her bionic red eye, only she could read.

The mole had been caught.

"Then ask yourself this," Red-eye said rhetorically, "why would we create an insular caste of inbred elites when there is already an insular caste of socially inbred elites who think they rule this planet?"

"Good point," Galton conceded, "and one which leaves me none the wiser."

"Then I'll rephrase the question," Red-eye replied, raising a hand and expanding one of the holographic faces to full-screen with a single hand gesture, "if the goal were to create an insular caste of ruling elites out of the voidstalkers, why would we allow them to marry and breed with 'ordinary' Humans like Dr Aster Thorn?"

The answer slowly dawned on Galton like the rising sun.

"Keep up the excellent work," Red-eye ordered, "you have no idea how important it is."

With that cryptic command, she turned around and departed the chamber.

Galton turned back to the screen to see Aster Thorn's face staring at him. She had been assigned to one of the aerospace engineering teams and was apparently doing good work. She was a frontier girl from a back-of-beyond mining colony who had risen from nothing to a prominent place in whatever multi-dimensional chess game Red-eye was playing.

Galton summoned the family's photos to view them together, and seven profiles expanded to fill the screen. Colonel Gabriel Thorn, Dr Aster Thorn, the grinning faces of four of their children with their glowing green eyes, and a fifth profile with no photo yet.

"Human-assisted evolution at work," Dr Francis Galton murmured to himself.

* * *

The Hive-dwellers were panicking.

A lone intruder had infiltrated their hive and embarked on a one-man rampage, killing tens of thousands of their best soldiers. Not only that but after being captured, the intruder had somehow destroyed the lightning conduits and instantly massacred thousands more – and he still wasn't dead. Gabriel was still on a rampage, and in no mood to be merciful, but it seemed as though the Hive-dwellers had more important things to worry about.

The discharge of billions of volts from the ruptured power conduits must have resulted in a ship-wide feedback event, destroying key systems, and resulting in catastrophic damage across the ship. In every chamber Gabriel passed through, the machinery in the chambers was either malfunctioning or had overloaded, blowing open with the force of several tonnes of explosives and killing any Hive-dwellers nearby.

There was also a palpable lack of resistance. The Hive-dwellers were no longer trying to eliminate him; instead, they were trying to evacuate their doomed ship. Hive-drones scurried in and out of tunnels, fleeing for safety as quickly as their legs could carry them. Some were carrying back-mounted containers full of supplies while others were transporting wriggling larvae, the future of the hive clearly at stake.

Bands of hive-warriors continued to ambush Gabriel nearly every step of the way, but their attacks were tinged with desperation as they put up a vicious rear-guard action to protect the fleeing hive-drones. Gabriel wasn't interested in killing the hive-drones so much as he was in following them to the exit, and the hive-warriors were trying to slow him down.

His final heavy weapon was a two-handed flamethrower that spat a pressurised jet of liquid fuel at the target. The fuel was ignited as soon as it left the barrel, producing a fire that burnt at close to 1800 Celsius, devouring the targets with flame. They choked and squealed in hideous agony as they burned before being reduced to crispy corpses.

Gabriel was much faster on his feet without the Juggernaut armour weighing him down. At the same time, his conventional armour was precisely that: conventional. His shields were strong enough to protect against most needle-rounds, and his armour kept him more or less safe against the ones that got through, but he was far from invincible. Were it not for the sporadic nature of the resistance, he would be massively outgunned.

Finally, Gabriel reached the end of the tunnel and jumped off a ledge, landing in the middle of a crowd of evacuating aliens. They scurried away to the escape pods as an enraged hive-scorpion dropped down from the walls to confront him. Gabriel took aim at the hive-scorpion and squeezed the trigger before it could close the distance, drenching the alien monstrosity in scorching fire.

The fire feasted on the rich oxygen in the air, the extreme heat compensating for the near-saturation levels of moisture as it burned its target. The hive-scorpion raged and thrashed and rolled around as it was doused in flames, its energy-dissipating shields useless against conventional fire. Gabriel kept on spraying flames at the beast until its dying cries ceased and it collapsed into a smouldering heap on the floor.

The flamethrower would have saved him a great deal of trouble earlier.

Looking around, Gabriel found himself in a hangar bay with dozens of boarding pods suspended from docking claws on the ceiling like so many bean pods. One by one, the docking claws were opening up and dropping the pods, allowing them to fly away under their own power. They flew straight through an open hangar door into space beyond, lighting up with a flash as they passed through an atmospheric containment field.

It was obvious that he would have to hijack one of the transport pods in order to escape, it was less obvious how he was supposed to pilot one given the alien nature of their intended pilots. To make matters worse, he only had a few minutes left to figure out how.

5:00

4:59

4:58

"*Incoming,*" said a voice suddenly crackling over the comm.

Gabriel blinked. It was a female voice. As he watched, another shape appeared in the distance. It was the Firebird gunship, flying straight towards him as he stood on the ledge. As it approached, it swerved around close enough for him to reach the handrails if he jumped. This method of extraction was far simpler than somehow hijacking a Hive-dweller pod, and yet Gabriel couldn't help but wonder why she had come to save him.

"*If you'd rather stay and die–*" Aetherea began to say.

"*No, I'm coming!*" Gabriel quickly cut her off.

Gabriel dropped the flamethrower on the ground and took a running jump, grabbing the handrails and clinging to them. The gunship swerved around and gunned its engines, following the remaining Hive-dweller pods out of the doomed hive-ship. Before long they were clear of the hangar and cruising through empty space to safety.

* * *

In the heart of the hive-ship, a new sun was born.

When the timer hit zero, the magnetic bottle within the bomb was deactivated, causing the antimatter globule to drop and touch the side of the container. The resulting annihilation of matter and antimatter released almost 100 kilotons worth of energy in an instant. Running on a fraction of the power it needed, the energy containment field was nowhere near strong enough to contain the force of the explosion.

A blinding ball of light engulfed the hive-ship's mid-section, completing annihilating the fusion plant as well as the central chamber and magnifying the force of the explosion as the ball of light transformed into a ball of flame. The shockwaves sent tsunami-like ripples racing out across the gas giant's atmosphere, and massive streaks of lightning radiated out from the detonation, lashing at the heels of the atmospheric shockwaves.

The entire middle and rear sections of the hive-ship disappeared in a cosmic maw of ultra-hot fire. As the explosion progressed, it showered pieces of debris into space and across the clouds of the gas giant, glowing like a swarm of countless fireflies as they burned. The front portion of the hive-ship was propelled forwards and then downwards by gravity into the gas giant's atmosphere.

As the bow of the hive-ship tumbled to its doom beneath the clouds, a million tiny fires ignited inside the ship itself, feeding on the oxygen-rich atmosphere within. Under the light of the field of flames, little dark specks could be seen fleeing the destruction: Hive-dweller pods that had escaped the blast and were travelling as fast as they could to safety.

The filters in Gabriel's HUD protected his eyes from the glare of the twin suns as well as the cosmic flash of the hive-ship's destruction, but it retained full-colour vision. Even at this distance, he could still discern the innumerable fires that burned within the blazing carcass of the hive-ship as well as the countless Hive-dweller pods fleeing the destruction. It was an awe-inspiring sight to behold.

It was also a deeply sobering sight to behold. Gabriel was solemnly aware that he had just single-handedly snuffed out millions of lives – alien lives, but lives nonetheless. Killing was a filthy business to be done with as little feeling as possible, otherwise you might be driven mad by the choice between cowardice and sadism.

So what did that make Aetherea? This entire mission had been undertaken over her objections on the grounds that it would be better to kill billions of Hive-dwellers later instead of millions now. For all her irritating flippancy and propensity for manipulation, she was still exceedingly good at what she did and clearly was neither a coward nor a sadist.

"*How did you know where I was?*" Gabriel asked her over the comm.

"*There are two tracking devices, one in the bomb itself, and one inside your regular suit,*" Aetherea explained, "*the bomb signal stayed next to the Swarm signature, and your suit's signal fled back to the hangar, which is where I picked you up.*"

That was a backhanded way of putting it, but Gabriel let it slide. Then something else she'd said caught his attention.

"*What a minute,*" Gabriel demanded, "*are you saying the Krakenscourge was able to track the Swarm inside the hive-ship this whole time?!*"

"*Not the whole time,*" Aetherea responded, "*but shortly after you boarded, the techies figured out how to track the Swarm's signature using the Krakenscourge's sensor array. And since the signature disappeared as soon as the bomb went off, that's how we know your plan actually succeeded.*"

That was an extremely convenient turn of events, but it meant that his decision to flee the central chamber had turned out for the better. Even so, he couldn't rid himself of the feeling that Aetherea would have been happy to let him die aboard the hive-ship.

"*Thanks for picking me up, by the way,*" he said gratefully.

"*Since the would-be martyr got cold feet,*" Aetherea sneered, "*you're welcome.*"

The comment was snarky rather than teasing, and had a sharp edge to it. She was annoyed, maybe even bitter, and she had no right to be. Gabriel, on the other hand, wanted to be angry with her but found it awkward given that she had just saved his life.

As the blazing remnants of the hive-ship disappeared below the clouds of the gas giant, Gabriel decided that for the journey home, he would rather sleep on the floor.

* * *

Older freight barges like this one had been launched decades ago and given numerous refurbishments to keep them space-worthy. Even so, they were still sturdy enough to use, and once the last of the barge's cargo had been loaded, it broke from orbit around Asgard and sped towards the edge of the system, preparing to make the jump to Q-space.

Keeping out of sight, several crewmembers used the cargo cranes to remove a single container from the storage racks and place it on an inspection platform. They opened up the container, stepping back as a hiss of cool air was released. The container had a biohazard symbol on the side, but the cargo was a life support casing with a respirator unit.

The man inside had fallen asleep during the trip, and his steel grey eyes fluttered open as the crewmembers unzipped him from the casing. Carefully, they removed the nutrition tubes and then the respirator mask. The man they were smuggling hyperventilated for a few moments, taking in lungfuls of already-stale spaceship air.

Slowly and groggily, he sat up in the container, smoothing down his grey hair and silver moustache before letting his smugglers help him out of the container.

"That was a horrible trip," Mortimer Shelton opined.

"It was the only way to get you off world undetected," one of the smugglers explained.

"I understand, and I'm grateful not to be under the DNI's thumb anymore," Shelton replied, "but still, being stuck in a container like that for days on end is awful."

"We've still got to clear the system," said another smuggler, "then we'll be safe."

"Speaking of which," Shelton added, standing up straight and giving his back a stretch, "are you going to tell me where we're going?"

"Somewhere beyond the DNI's grasp," a smuggler responded.

"So your boss has the technology to transport us to the Andromeda galaxy, does he?" Shelton laughed, his joke making plain his scepticism.

"Technically, he's your boss now too," someone answered.

"Well, I'm not really in a position to contradict that," Shelton replied, "but will I at least have the pleasure of meeting him?"

"Yes. In fact, this whole operation was organised in order to recruit you."

Shelton did a double take.

"So the hallucinogenic chemical you had me develop, and the extra helpers you had me recruit," Shelton asked, "all of that was purely to get me off Asgard?"

"You were the objective all along," a smuggler confirmed.

"That's a lot of effort to go through for just one man," Shelton remarked.

"Evidently, the boss thinks you're worth it," the smuggler replied.

"Well, I know why he'd find me valuable," Shelton said hesitantly, "but who is he?"

"We can't tell you that here," one of the smugglers replied, "but you'll meet him face-to-face once we reach our destination."

"I'm flattered," Shelton said, turning to leave, "and for the record, I'm also glad the gas wasn't necessary after all."

His back was turned and he never saw the wry grimaces on the smugglers' faces.

* * *

Prisoner no. 11631 entered the interrogation room and sat down in the prisoner's chair. She barely flinched as the cushioned restraints closed automatically around her wrists and ankles. As soon as the prisoner was secured, the escort androids departed the room and sealed the door behind them.

"Jezebel Thorn," said the operative sitting opposite her.

"Yes, that is still my name," Jezebel Thorn replied with lofty sarcasm.

"Do you remember what you were told after the incident?" the operative asked.

"Could you be more specific?" Jezebel asked with a raised eyebrow, maintaining a look of implacable superiority despite being dressed in prison overalls.

"Yes, I can," the operative answered, "do you remember what you were told after you shot and killed your husband?"

The question cut like a knife through Jezebel's composure.

"Well, do you remember or not?"

"Yes…" Jezebel replied through gritted teeth.

"And yet you still thought it acceptable to divulge sensitive details to your daughter-in-law," the operative said with an icily stern voice.

"I did no such thing," Jezebel retorted equally icily.

"You told her the name," the operative said.

"Yes, Alexander Thorn," Jezebel replied, defiantly uttering the name.

"Why did you tell her the name?" the operative asked.

"Because she asked," Jezebel responded.

"And in so doing, violated your non-disclosure agreement," the operative pointed out.

"Are you going to send me to prison?" Jezebel asked ironically.

"We can keep you in here for longer," the operative answered, "for the rest of your natural life if necessary."

"Then just kill me and be fleeking done with it," Jezebel spat contemptuously.

"We have no reason to take your life from you," the operative replied coolly.

"You've taken more than enough from me already," Jezebel continued, what remained of her composure dissolving away, "first you took my husband and turned him into a raging monster, and then you took my son and turned him into a humourless killer."

The operative raised an eyebrow.

"'Humourless killer'?" he said, the ghost of an ironic smile flickering across his face, "coming from an actual convicted killer, that's hilarious."

Jezebel didn't smile back.

"In any case, you seem to have done rather well for yourself since the incident," the operative continued, "using the hush money as seed money to start your business empire. You've become one of the richest women on this planet, and all while a blind eye was turned to the less-than-legal methods you used to become rich."

"What's the point of all this?" Jezebel demanded.

"The point is that all that was required in return was that you keep your mouth shut," the operative replied, "something, it seems, you're no longer able to do."

"Are you making similar threats to my daughter-in-law?" Jezebel asked, "She was the one who reached out to me, after all."

"That's no concern of yours," the operative replied.

"I don't really care if you are," Jezebel said dismissively, "she may be the mother of my grandchildren, but she's still a colonial bitch. I'm more interested in why the DNI is still so touchy about Alex's name being mentioned."

"That's definitely no concern of yours," the operative replied, "or mine."

"The spooks keep their dogs on a short leash," Jezebel sneered.

"Yes, it seems they do," the operative replied with a smile, "which is just as well."

A series of clanging sounds echoed from outside the room like a set of giant latches unlocking, and the entire chamber began to move.

"What the fleek's going on?" Jezebel demanded, casting around the room in a panic and struggling against her restraints.

"This facility was built as a series of modular blocks, where each room and cell can be repositioned according to the whims of the prison management, or whoever gains access to the controls," the operative explained, "in other words: we're moving."

"Is this your idea of a prison break?" Jezebel demanded.

"That would be the technical term, yes," the operative answered calmly.

"Whatever you DNI spooks are planning, you'd better tell me!" Jezebel shouted.

The operative raised an ironic eyebrow.

"Did I say I was with the DNI?"

* * *

The shortlist of potential moles had been narrowed down to three suspects. One worked in data analytics, and one was a software engineer. Both were taken down to the interrogation wing of the Spire, locked in separate chambers, and worked on until they broke.

The software engineer broke first. He explained – truthfully, according to the readouts – that he had been blackmailed into providing details on specific weaknesses and blind spots in the Directorate's surveillance network. It was a serious infraction, but one committed under duress. The data analyst was the true mole, and after an hour of interrogation, he didn't break so much as finally relax and give away what he had to say.

"*One of the principal ways we detect blind spots is through detecting anomalies in the data,*" the mole explained calmly, his voice projected through speakers in the observation room beyond, "*but if those anomalies aren't statistically significant, no one will find them.*"

Instead of a chair, the prisoner's hands and feet were secured to the ceiling and floor by clamps that kept him suspended like an animal on a spit. He didn't struggle. It was useless to struggle, and the slightest flinch could be punished at the whim of the interrogator.

An assortment of equipment was arrayed around the chamber, some for monitoring the prisoner's vitals, some for administering the pressure required to break them, and some for ensuring that they remained alive long enough to be useful. The life support equipment could keep the prisoner alive and conscious for weeks on end.

"*So you manipulated someone in the software team into creating these blind spots,*" the interrogator asked, "*and then concealed them using your own skills in data analytics.*"

"*You flatter me,*" the mole replied with disturbing calm, "*but that is correct.*"

Watching the interrogation from the observation room were the head of the Internal Security Department and the heads of the two divisions where the moles had been found. The director-general herself was also present.

The mole's neural activity was being recorded and displayed in real-time to distinguish truth from lies. The numerical readings that were actually analysed were far more nuanced and precise, but the colour-coded version displayed on the readout was more visually intuitive. Blue stood for truth, orange indicated a half-truth or evasion, and red was a flagrant lie.

The readout remained a serene blue.

The Directorate had to be constantly vigilant against security breaches and data leaks, but such threats were few and far between – and simple enough to pre-empt and prevent. Never in living memory had such a threat come from a mole within the organisation, let alone one who had succeeded in so severely compromising the Directorate's capabilities.

"*What specifically was the purpose of installing these weaknesses?*" the interrogator asked, preparing an interrogation implement using the drop-down menu.

"*To ensure that someone could escape undetected,*" the mole replied.

"*Who?*" the interrogator asked.

"*If you've caught me then you should already know,*" the mole pointed out.

The interrogator activated her chosen tool, and a robotic arm descended from the ceiling, applying stimulation to a specific nerve with a precision that no Human hand could match.

What the mole felt wasn't conventional pain, more like an extreme loss of feeling and orientation, like vertigo stirred together with pins-and-needles but a hundred times worse. His eyes went wide and he gasped in total silence, feeling too much agony to cry out.

"*You should know by now that every lie, half-truth, partial-answer, and attempt at evasion will be punished,*" the interrogator explained as the device was withdrawn, "*now answer the question: who did you help to escape undetected?*"

"*Some...medical doctor called...Shelton,*" the mole answered, breathing heavily as he recovered, "*Mortimer Shelton.*"

The neural imaging monitors used by the DNI were so sophisticated they could even parse out which parts of a sentence were lies, known truths, beliefs, or guesses. The readout remained clear blue, indicating that the subject believed what he was saying was the truth.

"*Where is Mortimer Shelton now?*" The interrogator asked.

"*I don't know,*" the mole replied, truthfully according to the readout, "*my only task was to ensure that he had the opportunity to escape when the time came.*"

"*Did you have any contact, direct or indirect, with Mortimer Shelton?*"

"*No, I didn't,*" the mole responded, again truthfully.

"*Who directed you to facilitate Mortimer Shelton's escape?*"

The mole was silent.

"*Silence will be treated the same way as a lie or evasion,*" the interrogator warned.

"*It doesn't matter,*" the mole replied, unfazed by the threat, "*he planned for my capture and made sure that anything I tell you would be useless by the time I was caught.*"

"*Who planned the chemical attacks?*"

"*The same person who directed me to facilitate Mortimer Shelton's escape,*" the mole answered calmly, "*or so I assume.*"

The readout registered a tepid orange spike, indicating a lack of certainty.

"*And who was that person?*" the interrogator asked.

"*Someone who sends his regards to Red-eye*," the mole answered, smirking a little at using the director-general's nickname.

"*Who?*" the interrogator demanded.

"*Gabriel Thorn*," the mole replied.

Before the interrogator could follow up, the mole bit down on something.

An alarm blared and medical warnings flashed. The machines used to keep the subject alive whirred into action, rapidly administering scans and antitoxins. The suspect's eyes rolled back in his head as the blood vessels in his mouth turned black, spreading across his face and into his brain as the poison killed him faster than the machines could save him.

A minute later, he was dead.

A stony silence descended upon the observation room. The three department heads and the technician supervising the readouts all quietly turned to the director-general, waiting with barely bated breath for her to say something. The Internal Security chief was particularly tense, being the only other person in the room who recognised the name.

Red-eye's lips pursed and a twitch could be seen in her Human eye, while her bionic red eye glared at the holographic screen like a targeting laser.

"Apart from the head of Internal Security, you are all dismissed," Red-eye informed the room without so much as turning her head.

No one needed to be told twice – let alone about their obligation to keep their lips sealed – and they departed quietly. Red-eye and the Internal Security chief watched the readout of the mole's neural activity. It had paused at the moment of his death.

The last segment was clear blue.

"The fact that the subject genuinely believed it doesn't necessarily make it true," the Internal Security chief clarified.

Red-eye knew that, but it did little to refute the simplest explanation: that Gabriel Thorn – one of her best operatives, and a key part of the Voidstalker Programme – had betrayed her and the organisation he had served for decades.

The only other explanation was that the mole had been led to believe that someone by that name was the instigator. That merely opened the floodgates for numerous other questions: who was the real instigator? Why would they want to frame Gabriel? Did that necessarily mean he was innocent? If not, why did the mole sell him out? The answers were a mystery, and wouldn't shed any light on the motives or goals of the perpetrators in any case.

"Snatch him as soon as he returns," Red-eye ordered, "in the meantime, dig through everything we have regarding the mole's personal history. We need to find out how he came to be turned in the first place and by whom."

"Understood," the Internal Security chief answered in acknowledgement, departing to execute his orders and leaving Red-eye alone.

The dead mole was still in his restraints, his head lolling to one side as venom-stained drool dripped from one corner of his mouth. All Directorate field operatives had to be willing to give their lives for the sake of the mission, and if this particular agent hadn't been a traitor, his commitment to the cause would have been admirable.

But it was clearly far more than that. A willingness to be captured, divulge potentially misleading information to the enemy and then take one's own life in enemy custody implied far more than commitment to the cause. There was something fanatical about it. What could inspire this kind of fanaticism? Who could inspire this kind of fanaticism?

The obvious emotional response to the mole's revelation would be either willful denial or a deep sense of betrayal, or a gut-wrenching combination of both. Red-eye barely felt either, she wouldn't be very good at managing the Directorate otherwise. Besides, there were plenty of unanswered questions about whether and to what extent one of her most capable operatives was involved in this conspiracy.

Nonetheless, the conspirators had succeeded in puncturing the Directorate's aura of omniscient invincibility, making it clear that they could strike right under the noses of the supposedly all-knowing DNI. The very fact that the Directorate had been infiltrated in the first place was disturbing in itself, and the possibility that a voidstalker might be implicated in it – or behind it – was all the more disturbing, rattling even.

Maybe that was the point.

* * *

The fiery ball rippled and pulsed, its core seething with the energy of nuclear fusion. Dark patches of abnormal coolness speckled the star's surface, blooming like blotches of mould before shrinking and receding again. Great plumes of orange fire danced across its surface, leaping up from the depths below before plunging below the surface again.

It wasn't a real star, of course, just an elaborate holographic simulation accelerated by a factor of 10,000. Even so, the hologram was so sophisticated it almost looked real, and the interleaving beams of light that generated the image gave off a faint aura of heat as if he could touch the fiery substance of the star without being burnt.

An alert chimed, signalling an incoming message. He withdrew his hand from the glowing simulation and opened the notification.

His operatives had successfully exfiltrated both marks from Asgard, but one of the moles had been exposed and the network's existence was no longer a secret. More seriously, the network's ability to operate in the DNI's own backyard was no longer a secret. Discovery had been inevitable, but it was a reminder of the need to stay at least one step ahead.

He dismissed the notification and turned back to a half-finished game of 3-D chess.

It looked like he was losing the match, having lost half his pieces while eliminating a few of the computer's pieces. But there was an opening that left the computer's king vulnerable, a vulnerability resulting from aggressively trying to dominate every corner of the board. He moved a piece across the board and cornered the enemy king, and when the computer moved another piece to block the path to the king, he eliminated the blocking piece.

The game grid flashed green and displayed a message: '*checkmate: player wins*'.

That was his tenth win in a row, and all on the highest difficulty setting available. It was getting dull, frustratingly dull.

Before he knew it, the rage began to build in his chest like the magma chamber of a dormant volcano. The urge to punch or break something became an insuppressible upwelling of fury, but he remained rational enough to snatch something off the table and press it against his nostrils, holding the trigger down and inhaling deeply.

Ten seconds of volcanic fury seethed and bubbled in his mind as he scrunched his eyes shut and squeezed the inhaler in his hand, waiting for the treatment to take effect.

Like an ebbing tide, the rage receded from his mind until it was as clear as water.

That episode was worse than usual due to waiting longer between treatments, but he would rather have a stronger than normal episode than grow dependent.

He put the inhaler back on the table and walked over to the mirror, taking off his shirt and tossing it to one side. The muscles of his chest and arms resembled chiselled marble with a fleshy tone, the product of numerous physical and genetic enhancements. Spread around the centre of his chest were seven patches of scar tissue, long since healed but still faintly visible under the dim light.

He stared at his reflection, and a pair of shimmering emerald eyes stared back.

THE END

About the Author

I'm not a full-time author, few of us are that lucky. I have a five-day-a-week job which pays the bills, including the book-related bills. I enjoy writing and science fiction as a hobby and an escape, and the result of unwinding at the end of every day, and over every weekend, are the stories I write.

CPSIA information can be obtained
at www.ICGtesting.com
Printed in the USA
LVHW090502100719
623655LV00001B/64/P